THE LEGEND OF THE BROTHERHOOD

CLAN MACLAOCH CURSE SERIES
BOOK III

BECKY BANKS

Published by:

Maui, Hawai'i | Portland, Oregon
haiku-press.com

Cover design by James T. Egan of Bookfly Design.

beckybanksbooks.com

ISBN: 979-8-9890889-0-4 (e-book)

ISBN: 978-0-9882614-9-5 (paperback)

Prologue

CASTLE LAOCH, 1989

Up the black-rock beach the boats bobbed and shook. Half-cabin wooden fishing skiffs were being filled with five-hundred-pound barrels of untaxed whisky on that moonlit night. The wet cold bit at the men's heels as they worked, back and forth between castle and boats. The rumor of authorities planning to raid MacLaoch castle that night had loaned a frantic rhythm to the otherwise peaceful pace required for aging raw spirit into Glentree's golden whisky. Clansmen sporting tight stone-washed denim, cigarettes between equally tight lips, muscled the oak casks from their racks in the castle's caves, swatches of red tartan tied around their wrists and forearms to protect them, and rolled them onto every available clan fishing vessel. The rocky shore made loading the boats hard, and harder still when their high-tops slid on the wet stones.

Rowan, a young boy then, remembered the way the tobacco smoke hung in the air like mist, creating a protective blanket cloaking their secret activities.

Then, the two-way radios squawked: Police were racing through Glentree toward the castle.

Men flew down from the castle, throwing their arms out at those loading MacLaoch gold onto the last beached skiff and yelling to: "Go! Go! Go!"

The last one, *Chief's Desire*, was Rowan's uncle's skiff.

Off in the dark, watery distance, out beyond the break, a motorized ship, something large judging by the low hum, was coming up from the south. Its searchlight became a ghostly dot on the horizon. The last barrels were loaded when the yacht-sized diesel-powered vessel with the words *HM Coast Guard* emblazoned on the side crested into view beside the distant cliffs.

The incoming tide had lifted the rest of the boats, but *Chief's Desire* was too heavy for the water lapping under her flat wooden hull.

The white sneakers of Alex Alexander, nicknamed Double-A, flashed as he sprinted toward the skiff. "Oye! Giver!"

Cigarettes were flicked to the ground. The men rushed the bow. Aided by their force and the buoyant lift of the water, the skiff moved out with the next receding wave. The men gave her a final shove before climbing in; their jeans were soaked up to their thighs.

Rowan remembered the starting roar of the outboard motors on his uncle's boat. Those unusual shiny white motors, two hundred horsepower in total, had been the talk of the clan, his uncle's Whisky Boys discussing the massive crates that had arrived from the US, how it was all so American. How, somehow, *Miami Vice* had gotten the better of his uncle all the way out there on that northern port of Skye.

Still, as Rowan stood on that beach, the searchlight of the incoming powerboat washing over the waves like an accusatory finger, he felt that his uncle's boat couldn't possibly outrun their English over-lords. That even with its Don Johnson overhaul, it was still a blunt-nosed, sleepy wooden vessel whose original design had been for quiet fishing in the late nineteenth century.

His uncle, clan chief, and mentor stood next to him, cigar clenched between his teeth. Around it, he uttered a Gaelic prayer just as the winds changed.

The Coast Guard bellowed: "Cease and desist all activities and return to shore."

"They'll make it?" Rowan asked.

"Lady MacLaoch willing."

Those words hadn't soothed him; in their legends, Lady MacLaoch was a woman who cursed every chief in her lineage, including him— the chieftain who would eventually take his uncle's place.

Then his uncle added, "And pray those engines don't rip tha' boat apart."

Rowan was watching the struggle in the loch when his uncle's words sunk in. "What?" he squeaked.

Just then, the skiff's motors caught and were thrust to full tilt. The boat jettisoned forward through the chop. The nose lifted dangerously at the first low, sloppy wave that struck the bow, making the men shout. The engine went slack, and two men were ordered to the nose. Double-A put power back into the motors, and with the nose weighed down, they broke through the waves.

The boat wave-hopped toward the channel and then the wide mouth of the outer loch. There, out of the protected bay, they'd catch the coastal rip current that sped north to the Orkneys.

The Coast Guard boat pierced through the outer chop, its own motor built for high-sea chases. It closed the distance to the skiff like a boot about to bash a roach into the rocks.

"Uncle..."

"Dunnae worry. Even with her load, she's made for the shallows. Her Majesty's ship cannae be foolish enough to attempt what they are pretending to do." His uncle let out a low growl. "I hope."

Rowan heard his uncle whisper in their mother tongue for Lady MacLaoch to keep the men safe, for the water to guide them, and for the MacLoach marshes to be ready to receive them.

Young Rowan, losing sight of the chase, ran to see them again, his uncle's last words lost behind him. Across the rocky beach, up the cliff trail. The smell of spilled whisky was heavy in the air. He looked down from the top of the cliffs, again following the boats.

The large British ship looked to be preparing to ram the skiff; Rowan's heart went into his throat. He shouted for Double-A to stop. Stop this madness or they'd surely die. Of course there was no way that Double-A could hear him, and Rowan knew he would not listen even if he could.

Double-A kept to his course, following the rocky arm of the outer loch. Suddenly, the Coast Guard banked hard away from the shallows, allowing the skiff to fly by.

Rowan shouted and punched his fist in the air. He ran to the next lookout, his feet stumbling over loose rocks on the trail.

In Rowan's next clear view, the Coast Guard was once more on Double-A and his men. The skiff veered away from the safety of the shallow waters. It wasn't a move Rowan thought they should have made.

Rowan heard Her Majesty's commands echo off the basalt rocks of the cliff's shoulders; they reached him in broken bites, sounding harsh and mechanical through the loudspeakers. There was an "or else" underlying the tone of the command to stop.

Rowan lost them again, and he took a shortcut through the forest following the trail, popping out in time to witness the skiff dodging left again, pushing even farther out. Rowan bellowed, "Nooo!" It was farther into the bigger ship's territory and a sure way to drown when the skiff was exploded by the larger vessel's piercing hull.

The Coast Guard vessel followed and, anticipating a cut-back by Double-A, who would surely want to be closer to the shallows, turned at the last second.

Rowan screamed. The water frothed. From where he stood, *Chief's Desire* looked to have been obliterated by the massive Coast Guard hull. Covering his mouth, as if the authorities could hear him scream-ing, Rowan felt hot tears sting his eyes. His uncle's men, his clansmen who were like fathers to him, were surely killed. And he'd borne witness to the English authority's brutality against an already brutal-ized clan. His stomach went sour.

Then the searchlight went mad on the water below, and as the clouds moved on, letting weak moonlight shine down, Rowan saw *Chief's Desire* running like a skater over the water. The English boot had tried to crush them but failed.

Rowan whooped, punching his fist in the air, tears still wet on his cheeks. He sped along the cliffside trail once more. The skiff, lit by searchlights, was headed directly toward the towering basalt cliff face.

Double-A kept the motors blazing. He tore into the shallows and swerved north again. While Rowan was relieved, the water there was riddled with underwater boulders that could crack the skiff in half. The men were literally between a rock and a hard place.

The Coast Guard vessel didn't attempt to enter the shallows but instead paced them, likely believing that a crash was inevitable, and they would then pluck them from the water. Those who survived.

Double-A and his men began to pull away. It was as if they had discovered they had another outboard motor and just then remembered to turn it on. Farther and farther ahead, the skiff led the Coast Guard. Rowan grinned. He understood what Double-A was doing. He'd finally found the rip current that traveled north toward the Orkneys. It was unexpectedly close to shore that night.

The vessel kept on them, its massive searchlight trailing them, their diesel motors competing with the crash of waves below. But then, in a blink, the skiff was gone. Rowan knew that Double-A had made a hard right out of the spotlight, and in the few moments it took them to readjust, the skiff was gone. The Coast Guard worked the rocky cliff face for some time. They searched the water and the rocks for parts of the boat, and eventually, they discovered what his clan had learned over a millennia ago: There were narrow cracks in the cliffs that weren't large enough for them to gain entry. Only sleepy old fishing boats fit.

Smiling and feeling righteous, Rowan ran back to the castle in a stream of whoops and hollers. They'd done it. They'd saved the whisky in the boats; they'd be able to continue to serve their clan's needs by using the tidy profit to fix the castle roof and help their people when they needed money for school or medical bills, like his uncle said they would.

Rowan's feet slowed as the castle came into view, and his jovial mood evaporated. Blue and red lights from police vehicles bounced off the upper turrets of Castle Laoch, a reminder that they'd not wholly gotten away with it.

The rest of the night was a blur. He remembered finding his uncle's hand and slipping his smaller one into it. That firm grip gave him the reassurance he needed as authoritarian boots moved up and down the basement stairs and then out to the loch beach and lower cave. The rest of the MacLaoch gold was forfeit.

There was one more pungent moment that Rowan hadn't recalled in a long time. Only his current circumstance decades later pulled it out of his deep subconscious.

There at the front of the castle, some of the Whisky Boys stood stoic and proud, flanking him and his uncle as officers interrogated them. They'd not cause a scene if it weren't necessary. Still, the current law of the land wasn't the law of their hearts. The MacLaochs had centuries of history on that land; they'd fought for it, including castle and country. Their confidence ran through their blood and into the soil beneath their high-top sneakers.

So, when one of the officers crossed an invisible line, the men responded. And Rowan's uncle was a particularly colorful one who wasn't one to shy away from responsibilities, a party, or a fight.

Rowan remembered his uncle's words to one of the officers that night: "What'd you say, Murdoch?" His tone was aggressive, and it made young Rowan's stomach churn. Then in his memory, more words sneeringly spit out, his uncle's next answer to the comment Rowan could no longer remember: "Is that right?" Just before the officer had his head knocked back.

His memory of the exchange, and then the mayhem that ensued, wasn't clear. But Rowan remembered that name, *Murdoch*.

Now in his library office, he looked at the empty chair across the desk from his, whisky in one hand and foreclosure paperwork in the other. It had been too recently that another vindictive Murdoch sat before him.

"This is long overdue, isn't it?" the banker had said. In a blink, his vile grin had come and gone, as if he wasn't sure he could achieve his lofty, horrible goal but was thrilled he was getting close. His suit was a beige, boxy thing much too large for his shoulders but buttoned snugly around his rotund middle. It stretched as he slid loan foreclosure paperwork across the desk to Rowan. "Ye can't outrun your bad blood, MacLaoch. And yer uncle was the worst kind. I'll finish what my own uncle started and take the castle from you and yours as you justly deserve."

Rowan rotated the crystal tumbler and watched the long legs of amber alcohol drip back down to the bottom of the glass. Soon after the banker had delivered that judgment to Rowan, Charmaine had showed up and fucked things up further for him by playing keep-away with Cole's ring. A lot had happened in not much time.

That second bit, at least, had been settled. The gold on his own ring finger winked; its match sat warm and comfortable on Cole's finger. But the banker, Richard, aka Dick Murdoch II, wasn't. If they had that confiscated whisky now, it'd be worth a fortune, and he could be done with the Murdochs' iron fist, first powered by the law and now by money, once and for all.

[illegible] [illegible]

[illegible] [illegible] [illegible] [illegible]
[illegible] [illegible] [illegible]
Edgar had appeared [illegible] the [illegible] [illegible]
had that confirmed [illegible] [illegible] [illegible]
[illegible] [illegible] [illegible]
[illegible] [illegible]

Chapter One

R owan and I sat on the couch, dust motes hanging lazily in the air as we stared blankly out the picture window of our cliffside cottage. We'd just hung up with my mother and father in South Carolina who'd informed us that TJ, who was stationed in Germany, was about to step off a C-130 in Scotland. Them sending TJ was tantamount to sending in a covert agent with headquarters' agenda their only mission.

"Can a C-130 land at Eli's airfield?" I was gauging how much time we had to fortify our defenses.

"Only if it wants to end in the water—there's not a runway long enough there. They'll land down Glasgow and then make their way north. We have a few hours to set the welcome mat and clean things up."

I looked around as Rowan stood and started to cross the room away from me. "Welcome mat? I was thinking razor wire. And besides, we don't need to sweep and mop to impress TJ."

"No, not that."

Then I remembered. "Oh, the field." Then: "Oh, the castle still has our clan in the upper halls."

"Aye, we did just fight mystical beings, get married, and turn the library into a makeshift hospital."

He seemed calm when he started the sentence, but by the end of it, he had turned back to me and was looking panicked. And by something, it turned out, wholly different than what was causing me to panic. "I'm meeting your kin."

"Right, and—"

"And the place is a bloody mess. Literally." He shoved his hands through his hair and looked around as if he hoped the answer might show itself from under the couch cushions. "Ugh, fuck!" Then he winced and put a hand on his abdomen.

I went to him. "Are you all right? Maybe we put all this TJ nonsense aside and get you properly checked out at the clinic over the hill? I wanted to do it last night, but—"

"Nae, it's nothing." He added, seeing that I wasn't wholly convinced, "I think my ulcer came shooting back."

That, I understood. "During the chat"—I pointed at the now-closed laptop—"they knew we were married, which, damn, that news traveled fast, and for my mother, going through that without her is unforgivable. She'd prefer I commit murder before getting married or having babies without her input. I think your ulcer may be contagious." I felt a nervous giggle bubble up. I was a grown woman, but my parents' opinion still held sway over a small but consequential part of my brain. My plan for a wedding with them post-supernatural event just sank into the sea.

"I'll change clothes, and we can head up to the castle and get things tidied. The field...can wait."

Luckily, it wasn't my mother coming. TJ was amiable, and the secrets I had on him were akin to what a priest had on his local parishioners. Still I was changed and back in under a minute, tugging on fresh woolen socks.

"Row—" I cut off. He was on his phone calling in favors, one of which sounded like fixing the newly ruined bridge. Our Glentree residents heeded their laird's call a few weeks back when he asked for ideas to keep the estate out of bankruptcy. They responded in vastly different ways. One was tampering with the Lady MacLaoch bridge. If the banker couldn't physically meet with Rowan, the foreclosure and ultimately bankruptcy proceedings could be stalled until "God only knew when."

As he hung up, I noticed his skin was taking on a sheen. His slate-blue eyes went pale and wide as he looked at me. "Ye have family."

I looked around the room as if they were standing there. "Yeah, of course I do—"

"No, you're not an orphan. Like me."

I nodded, unsure what he was saying. "Right. I have—"

"I've even spoken to them, but now it's real. They're real. The things I've done, the things we've done together. How do I face your da someday? And most importantly, now, your brother? They've every right to give me a proper hiding—"

"Whoa," I said, going to him and sliding my arms around his middle. I laid my ear to his chest and heard his heart hammering. "You've faced down much worse than a couple of country folk like us—you'll be fine."

"All right then, but if you allow it, we MacLaochs like our traditions, so I'll be rolling out the red carpet."

"Fine, but when we mess it up, don't come crying to me."

He laughed and kissed me again. "Ye know I'm a sensitive boy—dinnae make fun of me." I hugged him tighter, and Rowan hissed, "Not so tight."

"Oh, right." I gently touched his abdomen. "Are you sure we shouldn't see Dr. Moore about it? It looked rough this morning when you showered."

Even on a bad day, spying Rowan from the bed was always a good way to wake up. He was an incredibly early riser, something the Royal Air Force instilled in him that never left. The small bathroom off the main bedroom was tight enough that a man could—if so inclined—pee into the toilet and wash his hands in the sink, never leaving the comfort of the instant-hot shower. It was as wide as Rowan's shoulders and made for viewing only. The last time I attempted to join him in it, we ripped the shower door off.

That morning, I had enjoyed watching the way water blew off his upper lip as he exhaled within the pressurized spray. But the water dripping over his musculature had also highlighted the fist-sized bruise on his abdomen.

Now, against my lips, he murmured, "Nae, nothing but a few days of low abdominal work and I'll be fine. Dinnae fash yersel'," and his palm went to the round of my bottom. "But none of this"—he squeezed—"until I'm recovered and yer brother is tucked into a nice bed of his own far away."

That sounded like an eternity. "That could be...forever."

He kissed the end of my nose and said in a dry tone. "Then it's forever till we have sex again."

I grinned at him. "I think we're worrying about the wrong things."

"Aye, but it's a fun distraction. Shall we get to it, then?"

I took a deep breath and grabbed the button of my jeans. "Yes."

Rowan's gaze glittered with laughter at my antics and inability to hear anything from him as something other than a turn-on. "No. Cleaning and prepping for his visit."

I feigned a sad frown. "OK, fine."

Rowan held the door open for me as we stepped into the weak sunshine of the late-summer afternoon. Our fingers interlaced as we ambled up the trail that would take us past the cairn knoll, the name I'd come to use for the field after seeing what was below the meadow plants.

"I'd like to look at the field to see what's left and if we have to wrap up our research work with 'Everything is a charbroiled briquette. The End' or if there's an epilogue here. In college, I studied the aftermath of crown fires—fires that travel from treetop to treetop, leaving nothing but ash in their wake—and discovered solid ecological work still to be done. Even in the ash. Basically, we can study the regrowth. But with lightning from an ethereal being, I don't know what we'll be dealing with..."

Rowan simply nodded; his eyes were on the horizon. When he took a stabilizing breath, I looked up. The charred soil came down far across the research field, and after walking only several yards through green grass, we were crossing yellow, then brown, and finally, black-scarred earth.

I gripped his hand tight, and he squeezed mine in return; we both remembered the hellscape of the night before. That charred grass was a reminder of the near loss of everything we held dear.

"I'm sorry TJ is popping in at a time like this. I can take care of him and let you focus on the recovery of the clan and the foreclosure threats." Then I thought on it for a moment, "Or rather, lack thereof, since Sir Dick Asshat never showed." I was having trouble remembering the man's name. We were on day four of radio silence from the man, a record, to my knowledge. With the battle-wedding consuming so much of my attention, I certainly hadn't been itching for this early fight, but now I was starting to wonder about his absence. Maybe he was finding a printer large enough to handle the loan foreclosure documents.

"It's a matter of time. He reminded me of something in our shared history when he was here last. For him, what he's doing is personal; he's taking perverse joy in it."

"I'm sorry. He's an odd duck. Every banker I've meet—mind you, in the States—tries to help a long-standing client through the hard times. Outside of basic humanity, it's just good business: Get the loan back on track, and they continue to make money. Force a default and the opportunity for financial improvement, and just plain revenue, is gone."

"Ya, not sure what's wrong with tha man." He thought on it and pressed his MacLaoch gumption into it. "We'll see it through. I've no idea how, but we must."

"We could sell the Ulfberht," I said as the field turned proper black, with plant shadows blasted against rocks. The castle loomed over us as we made it up the low slope and approached the Circle Garden.

"Och," he said.

With everything that had happened, a foreclosure proceeding was the one thing that seemed fixable. "I'm just saying, the Ulfberht sword—"

"And I'm just saying, while tha' may make a fine collectible in a posh Bronze Age Viking nut's collection for several million pounds, I'll not sell the sword that is your birthright."

"Yeah, yeah, so you have said. I'm saying that if it will help save the castle from the banker's noose, as you so eloquently put it, then I think it's worth it."

"Och, no."

"Fine," I drawled the single syllable out.

"Anyway, it might bring tha' damned man back." He sounded like he was hocking the words from the back of his mouth like a foul taste.

That shut me up. No one wanted that. I squinted into the distance where the Circle Garden was rising into view. The beds had seen some trampling the night before but were incredibly intact. Pink, purple, and white cosmos nodded as the earth warmed up and the cool breeze off the cliffs ambled inland. And cutting a swagger along the once well-manicured grassy path was a brown-haired figure with a high, tight haircut. He wore a smirk as if he'd heard a good joke and took in his surroundings like an eager American GI on holiday in a new land.

Seeing his stupid, happy face, I was suddenly back at home in South Carolina laughing, trading bawdy jokes, and eating Mother's tooth-achingly sweet pecan pie. A pie she baked whenever my brother and I made her "stressed to the gills."

"My brother..." I breathed, the exhalation redirecting Rowan's gaze. I felt his fingers tense in mine. "He's not... That's not...actual skipping," I said as if I had to explain why TJ walked the way he did. "He walks like he owns the world and he's on a stage before millions."

We stopped, and Rowan released my hand as if scalded. He wiped it on his pants as TJ, in his civilian gear, holding a green camo rucksack over his shoulder, came at us.

"But it's never a good sign to see TJ smiling like that," I whispered through the teeth of my own smile. "He's up to something."

His eyes were bright and clear. He was on cloud nine, and when he saw me, his smirk broke into genuine joy. I felt it too. We were two peas in one pod coming back together.

"Well, my, my, if it isn't Miss Nicole Ransome Baker!" he shouted.

I couldn't help but laugh. It was as if just seeing him made me relive every funny moment we'd ever shared. "TJ, you jackass!" I exclaimed with love. "How the hell are you?"

"Great!" he said. "And this must be Rowan."

"It is." I opened my arms for a hug. Instead, he said, "Hold this," and tossed his rucksack to me.

I caught the fifty-pound sack with an "Oof," just before TJ socked Rowan in the stomach.

Chapter Two

Rowan's breath shot out as he doubled over. TJ smoothed his hand over Rowan's back. "That was from my folks. They didn't like you getting my sister pregnant and marrying her without Pop's consent. Mom, though, wants the baby to be named"—he paused, looking at something written on his palm—"Fredrick if it's a boy and Francine if it's a girl."

He gave Rowan a pat as if that settled it.

I loved my brother, I really did, but when he socked my husband only hours after we'd survived a mythic battle? I returned the favor.

I dropped his rucksack and lunged. My fist caught his cheek. "You mouth-breathing pissant excuse for a human being! He's injured—"

TJ blinked in surprise. He grabbed a handful of my sweater absently as I tackled him into the cosmos bed. Pink and white petals blew up into the air. I sat on him and tried to sock him in the face again. TJ dodged to the side again and again.

"Whoa!" he shouted.

"And," I said as I again punched air, "I'm not"—*punch*—"PREGNANT!"

He was surprised enough to forget his defense and said, "What?" as I clipped his jaw.

"*Ow!* Stop it!"

"*You* stop it! You hurt him! I'm not pregnant, and if you were born with ears that worked properly and an actual brain between them, you'd have asked! Goddamn you—"

"You OK, man?" TJ looked beyond me to Rowan.

I slapped TJ across the head for good measure and looked back at Rowan myself. He was on all fours on the gravel, one hand clutching his abdomen. He'd gone ashy and was struggling for a breath.

"Shit." I scrambled off TJ and gripped Rowan's shoulders in time to catch him from fainting face-first into the gravel. I murmured to him, "Rowan? Honey?" As he went to dead weight, I caught his head on my thigh and pulled him into my lap. "TJ," I hollered, "you damn shithead!"

TJ, whom I sometimes forget is an army medic who buzzes into active war zones to save people, had his cell phone to his ear as he came toward us.

"What do you mean he's injured?" TJ asked, putting his fingers to Rowan's neck to make sure he'd just fainted and wasn't dead as a doornail.

As soon as I realized he was talking to me and not his phone, I said, "I mean, he got hit yesterday, hard, in the stomach, and it made a huge bruise. And why the hell are you here at all?! Mother and Daddy said you wouldn't be here for another day!"

He shouted back, "I caught a ride!" TJ cursed as he lifted Rowan's shirt and then gingerly rolled him to check his back too. "He's got cuts all over him. What the hell was he doing?"

"He was... A tree fell," I improvised.

"You suck at lying." He gave Rowan's abdomen a gentle *tap-tap* with his fingers. He cursed again and said, "Yeah, you still with the rig?" I almost responded before I realized he was talking to the person on the phone. "Roger that. Stand by." He pushed some buttons on his phone. "Can you get a geo-locate on me?"

I piped up. "Tell the paramedics we're at Castle Laoch. They'll know how to get here. At the Circle Garden." Panic slithered in. All I could think was how shitty it would be for Rowan to survive everything, only for a single punch from my jackass brother to kill him.

TJ said, "Yeah, you heard that? Know where Castle Loch—"

"Laoch."

"Right. You know where that is?" he said into the phone, then: "Roger that, ten-four."

TJ hung up and tucked away his phone before gently tapping Rowan's face, then his collarbone, calling his name. He checked his eyes, pulling his lower lids down.

"How long did they say? Sometimes they have an ambulance sitting at Glentree. Was it there? Shit, TJ, this feels serious. He's unconscious, Tee."

TJ put his ear to Rowan's chest and tapped. He stood abruptly and went to his pack and rummaged through it. He extracted another bag, the guts of the pack: his medic bag. He unzipped it, dropped it next to us, put his stethoscope to Rowan's chest, and tapped again.

I heard the distant purr of a machine and thanked the heavens that the ambulance had indeed been at Glentree. Only the purr of the motor got louder and turned into a *chop chop chop* as it closed in quickly. As I recognized it as the sound of a helicopter, TJ's phone rang.

"Go," he said. "Yeah, put it down in the flower bed. Yeah, the circle one."

Wide-eyed, I looked around us. "Here?!" I said, thinking of the Coast Guard chopper out where Eli worked; it wouldn't fit here.

TJ ignored me, and within moments, a frightening mechanical creature peeked over the trees. The helicopter was something out of the wet dreams of every child who wanted to decimate their opponent on the G.I. Joe battlefield.

"Good Christ, TJ, is that what I think it is?"

He didn't respond to me; it was obvious the black war bird he usually rode around in when he was saving asses was about to land in the Circle Garden...or on a castle turret. My head was definitely going to roll off from the force of the wind under the rotating blades as the bird paused high over top of us.

TJ stood as I ducked over Rowan's face, protecting him from flying debris, and tried not to think about what it meant if TJ thought it pertinent to have his taxi driver come get us.

I watched from under my arm as the flag atop the castle's parapet flicked and snapped in the wind until it gave up and ripped off. The thunder of the rotor wash pounded through my chest and roared around us. The expert behind the stick slowly set down, gentle as if he were lowering a snail into the garden—with a tornado attached to its shell. The blades relaxed to a whine.

Everything from there on was a blur of TJ running, the copilot assisting, and Rowan being braced for flight. When he was moved from the ground to the backboard, his eyelids fluttered, and he groaned. We were in the chopper and airborne in under a minute. I advised them on the nearest hospital, over the ridge, where our lone surgeon was in residence. The same hospital I flew with Rowan to the year before when he'd needed his bullet wound stitched shut.

There was radio chatter of Rowan's description mixed with acronyms, numbers, and the occasional *unconscious* and *pain stimulus*.

The drone of the engine and helicopter blades became white noise as I watched TJ go through his expert motions of listening to Rowan's breathing, checking pulses, and monitoring his blood pressure.

If the pale gray of Rowan's face didn't scare the piss out of me, I would have found the quick trip humorous. We were on the hospital's concrete helipad two minutes after we left the garden, and for the second time in my life, I never again wanted to see that chipped white paint of the air ambulance cross on the tarmac or the weeds that were still crawling up through it.

We were out. Rowan was put onto a waiting stretcher. TJ was running alongside the stretcher, yelling things over the rotor wash to the surgeon. Once inside, I was stopped at the surgery doors and asked to sit in the waiting room.

No matter how many times it happened, I would never get used to that feeling of despair when those doors shut on me.

This time, though, my brother was there. Seeing him through the window on the helipad, I stood and hurried back outside. By the time I reached him, the chopper was airborne, and he was walking back to me, the sober, all-business brother in place.

I started the conversation. "You piece of shit—"

"He didn't fall out of a goddamn tree—"

"How could you? Two seconds you're with us, and you put my

husband in there." I whipped my pointer finger to the squat concrete building behind me in case he was as dumb as I thought he was.

"He should have been in the hospital yesterday. And don't fucking lie, Nicole. What the hell?"

I took a deep breath, and guilt crawled into my stomach. I knew Rowan should have gone to the hospital. Even though we were inland, I could smell the faint brine of seawater.

"Well?" he asked. "He's got level three contusions on his abdominal muscles, and when I hit him, yes, it ruptured something, probably a hematoma. And by the skin color there, I'd say that hematoma formed less than twelve hours ago. Did he catch a missile without his flak jacket on? It sure as hell wasn't my damn love punch."

I shook my head and crossed my arms. In the distance behind me, the purply Highland hills towered as my backup. "Love punch? That's what you're calling it?"

"He has internal bleeding, but yes, let's focus on me."

My hands flew up; the tears were there before my palms touched my face. "I knew we should have taken him," I said through my fingers.

"We who? And why didn't you?"

I dropped my hands and said with some heat, "I don't know if you noticed the scorched earth around us when we met?"

"Hard to miss. Forest fire?"

"Something like that. Look, it isn't very easy to explain. And knowing you, you'll have to see it to believe it, so I'll save the explanation for later. Right now, I need to contact Marion; she'll want to know why all the second-floor windows have been blown out. And maybe Clive," I mumbled, seeing as the clan historian had been Rowan's right-hand man these days. I returned to the hospital's side entrance, wiping my tears, TJ behind me.

"Nicole... Pipsqueak," he said, using his nickname for me, "if he sneezed today, whatever it is would have ruptured. I just happened to be the sucker who burst it. Don't be pissed at me."

I turned on him at the doors. "I'm not— No, wait, I am. Of course I'm mad at you! *You punched my husband!*"

"He deserved it! No one in our family knows who he is! He's some Harry Potter wank who's convinced you to stay up here in the boondocks in some ancient pile of rocks he's pretending is some functioning, historically important castle."

I was taken aback, way back, as in back the train all the way up to the station. "*Everyone* thinks that?" I hadn't realized my family had been worried. But then I remembered I was talking to TJ, so I amended, "*No one* thinks that!"

"Yes, they do. Mother and Daddy— No, check that: Mother is pissed. If you weren't in another country, she'd be sending you pie."

"Oh," I said. That was bad. Despite being raised to be a good Southern woman, my mom wasn't a baking sort of gal. She rebelled against her debutant nights and her pie days when she married my father, a farmer who liked to cook and never requested her presence in the kitchen. So when Mother stepped into the kitchen, it was a loud pronouncement that she was doing something she hated; therefore, everything that the kitchen produced under her hand was ire in edible form.

"What kind of pie?" It mattered.

"*Pecan.*" The word was a sharp metal dagger, and he knew it.

"Oh," I said, not liking the taste of even imaginary guilt-pie.

"Yeah," TJ said, gaining steam. "So, now you're lying to me about him being hit before. Did *you* hit him? You've got a nice slice on your head. Did he hit you first, and you got pissed and nailed him back with something big? You're all ready with the lies and not even a day into your marriage. Fuck yeah, I nailed him. When he's better, I'll do it again!"

TJ really knew where my big red button was and loved to jump up and down on it. "*FUCKER!*" I shouted as the receptionist inside—on the other side of the glass entry doors—heard me and looked up concerned.

"Tell me I'm wrong. Did you hit him?"

"Ugh! You don't understand!"

"Explain then!" he said, throwing up his hands.

"Ugh!" I responded again. "TJ, I can't just explain everything like it's instructions on how to make a peanut butter and jelly sandwich!"

"Try!"

"Fine!" I marched through the double doors into the waiting room and to the reception desk. I recognized the two women there from my last visit. "Hi," I said with an aspartame smile.

They gave kind but wry looks in return, first at my brother and then at me. They immediately updated me: "He's still in surgery."

TJ rested his elbow on the high reception counter and said to me, "Waiting."

Still looking at the women, I threw my thumb at him. "Would you be so kind as to tell this moronic paramedic who I am?"

The receptionist closest to me answered, "Nicole Ransome Baker, or Mrs. Rowan Douglas James MacLaoch."

"Ah, right," I said as TJ scoffed. "I meant, y nickname, please."

She crinkled her nose. "He won't understand."

"I know, but let's tell him anyway."

"Yes, well, in that case. You're the Minory lass."

I looked at my brother. "See?"

"Minory lass? Grandpappy's real last name? So, what of it?"

I waved her to continue, and she eagerly complied. "She saved the laird of Castle Laoch, Rowan Douglas James MacLaoch, by being his one true love and marrying him because she was destined from birth to break the curse."

I couldn't have said it better myself. I turned to him, smiling. "Still think you know what's going on here?"

He looked from the woman to me. "What kind of cult have you been sucked into?"

Chapter Three

Clive and Marion called to say they were on their way. A few minutes later, I met them outside. "He's fine..."

"Not again!" Marion exclaimed after giving me a hug. "We heard from Sal that she'd just admitted him and that he was unconscious! The stained glass above the entry doors is gone. My Lord Almighty! What happened? And not a day since Ormr was trying to kill us all!"

Clive cleared his throat and looked at my brother, who'd come up behind me, with a long, hard glare, then back to Marion as if in a pointed notation of his presence.

"Who's Armor?" TJ asked, taking in Marion and Clive.

"O-R-M-R, Ormr, Minorrison, jackass."

Clive looked to me in surprise, then to TJ.

TJ held out his hand to Clive. "Hi, I'm Jackass, but you can call me TJ."

Clive stood a little taller. "Yes, the resemblance is uncanny now."

"Beg your pardon?"

"Your sister shares your taste of humor, and some facial structure, if not hair and skin color."

"Last time I checked, she's also a girl with a rack and I am a dude with a dick. Not at all alike."

I chimed in. "Like I said, he's Jackass, and if you're feeling formal, elevate to Captain Jackass."

"Who's Ormr?"

"None of your business—"

Clive proceeded, "A legendary man who walked among us wearing your sister's skin like that of a selkie. She dealt us a mighty blow just yesterday; thus, we are all on edge. When your lethal aerial arrived and blew out the upper windows, naturally, we thought he'd come back and killed the two of them."

TJ took a long blink as if his eyes had absorbed too much light, then focused hard on Clive, expecting him to laugh and tell him it was all a joke. He waited. We all waited.

"You're not kidding."

"Young man, I've become accustomed to your sister, and I have to say your brand of humor is most juvenile. Of course I am not 'kidding,' as you say! And were you here just twenty-four hours prior, you might have seen what real men, dicks or not, can do. Your sister is one of the mightiest men I've ever encountered."

I held up my finger, pausing the conversation.

"Now, TJ, satisfied? You've been told everything I wouldn't tell you until you were ready. Ready to call the cops and report us as a cult?"

"Yes."

"Oh, for heaven's sake," Clive cried, "we were fine until you arrived and shattered the—"

"For the record, it was a good thing my ride to Castle Loch—"

"Laoch."

"—was available to hang a uey and grab us so I could get your boy's ass over here—"

"Thank you," I said to him and tried *not* to sound like I didn't mean it.

"Well." Clive held himself higher. "Had you called ahead—"

"And ruin the surprise? No, I was under strict orders to arrive without an announcement to see what was happening."

"Orders?"

We answered in unison, "Mother."

"Oh," Clive said, taken aback, "*Mrs. Baker*."

TJ looked like he'd swallowed a grape, and I knew I wasn't alone in hearing a sigh, of longing and desperation, when Clive said Mother's name.

"Well, in that case," Clive continued, "welcome. Will your mother be joining you?"

TJ gave him another long look before adding, "No, Mother *and Daddy* will be at home until further notice." Then he glanced at me and scrunched his eyebrows up and together in question.

I just shrugged. It was Clive—what was there to explain other than he needed more time outside his basement hovel? Aloud, I said to my brother, "Welcome to Glentree, fuckface."

I WAS HOLDING ROWAN'S HAND WHEN HE WOKE. THE GENTLE BEEP of the machines was the soundtrack. Rowan's hospital room was the hospital's only VIP room. It boasted a pasture view, an in-room bathroom, and paisley curtains that looked like station dividers repurposed from the emergency department. The hospital room was clean, but time had aged the corners where the vinyl baseboards came together into a sepia color; the ceiling tiles sported minor stains from a leak. The cabinets were faux wood. If I were a betting woman, I'd say that Rowan's uncle, the previous chief, infused it with cash when things were flush, before the big whisky bust in '89. Thankfully, the equipment was much newer.

The surgeon, however, was not. He was an old military doc and took advantage of having my ear all to himself when he checked earlier on a still-sleeping Rowan. He told me point-blank that whatever horse manure Rowan was constantly finding himself in, he needed to knock it off. Rowan's injuries were getting to the limits of their small country hospital. He gave me a list of things they couldn't do if we found ourselves in a chopper and thinking of landing there again. I winced at hearing a big fat no to cerebral trauma and pocketed the list for later, as in, never later. I was an optimist.

What they had taken care of this time, I was informed, was that

Rowan had had organ bruising, and like TJ thought, a hematoma had formed and then burst when TJ hit him. His body went into shock and shut him down. He had wide gauze wrapped around his midsection, providing support and coverage of the incision. And a reminder to take it easy for a while.

They had dialed back Rowan's pain medication an hour before, and he was now coming to the surface. He opened his eyes; the blue was washed out, making him look downright ill against the pale pillow and beige surfaces of the single-bed room. The sparse five o'clock shadow on his face showed how much time had passed since he'd arrived.

"Hi," he croaked.

"Hi," I said and got him some water.

He took a tentative sip, and when he got that down, I gave him another until he was strong enough to take the cup from me. His bed had him at a gentle slope, so I fluffed his pillows, adjusted his blankets, and fussed over his IV tube's placement where it flopped over his forearm until his other hand wrapped around my wrist.

"Cole, mo ghràdh."

I stopped, took a deep breath, and sat on the edge of his bed. "Are you OK?" I whispered.

He nodded and winced. "I am now. I'll have to thank your brother when I see him next."

I was sure my eyebrows arched so high they touched my hairline. "Demanding an apology was more what I was thinking."

"If I'm not mistaken, I was flown here?"

"You remember that?"

"I do," he said, and paused. "At least, I think I do; it's getting mixed with the last time I was on my back in one."

"Oh" was all I could manage. That would have been when he was evacuated to Germany after Vick, his navigator, was killed.

"If he didn't punch me, the doc said tha' it could have ruptured at any time. If I had to be driven here, I would have either bled out or had organ failure before I got to the ER doors."

I gripped his hand with both of mine and put his knuckles to my brow bone like I were laying my head on a prayer stone.

He continued, "You were right."

I looked up. "About what?"

"We should have gone to the hospital last night."

I shook my head. "You mean, two days ago."

He looked at the weak midday sun. "That was two days ago?"

"Yes," I said, smiling, "they had you sedated for half of it."

We made small talk as that settled in on him, having lost that much time.

"TJ wants to come by to check on you. I've told him to go pound sand until you're up and vibrant again. If he does show up, I've promised him another shiner."

Rowan tried to sit up and grimaced.

"Easy there, cowboy." I got the giant corded remote for his bed and hit the tattered button that had a faint up arrow on it. The room filled with the racket of the bed attempting to come to an upright position. It whined and growled, working under duress. I tapped the remote against my palm as if that would cure it; when it didn't, I tried another button. It made the bed vibrate.

"Whoa," Rowan said and grabbed the side rails as he shook.

"That can't be it," I mumbled and hit another button displaying an arrow. I was getting desperate. I needed to fix it. This whole situation of Rowan being in the hospital, I couldn't help but feel, was somehow on my shoulders. Ormr, who had initially punched him, had been in me; then it was my brother who punched him again. I had to do better.

I smashed the next button in a stress sweat.

The bed went flat in an instant—Rowan with it.

"Whoa!" he shouted. His feet flew in the air as he fell back with a thud.

"Shit!" I said and hit the up button again. The motor ground and shook the bed.

"Oh!" hollered Rowan as the nurse crashed through the doors.

"What in the bloody hell," she said, breathless.

"Oh my god, I'm so sorry, Rowan." Then, to her: "I was just trying to get him sitting upright, and it shook and vibrated. Then I thought maybe back would help get the motor in gear, and then it fell!"

"Aye, I see tha'. This bed is not meant to have weight on it when it's moving," she said, and with an arm around Rowan's shoulders, she had me do it again, and like a sloth through quicksand, the bed made its way to a slightly higher incline than it had been at minutes before.

My stomach churned while she took his vitals. When she left, I turned and delicately put the remote on the side table.

"I'm so sorry," I said and found his hand.

He looked over at me, and there was humor twinkling in his eyes. "Aye, let's not do that again."

"Deal. I'm pretty sure that after everything, you don't want your obituary in the newspaper to read, Killed by Wife with Bed."

He gripped an extra pillow to his abdomen and tried not to laugh. "I was just thinking of tha'. I'm going to bloody fucking die in some foolish way after everything we've been through."

I gave in to the stress giggles. The relief that he was going to be all right was followed by the realization that I needed to accept things as they were. Or I was going to make things worse.

Wiping tears from my eyes, I leaned forward and softly brushed my lips over his, "I love you."

His quiet laugh was sealed in our kiss. "Tha gaol agamsa ort fhèin." *I love you too.*

We were quiet for a while, our fingers intertwined, and absently, I stroked the side of his hand with my thumb.

"Your brother seems nice," Rowan said.

I looked up sharply; he was studying the ceiling, a grin on his face.

"Yeah, well, if you think he's nice now, just wait until you see him again; you'll get the impression he's trying to mimic Mother Teresa."

"No, he's a good older brother. I'd have done the same if our roles were reversed."

"And why should there be punching? How about a nice civilized discussion?"

But Rowan's mind was elsewhere. "What I can't shake, though, is the feeling I've met him before. Must just be the helicopter ride tha' was familiar."

I nodded. "You haven't talked much about Germany."

"No, I haven't. I try no' to. But now...there's something about how he moved reminded me of the medics on the helicopter after I crashed."

"He is a medic, as you know," I prompted, then waited for him to continue, but he didn't. He looked at the ceiling as if the thoughts he felt were written there.

After he crashed. After he was shot and Vick was killed. I didn't even consider until then that the airship that saved him would have been a helicopter. He talked of his time there in general terms, so now that he was in the memory and talking about it, it felt like a significant deal.

"Are you feeling like that helicopter ride was yesterday, or does it feel far in your past?"

He took a deep breath in and winced. "Aye, a little of both. I know it was a long time in the past, but hearing the blades beat the air is reminding me of things that make it feel as if it's just happened. The heat, the pain," he said, feeling at his side where he'd been shot, "and Vick..."

I nodded, listening.

"The smells... I couldn't eat a ham sandwich for years."

"You still don't prefer them."

"The smell is too alike. Flesh..."

He looked down then. "We weren't supposed to be in that air space. But we'd gotten good intel, good enough to send Vick and me in, but without NATO command sanctioning it, there would be no support. We knew what we'd signed up for, and after we crashed and I was shot, I was expecting another in the head before I wrestled a gun from them. Only I didn't have to. I remember the whir behind me and the sand spiking up as bullets came down. To this day, I don't know why they were there. I never learned their names; sometime during the flight, I lost consciousness."

I put my hand over his. "Remind me, they were your brothers in arms, weren't they? So, they wouldn't have left you there. You were RAF; they would have known you went down and come to get you. NATO sanctioned or not."

"You would think tha', only they were US military."

I scrunched my nose, did I remember that bit? "US military? How would they have known you'd gone down? The flight beacon?"

Rowan shook his head as if it wasn't that exactly. "I have plenty of theories, but the exact details of how, why, where, who…are all things I have to shake hands with and put back in my black box. Because of the nature of our mission, I'll never know."

"OK," I whispered, kissing the back of his hand, "let me know how I can help?"

He gave me a soft smile and returned my kiss, pressing his lips to the back of my hand. "Stay here with me, if you can? I hate hospitals."

"Done. Just try and get rid of me." I took a long moment to drink him in, the returning sea–slate blue of his eyes, the dark shadow beneath his sharp jawline, and the dark slashes that were his brows. He was the breadth and depth of my love, a human embodiment of it walking this earth. He was close, alive, and our future spread out long like an endless road before us. "Marion is coming up today to give me a change of clothes. Doc says tomorrow you go home."

He sighed. "Tha' will be nice."

Chapter Four

The morning started as it did every early morning since Rowan came home from the hospital: A solid bank of misty gray fog sat on the land, softening the edges of the forest, of our cottage, and of the path up to the research field. It created a creamy, dreamlike atmosphere, wrapping our part of the world in a gauzy mystique.

Actual dreams came for me. They began when Rowan returned from the hospital and everything seemed to be settling down. They roused me from sleep before dawn, and like the past few days, no matter the hour, today I brushed them off and went to work.

Walking past the field looking ominous and ghoulish, I noted the dew settling on the charcoal remains. Still nothing had sprouted—no lichen had started to grow, which was the first step in creating new soil. The field was inert, charred, a barren landscape that allowed my thoughts to drift back to a short while earlier.

This morning, Rowan had gotten up as early as I had. In the kitchen with our mugs of coffee he stood between my legs as I sat on the counter, the one time we were eye to eye. And as it happened, lips to lips. I was still gun-shy about putting his abs to work, but kissing, he said, was fine.

"Yer brother has been keeping tabs on my health, between threats to that same health. He says I'm healed, but I can't take another blow to the abdomen anytime soon. But I am cleared for sneezing and a good belly laugh."

"I didn't hear 'acrobatic counter sex' in there."

"Fairly sure ye never will from your brother."

"I did hear," I said against his lips, "PT for recovery in small steps, like this?"

I leaned in and pressed my mouth to his before opening and tasting him and the way he took his morning coffee. Heavily loaded with cream and sugar like a dessert. I smoothed a hand over his chest before grabbing a fistful of his sweater to keep him close. I heard Rowan's mug hit the countertop; then his hand gripped the back of my head as his other grabbed my thigh as he pulled my body in against his. Perched against his body there on the edge of the counter, I set down my mug and put my arms around his neck. With my feet crossed at the ankles, I pressed them into his rear. I had been with him for over a year, but I still felt in moments like that, it was the first time our lips were touching. My stomach dropped in that pleasant way a carnival ride thrills and breathed him in. He was safety, ocean mist, and that organic musk that was all him.

I heard his groan, one of lust and desire and this time, regret.

"Mo ghràdh..."

His eyes were drugged and hungry, and he gave me another kiss, one that was gently reminding me that there were tasks to attend to that morning.

"What?"

His gaze swept over my eyes and cheeks and landed on my lips that felt rough and wet.

"Nothing." He dove back in, firming his grip on the back of my head, his mouth drowning me in his love and devotion. The ring on my finger warmed as if enchanted by the power of his emotions.

He paused, nose next to mine, and caught his breath. I loved that he could get as blissed out as me, that his loyalty to us, our connection, was as powerful and equal as mine. But I did hate that he tried to be a punctual person.

"I have tae meet Double-A in five minutes, and the trip is fifteen from here."

I cradled his cheek in my hand and brushed his lips with my thumb. "Go. We'll have more PT time later."

He breathed up my neck before releasing my hair, and with both hands on my thighs, he squeezed. "Promise?"

"I promise."

ALEX ALEXANDER, APPROPRIATELY, IF UNCREATIVELY, NICKNAMED Double-A, was a scrappy older man with the perpetual energy of a rechargeable battery. He was trying to quit smoking every time I saw him. Something he'd tell me with one hanging from his lips. And he was the father of my research assistant, Holly. Alex and his cohorts, all mates from the eighties and earlier, had invited Rowan to a farm out on the border of MacLaoch estates. The crack-of-dawn meeting was to get their business done before it was time to get to work in the fields and distilleries. Rowan had a feeling that the older men, most of whom had known Rowan since he was a "wee bairn," had come together to help find a solution to the foreclosure.

My boots took me up to the castle. I bumped open the main door with my shoulder. Renovations had gotten underway restoring the historic stained glass above the door that the rescue helicopter had blown out. I noted that they were saving what shards remained stuck in the frame. The plastic sheeting covering the window on the outside of the building dulled their colorful shine. I stepped over the drop cloths under the scaffolding and made my way down to the kitchen. It was too early for the glass workers and Marion, Flora, and Clive, and I was sure TJ was still asleep where we'd put him, up in Rowan's old apartment tower. I had the place to myself.

TJ had been underfoot as soon as we returned from the hospital, asking probing questions. He'd done that for about twenty-four hours before he was set to work. For some time, Reggie, our head gardener, had needed help, but Rowan could not afford it. Moving heavy rocks, cutting out stumps, and other large projects had been sidelined, waiting for a strapping young human to make themselves available. Reggie relayed to me that Tee was just the human for the job.

In general, it was good to see my brother and smash together two realities into one: the reality of my home, heritage, and Southern roots to the new reality of Glentree and Rowan. Rowan said he received inquiries from Tee daily. They ranged from the objective, a medical professional asking about Rowan's condition, to all-out hostile, as my protective older brother. It was apparent TJ was still wrestling with not being involved in everything from my epic battle-wedding to my living permanently in Scotland. If it wasn't something the Baker family would do, then it was ill-advised. And since everyone in my family was happy with where they were in South Carolina, my being in Scotland was not recommended.

Moving through the castle to the quiet, sleepy kitchens, I started the wood-burning stove. With its massive, cast-iron glory, it anchored the long, wide, partially subterranean stone kitchen. In years past, the antique stove would have been left to smolder overnight and then be stoked in the morning to provide heat to the castle (before the furnace was installed) and a hot breakfast and tea for its inhabitants sometime before noon. Now, it was an unspoken rule that the stove should be lit by the first one who arrived each day.

When the main prep kitchen got an electric kettle sometime in the nineties, making tea became a whole lot easier. This left the stove to warm the castle's stones, dry out the subterranean kitchens, and stand available to bake cookies for the visitors who paid extra for tea service.

I set the kettle to boil and retrieved a handmade ceramic mug from Marion's pottery days from the cabinet above, then closed the sticking door with the side of my fist. As I prepared the imported loose-leaf tea that smelled strongly of bergamot and sharp tannins, I looked around for the antique cookie tin. The wood countertops held extra pitchers, bowls, a kettle, a porcelain cake stand for afternoon tea, and finally, I spotted the lavender cookie tin on the far side of the room. It had a relaxing country scene painted on the lid and sides. It was one of those tins that my grandmother might keep buttons in.

I lifted the lid and smiled; it was packed shoulder to shoulder with rectangular shortbread cookies baked by Flora. I retrieved a plate.

As I prepared my breakfast of champions, I thought again of the residual mysteries I'd yet to solve about Mickey, Charmaine, and the Murdoch banker. Without the field to occupy my time, other than it now showing up in my dreams, my focus needed a new target.

How had three people who had given us so much guff in the past few weeks gone totally radio silent? I'd spent enough time in our family peach orchard to learn about animal nature. And humans, despite our clothes, were animals. I knew that when a shooed fox disappeared and it didn't return to its foxhole, it was behind you.

Rowan had fired Charmaine Chevalier as the estate's liaison with Casswell, the estate planning and public relations firm that had worked with MacLaoch lands for hundreds of years. She'd taken it civilly, gracefully even, which made Rowan uneasy. He'd have been much more comfortable with her outright antagonistic attitude than the new "Yes, sir" human he encountered. But he also said she looked somewhat shell-shocked as if she'd seen something recently that cracked her brain right in half. I smiled to myself and thought, *I have no idea what that could have been. Lil ol' Ormr, perhaps?*

But then Charmaine had not reported for duty in Glasgow. A mystery Clive kept Rowan abreast of while in the hospital. Her boss had contacted Rowan via Clive, asking why the devil he was working her so hard that she couldn't return to the office. From what Rowan pieced together, Charmaine had checked in with her boss and sold him a lie that the MacLaoch estate needed more of her time. After leaving the hospital, Rowan cleared the air. Mr. Casswell, befuddled by the strange behavior of his prize agent, hung up without so much as an apology for her behavior. I mentioned that maybe Rowan should fire more than just Charmaine.

Mickey Gillian was also missing. Mickey had not returned the Fund's calls nor any of mine. Rowan was clearheaded on the subject: "He took one look at ye, full Viking, and is currently in Saint-Tropez starting a new life." I tended to agree. Protecting his lying, cheating hide was always what the so-called archaeologist was good at.

Still...had he gotten what he came for? That unresolved question made me want to take the next six months to do a deep inventory of the castle's artifacts. Rowan had checked on the more costly items, and all the exquisitely expensive artifacts were on my ring finger or under lock and key and accounted for.

Through the kitchen window, I heard a rustle. A bushtit and a black-capped chickadee flitted and strutted in the detritus of the flowerbed surrounding the window placed close to the basement ceiling. They looked for seeds and tasty breakfast insects. They called to their friends in the gardens beyond between pecks and wing flicks. The chickadee's classic *chick-a-dee-dee-dee* sound filled the kitchen as the kettle began to whistle. The morning was waking. Flora and Marion would be there soon.

One fox had begun to show himself. The banker, Murdoch, had started calling again while Rowan was in the hospital, and not via Clive. He'd hang up when I answered, which my Southern manners roiled in a fury over. But since Rowan's return home, the calls had stopped.

Sunlight began to break through the morning fog and stream into the kitchen. I waited the allotted time for the tea to steep, then pulled the strainer out. I promptly dunked my shortbread in. I smiled, thinking of my mother making a hiss of disapproval at my breakfast choice and my unlady-like slurp of the softened cookie.

Chapter Five

Rowan arrived at the farm in the middle of what was proving to be a difficult week back to work as chief. The foreclosure threats from Dick Murdoch had escalated while he had been in hospital, but now all had gone silent. Even Rowan's requests to have another bank agent assigned to him had gone largely unanswered. Their responses had been "Yes, shortly" and "We're looking into it."

Then, since Cole's brother's arrival, TJ had set the tempo of the household: anger tangled with proper manners. Rowan respected the man for his anger; the polite inquiries to his health concerned him. To be in a fury with Rowan over marrying Cole before anyone in the family had had a chance to meet him? That, Rowan understood. And believed. Regarding the pleasantness, which did seem contrary to TJ's God-given temperament, Cole assured Rowan that her brother had been raised to be a gentleman and, every now and again, TJ remembered it. Nurture over nature.

Stepping out of his boxy old all-terrain vehicle, Rowan pocketed the keys and approached the barn that was nestled at the base of the purple-dusted hills, a burn carving through them, the gravel from the freshly mended driveway crunching under his boots. The barn was on the old MacMillan property north of Glentree; the tall grass pastures and moss-coated rock walls were a testament to the time since the last owner had been there working the land. MacMillan left in the forties for the Second World War and never returned. The MacLaoch clan had been caring for it ever since. The wood building had aged to a silvery gray matching the sky that morning. Mist hung low as the burble and splash of the stream filled the air.

Double-A, who had been Uncle Jacky's right-hand man when he was in the chief's seat, stepped out from inside the partially open barn door. He gave Rowan a grin and stubbed out his cigarette in the gravel before coming up to him, hand outstretched.

"Ye all right?"

"Aye, good, and ye?"

"Good. Good." He stood there, and Rowan waited with him. Then, as if realizing he'd invited Rowan to him, that he was in charge of the moment and not his chief, he added, "Glad ye've come."

"Me too. It's good tae see you." Rowan made a point to look around him. To the barn, to the cars parked on gravel, then back to him. "What's going on here? I'm worried."

That made Double-A chuckle and reach back toward the barn door.

"No worry, Guvna." He mimicked a Cockney accent; then in his learned Scots: "Nae more worries. We got that little problem you had solved."

"Which one?"

"Ye've more than one?"

"Aye, so I have."

Double-A considered. "That Mickey bloke come back?"

"Him? Nae. He's in a nonextradition country after seeing...Cole."

Double-A nodded, happy with the answer, but also: "I'm sorry I missed it. I would have been there, had I known."

"It's all right, Alex," Rowan said, skipping the nickname to indicate his seriousness. "I know that. And I'm glad you and Holly weren't there—it was a bloody mess."

"I dinnae wish for another skirmish, but I'll not miss the next one, I promise."

Rowan gave him a reassuring smile. "I believe, ye, Uncle. Now, tell me, why am I here this early?"

Double-A grinned before he pushed against the sliding door. It rattled and complained as the old oak panel moved to the side and slid to a stop with a screeching groan like a rail car. Rowan stepped forward and squinted into the darkness. In the damp, dark innards of the barn, he was immediately awash in a cool tannin smell he was intimately familiar with. He'd expected the smells of a barnyard but was welcomed with the golden memory of oak aging spirits within banded confines. The overhead lights flickered on. Inside the cavernous space were hundreds of stacked barrels breathing in the salty hillside air. They towered throughout the barn, replacing the horses and nursing calves he had expected.

"Is tha' what I think it is?"

"If you're thinking pure Highland gold, then aye."

"No," Rowan said, taking in a long, tasting inhale that invoked memories: The feel of his uncle's rough and calloused hand in his— walking down the damp halls of the castle's subterranean floors. Then excitement, jubilation, and that crisp oak smell saturated with grain alcohol that was being let to rest and metamorphose into liquid gold. "No, what Jacky called it...MacLaoch's Glentree Gold."

An excited shiver ran through the group of men who had gathered and on whom Rowan now focused with renewed curiosity. "Aye. Tha's the one," Double-A said. "So, ye do remember, then? Ye were just a wee lad when the law came and took the holdings at the castle. Didnae think you'd remember any of it."

Rowan was shaking his head, trying to tease more from the memory. Did he remember damp, gritty boots on the stairs? Or barrels being hoisted out, two men each?

Yes, he thought, the beach, the ocean chase... "I recall. And I remember the smell of whisky in the castle below ground."

"Aye, tha's where we stored the majority of it. And some in the outer caves...where you and the missus had your first snog."

Rowan grinned at the memory and was not at all surprised that the man knew about his first snog with Cole. Holly, Double-A's daughter, was Cole's closest friend—and also the best way to share information to the entire clan at lightning speed. "Yes, I remember," he said, meaning both his lips on Cole and the sight, decades before, of stored whisky. "What happened to it, the barrels?"

The men crossed their arms; some smiled at the memory. "Ye don't remember tha', then? You were a wee one, your uncle tried to keep it from you, and made us swear on his deathbed tae not involve ye until the staute of limitations was up."

"Statute!" came from the back.

"Aye, statute of limitations. He was protecting you." Double-A gave Rowan's shoulder a squeeze. "That night the authorities confiscated 204 casks and placed them in the quickest place they could, the bunker at the fort left at the fork on McGillvery's farm on the mainland."

"I know of it."

"Aye, well, just as they got the last barrel tucked in nice and tight, there come word of a coke seizure large enough tae supply Glasgow to Miami, and it was all hands on deck... And so goes the story of 204 barrels of whisky in the fort across the bay, long forgot and handily aged."

Rowan nodded and did a rough count of the rows of barrels in the barn. "There's more than tha' here."

"Aye, and more stored across the county. We pool our monies each year and buy as much raw spirit as we can then barrel it. With you bein' away in the military, well, it was just last year we started making plans tae tell you. Then with everything that happened at the gala then after, it seemed like we should wait—yer plate was full. Now, though, with the seriousness of the finances and all, if you'll agree to it, we'll bring all the casks back home to Glentree. We can start Glentree Gold. Legitimately." Double-A motioned for Rowan to follow him and the men.

Rowan had often mulled over the idea of restarting Glentree Gold. Even if only enough for the clan's personal use, a cost-effective option for weddings and parties at the castle. But time had been perpetually against him. Now, here were the men who'd worked in the big distilleries asking him to start it up. To continue his uncle's legacy, to dust off the old stills, and by the looks of the charts and graphs being projected on a hung white sheet they'd led him to, there was a road map to get there. Small bar tables had been set up near the screen with tasting glasses on each in various shapes and sizes, as if the men's home cupboards had been raided, and each held amber liquid of varying shades.

"How many barrels do you have now? As ye know we'll need a continuous supply—"

"Wee Rowan, don't be getting ahead of yourself." Double-A was at the laptop, a set of half-lens reading glasses perched on his nose. Rowan's insides warmed. It had been since Jacky that anyone had called him Wee Rowan. "Take a seat, and we'll get started…"

But Rowan was looking at the screen. "Two"—Rowan squinted— "thousand?" He felt lightheaded. "But how?"

"We ran the numbers with yer uncle before he left us—God rest his soul—and came up with the plan tha' the estate purchase grain alcohol and barrel it, hundred barrels a year, roughly, and then in twenty years we'd be able to start bottling it and commit the funds to the town for upgrades. Maybe even high-speed internet. After he passed and the estate stopped purchasing the raw spirit, we improvised and bought our own."

Rowan murmured, incredulous, "Ye bought them on your own?"

"Then we thought of the confiscated whisky barrels, and how we could meet our goals faster with them. Though we weren't sure if the barrels from the seizure were usable and didn't want tae drag ye into it if they were still hot. Just had a solicitor confirm tha' enough time has passed: The barrels are free and clear. We got special permission tae take them back, no tax owed."

"Aye, so now we can start talks of updating the old stone bridges?" That came from behind him.

Rowan turned and gave Shepherd Rupert a smile.

"Aye, or reopen jobs on the estate?" It was Josh, the estate's gillie, whom he'd had to lay off the year before. Rowan felt his cheeks warm with shame at the memory. But the older man had just given him a quiet, knowing look that said he knew Rowan had no choice in the matter. As had Simon, now seated on a crate next to Josh, who had overseen the docks, as his father did before him, before the estate had cashflow problems.

"And free drinks for townsfolk!"

The group turned as one toward the man who'd spoken. Charles's red nose and cheeks gave away his preferred hobby.

"Och, Charles, there will be nae drinking of the profits—"

"Charles, ye taste as ye go as it is; you're a liability!" Double-A hollered from the projector.

"Thoroughly tasting is the only way to truly know the continuity of the aging spirits—"

Rowan cut in before Charles was hung from the highest beam. "Where are the rest of the barrels now? Are they ready? Where do we—"

Double-A interrupted him. "If you please, Wee Rowan, we have a whole slide deck tae show ye; it'll answer all your questions."

AN HOUR LATER, THE PRESENTATION ENDED AND ROWAN STOPPED pacing. He pulled over an old wooden milking stool and sat. He put his head between his knees and took long deep breaths. If the data and the buyers lined up to purchase their first bottling were to be believed, the castle estate would be solvent by year's end and, in another two years, have enough to rehire every one of the estate's positions back, refurbish the town schools, and hire more teachers. And in twenty? Who knew... The possibilities were making his head spin. The level of this planning for the clan and its fortuitous timing couldn't be over-looked. Nor the details that had already been painstakingly handled.

He scrubbed his face with his hands to clear his mind and looked up. All eyes were on him. These same men had been by his uncle's side. They'd been there all along helping out. He just needed to be here, in Glentree, not in Glasgow or London, looking for fiscal help. He had to be here and here long enough to see them.

"Yer a blessing. All of ye." He felt his throat clog with emotion. The castle and everyone's way of life had nearly buckled under modern pressure, and here it was being handed back to him on an amber platter.

"Ye'll do it?"

Rowan stood. "Do it? It's done. Ye've all done it. If all you have goes as you've planned, this will save the clan, the estate, and our way of life." He shook his head at how daft he'd been not to first talk with the people who mattered most to him. "Ye have my support. Do ye need lands? I can source warehouses too."

"Aye, good." There was a shiver of excitement that ran through the crowd. The idea was shaping up into something real. Something tangible. "But we'll need more than tha' from ye…"

"Anything."

Double-A cleared his throat and pulled off his reading specs. "If ye'll excuse the blunt language. We need yer credit and good name, Wee Rowan, and no' much else."

Rowan felt the first speedbump in their progress. "The estate is dodging foreclosure but likely headed toward bankruptcy at the moment. I'm afraid our name and credit aren't what they once were."

"We know, but the MacLaoch name has been around longer than we sods"—he twirled his finger to include the men in that room—"and it was only at the mention of *your* name that we were able to secure the buyers, the distributors, the network. They knew of yer uncle, and it was him that they were keen to work with. You? Just as good."

Rowan was having difficulty understanding. "But you did all the work, and surely they know of you from when you worked with Jacky, aye?"

"Aye."

"Ah," Rowan said, grasping his meaning in his tone. "We've left the past behind but not at all, have we? They'll take an unknown laird and chief over hardworking—"

"Nobodies. We're nobodies."

"Ye have it. My name is yours."

Charles piped up. "How about yer signature?"

Charles was booed and cuffed on the shoulder.

Double-A spoke up. "Be our chief…executive officer." He gave a rare toothy grin. "If ye don't mind, we'd have ye take the business in under the castle estates and run it from there. We have a mind to do the work, but we've no stomach for the taxes and political handshaking."

He didn't either, but he'd take it on with verve. "Aye, point me in the direction ye need and set me loose, boys."

Double-A grinned back at him. "I knew ye would; we knew ye were your uncle's lad. He'd be damn proud."

Chapter Six

Iwashed my breakfast dishes and took a shortbread for the road before heading upstairs, where I heard raised voices. We had been getting visitors early, trying for a glimpse of the chief or me as word spread to clan members far and wide that another paranormal event had happened. And while we hadn't formally announced the news, word of our extraordinary wedding was also spreading, and felicitations were starting to trickle in. However well-intentioned the congratulatory visits, Marion and Flora had no tolerance for non-paying lookie-loos. If visitors couldn't connect their family tree to Marion and Flora's satisfaction, then admittance was cash or credit. The castle's crumbling foundation wasn't going to fix itself.

Dusting the last shortbread crumbs off my chest while I was still making my way around the back of the main staircase, past the old books and glass curios that held artifacts, I finally saw Marion and then Flora arguing and pointing up the main stairs. They were beautiful stairs, regal, wide, and carpeted in the red of the MacLaoch formal tartan. And recently redecorated with stained glass from the blown-out windows. But that was not what they were arguing about.

"You go up there and tell her tae git out."

"I already 'ave!"

I interrupted. "Who's up there I have to shoo out? Clan member?"

"Oh, my lady—"

I squelched the desire to snort at that. Marion and Flora liked the old-school way of things, and calling me "lady" was one thing they strictly adhered to, but it also made my tomboy American brain crack right in half.

"She's gone up there. We told her not to tae, but she did it anyway. We're so sorry but—"

Flora cut in, "She's lost her faculties."

"Who has?"

"That conniving—"

"Ms. Chevalier tae us." Marion's lips puckered as if she'd had something sour cross her tongue.

It took me a moment to get past the déjà vu; Charmaine had been up in that room before, and I'd needed to get her down then too.

"Like a damn cat in a tree," I mumbled.

"What's that, m'lady?"

"Nothing. Rowan knows she's here?"

They shook their heads.

"He'd skin 'er alive if he caught her here. She's supposed tae be back down in Glasgow or the London offices, but she's not been. Says she has papers for him tae sign about the loan and will wait until he returns."

Flora piped in. "Saw her skulking about the other day, but the laird was in the hospital, and ye were blue with worry for him, so we didn't tell ye. You'd think she'd be here fretting about his health, but instead she's been mumbling to herself and assessing castle assets."

My brow pinched with worry. I started up the stairs as Holly came around from the basement staircase and hall as I had done. She looked so rough I stopped in my tracks. Dark circles creased under her eyes as if she'd stopped sleeping, and her expression looked as if she'd seen a ghost repeatedly.

I asked her, "Are you all right?"

Seeing us, she dropped an emotional mask over her features and brightened her eyes. "Aye! There ye are. Been looking all over."

Holly's arrival didn't divert Flora, and she was back at me: "Yer brother is one tae get up early and wander." She made eyes up the stairs as if it was urgent that the twain should not meet lest he be scratched when he used his Southern manners to try and pet that particular kitty.

Holly asked, "Who's up there?"

"Charmaine," we said in unison.

"Ah." Holly adjusted her sweater cuffs. "Saw her the other day, wandering about. She was stuck in the Circle Garden tidying up."

That made no sense. "Why is she still here?"

"Dunno, but she was picking up after the helicopter visit. She was taking flower petals—one by one—of the thousands that got blown around and tossing them back into the garden beds."

Our collective looks were: "Why?"

Holly's tone was matter-of-fact: "She's nutso."

"Aye, trying to control nature is now on her CV. She's gonna break."

"If she hasn't already."

"I think she saw"—and I pointed to my face—"*him*. She was probably the one who triggered him, actually."

Holly leaned close, her keen brown eyes searching my face. "Sorry I missed him. He...comes back other times at all?"

Marion genuflected as Flora gasped, clutching her necklace. Ormr was not far enough in the past to joke about.

"No."

"Not even a little bit?"

I crossed my eyes and stuck my tongue out.

"There he is!" she exclaimed and tried to grab my tongue.

"Ack!"

"Shall we?" she asked and nodded up the stairs.

"No worries, Holl, I got this."

"Ye mean to say I can't come? Yer brother is wandering around helpless upstairs, and you've got a missus who's one split end from going completely horizontal off the plane of reality; what's one more?"

"Fine, OK," I said, starting up the stairs, "let's run Charmaine out of Dodge once and for all. Then we'll get back to work." As I plodded up the stairs, I muttered, "She makes the most basic things feel herculean."

A few steps up, Holly asked, "But Dodge, where's that, and how do we run her out of there?"

I whispered back to her like we were the Ghostbusters entering a warehouse to meet a wild paranormal monster. And it might eat us if we didn't get the moment of surprise 100 percent right.

"Dodge City, Kansas. Rough-and-tumble town in the Old West—I think it's from a TV show. Criminals are run out of town, or Dodge."

"Gotcha. Bless ye Yanks and yer cowboy shows." Then: "Remind me tae show you my pink cowgirl boots."

"You have cowgirl boots?"

"Kinda."

"Kinda..." I murmured and let that sink in as we made our way up. "I don't want to know why they're 'kinda' cowboy boots, do I?"

"Probably not."

A night out at the pub earlier in the summer came to mind. "Are they those pink stiletto boots?"

Holly scoffed, confirming yes despite her "No..."

It was quiet as we got to the top of the steps. I looked right down the hall to the fairy tower rooms where Rowan's old studio was and where TJ was currently staying before looking left down the hallway where the anterior rooms were.

"They're still considered cowgirl boots, aye? I mean, not all of them have to be worn doing cow stuffs?" Holly whispered.

Over my shoulder: "No, Holl, sorry, those aren't cowgirl boots. Those are stripper boots, cowgirl *style*."

"Shit," she said and clarified why she was swearing. "Not about the boots, but he's in there."

The door to Rowan's office was ajar. In the sliver of visibility, my brother was scrutinizing his desk, an apple in hand, before he looked up in the direction of the adjoining conference room.

"What's he doing?" I said to myself.

"He looks like he's investigating. Digging for dirt."

"Proof we're a cult so he can take me back to South Carolina."

"Well..."

"He should be out helping Reggie." I took a deep breath, hating what I had to do. Plants gave me zero trouble; humans did, though, all the time. "No time like the present." I came off the top stair and made a beeline to the conference room, where Charmaine likely was, to head TJ off. I gave the unlatched door a good thump with my boot toe. The door swung open, hitting against the wall with a bang.

Too late, TJ had meandered through the doorway that connected the conference room to the office. At our door screaming open, he froze with the apple halfway to his mouth, staring at us.

Charmaine was also there, pretending she hadn't been startled out of her skin. I stopped the door as it swung back. As she had been rumored to be, she was unusually unkempt; even the silver hair clip she usually wore had been replaced with a regular rubber band. I winced for her. She had curly hair like I did. I knew she'd need a surgeon to remove it.

"Oye, I see it now," Holly mumbled. "She needs a hug. Then, after a beat, she added, "Or an exorcism."

"What are you doing?" I aimed at Charmaine, then gestured for my brother to get out. This had the opposite effect: It made him come stand at my opposite shoulder. He gave Holly a wink across me.

She responded to him under her breath behind me, "Want to see an exorcism?"

He leaned back and whispered, "Absolutely."

"You're about to."

Tee looked at me, eyebrows raised.

Charmaine pushed back the hand-carved Chippendale chair from the long, solid wood table with the air of a person she no longer was. Her mascara was smudged thickly below her eyes as if she'd applied it a week ago, forgot it existed, and then reapplied it every morning. Something had fallen onto her skirt and been wiped away, but not enough to eliminate the mustard mark on the soft gray of her couture skirt suit.

She gestured to a chair beside her, saying, "Please have a seat."

I didn't.

"Charmaine," I started, "Rowan's instructions were clear, but since you've taken to giving him the bird by staying here, let me try another way. Get. The fuck. *Out.*"

Holly hissed with joy under her breath, a sound like *yes*.

"Ms. Baker—"

There was a crunch of the apple from TJ, like a crack off the back wall. Charmaine eyed him, then me.

"As I was saying—"

Another crunch.

Mentally, I groaned; TJ had never met an argument he didn't thoroughly enjoy.

At him, I said, "Tee, no. That wasn't an invite—"

"Who's getting the *fuck* out of where?" he asked, homing in on my single curse word like a laser pointer. "Isn't *fuck* a verb? So, technically, you can't get the fuck out of something, but rather fuck the fuck out of something?"

"Tee, no one is—"

Charmaine's tone was like acid on a wound as she said, "And who are you?"

"Who are *you*?" he mimicked, then threw a casual hand over my shoulder. The Baker kids—including Holly—united.

"Ah, yes. I see now. I know who you are. Let me educate you on who *I* am. I'm Ms. Charmaine Chevalier, esquire, agent, and clan representative."

I let some air out of her balloon. "*Ex.* Rowan fired you days ago. And you are here why?"

"And yet," she continued, "as things stand, I've not been replaced; therefore, I must do my duty—"

"Doody." TJ reinserted himself into the argument and set to put the final nails in the "I'm going to ram this entire confrontation into the ground" coffin.

Holly strangled down her chortle, putting her fingertips to her lips to cover a smirk. Charmaine was ill-equipped to play any game, much less the one TJ had set in motion, and was possibly going to lose her head.

"Du-tee," I said, playing my part, "not doo-doo doody."

TJ nodded. "Right. Doody, as in poop."

"Stop. You both are the vision of idiocy."

TJ took another bite of his apple and moved to the end of the table and rested a hip on the edge, effectively putting himself between Charmaine and me. "I don't mind being called an idiot, but were you calling my sister an idiot?"

She put her pen down with great care and looked at him with a self-satisfied smile: "If the shoe fits...Tiberius Jerome Baker."

He and I both flinched at his ostentatious name, which no one but our mother called him, and only when he was in deep dog doody.

"It's TJ," he said around a bite, "unless you're aiming to spank me."

Her eyes narrowed. TJ was used to entertaining all humans—except his commanding officers—with his charm, albeit childlike. They could be in a deadlock for days. Charmaine would try to prove to him that she was the most powerful human on earth, and TJ would try to make her laugh.

"I see you have an overinflated sense of self, like your sister. Do you also take things that don't belong to you, *Tiberius?*"

He gave her a long, analyzing look, one that, to someone unfamiliar with it, might suggest that he had been bested.

I groaned. "Pick one, TJ. You can't have a rebuttal to the 'overinflated self' comment and squeeze in a 'You called me Tiberius, so now you have to spank me' joke too."

"I can try," he said around a bit of apple.

Charmaine let out an exasperated sigh.

"You used Tiberius again; now you have to spank me."

Holly murmured, "Aw, he picked one. I was hoping he'd do both."

"To keep my ego in check—and because Pavlov demands it—I'm programmed to receive punishment when I hear that name. Spank me." He stood, putting his apple in his mouth, his hands going to his belt buckle. Holly threaded her fingers together in prayer or to keep from clapping in glee, I didn't know.

Around his apple, he said, "Here? Or do you have somewhere more private that you'd like to do it?"

"Tee..." I halfheartedly pleaded. A serious part of me was done with her soap opera antics and was fine with a new kind of tact to get her to leave. *I* couldn't get her to leave, *Rowan* couldn't, maybe Tee could. It would be a scientific experiment to see which option got her to respect our request.

"Mr. Baker, you cannot be serious!" Charmaine's eyes were wide, yet her anticipatory gaze was glued to my brother's hands.

I pointed at the door. "You can always leave, Charmaine. In fact, I urge you to."

He got his belt loose. "Here is fine, I suppose. I tend to be a shy man, but it must be done," he said, looking down at his hands, making slow work of it, giving her time to run from the room.

Holly looked at me, then him, then back to me. "Is he gonna..."

"Oh, he's gonna. Unless Charmaine leaves."

Charmaine, though, didn't hear us. Her own hands were frozen on the arms of her chair, her chest sucking in air with an expression on her face that was a mixture of high astonishment and a strong desire not to look away. "Is this happening?" she asked no one in particular.

I shrugged. "It's your decision to stay. You're actively participating in this charade, Charmaine, because you didn't do as he requested. You haven't done what any of us have requested of you. TJ, you should know, is a man of his word. Now, you can get your things and leave like you've been asked to—"

TJ's pants hit the floor.

Charmaine squeaked.

Chapter Seven

To see Charmaine's face at that moment was a thing of beauty. The same woman who hounded and bit at me, telling me I was a liar and a fraud, before engaging in all-out political warfare against me, was eye-poppingly staring at my pants-less brother. It was satisfying. I was grinning from ear to ear when TJ turned his fabric-covered butt to her, waiting for his flogging.

TJ was wearing benign blue-striped underwear that covered him as much as a pair of shorts would.

"Still a boxers guy, huh?"

He grinned at me. "It was a rush job packing. I'll have something more presentable tomorrow. My apologies."

"Excellent. I know Charmaine will be interested, seeing that if she pops by, she'll get another eyeful. Or should I say, *trespasses* tomorrow."

"Please!" Charmaine squealed, finding her manners side to her brain. She put her palms out in front of her face as if my brother's butt was a projectile about to crash into her. "Cover yourself; this is most indecent!"

Next to me, Holly kept her face impassive, something I was wholeheartedly impressed with, but her eyes said she was making a movie in her memory and would replay this scenario down at the pub for a week until all of Glentree heard about: *The Baker Kids and the Casswell Agent Who Wouldn't Take No for an Answer.*

I looked back at Charmaine. "Come on, Charmaine, put TJ out of his misery and spank him, or promise to call him TJ in the future."

"Yes! Fine!"

He was now resting one elbow on the table, his chin propped on his fist. I nodded to his pants on the floor. "Britches up—she promised."

"I'm not sure. She didn't sound convincing."

"I'll tell you what: I'll get a device out of the dungeons that will give you one helluva spank, then pull your britches up for you."

Holly nodded out the door. "Want me tae grab it?"

"Would you?"

"Oh, look," I said as my brother started to move, "he's got it. Don't you, Tee?"

TJ was pulling up his pants, tsking. "You're so violent sometimes."

Holly scoffed. "Ye have *no idea*."

TJ buckled and turned to Charmaine, his apple back in his left hand. "Now, where are my manners?" He held out his free hand. "The name is TJ, and I'm Nicole's *older* brother."

Charmaine stood, "I'll not be shaking your hand. *T-J*." She pronounced the letters like she was reciting the alphabet. "You deserve no such honors from me, and soon you and your loathsome sister will be far from here, mark my words."

I groaned and looked up at the ceiling as if the answers for how to get the hell out of this predicament were written up there. "Oh, please don't do that," I complained.

"And what, Ms. Baker, is *that*?"

I shook my head at her. "You keep doing these things... I can't figure out if you're doing them intentionally, or are you that ignorant?" When she said nothing, I continued, "Charmaine, you served him an ultimatum." I nodded to TJ. "There's no one more loyal *and* hard-headed than him."

TJ was grinning and looking at Charmaine. He was happy to have someone call him out so his actions could be applauded, and the subtext didn't need to be explained.

"I did no such thing."

"'Mark my words'? This guy," I said, gesturing to the grown man-child before her, "will prove you wrong."

Charmaine's chin went up as she looked my brother in the eye. He gave her an equal stare back. Then, she did it again. "I'd like to see you try."

"No. Tee, she's leaving. She's a dishonored ex-employee and no business of yours. Goodbye, Charmaine." I got between her and Tee and, arms out wide, kept him back as if he couldn't see her around me, and ushered her and her things out the door.

Bulging satchel on her shoulder, she paused at the doorway. Her brown eyes flashed. "You'll drown Rowan in your ineptitude, and he'll lose everything he's held dear. Only at the bitter end will he finally see you for the charlatan you are."

Her words had the bitter jab of a curse, and I was reminded of what Great-to-a-Billion-Granny Ethel said weeks ago, that there would always be a MacLaoch agent set to destroy the union between the Minory and the MacLaoch.

I suppressed the urge to head-butt her into the doorframe and instead snapped the rubber band on my wrist and said, "I'm sorry you can't see the passion and connection Rowan and I have for each other. I'm sorry you'll live your days with unrequited love and the inability to love yourself enough to move on to someone who cares for you as much as you do them. I wish you a better future than the one you see for yourself."

Her eyes hissed in response before she stalked to the stairs. I followed to make sure she left. At the top of the stairs, I could see Marion and Flora below swiftly doing busywork arranging pens and the guest book, covering what they had been doing, which was eavesdropping. I opened my mouth to ask them to open the main doors to flush Charmaine out when something caught my eye down the hall that I hadn't noticed from the angle I'd been facing when I came up the stairs.

My new vantage point showed me the southern side of the long, elegant hall. Most was an everyday sight: It was lined with petite cherrywood tables topped with porcelain vases. Each Queen Anne leg gracefully ended in a wooden paw kneading the Persian rug that ran the length of the hall. That rug had been a gift to the MacLaoch clan chief in the eighteenth century. The wide, carved wood panels of the walls were bisected by doorways that stood open on either side, letting soft daylight spill onto the red and indigo of the patterned rug. Portraits and landscapes in brass or gold filigree frames adorned the dark walnut of the wall panels. The largest of them Rowan had once seriously considered putting up at auction to cover the estate debts. He'd ditched the idea, realizing he'd never forgive himself if he did. The painting was a gift to his clan nearly four hundred years earlier by a Mr. Harmenszoon van Rijn. To his friends, Rembrandt. Though I'd taken to caring for it as well, at first, I knew it was a Rembrandt only because his name was on the brass wall plate. The brass plate that had been installed below the painting, which was now just a brass plate because the square of wall above it was empty.

"Where's the Rembrandt?" I blurted.

The person who answered took me by surprise. Charmaine made an indelicate scoffing sound. "My, my, Ms. Baker, I'm surprised you even noticed."

She stood midway down the steps. I looked from her down to Marion and Flora, who called up to me, "It was there last night when we closed up! Is it really gone?"

Feeling my eyes narrow in suspicion, I rested my gaze back on Charmaine.

"What have you done?"

"The thing you could never do."

Holly read my mind and said under her breath, "Want *me* to give her a push? Such tiny stairs, and they're carpeted—she won't get but a few bruises. Been down them myself after a party here in my youth."

"No, if she takes a tumble, it'll take her longer to tell me why the fuck she seems so smug." To Charmaine: "Why are you so smug about that?"

"Why do you think I'm here, Ms. Baker?"

She'd said it several times now, *Baker*. I was still officially Baker, but it felt like she was using it as a dig—as if, in her eyes, I'd never be worthy of the MacLaoch name.

She continued, "Well, it certainly is not to get into another round of fisticuffs with you; it's to do my job. And even if Rowan thinks he can go it alone, an idea no doubt you put into his head, he cannot. Mr. Murdoch—"

"The banker?"

"—reached out to me to see if we could come to an agreement, and I've spearheaded efforts to pause the loan's foreclosure proceedings with a good faith payment in the form of the Rembrandt. The chief knows of this and approved my idea before you came along, and I'm seeing it through to the end. You're an annoyance, and if I have to subjugate you to do my job, I shall."

"Wait." I held up a finger. "One, subjugate? Fuck you." Then added another finger. "Two. You *stole* the Rembrandt?"

Her face flushed, and her chin tilted up in defiance. "I've stopped the bankruptcy proceedings by seeing to the financial expectations set in place when the laird took on the estate debt and ignored the prosperity he could have had through other means."

"You're unbelievable." I was seething. "You don't work for us anymore, so this is theft, *and* trespassing. You stole a prized heirloom from the castle. Don't congratulate yourself."

TJ piped in, "Quick question for those of us who need the Cliffs Notes version: What does she mean about some ignored prosperity through other means?"

Holly clarified, "She wanted the chief tae marry her, and she'd use her finances for philanthropic means around the castle, etc."

TJ and I were raised on Southern interpersonal drama, so he quickly grasped the basic meaning. "Oh, she was going to pay him to marry her?"

Glaring at Charmaine, I answered, "Yes."

Her triumphant brow crashed. Red blotches of rage moved from her neck up to her cheeks. When she spoke, her voice was uncharacteristically loud. "How disgusting—"

Tee moved down the steps toward her; his body language was like that of a man put into the stable of a wild stallion. With a calm, cool-headed tone, he said, "I bet you're smart enough to know when you're being baited, Ms. Chevalier." He moved slowly, landing one stair down, so she stood above him. "This isn't a place to air our dirty laundry, now, is it? My sister won the game of hearts; Rowan is hers; he loves the almighty hell, pardon my language, out of her, and I reckon, come hell or high water, he will do anything, and I mean *anything*, for her. So, you take that beautiful wreck that is your honor, and you protect it. Don't get into it with my little sister anymore, you hear?"

Holly whispered, "Can your accent get that thick too? I don't think I understood a word he said."

Charmaine sneered at him. "You both are absurd."

"Thank you," he answered. "Now, share with me these details of the Rembrandt you fixed the loan with. If we can get that sorted before the chief comes back, I think we can avoid some serious trouble. Don't you think?"

I hadn't focused on how close Tee was to her until he stepped up to her stair and gently laid his palm on her shoulder and gave it a squeeze and a soft smile before letting go.

Charmaine didn't look like she wanted to give up the fight, but TJ had his face arranged all pleasant like. With his tan skin, dark brown hair, and the family's blue eyes, he was what my aunts called a looker. And right then, he had those good looks aimed directly at Charmaine, and he wore an expression that said she was his last saving grace, and he knew—just knew—she'd make the right decision. And surprisingly, she tried.

"The Rembrandt is on loan until back payments can be made and regular service to the loan can be reestablished. I have the paperwork."

"Sounds fair." TJ gave her a smile that lit his eyes.

She looked to him with wary concern, then to Holly and me, then back to him. "They think I stole it." To us: "I didn't, it was an agreed-upon—"

"Agreed upon?!" I hollered, and my exclamation boomed around the stone cathedral ceiling of the foyer.

Tee patted at the ground. "Shh, let's hear her out. You're making her question her own judgment, sis. You're a damn bulldozer—let her have her say."

Holly snorted, "Bulldozer," as I ground my molars. Loath to let the fight pass, I searched my wrist for my band and reminded myself that anger was an emotion, not a state of being, and that it too would pass. Then snapped it.

Charmaine continued, "The chief is under the assumption that I'm no longer an employee of Casswell, but I am, and my supervisor approved the decision to move forward with the Rembrandt as collateral. The castle and all its assets are safe. It's time to improve the operational costs here at the castle to show an increased revenue stream and resume regular payments, putting all this foreclosure and bankruptcy nonsense behind us."

I had a feeling she included me in the "foreclosure and bankruptcy nonsense."

"There, that sounds like some highly intelligent business savvy." He smiled at her in a way that made her look pleasantly at his mouth. But what TJ always had was my back, and she wasn't going to like what he had to say next. He was wearing his "yeah, but" smile. It was meant to make the observer feel good because what he was about to say wouldn't.

He continued, "But. You've neglected the body count."

"I beg your pardon? Body count? This isn't a military operation; no one has died, T-J."

"That may be so, but your reputation took a swan dive off the tallest turret of this castle the moment you moved behind the back of the owner of this place."

She scoffed, resuming her mask of contempt. "My reputation is solidly intact because it's based on the three-hundred-year-old legacy of Casswell to do right by the clan whether there be a chief of legendary import at the helm or one who gets sidelined by an American tart."

Holly stepped toward her, and I held my arm out, stopping her. The name-calling was new, putting both of our backs up. "She's baiting. Let's have her explain to my brother what tart means."

TJ looked sad. "You're an intelligent woman, Ms. Chevalier. Calling my sister that is beneath you. I know what tart here means."

She looked smugly at TJ. "You Americans—" She broke off with a surprised squeal as TJ picked her up, tossed her over his shoulder like a sack of potatoes, and headed down the stairs.

Over her squeals, he continued, "You can't call my sister a tart, Ms. Chevalier, and think I'll let you get away with it. Let's get some air and talk about this."

Marion and Flora were shocked and gleeful as TJ walked beneath the workmen's scaffolding—they were thankfully late to work—and out the front door.

When the front door shut, Holly's laugh burst out. It echoed off the arched stone and reverberated back to us as Marion and Flora began to tittle.

I was shaking my head. "She called me a tart... I wish that meant pastry."

"TJ! I love yer brother! He just"—Holly made scooping motions with her arms—"up and grabbed her, then, right over his shoulder!" Holly wiped her eyes. "I hope he takes her down to the docks and tosses 'er in."

"I wish. He's probably just taken her to her car. And either she drives out or he'll drive her home. I wish this were the first time this had happened to us. Maybe it's something about us Bakers that makes people irrational."

Holly was thoughtful before turning to me. "Do ye think I can borrow him? I have a family thing tomorrow, and tha' skill set would come in handy."

"It's not a unique skill set. I know you can do it too, Holly."

"Yeah, I'd have initiated my own tête-à-tête with her, had he not stepped in first."

I knew she would have.

"But," she continued, "I was talking about that sack-of-potatoes move. My uncle who spouts garbage about my mum's family when he's pished is over fifteen stone."

I'd been in Glentree for over a year, but stone measurement still threw me. "So, huge."

It was the correct response. Context and good guesses got me through a lot in this place.

"So, can I borrow him?"

"You bet."

Chapter Eight

When Rowan heard that the Rembrandt had been "given" to the bank, I didn't have to be spiritually connected with him, as I was, to know he was livid. The whisky in his belly soured quickly when I filled him in, and he spent the rest of the day growling and skulking around the grounds, his cell phone to his ear. We met back up in the cottage that evening. The late-summer sunset was laced with a crisp breeze that ambled through the window reminding me that fall was approaching. The researchers would be heading back to school, and the Fund would want a progress report.

Rowan was still processing the fact that his ancient uncle's portrait was stolen to pause foreclosure proceedings. "I've spent all bloody afternoon trying to get a meeting with the two of them. Charmaine is simply telling me tha' she's indisposed and hanging up, and Murdoch is still refusing to answer my calls. Something is off, I can feel it in my bones. I'd expect him tae call and rub it in my face that he has it and give me the backhanded compliment of avoiding foreclosure of the loan."

"Maybe he gave Charmaine that speech. I imagine them toasting and high-fiving, not realizing you had other plans. Or, excuse me, not giving a rat's patootie about your plans."

"They need tae know what they've done." Rowan wanted to watch their expressions when he told them what taking the Rembrandt meant to him and precisely what he would do to them as penance. It sounded, on the surface, as just. He wanted to tell them they would no longer do business with the estate. But I thought the subtext of his body language—"and if I get an opportunity to torpedo your career, I'll take it"—made the in-person part critical.

I pulled my university tee over my head and slipped in under the covers as his phone chimed. "Is that one of them? Is it Charmaine apologizing? Murdoch texting you that Charmaine was out of line and that he'd love a sit-down with you to apologize and work through what new direction the estate can take to avoid foreclosure?"

When he laughed, I had my answer.

"No. An old friend is coming to visit." His fingers texted back as I waited.

And when I couldn't wait any longer, I asked, "Who?"

He put his phone down. "A verra good distraction and a research fellow who has heard from Clive that we've had another paranormal event."

I grinned back at him. "Peabody!" I loved Peabody. That is, I loved Peabody *after* I got over him pinching me at the gala when we met the year before to prove his point that Rowan's and my energies were connected. There was no one in my sphere who was more joyful and enthusiastic in his dedication to his pursuit than Peabody.

"Tha's right."

"When is he coming?"

"He doesn't know."

"Next month? Next year?"

Rowan shook his head as he toed off his shoes. "Something about grants being funded, and he will come once they did."

"Ah, so this decade, then."

"Aye."

"Speaking of people visiting, have you seen TJ?"

Rowan paused in unbuttoning his cuffs, thinking. "No. Haven't been threatened by him either. Odd, aye?"

I adjusted the covers, then plopped my arms on top, letting them slowly descend into the feather comforter. "Charmaine killed him."

His cufflinks clinked into their holder on his highboy dresser. "Or he's making passionate love tae her while she scratches his backside off."

I made a retching sound. "Gross."

"What?" he asked absently, his mind elsewhere, "ye don't think she'd scratch him?"

"I dunno, you tell me. You're the only one here who's slept with her."

He was working the buttons down his front when he stopped and gave me a long, dry, unamused look. "I know tha' comment comes from a place of jealousy, but we both know I learned tha' lovemaking could involve scratching when I met *you*."

I smiled at having been called out; it was true. I smoothed down the covers and was back to: "Charmaine murdered him."

"Likely."

"Tomorrow, I'll call the police and report him missing." I made a mental note to remind TJ that Charmaine was one nut he'd not be able to crack, certainly not in the few days he had left at Castle Laoch. He had to return to service for Uncle Sam, so he should not dally with my mortal enemy. Unless he was investigating her for a weakness I could exploit.

Rowan shucked his pants and slid into bed with me, buck naked.

He pulled me in against him, and I smiled against his lips. "You're a Neanderthal."

He kissed me down my neck. "And why's that?"

"You left your pants wadded on the floor."

"I'll get it in the morning."

"And your shirt?"

"Morning."

"And what happens now?"

"I sleep long and deep knowing that in just forty-eight hours, I'll likely spend the rest of my life in a box."

I turned over and tucked my pillow under my cheek while I

analyzed the contours of his cheeks in the low light in the room. "Is that a prison cell for murder?"

"Double homicide."

"Two more cairns on the knoll and no one would be the wiser," I hypothesized with him.

He lightly touched my lips with his. "And tha' is why we're better together."

I grinned. "Some might call us homicidal maniacs."

He murmured against my lips. "Just misunderstood."

Rowan ran his hand down my thigh before gripping my knee and bringing my top leg over his. He pressed his pelvis in, whispering, "I missed ye all day. There's so much I wanted tae share with ye, then the Rembrandt." He sighed long and loud. "Now, though, all I want tae do is be with you."

"Good." I kissed his lips. "I'll be here all night."

He found the breast closest to him and, between the backs of two fingers, gently pinched to see if she was awake. Then bent to kiss her, as if apologizing for his rough behavior. After his soft, warm peck, he slipped her into his mouth and suckled.

I swallowed my deep-throated laugh and clutched him to my chest.

"Och, god, I love that laugh. Feels like I'm in deep trouble and also about tae find out how long I can last before coming."

I captured his smile with my lips and fell into our connection. He smelled of sea salt and the pine-scented soap from the shower he took earlier in the day. His tongue danced with mine as he grabbed my ass and brought me in even closer. And with a skim of the backs of his fingers down my stomach, he caressed until he dove into the auburn curls between my legs. I gripped him to me as his fingers found my entrance and slipped a curious finger inside.

I groaned and slid my fingers into his hair and gripped tight. "Rowan..."

He slipped in another finger, then a third, before giving a slow slide in and out, warming up my body and creating a slip and slither for his hardening erection that lay between us. I gripped him harder to me, and Rowan responded with a gentle strike of his palm to the front of my opening. He made quick work waking up, stretching, and calling out my lust from outside in. I arched my back, trying to get him to dive in, climb higher, go deeper. There was one more erotic pleasure to be had deep inside, and it could only be touched by his thick erection.

Holding fast his hair, I bent his head toward mine, put my mouth onto his, and devoured. I wanted him, his hands, his hard-on that lay between us, all of it, inside of me all at once. I wanted to, like I had since the moment he tied my wrists to his a year ago, inhale him into my lungs and have his blood become mine.

He pressed me back into the pillows, matching my aggression with his own desperation. It had been days since we'd connected, and his hand still within me thrust in again and again. My body warmed, and I felt that sizzle in my veins that was both my own building orgasm and Rowan's need; we were a matched set of bodies in desire. His hard cock lying across my abdomen was too much of a tease: I needed him, wanted more.

Rowan's voice was warm over the shell of my ear. "Come for me."

Holding onto his wrist, I helped him ram his fingers harder and farther. The meat of his palm hit my clit once, then twice, and I felt the orgasm bloom.

Warmth starting between my legs moved out like molten honey into my veins; the call of him, his request, and I closed my eyes and rode his hand as I felt his breath catch and his pelvis begin to pump.

His thrusts seemed lonely, though, and as if we had one mind, he pulled his fingers out of me and turned onto his back with my leg still over his thigh; he pulled me over him and thrust himself inside. Straddling him, I felt my breasts bounce as I rode him and our orgasm hard. Euphoria unraveled in my veins.

"Rowan..."

"Cole..." he groaned out as his grip on my hips dug in, and in rhythm with me, he arched his hips up while pressing my pelvis down. I braced a hand on the headboard as the bed shook, and our skin-to-skin contact clapped. My abs scrunched as the full-bodied orgasm shot through me.

Rowan's eyes were half-mast, taking me in like a drugged man. His healed abdominals were cut like bricks as he put them to the test.

A voice that sounded a lot like mine filled the corners of the night-lit room as I, she, we cried out in release. Rowan clutched me to his chest and, with a hand firm on my thigh, kept me still as he drove into me. His thrusts hit hard before he clutched me to his chest and bit my shoulder. Groaning, warmth filled me as he orgasmed.

Holding each other, we lay there, breathing heavily and letting the glow of our connection mellow around us in the puddled moonlight. Rowan sighed and pulled me in tighter against his chest. "Tha gaol agam ort, Cole."

I recognized the roll of consonants that sounded nothing like they were spelled: *ha g-eul ah-kum orsht*.

"I love you too," I whispered back before sealing it with a warm, gentle kiss.

THE WIND WHIPPED ABOUT ME. I WAS IN THE FIELD AGAIN, LOOKING for something, needing *something*. Only I had no idea what it was, much less where it was hidden in the charred field. The moonlight cast deep shadows on the burnt stones of the cairns. Something tugged deep in my core, an ancient call sounding like the one Rowan used. I saw Orabilia in her white ethereal linen, plucking her way across the site toward me. Her lips were moving, but I couldn't hear her words. I tried to move toward her, to hear her better in the chaotic atmosphere, but my movements were sluggish, as if I were moving through a vat of molasses.

"It's yours now" carried over the wind. "It is here that you will find what you're searching for. It is here that you'll finally be at peace." I watched her gesture to the field, then turn back to me, a quiet smile on her lips. "Child of my love, the power rests in your hands."

I looked down as my hands began to warm, then began taking on a golden inner glow—a glow like that of Ormr during our battle.

I swallowed the bile that came up from my churning stomach. I clenched my hands into fists. *No, not again.*

"Please," I begged, "not again. Take him...take him to Valhalla and keep him there."

She just smiled, then electrocuted me.

I shot awake, gasping for air. I sat clawing at the sheets before I realized I was still in bed. Panting, I closed my eyes and willed my heart to slow down. I noticed then that my skin was as wet as if I'd stood in the rain and that the room's heat was suffocating. Quietly I pushed the damp covers off to stand at the open window. Cold evening air refreshed my burning skin and reminded me it had been just a dream. But I felt Orabilia's power in my heart and down into my gut; somehow, I had touched her within that dream.

My heart settled and I turned to slip back into bed. It was then that I got a look at my surroundings. Rowan's arms were dropping back onto the bed as if he'd been hovering above it. And as he settled down, so did the moonlight glow that had lightly tinged his skin.

I smothered a groan and went to him. Quiet as a mouse, I listened to his breathing and watched the pulse in his neck. He was fine and in a deep sleep. Whatever had happened in my sleep was now gone.

I bit my fist, keeping my relief from escaping in a little cry. Slowly, I worked my way back to my side of the bed, keeping an eye on him.

I slipped back in. Next to him and with a hand under my pillow, staring at him, I told myself I was fine. He was fine. All was just fine.

Chapter Nine

After dropping Rowan a coffee and a kiss in bed and, because it was before sunrise, successfully avoiding his typical morning question of if I slept well, I was in one of my happy places: the castle artifacts room. After the Rembrandt, I wanted to double-check our inventory. Open to the public, it also contained the items we'd unearthed from the midden before I went Viking and set fire to the hillside with my Ulfberht sword.

The Ulfberht was an artifact I was loathe to see again, but equally desirous to carry at my hip at all times. I had to see her.

The Ulfberht looked beautiful in her plexiglass case that Marion had found for her. The sword still subtly called to me, the song of a beautiful thing to her owner, and as I crossed the room to her, I fought the urge to break the case and hold her. The runic symbols running down her spine spelled out her name. Her edge was still sharp.

I forced myself to turn toward the other cases. Broken bits of pottery, carved bone, and shards of wood were laid out on cloth. An educational card next to each item told guests what they were looking at, and with Holly's help earlier that summer, there was an artistic sketch to show the original form. All was in its place in the basement room.

Along the back wall were the boxes of artifacts we still hadn't identified or that were waiting their turn in the display rotation. I reviewed each box to ensure no item on the inventory sheets was missing. The last case was larger than the rest. It was about the size of a steamer trunk, and at the bottom of it was a boxy item covered in a stained muslin cloth.

As I reached for the protective cloth, something in the walls groaned. My hands froze halfway to the item. The sound set my hair on end, and only after a few heartbeats did I realize it wasn't the walls groaning. They were...hollering. The hair on my arms stood on end, and I sat still, wondering if my mind was playing tricks on me. In a few seconds, I heard it again. I was out of my chair and at the far wall. I put my ear to it and waited. Just when I thought I was going mad and should leave to find another human being, I heard it again.

Feeling my heart race, I walked to the room's entrance, waiting.

It was coming from below me. It was coming from the fairy hole—the lower dungeons.

"What the... Oh, fuck." I ran down the hall to the end room where I had, days before, fought as Ormr with Eli, Rowan, and Mickey. I yanked the old wooden door. The door that led to the stairway down. The door opened with its own groan. I slipped two at a time down the stone stairs that were now damp with dripping seawater—a sign that it was high tide in the loch. I thought the inevitable had happened. Someone had caught the banker and had thrown him into the fairy hole. With Holly aware of the Rembrandt's disappearance, everyone would be on high alert, and there were some members of the clan who were all too glad to take matters into their own hands. I skidded around the corner and into pitch-black.

I had *not* thought this through. From the initial grand tour that Rowan gave me, I remembered there was a pull cord for a bulb *somewhere*. That *somewhere* went outward like a question, and as if he were there with me, Rowan responded.

What are you doing?

Fairy hole light?

Four steps into the hallway; wave your hands around.

OK.

Why are you down there?

There's hollering. Did someone put Dick Murdoch down the fairy hole?!

Mo ghràdh, you aren't making sense. Call me.

Bank-er. Fair-y hooole.

You're really not making sense.

THERE IS A HUMAN IN THE FAIRY HOLE.

Oye, fuck. I heard that. I've just arrived. Wait for me.

I waited a beat, waved my hands for the light's string, found it, and then pulled, illuminating the narrow, dank space.

From the end of the hallway came "Hello!?" It was a voice I recognized.

"Mickey?"

"Hello! Who's there?! Let me *out of here!*"

He wasn't in the fairy hole. He was in one of the sea-level dungeon rooms that Rowan's uncle used to store whisky in. I stopped short in my rush toward him. "Oh, shit," I whispered to myself. Did *I* put him in there, as Ormr?

"Mickey! How long have you been in here?" I fumbled with the ancient iron door latch, cursing as I went.

"Just get me out of here!"

"I'm trying! I can't get the latch to give at all." With both hands around the latching mechanism's handle, I squeezed with all my might to get the rusted metal to move.

"Kick it like Holly does!"

"OK," I said, standing back, ready to kick. "Wait, *Holly?!*" I kicked the door, not hearing his response. The latch settled, and I attacked it again, "Holly put you in here?" I hollered as I threw open the door.

The room seemed plush for a dungeon. It was warmly lit by several camping LED lanterns that hung low off the wooden rafters in each corner, and in the glow, there was a round hand-loomed rug on the floor, pillows and plush blankets on a camping cot, an assortment of snacks and an orange-colored drink, and stacks of books. The flicker from a candle, making the room smell like vanilla baked goods, wavered in the corner on a small wooden stool. But writing paper and pen were scattered onto the rug as if thrown down in a hurry. His wrists were bound together with silky rope, and an ankle chain was around his boot. Dirt coated his cuffs, and the knees of his pants were encrusted. It was as if he had been midway through a gardening session and got trapped in that room to write a dissertation on isolation. Only that room was solid stone. Where had he been digging?

"What is going—"

"Thank the Lord you're here. Undo me and get me the fuck out of here; she's fucking out of her nut!"

"Are you living here? Who's out of her nut?" I asked aloud at the same time my mind was processing "undo me." So stunned by seeing him in that room and a chain on his ankle when we'd all thought he'd left for some tropical paradise.

"Holly! She hit me in the back of the head and stowed me down here—"

"Holly-*Holly*? Our Holly, researcher Holly? She hit—"

"That cow put me down here, and when I—"

"Hey!" I cut him off. "Don't call her that. I'll get to the bottom of this, but tied up or not, you'll not call her a cow." I hadn't forgiven him for hiding the Ulfberht sword. I was *trying* to be calmer these days but was no saint. I snapped my rubber band and exhaled: "What happened?"

"I dunno, she's gone mad! Get me out of these ties!"

"Yeah, yeah, OK," I said and reached for his bound hands, mumbling, "This isn't weird at all."

"Hold on a moment."

I hadn't heard Rowan enter; I jumped when I heard his thick Scots.

"You..." Mickey squinted at Rowan, his multicolored eyes taking on the dark of the room. Then pressed his wrists toward me. "Hurry."

"Aye, me," Rowan said to him, "If I didn't know better, I'd think ye were back to steal the sword. But you've seen Ormr's face. Ye've seen what he can do, so what could have possibly motivated you to return?" I wasn't sure about Rowan's tone—it was as if he was leading him into a confession, and the full story was one he knew.

"I was trying to leave when—"

"Trying to leave? Ye mean you found something that's keeping you here. Save your lies." He looked at the silken ties that bound his wrists. "Purple looks good on ye. And that chain around your ankle is so rusted a quick kick would snap it off the wall. So the question is, why are ye still here? Buying time?"

Mickey opened his mouth to respond when Rowan added, "Again rhetorical."

Rowan then gently took my arm to turn me away from Mickey as he lowered his voice. "I have a fair good reason why he's here. Holly's sobbing up in the artifacts room; I caught her on the stairs coming down."

Eavesdropping, Mickey interjected, "That ungrateful hag—"

"Oye!" Rowan's brow cleaved as if he couldn't believe the decorum of the man in bondage ties—now I realized where I'd seen the silks before—and chained to the wall. "Have some pride, aye?"

"Pride? Pride?! I'm being detained like a *prisoner*."

"Again, give it a kick and be done. I'll walk ye up to the constable; there's much to discuss on why you're here. The Fund is mighty eager to get to the bottom of it as well."

This had a subduing effect on Mickey, but his response was saturated with loathing. "Unchain me, and I'll get out o' everyone's hair and *not* press charges."

Rowan went to Mickey, slid his hand over his shoulders as if he were about to confide something to him, and softly said, "I've never been a big fan of ye after everything you've done; so how's about I'll *not* knock yer teeth out, *and* I will keep this door open in a show of good faith while we sort your story out, aye?"

Mickey's response was a molten glare.

"Aye, there's a good lad." Rowan patted his back.

Rowan and I found Holly in a crying jag to beat all crying jags upstairs at the table near the heavy boxy object I was going to uncover when I first heard Mickey. Tears ran out her eyes and nose and off her chin. Her eyes were red and swollen.

I rubbed her back. "What's going on, Holl? He's saying you locked him up?"

She looked up at Rowan and sputtered something that sounded like "So sorry..."

Rowan shrugged as if finding people tied up in the dungeon was something that still happened in modern times. "Och, never mind it.

After all he's done... Trying tae convince Cole tae break it off with me for payment from Charmaine, falsely claiming he was sent from the Fund just so he could nose about—"

"Taking the Ulfberht," I added.

"I wish I'd done it. The stones it took to do it..." He shook his head and grinned at her. "Bella ad mortem. If we were still a skirmishing country and clan, Holly, I'd declare ye chieftain."

Holly gave a wet laugh and wiped her nose on her shirt. "Tòiseach? Or just plain chieftain?"

"Tòiseach with a shoo-in for tanist. With a land swath from here to Portree."

"Aye, second-in-command." She smiled, and then her face fell. "I shouldn't have done it, but he was going to take this"—she pointed at the cloth-covered item—"and he thought that I wouldn't stop him."

Both Rowan and I digested Mickey's assessment of Holly and how far off base he had been in thinking she wouldn't stop him if she felt she had to. He had seen her as a student who asked for advice on even the smallest decisions. He hadn't seen her as a MacLaoch with a crush who found little ways to talk with him.

"I see," I said, even though I didn't, not really. I watched her relive the moment in anguish.

"I had no choice," she pleaded and swallowed down her tears. "I arrived too late to help; the field was charred. I couldnae believe it. I started picking up tools because I didn't know what else tae do. I felt so useless... I'd pieced together the battle, from the bazillion texts I had once I was back in cell range, but until then, I didn't really understand... I couldn't believe we'd fought with just the tools in our sheds..." Her story had flowed out in a strange rhythm, fast at times like a tap turned on full blast, halting at others, interrupted by her tears.

"So I wasn't thinking straight. And that's when I saw Mickey across the field... He was definitely not just picking up. He was at this..." She reached over and uncovered the mystery item.

"What the..." I murmured. "Is that a—"

"Babe's coffin, originally? I've no clue. I told him to drop it. Then, when he wouldn't, not to open it. But he did. And then...*bash.*" I winced as Holly mimed swinging a shovel. She continued, "My da knows of him; he's an archaeologist all right, but some of my da's friends from down in Glasgow... They say he got his start in his *other career* during uni... He's a pilfering archaeologist." Holly made a fist and looked at it like she was done keeping secrets and the relief suddenly made her tired. "His last big score was a gem. Word was he was getting to the end of the thing—selling off bits of it—and was looking for his next prize.

"That's what my da had wanted to talk with ye about last month, plus whisky business," she said to Rowan. "But mainly they knew him, and they figured I could keep an eye on him." She shrugged. "Not a bad assignment as far as missives go from your father, aye? But then, the second I turned my back, he'd snuck off and found something. That ground-penetrating radar he'd ordered had come, and he was elbow-deep in the soil. I just couldn't. I felt betrayed that he wouldn't listen to me, and he was all the things I was worried he was and...and... I might have lost my cool and cuffed him harder than I expected. My stomach had been in knots for days; he was unconscious for like an hour. Oh, my lord of days almighty, am I glad this is out. I didn't know how long I could keep him until it became kidnapping."

She dropped her hands into her lap with a soul-shuddering sigh.

Rowan nodded in understanding. "Aye."

I gave her a sad smile. "Babe, when you put the restraints on, that's the kidnapping part. And the door locking and...and yeah, all the things that were against his will."

"Aye, I had a moment dragging him down the stairs... I really wondered what the actual fuck I was doing, but I'll not commit myself to a task and not see it through. I thought maybe tie him to a guest bed in the upper hall, but everyone from the battle was using 'em. So I figured down here would be safe. He and I could have a tête-à-tête; then I'd make sure he left his life of crime, and he could come live with me. It kinda worked for a bit...but now he just hollers."

Looking at the coffin, I asked them, "Which comes first: Offering our prayers and reburying this poor babe or calling the constable?"

Holly took a big sniff and wiped her nose with her hand then her hand on her shirt, well past caring about decorum. "Well, aye, it's filled with gold."

"It's what now?" came tumbling out of my mouth just as the earth seemed to tilt beneath my feet.

She nodded as Rowan pulled out a chair. "Gold?"

"Oh aye, gold. They're stamped, looking like Roman coins."

Rowan sat hard on the chair. And wavered there as if he had been told Orabilia was back.

He got a long-off stare and whispered something that he and I constantly wondered about Ormr: Had he stolen Orabilia, the clan chief's daughter, or had he negotiated for his one true love? "What's the price for a war chief's daughter in the thirteenth century?"

"Yes," I said, keeping up with his thinking. The skeletons in the field were Ormr's men, and they had traveled with Ormr centuries ago, supposedly to assist in taking Orabilia. Still, Rowan and I knew that they'd been in love, and likely, Ormr was, for the first time in his life, bartering for what he truly cared about. "But why a babe's coffin?"

"Maybe he grabbed what he had on hand?" Rowan mused with me.

"Did he hear 'coffers' and pick up a coffin?"

Rowan said to me, "I'm not sure the wordplay is the same in his language..."

Holly cleared her throat. "Oh, it's a coffin; there's bones in it too."

All three of us looked at one another and then at the soil-encrusted coffin.

I whispered, "What the fuck?"

Rowan answered, "Oh nae..."

Chapter Ten

It was obvious that Mickey was the best person to give us some immediate answers.

Up in the artifacts room and standing over the coffin, he gently lifted out its contents and set them on the canvas-covered table we'd set up. It was, as Holly had said, coins and bones. His wrists were pink where the silky bondage rope had been. Holly stood farthest away from him as if he had something catching, or like a well-placed accusation, which I thought he was maybe, probably, likely, owed.

While he worked, he yakked. "I'd like a bath, a proper meal"—his eyes slid to Holly—"and to never see the likes of her again."

Holly glared back, "I wasted so much time playing captor and captive with you."

"You!? What about me?!"

"You were having a grand ol' time until you realized I wasn't going to show you the casket."

He twisted it back onto Holly. "I thought you said you loved me! Caged animals don't feel love!"

"Well...ye crapped on the carpet, Mickey Gillian! So, into a human-sized crate ye went until you could promise tae not do it again."

"I promised."

"Oh aye, I heard ye. I also heard you when you asked about how heavy that casket was and what did I actually see when I opened it? Or if I had opened it? I wanted to let you out, but I love ye too much tae. A life of crime is not for you—don't make the old men right about you."

The plea in her voice left me feeling for Holly. She sounded deeply profound and vulnerable. She wanted Mickey, so desperately, to change.

Mickey was sullen, and his only response was: "I'm no criminal."

Rowan interjected, "You say that, but then why were ye digging this up? Scientific inquiry at midnight on a battle-wrecked field?"

"It's not a crime to be curious, is it?"

"Is that what you were, in the middle of the night, with dirt up to yer elbows?" He nodded to Mickey's half-cleaned appearance. "Being curious?"

"Look—"

Rowan interrupted. "I'd like to know what the coins' value is, whose name belongs to these bones, and why you thought you could steal them from me."

"There is that," I murmured to Mickey.

Mickey sighed and rolled his head as if loosening his neck muscles. "These are Roman coins."

He made us wait for more by first returning the bones to the coffin and closing it. He then picked up a coin with his gloved hand. The coins were grime-encrusted, but it was obvious from an exposed edge here and there that they were either brass or gold. Mickey dug around in Holly's toolbox and came out with a container of swabs. He wet one of them with distilled water and gently rubbed the cotton tip on an edge.

My breath caught as Rowan cursed. The coin was gold—not dull, brassy gold but the kind of gold jewelers beg for, which billionaires decorate with, and which sunlight glints brilliantly off.

"This is a—" Mickey started, coughed, then mumbled under his breath.

"Sorry, what?" I asked. I was right next to him and hadn't heard.

"It's a..." he said and uttered the rest.

"Louder." His hands began to shake, and if I wasn't mistaken, he had a look of deep, profound regret. As in, he could've been in Glasgow with a casket of undocumented gold right now. This was not, as I could only assume he'd tried to convince himself of over the last few days playing captive with Holly, useless scrap brass coins dated last year. "What'd you think it was? Just rocks?" I whispered to him. "Prayed it was mostly worthless? They're not, are they?"

"Aureus Roman coins. I'll have to research the current estimated value, but this has the Colosseum on it. This minting can be worth close to five hundred thousand pounds each. On a bad day at auction, when the cost of gold is down."

Rowan began a slow, deep inhale.

I looked at the pile removed from the coffin. "There're several hundred coins here."

Mickey swallowed the last of his dream down.

"That's a fuck load of ancient gold," I whispered to him, watching his reaction, "and you were just going to pack it up, and what? Start a new life? Pay off all your friends' credit cards? Pay back your parents for you being a shitty kid?"

His eyes narrowed at mine. "If anything, they owe me—"

"Sorry, I don't care what you had planned, actually. What I do care about..." I said, feeling like this lifeline for Rowan was a single, solitary moment away from being dust in the wind. This one thing that was going to bring the castle, the MacLaoch clan, and the town of Glentree back to a thriving life was almost taken by this pain in my ass. This second item he'd nearly pilfered. "What I do care about is that you pay penance for attempting robbery on us—the clan—*twice*."

"I was imprisoned," he hissed.

Rowan exhaled, "But not dead."

"Right," I said, giving Rowan a quizzical look over my shoulder and glanced at Holly, who had regained her confidence as I grilled Mickey. Rowan had spoken with the kind of tone that made me question how often he actually killed people. Back at Mickey: "The town will know what you've done by nightfall. Now, what do I put at the end of that story? He tried to steal all our gold, but he's helped us—"

"It's blood money, *Nicole*. Why would someone like you, a scientist, be interested in money that a Viking came here to buy out an old chief with? This belongs to a museum. Not in your coffers for only you and some greedy lender to have."

Rowan lunged at him, knocking me back in the process. The two careened into the desk as Holly shouted obscenities. The coins flew, and the casket threatened to tip over as the chime of coins hitting the stone floor filled the room around the shouts.

I landed in a chair. Rowan had Mickey by the collar and shook him as Holly shouted, pointing her finger at him, "Blood money?! What do ye call that fist-sized ruby ye snuck out of Egypt? A gift from the Lord?"

Rowan held Mickey tight and bent backward over the desk. But Rowan's gaze was on Holly. "The gem was a fist-sized ruby?"

Only Holly was on a tear and was laser-focused on Mickey. "Decide to enter the family business too? You sold me a sack of lies! You only fancy yourself an archaeologist when it suits you."

"I am an archaeologist!"

"Fuck you! I trusted you." Holly wailed.

"Yeah, well, it's not my fault you've poor judgment."

I groaned for him. Rowan's patience toward Mickey was being held back by a hair, and he snapped, defending Holly's honor.

Rowan twisted, slamming his elbow into Mickey's jaw. Mickey's head snapped to the side, and he fell to the floor on all fours.

"You piece of shit!" Holly lunged for him, and Rowan caught her and pushed her back.

Out of my chair, I gave Holly a hug from behind and, against her hair, said, "It's done. Breathe, it's over." Then to Rowan: "We need to call the constable. This is out of our hands."

Both of them were seething. But Holly cleared her head first and took a few steps sideways and out of my embrace, going eerily calm. "Aye, let the police sort him out now."

Rowan took out his phone. "No signal. Come on, Mickey, let's go. You can use this time to make up a statement."

Mickey rested his hand on his jaw as if nursing a wound. "No, I'd rather be done with you lot."

Holly scoffed. "Done? Just like that? Ye want to run from here and never look back?"

"Don't talk to me," he hissed at her.

"Check his pockets," she bit back.

Rowan shook his head and spoke quietly to Mickey. "After everything, you still haven't learned, have ye? I'll tell you what—keep the coin we know you swiped, a little something to remember us by? And if tha' Viking ever comes back"—he glanced back at me before returning his thundercloud gaze at Mickey—"it'll be a talisman to take him right to ye. And we both know what that Viking will do to ye. Already you've escaped from him, what?" His gaze held venom. "Twice? Good. Take it. Let's see if the third time really is a charm."

Mickey had the decency not to meet his eye. "I don't know what you are talking about." Only his throat worked at something as if he were swallowing down a vivid memory that made bile rise into his throat.

"Aye, sure." Rowan grabbed his arm and led him out of the room.

Holly blew out a breath and sat hard. "He's got that cleaned coin, ye know."

"I do know. He must be some kind of desperate."

Holly nodded. "He told me one night when we both were completely blootered that the 'beauty' of archaeological digs is that they are discovering undocumented items. That they're 'ripe' with 'opportunity.' When I asked what kind of opportunities, he laughed it off, saying he was kidding, just a fantasy he had."

"But then, why come here? Why not head down to those more archaeologically interesting and lauded sites?" I shook my head. "How'd he even know this was here?" I gestured to the coffin.

"Some kids at uni said there was MacLaoch gold here at this dig. Like ye said, it was a long shot, and he took it. Lucky is what he is. I won't make a dig about him being Irish and lucky. But if tha' leprechaun shoe fits..."

"Good job on not making that dig," I said sarcastically.

Holly grinned at me. "That fucking sod has debts up to his eyeballs and finds a way, each time, tae pay them off so he doesn't lose a finger or his kneecaps."

"Industrious."

"Lucky," she corrected.

I remembered him saying something about gold when he pressed me for a job a month before. I had to hand it to him—he was a dangerous mix of handsome determination and desperation.

"More tae the point, he isn't getting invited to digs. Bigger projects are rejecting his CV. And he can't get funding for his own. His professional career has stalled. Word from my da's friends is that he got too greedy, and rumors spread about the ruby. There are only so many times you can sell off a chunk of ruby and no one asks questions. Really, tho?" Holly leaned forward. I smiled inwardly—hearing a story from Holly was like peeling layers off an onion. There was always another one. "His da, Lou Gillian, is shit, been in prison for art theft, and when he got out, he wanted some of that ruby, and when Mickey didn't give it up, he started causing trouble for him. Then our wicked witch of the south came in—"

"Who?" I feigned ignorance.

"Charmaine hired an investigator to dig up dirt on you, and they found it on Mickey instead. She got a guy with photographs willing to talk for a big stack of cash."

I had been worried Charmaine would try something like that, and I suddenly had a burning desire to hear what this investigator found.

"So, that guy was Mickey's dad, and he told Charmaine's investigator about the ruby?"

"Aye. I'm sure for a big stack of cash of his own. At first, I was livid for him, thinking we were on the same team, Mick and me. I thought he would be done with all the scheming and he'd be livid that his dad gave him up...but no." Holly gave a soul-rending sigh.

"Sorry, Holl."

"Aye. The heart wants what the heart wants. I want his pretty face to look at me with trust and respect—and then have that agile academic hand grab my ass and show me all the ways I can be persuaded to scream his name."

I felt my eyebrows graze my hairline with surprise. "Well, now... when you put it that way."

We were quiet for a while, and then I realized she'd said something that might have a bearing on our pressing issue of a stolen Rembrandt.

"Did you say his father served time for art theft?"

She wiped her eyes clear. "Yeah, what are you thinking?"

"Let's say, for example, you're a—"

"An anal miss who wants to take a Rembrandt from a locked building, but you haven't done much after-dark work, much less nab a rare artifact." Holly was a mind reader.

"If she contacted him with a fat wad of cash to rat out his son, what's to say she didn't show up with another fat wad of cash and broker a deal to achieve her overreaching goals?" I remembered asking her when I was shooing her out of the castle what she'd done and her reply, *The thing you could never do.* "I mean, it's the one piece to her 'I've saved the day' puzzle that didn't make sense. How'd no one see her? And it proves she knew she was being sneaky—that she knew she had to be sneaky."

"She wasn't the one who took it off the wall."

I made a sour face. "She wouldn't be dumb enough to hire a known art thief, would she?"

"Take it from me, the things we do for love is downright bonkers. If she's still got Rowan on her vision board, I'm thinking she'd hire the devil himself if he promised her what she wanted."

"I dunno."

"This could explain something Johnny at the pub told me a few days back."

"What's that?"

"One of the stained-glass craftsmen repairing the window—alleged craftsman," she added, "showed up for a pint. Bartender Johnny chatted him up, asked him for a quote on his own windows." Crickets. "Mind ye, you're still new here, so this glass man not wanting to get into the particulars of glass on his break would sound fine, but it's downright odd. If there's anything we love tae do more than talk of ourselves and the things we know, it's drink and talk of ourselves and the things we know. Johnny thinks this man is a stained-glass craftsman to the same degree he thinks horseshit smells good. That's how much he knew about glass."

"Could it be that easy?"

"I think it is. He'd have to be good enough to get around the alarms, but not *Ocean's 11* keen because we're not the Louvre. Then, he can't help but have a pint for a job done well."

"But that doesn't tell us where he took it."

"Aye. The banker must have it. If Charmaine gave it as collateral?"

"Rowan would have gotten a notification about it if it was applied to the loan, right?" I groaned. Not hearing from the bank yet, and now suspecting that Charmaine had the painting removed in an underhanded way, I was definitely beginning to worry this was not as "Everything's fine!" as Charmaine led us to believe. I'd have to chat with Rowan about all of it, and none of it would brighten his day. To Holly: "One part of this whole bankruptcy ordeal is sketchy as fuck, and the other half is by the book."

"Welcome to my life, mate."

I gave a short laugh, glad her dark humor was back. "Now we can sit down with Charmaine and the banker and have it out—with the constable on speed dial."

"That Murdoch, he's not going to just give it back, do you think? Da says he has a beef with the MacLaochs that was taught tae him."

"I'm sure he will, wouldn't he? Bankers live by a federal code of conduct, and any misstep is a fireable offense, or at least would get you demoted to the mailroom. At least, in the US."

"Aye. Here too. But only if he's sane. Most Murdochs are, but there's history there. And you know what history does to some folk around here. Quirks a few of 'em. This one might be itching to give Rowan trouble."

I racked my brain. The name Murdock had always been, on Rowan's lips, less about banking and more as some kind of idiom for unsolicited anger.

"Do you know of the police raid in '89?" Holly said, again seeming to read my mind.

"Rowan told me they'd been making whisky the same way they'd always had for centuries, but in the eighties, the government cracked down hard on the small, independent distilleries."

"And?"

"That's all."

"Oh aye. Not a natural-born storyteller, that one. I'll catch you up: In the eighties, they were ordered to pay taxes on their private whisky operation *or else*. When the police come, though, half of it is gone. They confiscated what was down 'ere and interrogated the clansmen. Da said the lads were all being good boys, saying 'yes, sir,' and 'no, sir,' next to their chief out there on the castle steps." Holly pointed behind her in the direction of the castle steps. "Now, mind ye, they've got Rowan with them, holding his uncle's hand. Then, seeing how they're just a solid wall of shrugging shoulders, claiming to be not knowing where the other half of the whisky went, one copper goes too far. He gets in Jacky's face—"

"Who?"

"Seac."

The name sounded like *Jacques*. And the only one I knew was Cousteau.

"Again, who?"

"Rowan's uncle, the chief. Has he no' ever told ye his name?" Her face contorted into a weird angle, confused on how daft one of us could be.

"No, of course he has," I lied.

"Right, so Jacky was getting grilled by the officer. He's asking, 'Where's the rest? Where was it taken?' But Jacky didn't give an inch. Then"—Holly waggled her eyebrows at me and let the pregnant pause add drama to her story—"then," she said again, "he stabbed a finger into Jacky's chest and said, 'How's about I take yer little boy, and we'll see if you'll start talking?'"

I sucked in air between clenched teeth. That was a gauntlet only the foolhardy would throw down at a posse of MacLaochs.

"What happened?"

"Oh aye, my da says, it was electric. Jacky knocked the man's head back, and they all went nuts. Take Rowan from the clan? Over their dead bodies. Da says they were punching their way into the backs of patrol cars. Then, at the station, they were let go. Get this, 'for good, cooperative behavior.'"

"What?"

Holly was nodding now, into the retelling as much as I was gobbling it up. "Turns out there was another matter—coke, a much bigger deal than untaxed whisky—needed all hands on deck. I'm sure some money still exchanged hands—the coke distraction just allowed the cops to entertain being bribed." Holly winked.

"What the..."

"Aye, isn't it the best? And here I am, having missed tha' *and* the battle." She sighed with longing.

"That's incredible."

"Surprising that the laird hasn't shared it with ye."

"Not that level of detail. Your dad had a front-row seat to it all. And was an adult. Unlike Rowan."

"For sure, but back to the banker. He's a Murdoch. His uncle raised him, like Rowan was raised by his. His uncle is—"

"Oh no," I said not believing where this was going.

"Oh yes."

"Not the officer who threatened to take Rowan."

"One and the same man. The same man who ate fist and pride for it."

I marinated in the story for a few beats more, then realized: "Even if Dick Jr. did take payment in the form of the Rembrandt, any institution would be allergic to accepting stolen goods for payment. Once they've been publicly notified, of course."

"Aye, the laird will make sure it's public all right." She thought of something I was mulling over. "He's still going to need payment, though, either way?"

I reached down to the coins that had spilled onto the floor. Turning their crusty edges over in my fingers. "I'm sure he is. Especially since Rowan refuses to sell the Ulfberht. A solution I keep suggesting, even now with the whisky business. It'll take time we don't have before it's operating in the black."

"Oh?"

"He thinks selling the Ulfberht will bring the Viking back."

"Oh..." she said, looking over to it in its plexiglass case. So that's how I bring him back?"

"Please, no, I need to sleep through the night sometime this century. The more he stays gone, the better I'll—we'll all—be."

Chapter Eleven

That night, the dream came again, the heat of Orabilia's power coursing through me. It was as if the coins, the stolen art, and my brother wandering into my life thinking I was in a cult kept stirring it back up. I sat up gasping. I made sure Rowan wasn't hovering in midair. Again I went to the open window. Cool night air caressed my superheated skin.

I gripped the windowsill as I heard, from behind me, Rowan turn over and, in a low voice, call over to me, "Ye all right, mo ghràdh?"

I could only nod. I had no idea if I was all right. Seeing her over and over again made my body shake in fear, especially if she brought *him* back. It felt as if something were escalating. Again.

I looked down at my hands. Were they still glowing? They weren't, but they felt hot.

I heard Rowan's feet pad along the floor before he was gently pressing against my back and pulling me into his embrace. His naked skin was warm against my back through my T-shirt, and the soft touch of his fingers as he brushed damp ringlets off my neck was soothing to my freaked-out mind.

"Nightmare again?" His low voice warmed my shoulder before he kissed it.

I could only nod again.

He held me tight around my middle, and I gripped his arms in return, leaning back into him like the refuge he was. I was a ship caught up in a midnight gale, and he, the calm port, stilled me.

I closed my eyes and whispered, "It feels like chaos in here," and tapped the side of my head. Then I added, "Feels like a bit of Ormr was left behind."

"Mmm."

"I hate it."

He gave my neck a sleepy kiss. "The chaos has a few names."

I turned to face him, staying within the circle of his arms. "No, I don't want it... No, thank you."

He gave me a sad smile. "Aye, we don't get asked if we want it, do we? We're just given it through our experiences, and then we must figure out how to quiet our minds so we can do basic things again." He paused, thinking. "Mine is called PTSD, and it can wreak havoc on my consciousness. Like a smelly, twelve-hundred-pound sow ye have to take everywhere, and she tries to run amok in the most inconvenient times. And just when ye think, *Oh aye, fine, go, run off!* ye realize she's tied to your ankle. And she drags ye through her rompings, out of control. She especially waits to cause chaos when I'm my most tired. Her favorite is when I sleep."

"Yeah... Well, I can stop sleeping," I whispered like a fool.

Rowan kissed my temple. "Ye can't."

"I don't like feeling like any moment is a fight-or-flight moment. How do I turn it off?"

"That's ye minding your sow. You have to find a way to get her to be happy, fed, exercised, and safe so she doesn't run wild. And eventually, ye can leave her grazing in the forest."

I thought of his pig, fat and happy in the cool of the woods. "Is that where yours is?"

"Och, no. She's rummaging through the fridge. A Viking recently inhabited you with the strength of the Hulk, and when ye came down that hillside in that silk gala dress, my sow came tearing back to me from the woods."

I gave him a sad face. "She was happy there."

"Aye." He tucked a group of my ringlets behind my ear. "But what ye'll come to find out is that she's devoted to you and charges back home when things aren't right. She's a protector, but when she's done protecting, she has difficulty remembering to head back to the forest."

"So she eats out of the fridge?"

"Well, mine doesn't want to go too far, but she's also a pig and hungry, so, aye, she's in the fridge eating the cornbread you made and listening to our conversation."

"Nosy pig." I smiled against his lips before kissing him.

He asked, "Where would yours be right now?"

My answer made him laugh.

"She's taken one look at my situation, jumped in a boat, and is rowing for all she's worth back to South Carolina."

KNOWING IT WOULD BE ANOTHER SLEEPLESS NIGHT, WITH ORABILIA snaking across my skin, I thought how I'd like to see the field in the moonlight. I slipped from the bed, leaving Rowan safe and asleep. I put my wellies and a heavy sweater on and walked up to the cairn knoll. There on the hill, I paused by each of the rock piles marking the dead souls that had risen up to fight us. Despite their aggression, they were to be pitied. They had only been doing as they were commanded by my Viking grandfather and his Ulfberht sword. Then Rowan's grandmother, Orabilia, sent them off this astral plane and into their dream world, Valhalla. The power that woman wielded was something I wasn't sure I ever wanted to see again, and yet I had seen it twice. During the battle, she'd sucked the life right out of the soil beneath my boots to send my ancestral grandpappy, his crew, and herself into the afterlife. How did that affect the field? Did it at all? I still didn't know.

We had taken soil samples and sent them off for analysis, and I had rehydrated some in a petri dish. But I could see nothing in it under the microscope. Pool water had more bacteria than the slide I'd looked at. I made a mash of soil and distilled water, spread it on agar in a petri dish, and sealed it up. Days later, still *nothing* had grown. It was as if I'd squirted hand sanitizer into the petri dish and not what should have been microbe-laden, fertile soil.

Holly and I had bantered about why the soil was inert.

I had commented, "It's as if even the microorganisms were killed, but more than that, new bacteria and yeast aren't growing. So whatever is left in the soil isn't bioavailable to the microorganisms that land on it."

"Or it's poisoned? Radioactive?"

I had wondered that too. "I have a little radiation meter I kept from grad school when we were working around the Hanford nuclear site. I took it out to the field, and it registered regular levels, only as much as the sun creates. That's it."

"So, poisoned, then?"

"I've got a sample off at the labs. We'll check for heavy metals and common poisons, but this event was supernatural. I think we both have an inkling of why it's not growing."

"Cursed," she had said before stuffing an impressive amount of one of Marion's strawberry scones, reserved for paying guests, into her face.

"Something like that."

Around her bite, she said, "Best go talk with your granny."

Supernatural event aside, I had the sinking realization that it would take quite a bit of verbal gymnastics to update the Fund with my current findings about the field and also keep our research grants. I planned to delay by instead giving them salacious details about Mickey Gillian. In the meantime, the students were occupied on the fallen tree that had had its tip scorched; it had enough biological interest below the scorch line to keep them busy until fall term began in another month. But the Fund's inevitable inquiry weighed on me.

Many of the students had joined us in the battle. It was a bonding moment for us all. Of those who'd received Rowan's call, most had cuts on their cheeks or knuckles; some were still limping. It was the MacLaoch way: to wake up the next morning and set to task no matter what happened the night before. I'd given them time off while I was away with Rowan at the hospital, but Marion said they showed up anyway.

Now, on the cairn knoll, illuminated by moonlight, I held out my hands and looked at them, remembering my dream. Would the field make them glow, or did I need my hands to glow to make the field regrow?

"It's fucking cold out here, Pipsqueak."

I turned at the sound of my brother's voice. He was in a heavy, drab-olive, military-issue coat that had been our dad's until Tee enlisted. It had that worn-since-the-sixties feel, the soft comfort of a father's hug. I had one of Daddy's old field coats; I was familiar.

"You're back. Where you been hiding?"

"What are you doing out here?"

TJ was dodging the question, but I let it go because I was just glad to see him.

"Taking in the beauty," I said, extending my arm to encompass all the dead char. "What are you doing out here? It's midnight."

"It's six back home."

"Yeah, it is, isn't it?"

But he'd come from Germany, only an hour's difference from here, another point I didn't press.

He came to stand next to me, blowing into his hands to stave off the evening's wet chill. "Wanna talk?"

"Please, no."

"So you're fine?"

"Yup."

"Totally fine?"

"Hundred percent."

"This isn't the aftereffect of a Viking dude taking up in your body and giving you nightmares?"

I blew out a breath to try not to feel in my memory Orabilia electrocuting me.

"You know," he said, "I distinctly remember you holding me back home after what I experienced, as I scream-cried."

I remembered too. In the middle of our family's peach orchard several years back TJ recounted a moment from the seemingly infinite number of moments he'd had in his years as an army medic one that had hit him hard. There'd been two men, a downed plane, blood was everywhere. They scooped one man out of the sand and put him directly into a body bag. The other lived only to die later. TJ had yelled and screamed as he'd relived it, sweated it out in the South Carolina heat, then collapsed in a heap sobbing from the horrors of it. We cried together that day. I walked alongside him within his darkness, and we dealt with it together. Darkness was like that; it was easier with a friend.

"Yeah, well, I'm at the scream part. I'm trying to put Ormr into a box and move on…"

"But?"

"My brain keeps remembering this one moment. It's almost like it wants me never to forget, not even for a second, and always be on guard. It's exhausting."

"The stabby part?"

"Yeah."

Over the week-plus that Tee had been there, he had gotten the battle story from everyone wanting to tell another Minory of the might of his own lineage. They loved watching his jaw go slack in disbelief, then buying him another round to ease him into the rest of the story.

We were quiet, looking out over the darkened field lit only by the peek-a-boo of the stars and moon.

"This time, though," I said, stretching my fingers out, "there's something Lady MacLaoch wants me to know; she's making my hands glow in my dreams." I pretended to shoot electricity out of my fingers.

Instead of mocking me, Tee watched with rapt attention, like a guy who had heard all about his sister's spiritual encounter and was about to see it with his own two eyes.

Then I watched as his hope crashed once he realized nothing supernatural was going to happen.

"Right."

"Yeah."

"Kinda disappointing."

I gave him a tired smile. "You're telling me."

My skin lit up then, and a shiver rolled over me. Rowan was coming up from the base of the field on the cottage trail, adjusting the elastic waistband of his soft flannel pants as if he'd yanked them on while striding out the door.

Tee and I were quiet for a while, and then TJ said, "He does know it's cold out, right?"

"He's born and raised here." As if that explained why he was barefoot and shirtless. His voice whispered over my skin, *There ye are.*

"Where's your shirt?" Tee said as Rowan arrived.

"It's a warm night." He stopped before me, put his palms gently to my cheeks, and searched my face. He offered, "It's a nice night for a loch swim."

The thought sent a shiver down into my bones.

"And hypothermia," Tee added.

"When you return to shore, you'll have nothing left in your mind— you'll be just a quiet body ready for sleep." When I didn't jump on that suggestion, he said, "Or a hike to see the sunrise over the Cuillins?"

I felt relief under his dark gaze; he understood, as did my brother, about the hellscape I'd walked through, and both were willing to stand there with me in the dark of night and do whatever needed to be done.

"You'll hike barefoot and shirtless too?"

Without taking his eyes off me, Rowan replied to Tee, "If she wants me to, I will. Her words are my command."

"Geez," I whispered, feeling suddenly tired as if the spirit that had caught hold of me had let go. "It's all right—I'm ready for bed again."

Tee opened his arms to me. "All right, Pipsqueak, bring it in." He gave me a tight squeeze and kissed the top of my head. "Sleep tight, and find your man a fucking shirt."

I gave a soft laugh and let him go. Just before I did, I caught the smell of clean linens—herbal lavender on a sea breeze.

Instead of asking him where he'd been doing laundry, I said, "See you in the morning. Thanks for hanging out."

"Anytime, Pip. *I'll* always be here for you."

Rowan watched him go, then followed me back to our cottage, the tone of TJ's remark on his mind. "Does he think I'm not here for you?"

"He's pretty transparent, huh."

"I love ye, Cole, and it boggles my mind that you two are brother and sister."

I felt my eyebrows rise. "Oh yeah?"

"It's just tha' I love you so much, I assumed your brother and I would get on like a house on fire."

"You will. Tee has to get to know you; once he's sure of you, you'll level up in his friend ranking, and he'll be the most annoying human you've ever met."

His fingertips traced the curve of my spine as we got to the path to our cottage. "I'm just disappointed that it took me a while tae notice ye weren't in bed. Then I came to find ye with your brother—he beat me to meet your needs. Again I'm subpar in his eyes."

"He's just jealous of your abs."

Rowan laughed out. "Aye, right." Then, at the door, he said with mock fatigue, "Now I have to spend the rest of the night exhausting you so ye can sleep."

My hand paused over the door handle. "Oh. Exhaust me?" I put the door to my back and turned the knob behind me. "Kind sir, please tell me exactly what that entails," I said, as I fell into the foyer.

He was still at the door. The evening light shifted, and soft moonlight threw his half-naked body in relief. The curves and edges of his body were highlighted as the shadows deepened the grooves, making him that Scottish warrior I'd met a year ago.

He rested his palms on either side of the door. "You. Me on my knees."

A pleasant night breeze ambled into the cottage off the cliffs far behind him, carrying his words to me. "I'm a visual person. For me to really understand, you're going to have to show me."

His hands came off the frame. "With pleasure."

Rowan came to me and, with a soft kiss on my cheek, picked me up. With me tightly hugged in his arms, he carried me to the living room and sat me on the plush couch. It faced the picture window that looked out over the cliff to the moonlit loch. He tucked me in with the cashmere throws before lighting the wood stove. The crackle and snap of the burning wood filled the air. Then, back at my knees, he lifted my right foot, tugged off its sock, and rested it on his thigh. He turned and from the little basket under the coffee table brought out the lotion I used to keep my hands soft after digging in the dirt all day. After rubbing his hands with the creamy lotion to warm it, he pressed both thumbs into my heel. Slowly, undoing each hard-worked muscle from my heel up through my instep, he relieved the pressure I hadn't noticed was there. With my foot warm and in Rowan's care, I sank into the safe, cozy couch, heavy with blankets on me. I felt my eyes close. He worked the pads of my feet, first my left then my right, digging his knuckles in until I felt the loosening up my legs and into my back. My mind went light with relaxation.

With the dedicated warmth of his touch mixed with the crackle and pop of the wood stove, Rowan lulled me back to sleep.

THE SUN BROKE THROUGH THE FOGGY, DAMP MORNING AIR. A pristine crisp morning breath kissed my cheek. I lay quietly. I'd had nightmares of being back on the cairn knoll again, obeying its command to return. There, as I stood on the charcoal earth, the first choking cry grabbed my chest and rent my heart asunder. I gave in to the darkness and fell to my knees. A voice I was trying desperately to keep quiet lest her very real fear take over did then take control. I dug my fingers into the earth and wept as she broke over me. Releasing myself to her and that feeling shook me until I succumbed to a gentle, dreamless sleep.

I blinked. Rapidly.

I was *outside*.

A low mist hung in the air, and a shiver rolled over my exposed skin when I realized I was back where I had been in the middle of the night. Over the fog, I could see the eastern flank of the castle.

I blinked away sleep and sat up as voices rose from below. Rowan's voice chimed over my skin, *Mo ghràdh. Where are you?*

"Chief, I'll check up by the tree." Holly's voice carried, undulating through the mist.

I opened my mouth to say something, but my voice croaked. I cleared my throat and said, "Up here."

In a few moments, I looked up at Holly and Rowan as they emerged out of the fog.

"There ye are!" Holly exclaimed as Rowan followed, now fully clothed in jeans and a flannel rolled up to his elbows.

He reached a hand down and pulled me to my feet, and Holly quickly took me in from head to toe. Then her eyes went to the ground beneath me.

"Oh."

Rowan asked, "Were you sleeping out here?"

I was about to answer when the ground where Holly was staring caught my eye.

Rowan looked around my shoulder as he tucked me in against his chest. "Ohhh..."

The ground where my body had been was a lush and vibrant green. Multiple species of plants were growing within the grasses, giving the green carpet a dynamic texture. The dominant species was the tri-leaf pattern of trifolium.

"Clover..." Holly whispered. "My god." She turned and looked at me. "Fall asleep with seeds in your pockets, mate?"

"I...I did not."

"My mum and I don't get on much, but she tracked me down yesterday to tell me that you need to go see your great-granny. I now think I see why... Mum said the rebirth might happen when ye least expect it—if ye don't understand it." Holly pointed to the ground. "Like this?"

"Right. This too."

Holly asked, "Too?"

Rowan answered, "These dreams yer having might not all be trauma."

Holly looked between us. "Dreams? Aye, ye would after everything ye've been through. I've been told by more than one who was there tha' ye took a Viking tae his knees and dealt him blow after blow, making him beg for death."

"Well..." I started, not knowing how to explain that I'd lost my damn mind when I'd had Ormr on his knees and I was trying to punch his lights out, but Holly continued.

"Yer a warrior, love. We'll take a quick trip to Granny's place and finish whatever this is there," she said, swirling her finger around the place, indicating everything.

"Now?"

Holly and Rowan spoke at once.

"Aye."

"No."

Rowan amended, "First, ye need pants."

Chapter Twelve

I was not looking forward to a conversation with Ethel, and the length of time it took me to choose one pair of jeans from another was evidence of that. I felt peaceful now; there was no need to dig around my brain and sort out why I was having the dreams. I did want to sort out getting the cairn knoll growing again. Or, the rebirth that Holly's mom had mentioned. But it all sounded like I might need to get in touch with my Ormr side. Something I did not want to do. So, when a call came in that Charmaine had scheduled a sit-down in the castle with the bank representative, Dick Murdoch, I took the opportunity to delay and instead join Rowan. Not that meeting those two squirrel-brained idiots would be fun.

Actually, maybe it would be.

Rowan was confident as we dressed. He'd get the Rembrandt back and switch banks, even though that meant breaking a centuries-old tie with the Scottish bank. The whisky business, the gold, and the long-good name of the MacLaoch clan had already garnered interest from other financial institutions. Something Rowan had worked on while waiting for his bank to call him back. And he now was no longer gunning just to torpedo their careers—he aimed to bury them at sea.

There was so much at stake, on both sides, that it felt to me like a modern-day clan battle. And if we lost, it would be equal to burning the castle to the ground.

Rowan, reliably, was dressed for the part of a twenty-first-century warrior. His crisp midnight-colored suit pants were tailored to his exact measurements, leaving enough room through his rear and thigh so they didn't tear when he sat but also leaving little to the imagination of his athleticism. More than once, the fabric had felt my hands as I came up behind him and checked, then rechecked, by running my hands over his lean hips and into his pockets that the tight weave indeed included some silk. The pockets were lined with cotton, sturdier than the silk blend, and more forgiving to my probing fingers that fluttered around his penis, asking it if it was as excited about those tight pants as I was. As it always turned out, he was. Very.

I resisted this routine since I had to dress as well, though it was difficult to stay focused on myself when Rowan's dress shirt was open by two buttons, showing the dip below his Adam's apple where his clavicles came together in beautiful unison. With his matching suit coat, he looked like a fashion model who had stepped out from the pages of *Scottish Prince Digest*.

I made a show of wearing a silhouette-hugging pencil skirt in MacLaoch plaid. As it turned out, the distraction went both ways.

"I've never loved the clan tartan more," Rowan said, grabbing my ass as he followed me from the cottage to the castle. When I kicked off my wellies and slipped on my heels at the castle's back door, his eyes went wide with wonder and lust, like a kid happening upon a candy store at the moment he felt a ten-dollar bill in his pocket. Going up the rear stairs was difficult in the constricting skirt, and my hips swayed to make room for my knees. Rowan sounded as if he were having heart trouble behind me. "Holy fuck," he said the moment my hips tilted at the second stair, "ye are a MacLaoch wet dream."

Over my shoulder, I saw him looking wide-eyed at my rear. He put his hands on me, his mouth to my back, and breathed me in. "I don't think I'll get over you in tight MacLaoch plaid, heels, and revealing white shirts."

"My shirt is revealing?"

"It is," he said and moved around me. With his nose on my neck, he looked down into my shirt and exposed lace camisole.

"I see," I said and smiled, turning into his embrace. "So if the banker puts his face against my neck, he'll—"

"Be dead before his eyes know what they've seen."

"Right," I said, kissing his lips. "I think we're good, then."

A few minutes later, as I sat across the table from Murdoch's obstinate form, I thought he was the kind of man who didn't go in for human contact of any sort—but if a dollar were hidden in a dumpster, he'd dive in to get it.

Most bankers I'd dealt with were sticklers for regulations—following the letter of the law was what drove them. The man in front of me seemed different. So many wealthy people had bowed to the power of the institution that towered behind him, and now he erroneously believed that power was his. And doing good by his customers, or clients, as we were, hadn't even entered his narcissistic mind.

Enter Rowan; he neither bowed to nor was humbled by the power of this one man. He knew the institution was in charge, and it was their rules he respected, but he also didn't lose sight of the fact that the bank was making a fine profit off him. So much so another institution was willing to take the MacLaoch estate on as a client, helping the MacLaochs through the threat of foreclosure and ultimately bankruptcy.

Murdoch, from where I sat, had the unpleasant persona of someone who'd lost sight of reality, and Rowan's refusal to see him as all-powerful in this potential foreclosure situation made him irrational. Which he applied to a vendetta a vengeful uncle taught him.

Dick, as I began to think of him, looked to be doing his best impression of a sweating eggplant in an overlarge black suit shiny with a purplish sheen. Or maybe he was a fresh bruise. His hands were leaving slimy smudges on the well-polished table. Rowan settled him with a dram of whisky, a finger of golden amber liquid that I thought should have been lit on fire prior to serving, before asking if he had the Rembrandt with him.

"No," Dick said.

After that, the three of us sat silently in the long upstairs dining room that served as the meeting room these days. Waiting for Charmaine's arrival, I decided we needed to cleanse that room spiritually. Too many times, Charmaine had driven me nuts in there. I recently had to shoo her out of it, and here we were again, expecting her arrival.

I was a piss-poor negotiator on my best days, and there was something about the man that brought out my inner Ormr. The Viking wanted to slip a rope about the man's neck and kick him out the third-story window behind him. I snapped the hair band on my wrist and focused on the view, out over the cliffs to the loch and the sea beyond. It didn't have the zing of a rubber band, but it went better with my outfit.

Eventually, Rowan pressed him. "That piece you have in your position was ill-gotten. That must trouble you, Mr. Murdoch."

"The piece was not ill-gotten, and once your solicitor arrives, she will explain it all. You will not receive it, or like funds in return, until the back payments are paid in full."

"We'll see about tha'," Rowan growled.

I was incredulous. "You're kidding. That's highway robbery to demand the entirety of back payments before you'll give the Rembrandt back. The last paperwork you sent us showed that back payments had climbed to five million dollars. Half of which seem to be in fees and interest. You can't be serious about demanding that kind of cash right now from us." We had the gold, not appraised, so we could only assume it would cover that, but mostly, the principle of the matter made me irate.

The man sniffed and looked at me. "What did you say?"

This was an annoying tactic he had used more than once with me when I'd taken his calls. And the one time I'd called him, trying to get a pound of flesh from the man for the nasty messages he was leaving for Rowan while he was in the hospital. I felt protective and on defense. I'd taken my rubber band off for that call.

Now, however, I tried not to take it as a sign that he was a misogynistic prick or that Charmaine had bad-mouthed me to him but rather that my American accent was too strong for him to understand what I was saying.

I snapped my band and reiterated slower while Rowan studied his side profile. His eyes had become hard gemstones laser-focused on Dick's face. I recognized his old self, though it was one I'd never met, the RAF pilot who was used to managing a multimillion-dollar aircraft at speeds that I could only dream about; he was plotting where to put a missile.

The man wiped the sweat off his forehead with his plain white pocket square. He dodged my reiterated question. "Where is your counsel?"

I looked at my watch, wondering the same thing, when I heard a commotion at the front doors. Then muffled heels on the carpeted stairs, and Charmaine breezed in. I still thought the constable should have been there, but Rowan wanted a metric for measuring the depth of her betrayal, which, I assumed, he knew was deep. Rowan wanted to see what these two did on their own.

Except we weren't alone with them. My brother was just behind Charmaine. I was about to ask what he was doing there, but then I realized he only had eyes for her, giving her back a look that was somewhere between longing and seasickness.

I looked at Charmaine too. Her mood was buoyant and gorgeous. There was pink in her cheeks, her eyes were bright, and she wore a clean, casual linen suit that whispered its color might be peach. She also wore delicate leather-strapped sandals. She set her bag down, an airy thing made of cloth that would look right at home at a yoga retreat for celebrities. And then she smiled back at Tee. Had they arrived together?

All three of us got the answer to my unvoiced question as she walked back to the doorway, gently laid her hand on his chest, and kissed him, not so gently. "I told you I was late," she said.

"I'm going to miss you. I need something to carry me through."

"This"—she kissed him again—"will have to do."

"One more."

She smiled and gave him another kiss that was like two mouths fucking. I heard myself retch, and "What the *actual* fuck" spewed out.

With a Cheshire grin that spoke volumes about the bombshell Tee knew he'd dropped, he saluted Rowan and gave me a wink, and to the banker, he said, "You're in deep shit," before leaving.

I was half out of my chair to chase him, my mind whirling, when Rowan rose, cleared his throat, and pressed into my mind, *Not now*.

Oh my god, I pressed back.

Agreed was all he managed before Charmaine floated over to him and gave him a double-cheeked kiss that he winced through.

"Rowan, it's a pleasure to see you again. My apologies for my previous behavior. I felt lost when your Nicole subverted my goals. I can see now that what I really desire is to fulfill my need to salvage ancient structures, and Tiberius has shown me that I can still do that. My actions jeopardized my true intentions with Castle Laoch. He's also taught me that love can't wait a year. I didn't love you. Ever."

Rowan's eyes were wide.

Dick crowed, "Ms. Chevalier! We have *business* to attend to. This is not a personal session for airing our feelings and wild displays of indecency."

Her eyes went cold. "My kissing my boyfriend was obscene?"

"Oh, he's your boyfriend now?" I interjected, not buying any of her horse manure.

Her gaze still held a chill. "You bring out the worst in me, Nicole. Tiberius says we can someday be friends, but—"

"I need you as a friend like I need another hole in my head."

"Exactly."

"There, look at us getting along."

"You will always be present to test my patience, and Tiberius will be there to remind me that with him, my patience is infinite."

"He returns to base in a week. I hope you learn all the lessons you can before he's out of your life forever."

"I've purchased a home near the base in Germany and will run my businesses from there. Anything else?"

I was about to ask how she'd like living on a peach farm in South Carolina when he wasn't on a tour of duty. Instead, I blurted, "You bought a home in Germany?" How many days had passed? Time felt meaningless anymore.

"Come now," the banker whined.

Charmaine looked resigned. "I love him."

"You just met."

She glanced at Rowan, then at me. "And you? Your love is any less because of how swiftly it arrived?"

Now I was out of my chair. I felt my lip curl back. "That's *real* different. Destined-for-centuries different. I don't know what you have planned—"

"I love him. I feel like a fool for the way I behaved toward you. Especially now that my focus is on him and chasing something that gives me joy."

I caught Rowan's gaze, and he was slowly shaking his head. He wanted me to table it.

"Let me be clear," I said to Charmaine, "if you hurt him—"

"I realize that trust will be a difficult thing for me to earn back with you both, but let me try."

Rowan gestured to an open chair.

Charmaine gave him a polite smile as the banker said, "Thank goodness. Let's get this over with. The Rembrandt has been furnished for the good faith payment but has satisfied only that our bank will not pursue foreclosure at this time. If the back payments are not made in the next thirty days, we will foreclose on this asset, and you will need to vacate the premises."

"You—" Rowan lost all of his cool all at once. His fist slammed down on the table, making Dick jump. "This is theft! Plain and simple. What is it about this castle tha' makes ye think ye can have it, Murdoch? Yer uncle didn't take us to our knees in '89, and ye'll not take it now."

His voice was still booming through the room and making me itch to go to war with someone.

"Chief MacLaoch, please," Charmaine said, her voice cool and unimpressed. She was still unloading her folio and writing utensils, lining them up just so. Charmaine pulled her hair back, and I expected her to secure it with the rubber band she'd been using of late, but instead, her pewter clip was back, and suddenly, she was the woman I'd first met. But this time, her ire wasn't aimed at me.

"Mr. Murdoch," she snarled, "let's get something out of the way directly. The Rembrandt was taken without consent. You cannot receive stolen art as payment. Or at least not once you've been notified the art is stolen. Consider yourself notified."

Chapter Thirteen

❦

Dick was agog at Charmaine's blunt words, and they seemed to torch the last of his reserve. "You gave it to me!" he exclaimed.

"I did serve the Rembrandt. Crated and delivered as discussed. And I'll leave it up to Chief MacLaoch if he will press charges against me, but setting that aside for a moment, I need to have you acknowledge the repeated attempts I have made to contact you regarding this subject. And the lengths to which you've gone to conceal your true motives. And I do not mean servicing the loan."

"I've no idea what you are talking about."

Charmaine was unfazed in the glare of his obvious lie. "As of yesterday morning, the cash I deposited onto the loan equal that of the Rembrandt's value was accepted. And yet as we sit here at"—Charmaine recited the date and time down to the second—"we can confirm that the Rembrandt has not been returned to the client."

She looked directly at Rowan for confirmation.

"Aye, it has no' been returned." His Scots was thick.

Back to Murdoch: "The return will need to happen today. The Rembrandt must be returned to the MacLaoch estate by four. End of the business day."

The man was going puce, and he did not agree. In fact, I pictured a little, childlike him throwing a temper tantrum from somewhere inside him: *NO! You'll never get the painting back!*

Charmaine continued. "Your inability to agree to these terms leaves me no choice but to air insider knowledge of the MacLaoch account that will leave you looking shamefully incompetent. Mayhap even devious."

The man sputtered. Rowan and I were glued to Charmaine's every word.

"After the Rembrandt was in my expert care, your courier took it to the Edinburgh branch, where antiquities are valued and stored. The paperwork was processed correctly, and the value was placed against the loan. It seems that was a show for me. As of this morning, the transactions are gone. The appraised value against the loan was reversed without a digital paper trail. Had I not attempted to apply cash value against the asset, something you had not anticipated, you would have succeeded in your subterfuge. I've discovered, much to my horror, that the Rembrandt was improperly handled. The crate arrived. The Rembrandt did not. It was as if it never existed."

There was a collective *uh-oh* that ran through the room. I could hear Rowan's internal roar and reached out. I grabbed his hand before he could get both hands around the man's throat.

"I must commend you on your assistant," she said, leaning forward as if in a conspiratorial whisper to Dick, "as he was quite a helpful person—to me.

"These things," she said, sitting back, "if revealed, can tarnish a man *and* his institution's good name."

Rowan's responding grip was firm.

Dick sputtered.

"I'm sorry," Charmaine said, sounding anything but. "I realize you felt like I was in some alliance with you. I was, for the service of this loan and moving Clan MacLaoch out of bankruptcy risk. My job is to protect this historic institution, and as such, this time around, that involved me taking stock of my failures and rectifying them. This is by far the largest error of my career. I failed to see your ulterior motives until it was too late." She wrote a few things down, which I could only assume was her lunch order since she was the only one in the room calm as a summer lake. "Where's the Rembrandt, Mr. Murdoch?"

His gaze was turning into double saucers, his face apoplectic. He looked at Rowan and skated over mine before going back to Charmaine. "What are you talking about? We have it safely in our possession!"

"As I've mentioned, that is not true."

"Lies! The account was unfrozen and allowed to receive payments. But that's just the beginning! This is what I've been saying. The good faith payment was to delay foreclosure proceedings to allow time enough for the client—"

"*The client?*" Rowan snarled. "I'm right here, Murdoch, the name is Chief MacLaoch, and—"

"Then repay what is owed! Never in the history of this institution have there been such lax rules for an account. Not on my watch, MacLaoch; you'll pay down the account, or I'll take this castle brick by brick."

Rowan went to ice. "Is tha' a threat?"

My stomach twisted into knots. I thought we should tell them that we had another institution that was going to take the loan off their hands and make this man go away, with his threats and all. But there was something larger at play now.

"Mr. Murdoch." Charmaine brought the attention back to her. "I'm not finished. It took me a long while to get someone with a high enough pay grade in the tech department to open the loan and tell me about the creative footwork that had been applied to it. The digital footprint, once revealed, is damning," she said with a smile.

I might not be Charmaine's best friend, but it was goddamn refreshing to have her working toward our interests instead of against them.

"I don't know what you're talking about. If you're trying to involve me in some sort of insurance payout for stolen art, I'll not sit here and—"

Charmaine continued, "The digital trail leads back to your computer, your log-in, your...what did the tech expert say? Ah, yes, your 'amateur-hour hacks' were easily traceable.

"Might I remind you the MacLaochs are not Casswell's only clients. Over the course of Casswell's prestigious three hundred years in operation, we've come across all kinds of dubious individuals. That is why, no matter where, who, or what I'm transporting, it's checked, logged, stored, and sealed to prevent tampering. The MacLaoch file now has photos of the crate, tampered with, on file. We can all assume where I'm going with this; I shall cut to the chase. You did not take it to Edinburgh. You are still in possession of it. What are you hoping to gain precisely? My apologies—that was a rhetorical question." And Charmaine plunged forward without waiting for a response.

"Five hours. That is the length of time you have to return it, or Casswell and Associates will begin a dastardly media campaign to expose you and will end with your arrest. I assure you, the client blowback will be unlike anything you or Scottish Trust Bank has ever experienced."

"You!" he shouted, snatching his briefcase, tossing his folio back inside, and snapping it shut. "You're to blame; you have shown that you're willing to dirty your hands for whatever it is that you want. You'll go to prison for this. You gave me an empty crate. This is all *your* doing."

She continued calmly as Rowan and I listened as his story changed. We were like two cats observing their exchange like the back-and-forth of a laser pointer. "Casswell is willing to overlook an overachieving agent as long as their goals are for the betterment of the client. What you've done is purely for personal gain. Return the Rembrandt. Money in equal value of the Rembrandt has been applied to the account, as I've said. There is nothing else you could possibly require."

I wasn't sure that something like this could be easily slithered out of. I was sweating for the guy now; he'd been cornered.

"You removed the tracking device and broke the chain of custody on a historically important and costly piece of art, and it seems you are purposefully hiding its location now. You know this. You know that I took the proper precautions. The crate was impeccably prepared for transport," she explained to him as if he were new to the whole thing. "Photographed and witnessed." She slid out from her folder photograph after photograph of the art in various stages of being crated up.

"If it is returned in any condition other than the one seen here, the dastardly media campaign will move forward, as well as charges for theft, destruction of private property, and damage of a historical artifact."

"This is— I'll need these photographs to report to my superiors."

"Take them—"

Rowan cut in, simplifying. "Discuss it with your superiors, discuss it with yer ma, but if it's no' back here in—"

Charmaine held up her open palm, fingers splayed. "Five hours."

"—I'll come for ye like a bloodhound tae a hare."

"What Chief MacLaoch means to say is that we'll press charges."

Sweat dripped off the man's brow onto the tabletop. I had the absurd thought that I'd need a boat soon.

"That's incomprehensible, everything you've just said. You're lying. You can't get access to the vaults like you said you did. You've taken it and now are trying to ruin *me*!"

I thought I could smell rubber the man was backpedaling so hard.

Charmaine said, "I have requests to meet with your superiors in one hour. They will be as concerned as I am."

I practically heard the little rat squeak. "Fine, a phone call, then. I'll double-check the asset logs," he said, doubling down on Charmaine being the perpetrator. "But it'll take time; Edinburgh is hours away, and getting things here from Edinburgh will take *days*."

Charmaine repeated, "You will have it here in five hours. I've had things shipped here from the continent in less time. Do not worry. I have a feeling it's close and in your possession. Shall I get you my courier's contact information?"

"Murdoch, ye look like you've had something spoiled tae eat. Be calm. I'm sure a simple phone call will set things to rights. Or have ye done something only ye would be proud of?"

Dick was skirting around the table. "This is most untoward."

The man was a puzzle. There was so much risk in taking it. If this was about the raid in '89, why now with his payback? We'd likely never see him again without law enforcement present, so I pressed.

"Dick, Mr. Murdoch," I corrected, "any innocent human in your position should be shouting with joy that his loan is back on track and not headed toward foreclosure. And that the misplacement of a precious painting was discovered quickly, not after months. We have a saying in the States that if it looks like a duck, swims like a duck, and quacks like a duck? It's a duck."

I lost everyone in the room. I clarified: "You look like you stole it. You're covering your ass like you stole it, and you're squawking like someone who stole it; I'm going to assume you stole it. So, *why* is the real question."

His gaze on mine went ablaze, surprising me with the anger burning there. "Don't address *me*, sassenach—"

"Careful." Rowan was behind me and his hand went to my shoulder and gave it a squeeze.

Sassenach, I had learned, meant English person, aka outsider. And while that definition alone wasn't insulting in modern times, it had history. The connotation and tone were everything. He was using it in its derogatory sense, when the British were bloodily ripping Scots off their land.

I'm going tae fucking murder him.

There's more here—hold on.

"Why are you gunning for the MacLaochs so recklessly?" I touched the band on my wrist.

He physically leaned into my question, having forgotten he was fleeing. "*You'd* never understand."

"You're right. I don't. I'm just a dumb Ameri—"

"You've probably never seen a thistle but for a weed... Ye don't know what it means tae be Scots."

Rowan's hand on my shoulder tightened. And I reminded him, *I gave him some rope, love; let's see what he does with it.*

It took three heartbeats before he sang like a sinner on Sunday.

"But ye come for a tidy visit after discovering 'Oh aye, I've a bit of Scots in me, so let me buy up land and pretend tha' maybe it was once mine?' But it wasn't, was it. It was divided up by clans centuries ago, and whilst now ye are in your romantic dreams of kilts and fucking in the pastures, the rest of us have to face the loss of lands tha' took both place and meaning from us. MacLaochs never had tae suffer like the rest of us. But now..." His gaze went to Rowan's. "Now your time has come, hasn't it, MacLaoch? I might no' carry a sword or a pistol or the warrior title like ye, but I have a pen. And come judgment time, tha' pen will see to it tha' you're humbled like the rest of us."

I could feel the growl before I heard it, and I thought, *Well, fuck, that popped that zit of a confrontation.*

Rowan, whose entire lineage had been cursed since the times of the Vikings, growled his response from behind me, "Come judgment time? And who's doing the judging? Ye? Because if it is, I'll curse ye, Murdoch. I'll curse ye with the good fortune ye think I've been strapped with, and maybe after a bullet or two has torn through yer body and another blown open your best friend's head, you'll see the kind of good fortune I'm most familiar with."

Murdoch kept his eyes on Rowan and walked backward toward the door. With one last scowl at the room, he left. We heard him thunder down the stairs and brush off Marion and Flora, offering him a freshly baked scone, before slamming the massive wood door behind him that shook the building. The workmen hollered at him from up on their scaffolding, "Oy! Git tae fuck, ya sodding arsehole!"

Back in our conference room, Rowan was seething. "He's a dead man walking."

Chapter Fourteen

"Please, Chief, no talk of homicide. At least while I'm within earshot."

I gave Rowan's hand a squeeze. After a moment, he visibly relaxed and sat on the edge of the table next to me. "His branch of the Murdoch clan is no friend to us, but the rest of them are fine. If he keeps the Rembrandt from us, he'll find himself pruned from their family tree."

I voiced something that had come to me during the meeting. "Look, we all have stories we tell ourselves and others, and he was so off base from my own reality—why I'm really here, my actual character—that it makes me think that he's a Murdoch in name only, and if he can take the MacLaochs down, he can win the ultimate merit badge: pride from his clan. Or at least his dad, or someone else who knows he's not a Murdoch by blood. Probably a relative close to him was English and married into the Murdoch family and told him tales of ancestral bravery and pride and left out the reasons for the darkness." As I finished, I saw Charmaine had a funny expression. Was it...was she impressed by me?

She said, "His grandfather was an Englishman and raised him when his father left. His mother remarried a Murdoch. He never did call him dad, but uncle."

"Wait, my guess was corr—" I said at the same time Rowan said to Charmaine, "How would you—"

"I, of course, made inquiries when it came to my attention that the Rembrandt wasn't applied to the loan."

"You have a habit of doing that. Digging up dirt on people."

"Yes, I do. It helps even out the mysteries of humans. We are all, ultimately, predictable."

I could feel my lip curl back. Now that one menace was out of the room, I could remember the awful news I'd learned before the meeting. "And now you're fucking my brother. What, pray tell, is your prediction there—"

"Holy fuck."

The new voice made us all jump. Holly in her work gear, tight crop top under flannel and jeans with reinforced knees, came panting into the room. She was trying to catch her breath while she pointed to her phone in her hand, "Cousin."

"Cousin?"

TJ appeared; the grime on his boots told me he'd been out in the field.

Holly pointed at him. "Tell them. Can't. Bloody fucking stairs."

He took the phone and waltzed over to Charmaine, who gave him a radiant smile; he gave her a quick kiss.

She looked at me and, with a blank face, answered the question I'd posed to her before Holly showed up: "Devotion. That's what I foresee."

TJ glanced between us. "What's that?"

Up to his ugly mug, I said, "What does it say?" and pointed to Holly's phone.

Keeping Charmaine in a one-armed hug, he read the text message: "Hanging over the mantel. And then something about dicks. Let's see, more dicks, and then, old Otey manor house. The Rembrandt is hanging over the mantel in the main foyer."

My connection with Rowan sizzled. Rowan, tumbler in hand, slipped off the table and pivoted.

"Oh no." I lunged for him and missed.

With an arm an outfielder would respect, he whipped the tumbler through the doorway into his office where it shattered against the far wall and dripped whisky down the dark wallpaper.

TJ asked, "What am I missing?"

To Rowan, I said, "Well, that answers that question."

Charmaine patted TJ's chest. "The MacLaochs have always been perceived as wealthy and unbeholden to laws or justice that other clans, particularly the Murdochs, have had to face. The feud with the Murdochs began when the clan stole cattle from the MacLaochs, well back in Shakespearean times. They battled each other every generation then went silent for about 150 years until it was rekindled at the whisky raid of 1989. If that was a purposeful rekindling."

Holly was breathing easy now and came over, giving Charmaine a once-over. "I have to interrupt, love—that pant suit is chic. Is that raw silk?"

"It is."

"Cool." Holly flicked her gaze from the suit up to Charmaine's eyes. "But still, fuck you, aye?"

Charmaine gave her a dry smile. "Holly. Still the vocabulary of a naval nurse, I see."

Then, to Rowan, as if Charmaine no longer existed, Holly continued, "My cousin works at the old Otey place. Dick Murdoch refurbished it into a modern nightmare. She's one of the cleaning crew, and she wants me to tell ye, she can take it down and bring it home, if ye like."

I wondered if we were all envisioning a several-million-dollar painting popped into the back of Cousin's Peugeot, bungee cords tying the hatch closed before they trundled on back home to the castle. Done and dusted. I smiled with pride; these were my people.

Charmaine confirmed she was indeed sharing that image, though with less delight. "The Rembrandt is highly valuable; it'll need to be properly crated for shipment and then couriered back here. And insured."

I wanted to ask her if that was what she had done when she'd hired an art thief to steal it from the castle, but I was more concerned with

Rowan. He was still turned away from the group, trying to catch his own breath and keep his frustration and temper in check. I went to him and put my hand on his back, giving him some of my calm.

As soon as my fingertips touched the hard rope of muscles lining his spine, his head went up, and his eyes closed.

"It'll be OK," I whispered.

He took a deep breath in and whispered to me in my mind, *My sow is running bonkers through the fields.*

"I bet she is."

When his hand slipped down off his face, it opened for me; against his chest, I put my hand into his and gripped tight.

We have this.

One more deep breath and he rested his forehead to mine, and I felt him relax.

Rowan, his hand still in mine, turned to Holly clear-eyed. "Yer cousin, she shouldn't take it; it'll bring her too much trouble to do. And, aye, if it's not returned today, I'll retrieve it myself. He cannae be so daft as tae think I wouldn't find out. The old Otey place is not thirty miles from here."

Holly said, "We'll get it back, my liege. If this is a trap, best it be us squirrelly folk tha' retrieve it."

"Nae, Holly, I appreciate ye wanting tae do this, but I'll not risk your scholarship nor your standing at university; it's not worth it."

Holly's face crashed. "But I need tae."

"Nae."

They both were getting thick into their respective Scots as their emotions heated up.

"Holl," I interjected, "it's all right. There's no debt to be owed or repaid."

Her gaze glistened with unshed tears. "Ye dinnae understand, Chief. I've failed my clan. I wasn't at the battle. This I can do. I have tae."

I felt Rowan melt. Holly's need overshadowed his own. He paid forward my abilities to calm him and went to Holly, his hand held up. She clasped it as he quietly said, "I know ye feel like ye've let down the clan, but ye've no'. Do ye see me? Look at me, Holly Alexander

MacDonagh MacLaoch. I know your desire tae help, and ye will, but your focus needs tae be on your studies. The slope into the world yer father left is a steep one, and all it takes is one second tha' ye take yer eyes off the road ahead for ye tae fall into it. I promised yer ma tha' ye'd not get into trouble when you're here. It's a promise I'll keep."

Holly looked out the windows, not wanting to meet Rowan's gaze any longer. She wiped her nose on her sleeve and muttered to him, "But I can help."

"And ye will. I'll need it."

Holly's gaze shot to Charmaine, then back to his, and it was only then that she relented. "Aye, fine. But for the record, I know a guy."

The way her eyes hit mine to check my reaction, then back to Rowan's, made me groan. We all knew a guy. "Holly, no."

"He owes us. Just like Charmaine."

"He's gone," Rowan reminded her.

"No, he's not."

This made Rowan's brow furrow.

"He's desperate," she said, and it sounded like she was pleading on his behalf.

"He's a fucking dead man." Rowan punctuated his point by stabbing his pointer finger at the floor, as if he were saying, *Bring him here and I'll show you a dead man.*

"He probably wants the gold, hon." I tried for common sense with her.

"Gold?" Charmaine and TJ said in unison.

Rowan looked to me, his question easy to read there in his eyes: *Should we tell him in front of Nincompoop?* The last word I inferred.

"What, those Roman coins?" TJ continued.

"Who the hell told you?"

He gave a Baker shrug. "I was down at the pub when I heard about it."

All eyes were on him now.

"What?"

"You know, Tee, you shoulda been a damn investigator not a medic for the crap you dig up everywhere you go."

"Not my fault people like to talk to me, but damn, in this town, *everyone* talks."

"Who told you?"

"Look, I was minding my own business when this huge dude came up to me and asked if I was TJ, your brother. Like, knew my name. I hoped you didn't owe him a shit ton of money because he looked like he could bounce me out of that place one-handed. Instead, he said he was coming by later in the week for a proper hello but that he thought it was fortuitous we met then."

Rowan's gaze went to mine then Tee's. "Big man, looks like yer sister?"

Tee held his thumb up to me as if squaring up a mental picture. "Ya, just like her, all burly and such."

"Jackass," I responded, then clarified further, "looks like Grand-pappy, you mean."

"Yee-up. Freaky like, how much he did, now that you mention it."

"What did Eli say?"

He snapped his fingers and pointed at me. "Eli, that's right."

"You're stalling. Spill."

"How nice do you promise to be to Charmaine?"

I got close to him and looked up into his stupid, ugly face. "I'll be super nice. Like super-duper," and gave him a wide, shit-eating grin.

"You look like Rex"—TJ said, naming our childhood dog—"right before he bit the mailman. So, no, you're not."

Charmaine watched the banter like a tennis match, wisely keeping her mouth shut.

"I'm the nicest peach in the orchard. Just not to you."

"What, come on— Oof!"

I had slapped his crotch with the back of my hand. When he was bent over, I put him into a headlock and sat hard on the floor, taking him down with me.

"Goddamn it!" he hollered as he hit the ground. Charmaine stum-bled into the table as Tee's one-armed hug was ripped from her.

I firmed up my lock. "What the hell did Eli say?"

Rowan had come around and had to shout my name to get my

attention. "We'll ask Eli," he said, not understanding what was happening.

"It's not about that! He sassed me."

Tee socked me awkwardly in the side—his fist glanced off my hip—and then tried to roll me over. I braced myself as best I could in the tight skirt and leaned back, putting more pressure on the hold even as he tried to pull himself free.

"You're outta your damn mind!" he garbled, his face going beet red.

"What'd he say?"

"Go ask him!"

"I'm asking you!"

"Goddamn it, Cole!"

Rowan tried to interject again. "Mo ghràdh, I can just—"

"It's not about that!" I roared, feeling the fight from earlier come flooding back. "You goddamn dimwitted fool, what the hell are you doing sleeping with the woman who tried to torch me off the face of this earth!?"

With that realization, I let him go. I was pissed enough to choke him, but he deserved a fighting chance to explain himself first.

He sat back on his haunches, his hand going to his reddened neck. "What the hell, Cole?! Are you...stronger now?"

He looked to Rowan then, as if he needed confirmation.

Rowan looked to me, then to Tee, and back to me. "I'm sorry, ghràdh." Then he said to Tee, "Not full-strength Ormr, but..."

I looked down at my arms. Were they lightly glowing? "*What?*"

Charmaine whimpered next to me as Holly scampered around and slid in on her knees. "Show me." She took my hands and studied my face. "He's here?"

I sighed, losing the fight in me. "No, Holl, he's gone. Mostly."

Charmaine whined again, making Holly snap, "Stop whining, you got to see a once-in-a-lifetime supernatural moment, and you handled it like a damn sissy."

"I...I can't if it comes back," she said and sidestepped away from me.

Tee looked me over then to Charmaine. "She's fine. She's just regular pissed now. But before, her eyes went—"

"Neon," Rowan confirmed.

"I was gonna say to slits, but neon would do it too."

Holly was crestfallen. "Bring him back for me, mate, just once?"

I gave Holly a resigned sigh. "No way." Then to Tee: "We'll talk about everything else once you can unhitch yourself from Charmaine for three minutes."

"You have got the mouth of a sailor, Cole," he admonished.

"You'd know—you taught me." I flipped back at him. "For now, tell us about the bar and seeing Eli. Or I'll put my Ormr strength to the real test."

Chapter Fifteen

Tee said, "There's nothing really to tell. Eli came in right when that Mickey guy was trying to leave—he was there with some older dude. Eli seems like a really nice guy. I got the feeling from people around us that people underestimate him and how much he knows because he comes off as a big loveable teddy bear, but he's—"

"A Minory."

"I was gonna say a Baker but, yeah, I suppose that's more accurate now. Eli made this Mickey fellow feel like he could be Mickey's one saving grace, and then Mickey told him everything."

Rowan had helped me up off the floor and was holding me in an embrace, both to calm me and to restrain me while Tee told the whole damn story at the pace of a slug. I gave Rowan a squeeze and breathed in his clean linen and salty loch smell and felt my bones relax. His right hand worked its way up my back and into my hair as Tee spoke.

I looked up at Rowan. *We both know why he unloaded his burdens on Eli.*

Yes, he hoped this very thing would happen, that word would get back to us.

Rowan massaged his thumb behind my ear, small but purposeful circles soothing me.

Over my shoulder at TJ, I asked for the final time, "What'd he say?"

. . .

Mickey felt small there in that dark Glentree pub. The kind of small that happens when a larger-than-life character from your past reemerges and fucks around. When he had been a child, no one understood that the sweet-talking man had been a blighter. A real piece of human flotsam.

Now, that man was saying, "If there's more, son, we could be rich. Put this piss-poor climate behind us and find a nice beach in the Bahamas to live out our days."

"For you."

"What'd you say?" His Dublin tone reflected his neighborhood, where his question would be a threat as well.

Mickey had built something of himself. Sure, it wasn't as posh as his colleagues preferred, but considering the tenement housing his father had raised him in with a hard hand, he was practically royalty now.

"Sounds like a pretty fairy-tale life for you. I'm not a fucking retiree, now, am I? I'll bugger off. You're welcome to stay and attempt to nick the gold that will put you back inside or summon a pissed-off ghost who'll cut your head off. It's up to you." Mickey polished off his pint, and the heaviness of the glass hit the table hard. The only outward sign that his temper was flaring. He stood as his father leaned back in his chair. The lines that etched the older man's face from a hard life with hard drink now had lines of their own. The son could still read the father by those cracks and crevices. A barometer of his mood changes. This expression said he was about to launch into what a piece-of-shit kid he was, and if he didn't do what he asked, then he was going to use his leverage to put him in prison with him.

Only the ruby was gone. And he'd properly dodged the constable, and Rowan had let him, watched with those keen, devil-blue eyes as Mickey had lied his way out of the grasp of the law and put himself squarely in MacLaoch's debt. Fuck that man. Fuck everything he owned, and the entire county of Glentree.

"So, that's how it's to be then, eh? Your father needs help, and this is how you repay him?" There it was, the Catholic guilt in a Protestant man. He was hypocrisy on two legs. "I spent my life trying to raise you right, trying to do right by you, and this is the thanks I get?"

"Blackmailing your own son for a couple of quid?"

"Couple of quid? Are you mad? This will put us up fine for the rest o' our days, son. And you? Just walking away? What are you playing at?"

"If you'd seen the things I have, you'd run. You'd run so far and fast that you'd never look back. It's what I'm trying to do, and you're keeping me here and they'll find me, and what I'd nearly escaped will get me. So, fuck off, I'm out. Far out. I'm transferring to a university in the Americas."

"America?" His father sat up surprise written on his face. It was as if he couldn't believe he'd leave him and all his good ideas behind.

"North, Central, South, doesn't matter, as long as there's an ocean between us."

"My son, running for his pretty life?" Something dark slithered into Lou Gillian's laugh.

The dig of how pretty he was sat like a red-hot button with Mickey. The same face that got slapped for looking like his mum. Mickey leaned in so close he could see the red veins in the whites of his father's eyes. "What you've done is fucked us. You took a Rembrandt from a place that is so haunted that its ghosts emerge out of the bodies of their descendants and murder in the name of their honor. I saw one, nae, I saw two"—he held his fingers in front of his father's face in case he was as stupid as he knew him to be—"breathing ghosts that ripped a hole in this life, so, no, I'll not be going back onto MacLaoch land. They know who I am and how to find me—I'll not give them more of a reason to. Though, again, if you want to, go right ahead. But before you do," he said, throwing cash down on the table, "tell me, white or red?"

"White or red what?" he spat back, his son's temper igniting his own.

"White or red roses for your funeral, you fuck. 'Cause that is the only thing I'll wonder when the police knock on my door and tell me you're dead."

"Oh, well, look who it is!" came a jolly voice from the door of the small pub.

Mickey looked up and groaned. He was too late; he'd never escape this place. Eli Campbell, cousin and sure as shit Minory descendant, was making his way over to their table, pint in hand and grin in place.

"Eli was there the whole time, then?" Rowan asked after he gave the top of my head an absent-minded kiss.

Tee nodded. "He was there having a pint on his day off, and he stayed when Mickey came in, then me."

"We need to find Mickey," I said into Rowan's chest.

He sighed. Pure resignation. "And lock up tha' gold."

I looked up at his face to find him looking at Holly.

Her face said it all: Mickey was with her.

Back at Rowan: "Does *anyone* leave Glentree?"

"No, we're a bit like tha' 'Hotel California' song." Something made him look at his phone.

Charmaine gave me one last look of apprehension before: "I've got paperwork to prep."

Rowan stopped scrolling through his phone and gave me a coy smile. "Ye'll never guess who has the worst timing." I tried to spy at the screen, but he tucked it away, saying to Tee, "I could use a strapping young man for what I have to do next."

"Who are you talking about? I'm neither strapping nor young."

"Oh aye," Holly protested, "looked in the mirror lately, love?"

This drew Charmaine's gaze, and Holly slung her arm around TJ's shoulder and waggled her eyebrows at her.

Rowan smiled and cuffed him on his free shoulder. "Aye, good. Come, we've a rescue to make."

At that, TJ was all business, shaking off Holly before falling in stride next to Rowan. "What's happened?"

Rowan assessed him as we went down the front steps then out the great front doors. "At ease. It's a simple, and, I'm hoping, uneventful rescue."

We got to the gravel, and I realized my heels weren't going to cut it. "Well, crap," I uttered and pulled my shoes off. "Hold up!"

I was back fast with my wellies on, and Holly and I jogged to catch up with Rowan and Tee.

Tee cut off his conversation with Rowan and dropped back to be next to me. "That thing you did back in the meeting room earlier, the close-your-eyes bit, what was that all about?"

I raised my eyebrow at him. "I'm not talking to you until you promise to stop humping Charmaine. Plus, I'm sure Marion, or someone at the pub, has filled you in."

"No deal. She's the one. Was it that communication thing?"

Rowan piped up. "Don't worry about it; the more ye think about it, the more it'll screw with yer mind."

"Do you have to close your eyes to talk to each other?"

"Nope, but sometimes it helps me to concentrate. Look numb nuts, Charmaine tried to torch my career and me out of existence not more than a month ago."

"I know, she told me."

"She told you?"

"Yeah, but she used words like 'my behavior was abhorrent and existed in a competitive bubble in which crushing you was the only aim.'"

"And you thought, 'Yeah, awesome,' and whipped your dick out to get some of that."

Holly tittered.

"You'd make a sailor blush, Cole."

"And yet you don't deny it."

"Hey, I get that it's really shitty timing, but can you pause judgment for one week? And I'll do the same for you." TJ nodded to Rowan ahead of us.

Rowan had keen hearing and gave us a look over his shoulder before: *One less body to bury in the cairn knoll. That'll save us some work.*

I gave a dark laugh. "Fine, sure, Tee. One week."

This made him beam, and he gave me his arm. I hooked mine through his and pretended he was a real gentleman.

He whispered out of the corner of his mouth, "He did it again, didn't he? Talking with his mind to you?"

"Yup."

"Just grunts or general feelings come through that?"

"Full sentences, emotions, and sometimes a bit of sensory information about where he's at. Like when he's at the loch edge, I can smell the brine of the water."

Tee was silent as we went through the tidy forest that Rupert kept from going full wild; we headed toward the bubbling burn of the Lady MacLaoch stream in the distance. Holly was enjoying watching Tee's mind break.

Tee tightened up his arm, thinking. "I'm not sure I'd get used to that. You could at any point interrupt him to tell him to pick up groceries, or you could tell when he's horn—"

I lightly punched TJ in the pectoral.

"Ow," he said with a grin.

Holly chimed in. "Ye weren't around when they were first dating, so ye don't know, but they didn't need a secret language for tha'. This one is always horny."

I feigned surprise at seeing her thumb aim in my direction.

Tee shook me off. "Disgusting. What would Mother say?"

"Atta girl?"

Tee scoff-laughed and caught up with Rowan. The four of us worked our way through the property, taking trails that forked off each other. Fallen leaves and damp soil were soft underfoot.

The sound of running water rose in volume as we got closer to the main bridge that separated MacLaoch grounds from the rest of the area. The air around us seemed wetter, as if the river were running through the air. We broke out from the thick forest to a green meadow dotted with tiny white roman chamomile blossoms and sunshine-yellow marsh marigolds. A while ago, the bridge had "mysteriously" lost four of its large timber treads, making it impassable for cars, and any walkers who didn't want to tightrope walk along the railing, but it had been "repaired" upon Rowan's request, for my brother's visit. So, it was interesting to see the treads gone again. And clarified why we were on a "rescue" mission. Someone we wanted to see was stuck on the other side of the river.

Holly read my mind. She patted her pocket where her phone was. "I'm so surprised folks knew exactly when the bank dude left. Huh, funny."

"Holly..."

She shrugged at her laird. "It'll be hard to serve bank papers when ye can't access the property."

"Holly..." he reiterated.

She beamed at him as if he were commending her on a job well done; then he returned the grin.

"Who are we meeting?" I called to Rowan.

His eyes sparkled as he looked back at me. "Someone who understands energy and was instrumental for you tae believe the unbelievable."

Just then I saw who Rowan meant. I began waving exuberantly.

"Peabody!" I shouted across the splashing water. "Welcome!"

TJ squinted into the distance with Holly next to him. "Who's Peabody, the old dude with glasses?"

"Yes!" I said and waved again as Peabody waved back with equal enthusiasm.

Rowan took Tee to the riverbank at the wooden bridge's footing and was messing with the floating dock, guide ropes, and pulley system attached to it.

I cupped my hands around my mouth. "It's good to see you!"

He gave me a thumbs-up and shouted back, "And you as well, Mrs. MacLaoch!"

Mrs. MacLaoch, I thought and smiled absently, looking over to Rowan; he paused to smile with me.

TJ ruined the moment by giving me a thumbs-up and a fake smile. "How's that for an atta-girl? Mother is gonna shit a brick when she hears that."

I sneered at him.

Rowan handed him a rope. "Pull."

He pulled. "She will, you know," he said to Rowan.

"I've yet to see a brick leave the anus of any being," Rowan replied.

Holly wandered closer, pointing to something Rowan wasn't looking at because he was too busy glaring at Tee.

"Tee," I explained, "we have a date set for a traditional wedding. Mother will get her day in the sun." My palms were beginning to sweat. Holly gave up on Rowan and waded through the tall grass down the embankment, her boots slipping here and there in the mud.

She stepped onto the movable dock like a pro and called to TJ, "Send me across, and I'll help him over."

Rowan put his hand on the rope, stopping Tee. Something was on his mind: "When ye arrived, you got to punch me in the gut. I deserved that from you and took it as payment for being with your sister before fulfilling my honorable intentions toward her. Now? I've rectified that, and we are trying to honor your family as we move forward. Dinnae threaten her with your mother's animosity. She feels it. Without your assistance."

"Guys, that's not necessary—" I said.

TJ just bared his teeth at Rowan, not quite a grin and not quite a growl. "Take your hand off the line."

"Your jabs are robbing Cole's face of her smile and making her panic, and I won't let it stand. Blood brother or nae."

"Boys..." I said in warning.

Holly was halfway across the wide stream when she shouted back, "Oye! Ye gonna keep pulling, or do I have to take over?!"

TJ repeated, "Take your hand off the rope..."

"Tee," I said, "if you sock Rowan again, I'll tie rocks to your ankles and pitch you into the river."

Keeping his gaze on TJ, Rowan said, "He won't get another crack in."

Tee yanked the rope hard. "Oh, really, Braveheart? I wouldn't bet on it."

"Guys! Can we focus on Peabody, please?"

At this Peabody waved again.

Rowan let go. "I prefer Rob Roy, and ye'll heed my warning."

Chapter Sixteen

TJ and Rowan's sparring died down to a scuffle as the guest, Peabody, crossed the river with Holly. He had just stepped out onto the muddy embankment, smiling and waving, when he fell back; Holly cursed and grabbed him. He gripped her as if his life depended on it as they both slipped on the mud among the slick reeds. Finally, with one look back to the burbling rush of the navel-deep water, and a gentle heave-ho from Holly, Peabody reached the crest, where Rowan and TJ grabbed the professor and hoisted him to flat ground.

The walk back to the castle felt quicker than the walk there, as Peabody, Rowan, and I fought for space in the conversation. Peabody was the most anxious of us all, excited to get inside where, he said, he could properly catch us up on a book he was writing about the MacLaoch curse. He thought the latest bit of "paranormal activity" in the field, as he called it, would be an excellent addition. Holly corrected him, "It's jus' magic, Prof." She said it with a wink before she headed out back to the field, but not before she leaned into me. "Want me to take Bro with me?"

"Maybe," I said then thought better of it. "Nah, I have a bone to pick with him. Then I'll be out."

Marion and Flora had brought tea to Rowan's formal office and set it up on the round table behind the settee. After putting back more cucumber sandwiches than was polite, I stood, hand on TJ's shirt to pull him up too. I explained that Holly had texted that the field was still growing, and I was eager to be up there. There were just a couple more hours before the shit hit the fan with the Rembrandt, and the rest of the day and likely week would be toast. This was all true—plus I needed to chew my brother out.

Peabody held up a finger. He swiped his mouth with his napkin before popping up. "Before you go, I have a request."

"How about at dinner? I'm assuming you're staying with us?"

Peabody said, "Yes, but I'm hoping you can do this now. It'll only take a moment, and I'd like to get it sent out in the afternoon mail." He lifted a vial from his case.

"What's this?"

"DNA!" he exclaimed with a jovial smile as if that explained everything.

Peabody handed me the vial to spit in, and I did as I was told. Peabody wrote on the lab's plastic envelope as I said, "In the States, even our pets are getting in on the DNA analysis."

TJ said to Rowan, "Bro, you should check it out, see what pedigree of asshole you are."

Rowan smiled and responded, "No test needed. I *know* I'm the biggest asshole there is."

Spoken like a man who'd spent his formative years prepping for the chief's seat, then his early adult life in the RAF learning to command a fighter jet. I bit my lip. I missed him being in command of me—it had been too long with everything going on.

Peabody smiled, pulled out another DNA kit, and lifted it to Rowan. "As a matter of fact, if you wouldn't mind, Rowan, I have one for you. Of course we know that your DNA concentrates right here on this very spot of land, but it'll help to bring more MacLaochs into the fold if you make your DNA public so that your clan people can find you." He watched Rowan with that air of excited scientific inquiry, then smiled. "Plus, it's heaps of fun."

He put the box down in front of Rowan, who was wearing the mask of a man at his leisure. But I could see that beneath it he was being careful, watchful, and I thought I had TJ to thank for that.

Peabody turned to TJ. "Tiberius," and I stifled a snort at his formal name and waited for him to attempt to drop his pants with Peabody. TJ gave me a grin that said he was thinking about it. Peabody continued, "I'm sorry, I didn't know you would be here. I will order another one and take yours as well."

"That's all right, Doc; my sister's will do fine for the both of us. Plus, I know what kind of asshole I am. The *likable* kind."

"Yes, yes," he said, though his tone said he was ignoring the "asshole" banter, "but it's always interesting to see what DNA each sibling picks up. You'd be surprised at the difference even biological twins have. This is more than what your makeup looks like in terms of geography. This is a test I've devised to look at specific locales on the genome and analyze the alleles there."

I had a feeling he knew which part of Rowan's and my DNA held Orabilia and Ormr.

TJ held up his hand. "Pass."

Peabody nodded and let it go but then had an idea that illuminated his face. "I'm curious," he said. Going to his equipment pile on the settee, he dug deep through the bags and cases to find the case holding his energy meter.

I grinned over at Rowan, who gave me a smirk back. One that said, if this didn't fully convince Tee that we were knee-deep in supernatural energies, nothing would. Plus, I wanted to witness Tee's first experience with Peabody's energy meter.

"What's that?" Tee asked, his brow furrowed in concern.

"It's a *real* asshole meter," I said as I stoppered my spit and sealed it into its plastic envelope. "Pants down and bend over, dickhead."

Peabody dryly corrected, "That's not where it goes."

TJ glared back at me, and I responded, "Call my husband an asshole again, and I'll use that energy meter as a suppository, so help me God."

"Now, now," Peabody interjected, "this is not going near anyone's anus. It cost me several thousand dollars, and I'd like to keep it in its current condition as long as possible."

TJ sauntered up to Peabody, rolling up his sleeves as if he were about to give blood. "All right, Doc, what's this thing?"

Peabody gave him a glance as he took the meter out and started connecting the sensors and cords that looked to be miniature microphones. At the round writing table, Peabody moved the overflowing platter of scones and sandwiches to the deep-set windowsill. He came back and patted Tee's arm. "Keep your sleeve down. There is no blood today. Just sit still and let me get some baselines to tune it, and then I'll take yours." He gestured next to him. "Cole? If you will?" and I saddled up and held my arms out as if I were at the airport.

"That's not necessary either," he mumbled—the Baker kids were an active bunch—as he turned dials and opened his notebook to see my last reading. It was hard to be with him and his equipment and not feel like you had to *do something*.

"Now," Peabody said, reading my low-level metrics, "we've got a slight mHz bump of energy; I take it that was the skirmish with Ormr, yes?"

I opened my mouth to respond, but it was a rhetorical question. He continued, "Yes, of course, and I've still got to get out to the field to take proper measurements, but generally speaking, we're on target," he murmured, the meter between us was giving off a gentle mismatched ticking that got more clicky as he put his senor next to me. I assumed it was in response to a rise in energy levels as it matched the triple dials on his meter. The dials reminded me of old car fuel dials. The wands in each jumped gently toward the quarter tank mark.

TJ was resting a butt cheek on the curved edge of the table, arms crossed, taking it all in. "So, what is that, like a metal detector?"

Peabody smiled at him and waved Rowan over. "Similar! Only what we're dialed in to detect is not metal but rather experiential energy that is left over from a tragedy. These electromagnetic field meters have been custom-calibrated to detect frequencies that are much too small for the average device. And energy that comes from high-voltage sources is not the same as the human body, especially the brain, when it experiences tragedy or is touched by death. The latter leaves an indelible mark."

"So, you've got Cole's. She's got some shit, I'm sure, with that Viking dude, and what's pretty boy here? Measured in nanometers?"

Peabody gave him a sad smile and looked back to Rowan who, hands in pockets, stepped up to the meter. I put my hand to his chest and went up on my toes, giving him a soft kiss; then I stepped back.

Peabody looked at him and asked quietly, "All right? Or shall we clear the room first?"

TJ scoffed and slid off the table. "Call me when it's my turn."

Rowan nodded at the meter and said, "Go ahead."

TJ was halfway to the door when Peabody turned his meter on Rowan. The machine screeched, filling the room with its alarm and violent clicking before Peabody shut it off.

"I always underestimate your reading, Rowan. It did short out my meter the first time we did it, and I've anticipated that with updates since, but it looks as if I'll have to unearth an old EMF meter that will likely be large enough to measure you."

TJ looked to the meter, then to Rowan, then back to the meter; quieter and with a dark curiosity, he took Rowan's place next to Peabody.

"What's that mean?" he said, nodding to the meter. "When it's up so high like that?"

"Simply registering a large load of energy. The kind of energy expulsion that comes from human death. Specifically, experiencing, in very close proximity, a death. Or multiple deaths."

I spoke up. "Or in this case, also inherited deaths." Orabilia had started the curse when she was forced to watch her beloved be killed with his own sword.

Peabody agreed then, happy to have a curious mind asking him questions. "These here"—Peabody pointed then recorded Rowan's metrics along with mine—"are the inherited energy readings; they have a lower, more of a deep thrumming, energy, the kind that is incessant and similar to those found in tectonic plates. These here are his experiential energies."

"They're all off the meter."

Peabody smiled sadly, giving him a moment before he moved on to TJ. "Yes, now, let's get yours! Isn't this exciting? We'll have two Bakers, or two Minory descendants, if you will, and what a magnificent addition to the research this is, isn't it!?"

TJ looked at Peabody and smiled, but his brow furrowed before he looked over at me, like, *Is he for real?*

I shrugged. "It's cutting-edge science, you'll see."

Chapter Seventeen

Peabody turned on the meter, and it screeched like Rowan's, also nearly immediately tapping out. He turned it off and looked in consternation at the machine. "I believe it's stuck on Rowan's."

"It's accurate," I said sadly. I knew it was a proper reading.

TJ cleared his throat then looked at me. "It'll pick those up?" he asked me.

I nodded to him then said to Peabody, "TJ is a medic in the reserves. He's been deployed to war zones."

Peabody said, "Ah, yes, that explains this one," and pointed at the middle meter. "This one, I assume, is the Minory heritage, but this one is a mix." With excited movements, he pulled out more meters, assembled them, and took more measurements. When he was done, he looked concerned and then turned his gaze first to Rowan then to TJ. "No, I'm sorry, but I think that this meter is still picking up on Rowan's energy. Rowan's energy signature is quite specific in its ratios, a kind of fingerprint, if you will. And I can see his imprint on TJ's readings. Rowan, will you please step outside?"

Rowan shrugged and walked to me as he took in the machines now consuming the surfaces of his office library.

"I'll call you when it's done," I said and brushed my hand up his arm.

He shivered as my connection lit up his synapses, then grinned back at me. "Or you can come with, and we can take our time coming back?"

TJ made a loud retching sound.

Peabody cut in. "No, no. This is both his and not his..." Then he pulled a ticker tape out and up, utterly confused, and to TJ said, "Let's do this one more time. Will you two," he said to Rowan and me, "go stand by the door? This is most confusing."

Rowan and I did as we were told, and TJ put his arms out as Peabody stared at his meters and put the wand back up to him. He clicked them on with one hand, and the far meter's hands hit maximum as violent clicking filled the space. Peabody shut them off and, dropping the wand on the table, picked up the ticker tapes again.

"Fascinating. It is the same as last time." Peabody's gaze went from TJ then back to his meters as Tee watched him warily.

"Not sure I'm getting the fascinating part, Doc."

"The one. The big one—what was it? Not the most carnage, but the one that hit you," he said, thumping his chest, "the hardest. The one that left the biggest imprint upon you, as if it took—and this is more psychology than metaphysics—a piece of your soul?"

TJ opened his mouth to say it, but no words came, then looked back at me in a silent plea for help, and I explained.

"It was a couple of years ago. One was dead when he arrived; the other made it to the hospital but died later," I said, then added when Peabody did not react, "There was lots of gore, blood, gunfire, and bullets."

Peabody took off his glasses and folded his arms, nodding. He was like that for a few beats, digesting this information and its implications for the data he'd recorded. Then, back to TJ, while his eyes said he was sorry, his mouth asked, "Why?"

TJ looked confused. "Why what?"

"Why is it this one? You are a medic, yes?"

"Yes, sir."

"This was the first time you had seen that kind of wartime ugliness?"

"No, sir."

Peabody nodded. "Then I wonder, why is it that this memory, this one, why is it, do you think, that it sits persistently with you?"

TJ shrugged. "Dunno... It was the last major one?"

Peabody gently pressed. "There's something more there. Tell me."

I said, "Tee, I remember you telling me that you couldn't believe that after everything, the guy died, right?"

TJ took a deep breath as if he were about to go underwater, and blew it out. "Yeah, things were shit, and he was, like, this one good thing I had in all that. That at least this nutso mission that nearly got us a black mark on our records meant something." He shook his head. "I can't explain it."

I squinted at TJ. "Black mark?"

"The COs, all the way up the chain, were all over our asses for going out without confirming that it was an RAF aircraft. The Brits weren't claiming it, but we had good intel that it was them. It was. Fuck them. Command knew," he said as if reliving an old argument.

Rowan spoke up from the doorway. "Two years ago?"

"Yeah, what's it to you, Braveheart? You wanna tell me I did all I could and should forget about it?"

"TJ," I cut in sharply, "Rowan's RAF. He likely knows who you're talking about."

Rowan, I noticed belatedly, had gone sheet white.

"Navigator, shot through the head. Pilot, hip wound, septic," Rowan said as if he were repeating a report he'd read. "I was the pilot."

TJ's gaze on Rowan went from dark to blank. I felt the room grow warm and lose focus, as if the press of history had fogged us into place, weighing in on what was being uncovered.

"The pilot's name was James." TJ had told me that, thinking back on it, he'd known the pilot was in bad shape, even there in the rescue bird. He'd given his first name when TJ had made small talk to keep him conscious. "You're Rowan. Fuck you," TJ said, guarded.

"Rowan is my Scots name. James is my Christian name, the one I used when I enlisted. I was the pilot who lived."

"Fuck you," TJ said again, but I could see emotion gripped his guts, as his brow creased. He might have been reluctant to tell Peabody the details, but now some kind of dam broke in him, and Tee slipped into the memory. "The pilot's dead. I was told in Germany that he wasn't there—he *died*, man."

"I didn't take to being in hospital well... I discharged myself as soon as my legs could hold me. There'd been a targeted strike that was bringing in bodies faster than they were leaving. I was able to discharge without hassle and updated my commanding officer on the way home. They'd already declared Vick and me dead because our plane went down and there were no orders to retrieve us." He laughed, a sound that was hollow and devoid of joy. "The paperwork, I hear, to undo that was not worth bringing me back from the dead."

"Rowan was the one who gave you hope," I breathed.

TJ stared at Rowan as if he were seeing a ghost. "It had been a shit week, month, year, and little hopes were all we had left. I applied for R and R after that." I could fill in the rest. He was in the peach orchard with me a few weeks later, unloading the burden of that memory. And now that memory and the interlaced events that led to it and followed were being rewritten.

Rowan and TJ, gazes locked, stood on opposite ends of the room, sinking into their shared memory with its new puzzle piece fitted into place. A silent communication was happening between them, and they were the only two who could understand.

"One shot in the head, the other—" Rowan shed his sport coat with jerking movements, tossed it onto his desk, and then, with a fistful of his shirt front, he yanked the hem out, exposing the scar at his hip.

"I saw that, the other night with Pipsqueak out on the cairn knoll... So that *is* a bullet wound." TJ swallowed, looking to the scar then back up at his face, as my own skin broke out in goosebumps from head to toe. "You survived."

I'd held my brother as he wept in the peach field, and I, too, had wept for the man he mourned. This man whose death tormented my brother wasn't some nameless, faceless human. He was the man whose history called to me from across the Atlantic. But now I knew that it was TJ who was the first Minory to deliver Rowan from his suffering, before I unwittingly answered the pull of the MacLaoch curse a year later.

Peabody's soft exclamation broke through the heavy weight of emotion in the room. "My god...this is absolutely incredible. *This*, this is the reason for the mixed energy reading. My stars... Rowan, Tiberius, do you realize what the event was? At the moment, the curse's requirements were fulfilled—"

"The Minory was there. *He* was there," Rowan said, following along in disbelief.

"Tiberius is the first Minory to be called to the MacLaoch chief." Peabody turned and smiled at me, stating a scientific fact. "Not you." Then back to TJ and Rowan: "How long was it until Tiberius showed up?"

TJ shook his head. "I'm sorry, what the fuck are you on about?"

"Tee," I said, settling down on the arm of the settee next to him. "Remember what Marion and Flora said? The thing I'm here for, the thing that changed everything? It's love, but it started out as a curse for the MacLaochs, for Rowan."

"Yeah, I remember. But that's just fairy-tale shit."

"Sure, but answer me this, who was that man you thought you saved? Who is Rowan to *you?*"

TJ looked over at Rowan, dismay clearly written in his frown.

"You know who he is," he whispered.

I nodded. "In the peach orchard, you told me about the dead man and his copilot."

"He," Tee said, nodding to Rowan, "didn't live. I've held that here," he said, putting his fingertips to his chest, and I heard the hiccup of emotion in his voice. That was a predecessor to tears for TJ. "We received that beacon, downed aircraft, and it was one of ours. The insurgents were going to be at their crash site in minutes. We had to go. No one would let us go, and at the same time, they weren't stopping us. I saddled up... Richy, Pat, and Carol all volunteered. We didn't talk about it. We just went. Everything was..." He paused, thinking about the right words. "It felt right. We were doing the *right* thing." He looked down at our clasped hands then to me. "I thought it was because you don't leave your man behind. They were our allies, our brothers in arms, right?"

"That's right."

"But now it might be more? I'm in this curse shit too?"

"Apparently" was all I said aloud. It was new for me too. This was the *why*. It was right, *and* it was a power beyond us that snapped her fingers and made it so.

Rowan made his way across the room and up to TJ, his shirt front as rumpled as his emotions. He put his open palm up between them. TJ let go of my hand and grasped his before yanking him into an embrace.

From beside them, each head buried into the other's shoulder, I could hear snippets of my brother's voice. That day had been a series of miraculous events: the odds that their chain of command let the helo go, that the helo hadn't been shot down by enemy fire, that they were fast enough, that the equipment was what they needed for that particular skirmish, that their medic skills in a flying ambulance in a war-torn land would be enough to save Rowan's life and their piloting skills enough to protect those manning the bird. There were a thousand little things that made that potential nightmare into a complete miracle. I heard Tee say that when he went to check on that pilot in the hospital, only to find his moment of hope in all of that endless war gone... Well, it was a gut punch to end all gut punches.

Now, here he stood. And here, Rowan, who held his own traumas of that day, was getting answers to unasked questions. Who had been those cowboys who had saddled up to save their allies in an unsanctioned mission?

For me, it was shocking; my brother had picked up the man I was destined to spend the rest of my life with, taken him out of the war-torn desert sand and used his skills to keep him alive despite the bullet wound at his side that was hemorrhaging blood. All while dodging enemy fire.

I felt the tears on my cheeks before I realized I was crying. This was the kind of beautiful born of the ugly that was rare.

Peabody quietly picked up another machine and, holding the nozzle up to Rowan and Tee, turned it on.

The sound of the vacuum broke the moment and sent all eyes to Peabody, who, engrossed in his work, murmured, "Magnificent!"

Chapter Eighteen

"Incredible."

I was crouched in the clover patch taking soil samples, or at least was trying to. I wasn't even sure what had tumbled from my lips. There was a rare late-summer sun, though the day was getting old. There were the sounds of students in the tree and at its roots—questions, laughter, and Holly telling someone to knock it off. And, of course, the patch of earth I had slept on was, as Holly had reported, still blooming. But also, had TJ really been the one to save Rowan?

Rowan and Tee were still in the library. They had more to say to each other; the details of that day, the details that followed when Rowan was in Germany, all needed to be shared. They were two stories melding into one, and they both were hungry for the details the other was missing. I let them have their time; Rowan would fill me in later. I took Peabody and headed out to the field. Peabody was reluctant at first to follow but with the data on the cairns still to gather he followed but not before throwing a longing look at Rowan and Tee.

I, too, needed a moment. My thoughts were still rearranging themselves in this new happy order.

TJ saved Rowan.

The man my brother was so heart-wrecked over *lived*.

And he was the man I loved, whose blood spoke to mine in an ancient chiming rhythm that we were still getting used to even a year later.

Joy and astonishment colored my thoughts and actions as I collected samples out of my mini green zone. Despite the charred earth surrounding my green patch, I felt a buoyant, joyous hope for everything.

I was closing a jar on a soil sample when TJ came up from the Circle Garden. I noted the time, date, weather, and sample number on the side of the container, and when I looked up to greet him, I saw his head was bowed the way he did with bad news, and he wiped his thumb across his mouth as if swiping away the stink of what he had to say.

This made me guess. I checked my watch for confirmation. "Uh-oh. The Rembrandt didn't arrive."

"Yeah," he said before hooking his thumbs into his pockets and squinting down into the field where Peabody was moving between the cairns, taking readings off the stacked rocks. "So, you need some magic to wake this field up...or something?"

It was obvious that TJ was dodging the topic, but I went with it. I had put a rosy halo on Tee as the human who had saved Rowan. I was sure he'd do something to knock that halo off sooner rather than later, so I'd enjoy the glow for now.

I tapped my pen on the side of the sample jar. "Holly and I are working on the theory that the field needs its energies restored."

"Right, so it needs to be woken up."

"In a way, I suppose—"

"Eh!" he hollered at the field before sticking his fingers in his mouth and piercing the air with a whistle. "Wake up!" He grinned at me as Peabody turned in the field and a couple students emerged from the forest.

I waved them back to work and gave Tee a look that said he was a dingus. It hadn't taken him long to attempt to knock his halo loose. "I think you just called every sheep in a twelve-mile radius to our spot. Great job."

He kept grinning.

"All right, out with it, it must be really bad news if you feel the need to make me laugh before telling me."

"Yeah, the banker is nowhere to be seen, same with the Rembrandt. Charmaine and Rowan are arguing about calling the authorities."

I knew which side Rowan was on with that.

"All right," I said, resigned to the bad news. "Thanks."

"AndMa'scoming."

"What?" My sample jar hit the dirt.

"Yeah, like I said, Mother is coming." TJ did not run his words together this time. "Daddy didn't like how slow I was to get things ironed out, and they now think I'm involved with the cult."

My guts twisted at the added complication. "Didn't you explain everything to them?" My voice squeaked on the question mark.

"Explain what? Explain that you broke a curse, and before I arrived, a Viking inhabited your body and attempted to kill your fiancé and the townsfolk who got in his way? And now there's this evil bank dude who's got a priceless artifact, and I'm pretty sure we're all gonna do a little B&E to get it back?!"

"No, ding-dong! How about the incredible thing where you've realized Rowan is a man whose life you saved and you now have found yourself the *love of your life*." I choked on the last part.

"You want me to tell Mother and Daddy that Rowan was the dead man I had a breakdown over and I met a woman who's gonna be my future bride?"

I could hear it. "Right, they'd *both* get on a plane then. So, when?"

"Like I'd know. Wait for her to text a flight number." TJ was still grinning.

"Just say it, Tee."

He grinned big enough that I could see the overlap of his incisors from not wearing his retainer after having braces for five years, or, as Mother put it, *five thousand dollars down the drain.*

"I met him first."

"And thank the good lord. But you're still a dingus."

"Met him first and was the one who really broke the curse," he said.

"Marion and Flora are about to burst with the news. Fairly sure they're calling a town meeting over it."

I agreed. "Live it up until Peabody measures Eli."

"Who's Eli?"

"Remember? Six-foot-five solid wall of man, heart of a teddy bear, Cousin Elias Campbell and Rowan's best friend from childhood?"

"Right, dude at the bar."

"I have a theory." I held up a finger. "It's a working theory, mind you. That a Minory has been at the side of the MacLaoch in every generation, and the MacLaoch just had to reach out for them."

"What about the same pain and all that?"

I was impressed with Tee's knowledge of the curse, down to the detail that Lady MacLaoch would only release the curse when one of the MacLaoch chiefs had felt her pain. "What are the odds that Rowan was the first to experience it? And what if he sent me off that day? What if he didn't heed the metaphysical connection?"

"Or what if he came on too strong?"

I was quiet, thinking how that would have affected things. I would have nut-punched him and continued on my way.

TJ echoed my thoughts aloud: "You would have pushed him off a cliff."

"Yeah, I'm not big on overly amorous gestures."

"That's an understatement," he said and put his finger to his ear, making a pretend call. "Lemme check in with Billy from senior year. 'Yeah, hey, Bill, how's your nut sack? Still sore?'"

I pinched the bridge of my nose at the vividness of that embarrassing memory. My voice was muffled as I said, "I forgot about that."

"Billy never has. Matter of fact, he doesn't attempt to stand and sing happy birthday to anyone anymore. Red Robin makes him clammy."

"Ooh, Billy."

"Anyway, he should really sing something that would bring out his new soprano."

That earned TJ a solid punch in the arm.

"Ow!"

"Butthead, that's not true, I didn't hit him *that* hard."

"You punched him in the dick!"

"Ugh. As I've said a million times—to him, his mama, our mama, and *you*—he wouldn't stop. I warned him: before we got there, during dinner, and after." I put three fingers in TJ's face. "No singing. No telling that pimply waiter it was my birthday. *Three!* damn times, and he didn't listen. He thought he was hilarious and my mortification was just as damn funny. I didn't see how else to get my point across, so what was I supposed to do? Leave without finishing my fries?" I shrugged. "Sometimes guys think shit is funny until someone teaches them it's not. Some use their brain, listen, and learn quickly. Some don't. Hence, nut-punch."

TJ looked at me with mock sadness. "Some smart people find nonviolent ways to communicate, Sis. Who's the jackass now?"

"Still you."

TJ looked mildly worried he'd gone too far. "Where's your rubber band?"

"Coming up through the Circle Garden behind me."

We then both heard Rowan's boots on the gravel as TJ muttered, "I hate it when y'all do that."

"When we do what? Touch souls so that we can communicate our love without saying a word?"

TJ braced himself on his knees and pretended to lose his lunch.

By the time Rowan reached us, I was wiping tears from my eyes from laughing so hard.

Rowan held his hand out to Tee, who, with a smile at his own antics, shook and gave Rowan a one-armed hug. They had turned the corner on whether or not to be enemies and settled on best friends forever. And ever.

"How're the abdominals?" Tee asked, genuinely concerned for Rowan, which made me think that maybe, just maybe, Tee was a decent human as well as stellar medic. And that he might never see Rowan as a regular dude but as a beloved patient who changed his life by living.

"Aye, fine. Nothing has changed since ye asked yesterday. And the day before."

"You're married to my sis—a lot can happen in a day."

Rowan gave me a warm look before again reassuring my brother that all was well with his guts, etc.

To me, Rowan asked, "Ye heard the news?"

"My mom's coming, yeah."

Rowan lost all the blood in his face.

TJ and I looked at him with amused concern.

Tee grabbed Rowan's wrist, and with two fingers on his pulse, he checked his watch. "Maybe you should lie down—your heart stopped beating."

"Your mother?" Rowan asked with an audible swallow.

"Yes," I said. I pulled his other, now clammy, hand into mine. "Don't worry—Mother likes you."

"Is tha' why she's coming here well before the wedding? Because tha' sounds like a mother who's not sure her first operative was successful and now is entering the field tae get the job done."

"Yeah... Let's run away?"

Rowan huffed a short laugh then took a deep breath.

Tee nodded, taking his fingers off Rowan's wrist. "Heartbeat is back."

Rowan's gaze was scared but a touch hopeful. "We'll be glad tae have her. She's most welcome here."

I smiled at his genuine attempt to be regal and welcoming and ran my hand up his arm to his chest, gave him a hug and a light kiss. "Yeah, you're not off to the hangman; it's just Mother. She'll get up in your business, interview everyone you know—"

"She makes it sound nice," Tee said. "Interrogate is more like it."

"And then she'll declare you fit or unfit for her daughter. But it's only for show; she loves me, and she'll eventually come around to loving you as I have."

"What if she doesn't?"

"Wear your kilt."

"Fuck, Pip, that'll give her a heart attack. Then Daddy will come." TJ gave me a pointed expression with his brows raised.

"Yeah, well. We'll just have to be ourselves," I said. "Tee was converted to our side—"

"That was different, Pipsqueak. This man is my brother."

"You make me sound incestuous. Say *bro, comrade, brother in arms*, or something."

"*Brother* implies a blood bond, and we got that in battle. He's my brother, not some dude-bro."

"You're a mess," I quipped.

"What? I'm not the one married to my own brother."

"See. That," I said, pointing at him, "is why you get smacked." I turned to Rowan. "We don't even have a flight number. Let's see if this is just a threat from the motherland."

TJ mellowed too and gave Rowan a kind look as he said, "Still no Rembrandt?"

Though it was an awful subject to shift to, Rowan seemed glad to get off the subject of Mother's arrival. "No, Charmaine is on the phone raising hell with high water, as Cole says."

Tee looked at me, and we shared a "that's not exactly the way to use that phrase" look.

He slipped his hands into his pockets. "The executives at the bank are sending recovery agents out. They've put notice on Murdoch that if he has done anything untoward, they'll find out."

"What? They just gave him the heads-up?"

"Aye."

Tee added, "He's just going to say thanks and move it."

"Aye, which is why Charmaine is attempting tae track down the agents and also monitor the Otey manor. After the meeting, she requested to sort this out herself and asked me no' to muddy the waters any more than they are with a breaking-and-entering scheme."

"That's frustrating." I gave him another hug, which he gladly accepted, pulling me in tight. "Are you doing that? Letting her take care of it?"

"Mostly." He added, "I hate tha' it's so close but I cannae just retrieve it."

"Maybe we can get someone to track it."

"Aye, my best tracker is on it."

I smiled. "Holly has all eyes and ears at her disposal, doesn't she?"

Rowan nodded. "Between her and her da, they should be able to.

Once the agents catch up tae Murdoch, we'll retrieve it from the boot of his car."

"Trunk," I clarified to Tee.

"I know what the boot is. Can I help at all?"

Rowan shook his head.

I let Rowan out of my embrace and said to Tee, "Then we should take care of something on my list before your R and R is up. Plus, your pelvic exercise instructor is busy."

"Haha." Tee didn't find my quip funny at all.

"We have a great-great-to-the-billion-great-granny to introduce you to. Let's see if Peabody wants to go on a field trip with us."

Rowan gave me a quick kiss. "Have fun."

Chapter Nineteen

The three of us sat in the car park at the Misty Cliffs Church, TJ and me looking at the white-washed building with its pointed spire with a reserved awe. Peabody was in the back seat rummaging through his bags and calibrating his equipment on the off chance that Ethel let him meter her. Or even let him into the churchyard.

"So, remind me again..." Tee said from the passenger seat, still staring at the church.

"She's our grandmother. Viking Ormr was her grandson, and we are his direct descendants."

"From the MacLaoch chick?"

"No, she was his one true love, but he was murdered before they could...you know."

"Get it on."

"Right."

"So, who's our mom in this scenario?"

"His sister-in-law."

This made Tee look at me, one brow raised in disbelief. "He banged his sister-in-law?"

"More like: 'My husband is chief and impotent, I need some sperm, you're virile and leading a life that'll get you killed sooner rather than later, so let's do the humpity to save my position and title before my last chance is killed.'"

"Mind you," came from the back seat, "all is assumed that Ormr's brother requested this of him."

"He was ordered to do the humpity with his sister-in-law? That's next-level twisted."

Peabody said, "You are applying values of the society you were raised in to a time when things could not have been more different. If she and her husband, a Viking chief, were to keep power, she needed an heir, and he needed to be viewed as virile. Your ancestor was doing her a service."

"Also, Tee, Ormr had *several* lineages that died out, save for ours and Eli's. He was, for all intents and purposes, happy to spread his... love. But, to the point I think you're trying to make, when he came across Orabilia for the first time, I think his personal directive shifted."

Tee turned in his seat to include Peabody. "How do we know all this?"

"Same way text messages will tell future humans of the world today. People wrote things down." He twisted one last meter wand into place before declaring with an excited smile, "I'm all set here—shall we?"

"Maybe. Let's take a moment. I'm not sure she's going to like an audience."

Tee squinted into the distance. "Is that her?"

Ethel, with long gray hair in a braid over her shoulder and garden gloves on, came around the front and through the gate to our car. I rolled down the window of Rowan's off-road machine as if we'd just come to a drive-through.

She didn't wait for hellos or introductions. It felt like she knew who everyone was already.

"Come on, then." She walked away but stopped and came back and pointed at Peabody. I expected her to say that his equipment had to stay in the car, but instead she said, "Bring the big one. If Orabilia's great-grandson," she said of Rowan, "was too much for your equipment, *I* shall break it."

When she was back at the gate, I looked back at Peabody, who was silent before his face broke out in intellectual excitement: "Excellent! This is perfectly thrilling."

I looked at my brother. "Well?"

"Shall we?"

"Let's."

Peabody trailed behind us, measuring the boneyard with his equipment. Tee had insisted on hefting the equipment bag on his shoulder. I thought it was mostly because he could use it as a shield, just in case.

I nudged his shoulder with mine: "It's perfectly safe. There's no need to be on such high alert."

"Yeah, but she's a witch, right?"

"So?"

"So? Aren't they mostly feminists who despise men? I've not dedicated my life to living in a gentlemanly manner."

"Is that why you've got Peabody's bag over your wiener?"

"Hell yes."

We descended the path through the field of gravestones and into the church. We both paused, observing Peabody as he went through the damp grass, analyzing gravestone after gravestone. We shrugged. Peabody was deep into his work, and even our waves went unnoticed.

"He knows where to find us," I said to Tee as we closed the church's massive oak door behind us; the metal ring of the door knocker clanged as we did so. We headed to the apartment where I'd spent a lot of time, at the back of the echoing church.

In the cozy kitchen, Ethel looked up and gave us a rare smile. "Tide and time wait for no man, but this woman is no tide. I've waited for your arrival with each sunup and sunset, wed and whet with the new life my grandson could never accomplish. Leave it to the reincarnation of his female self to accomplish what generations before could not."

Tee gave me a knowing look. This was the kind of feminism that he was scared of in a witch.

"Thank you," I said, taking her praise like a crown and proudly wearing it.

"And with you, your guests are thoroughly fascinating. This young chap," she said of TJ, then, with a wave of her hand. "Come, put that bag down; I want nothing to do with your family jewels, despite you giving them to the MacLaoch agent so freely. I see now that is your power, so like your great-grandfather in that way. A lover of women, all women, until you find the *one*. And just like fitting a gear into place, another piece of this MacLaoch curse gets set to rest. She herself has fallen for a Minory, giving you and the entire lineage peace. Well-done."

Tee was chuffed. "Thanks...er, Grandmama?"

She held out her hands to his, and he placed his palms on hers.

"What was that? Tell it again in your native tongue."

Our South Carolina English could be hard to understand at first.

"Well, back where I'm, we're, from, we use Mother and Daddy, Mama if we're feeling real kind. You're our elder, related to boot, so it's only natural that I call you Miss Ethel, or what fits a mite better, Grandmama."

Her regal chin tilted up, and she took in TJ. "You trust quicker than your sister."

He gave her a happy grin. "I do; she's got that stickler scientific gene Mother also has, which makes her ask why until the whole family goes screaming into the night. Me? Folks are just folks."

"Grand-mama. I shall have it." She looked to me then to TJ. "My grandchildren."

Something settled down into the room. Cogs in a timeline wheel fit snugly into place.

At our grinning faces, she said, "Good, sit." She gave Tee's shoulder a pat, then put the kettle back on the stove to reheat the water in it.

As she spoke, she took down plates that had seen decades of use, all decorative small saucers edged with gold filigree and chipped in one place or another. Then she took down a wide round tin filled with cookies.

"Nicole Ransome Minory MacLaoch, you now embark on a very special personal education in this world after having lived as your grand-papa?" She looked to Tee to see if she got the terminology correct.

Tee had no reservations about the cookie tin and popped it open to reveal buttery gold cookies inside.

"Thank goodness it's not buttons and thread," he mumbled. One buttery rectangle cookie his mouth and another in his hand, he replied to Ethel, "Grandpappy or granddaddy."

"Grand-daddy."

It sounded regal out of her mouth, the grandest of daddies.

"Ormr is fine," I mumbled, searching for the perfect cookie in the tin.

"Yes, he is your grandfather, but he is more than that for you, isn't he? He is also...you."

"He's a real piece of work who's left me nothing but trouble in his wake. I have a feeling he was like this in real life too."

The kettle whistled at my sour retort, and Ethel picked it up. In that thoughtful silence, she poured the water into a decorative pot that I was sure held the perfect Ethel blend: a powerful mix of black loose-leaf that could grow hair on one's chest, a touch of finely zested citrus peel, and creamy-blue cornflower petals.

"He haunts you still."

I looked down at my plate and pushed the crumbs around. I wasn't sure I wanted to admit that he had gotten my pig to run around manic-like. And *still* had my pig on edge, even though he was gone. But having your mind hijacked like that wasn't something after which you just skipped off into the heather-laden hills with a song on your lips and love in your heart.

Tee answered for me. "He does. Keeps her up at night. She's been walking the hills. Barely a stitch on, in this weather. He's still messing with her head. Can we do an exorcism or something and get that fucker out of her?"

Ethel pulled her glasses out of the nest of hair on the top of her head and put them on.

"It is easy for children of your generation to want a quick fix. It is all this society feeds you: take a pill, read a book, eat a certain food. But this is not the way, is it...*Cole*."

When she said my name, it blew across my skin and touched my nervous system, reigniting it like a forest fire. A forest fire for a second before being doused in water and going silent.

I dropped my cookie, and my hand shot out, and suddenly Tee's hand was in mine. We looked at each other and then to Ethel. I was playing catch-up when Tee went on defense. He might have put on social airs at first, but he had never lowered his guard.

"I don't know what you're on about, miss, but we're getting up out of here."

Ethel was calm, digesting the fallout of what she'd done, looking carefully between Tee and me. "Your bond is quite interlinked."

"No shit. She's my sister, and you just—"

"Asked her if she was still high on the energies of battle. She is, so much so that she is swallowing connections and energies around her to sustain herself. She is on fire with it. You should have been unaffected."

The cookie had been nice, but now it was too much. Too buttery, too sweet, too dry.

"I'm swallowing energies and connections?" I said and stopped, realizing something critical. "The field." Nothing grew there save for the one night I'd gone and poured my heart out. "Am I sucking it dry? Am I keeping it from coming back to life?"

Ethel didn't mince her words. "You are."

"But I can also make it come alive."

Ethel held a satisfied smile. "I see you've discovered that too."

"Now, hold on," TJ interjected. "She's not a witch or whatever. She can't just take stuff like that out of the dirt or put it back in."

Ethel nodded as if now the answer was clear. "The events on the field that night, you have not shared with anyone. You have not talked them out of your body. Not even to your kin. You are unsettled, and more than that, you are still wielding Ormr's powers."

I felt my face wince at exposing my brother to the gritty details. "He knows about it."

Ethel was shrewd. "So he knows that Ormr slipped your skin over his ethereal body and wore your face like armor into battle and wielded the Ulfberht as if he were a berserker once more? He knows how Ormr made you bring your sword, fist, and strength down on your one true love over and over again until I pulled Orabilia out of the clan chief to defend him against you?"

My mouth went dry.

Tee's voice sounded far away. "Sissy?"

"You have shared with your blood brother that the power you wielded that night physically bound Orabilia's grandson, the chief MacLaoch, Rowan, to you via blood and soul? I may have given you the elixir, but it's what's in your blood that held the power. It was also that power that Ormr brought forth in you that fed Orabilia, brought her back from the afterlife, then aided her in sending his warriors, her and my grandson Ormr, back into that plane of existence. Your blood brother, he knows of all this from your own lips?"

I squeezed my eyes shut as if I could keep the feelings, and myself, in. My pig was tossing pews in the other room. "How?" I managed. "How do I even begin to explain that?"

Tee gripped my hand like a hug, pulling my attention to his understanding gaze that was kind and serious for once. "You have done that for me, Pipsqueak."

"Yeah, but this is different. There's all this metaphysical energy—"

"Magic," Ethel amended.

"Yeah."

"And when I was there for Rowan, that was different?"

Ethel smiled at the mention of TJ being there for Rowan. "That thunderclap of connection was felt as far out as to this very soil. The singular instant your fingers touched his flight suit, yanking him into the war monster you flew in on, started the ripple effect that built the momentum to take this Minory-MacLaoch curse from whence it began to its end. I reminded Rowan James Douglas MacLaoch of this when we met over a year ago, even though his mind was foggy with the atrocities and the unraveling of the curse. I warned him, *it had begun.* And now, you know your part in it all. How close the Minory has gotten in every age, that for this MacLaoch chief, thrice in his life a Minory has come to him. And he is the first to reach out and accept the love that has been in lockstep with him since his mother's death thirty years ago."

Hearing my theory confirmed was humbling. I was just one of three Minorys who'd been sent to Rowan.

Ethel continued to explain to Tee about the Minory and MacLaoch connection as I closed my eyes and tried to quiet my mind and get my sow to stop tossing furniture in the other room.

In the quiet, I heard Rowan's inquiry chime over my skin.

I let go of Tee's hand and grasped my own arms and tried to quiet my mind further. Rowan had felt Ethel's power wash over me and wanted to know what was happening up there in that church kitchen.

I'm coming.

I'm fine.

Ye are no'.

I'm with Ethel. She's doing...stuff.

I can be there in a few minutes.

Tee is here. We're sorting through it all.

Good, I'll be there shortly. I need a distraction or I'll go to Murdoch's manor and break his neck.

I smiled as our connection faded, leaving an ocean glow lapping inside of me like a calm tide.

Ethel brought me back to the present. "And you freely speak with the MacLaoch through your connection, even though he is miles away." She held one of her silent conversations while looking at me, digesting the questions that came to her mind like a checklist until she said, "More than Ormr's magic has stayed. He was gifted with the spirit craft, knowing the movement of magic through all things and how to use those energies to heal, harm, and create. You have this as well, but it is unbalanced. You need to learn to balance it. Ormr learned this at my knee for the better part of his youth. You have been given it overnight and without instruction. Ormr has destroyed who you once were, and in his wake, he's made you into another facet of yourself. And yet, within all his destruction, he's left you with a gift."

I attempted to swallow my scoff, but it came out my nose in a huff. "Gift?"

"You have been left with his abilities."

I heard her say it but wasn't sure what any of it meant and simply said, "Abilities?"

TJ nudged me. "Abilities might be nice. Be able to reheat your coffee wherever you are? Golden."

He was trying to cheer me up. "I still don't think—"

"Just don't tell Mother or Daddy."

I did scoff then.

"Mother will make you keep her hair from frizzing in the Carolina heat, and Daddy will expect record peach production at top market prices every year."

This time Ethel scoffed.

Chapter Twenty

Rowan arrived then and after greeting Ethel with warm respect and sharing a handshake-hug with Tee, gathered me up out of my chair and into an intimate hello. Into my hair he said, "I'm just outside if ye need me."

"I need you," I said.

"Excellent, shall I take tea too or call forth my ancient great-granny tae explain things?"

For the third time in a row, Ethel scoffed. I wondered if she was more insulted that Rowan didn't think she was capable of helping me with my energy problem, not that bringing Orabilia back was impossible.

He bent to my lips and with a lingering warmth kissed them, reminding me that he was there, forever, and all I needed to do was to call his name to have him show up at my side.

"Bye," I said against his lips, looking into his granite-blue eyes. "Have fun with Peabody hoovering gravestones."

"I will, and for the record, I believe he's stalling. It's Ethel he really wants tae meet but is intimidated."

With another kiss, he was out the side door of the kitchen as if he'd been there before and knew it also led to outside, TJ in tow.

Ethel motioned for me to sit. "Tell me what you see, then what you feel."

I wasn't sure what I felt, but I told Ethel what I saw. While Rowan and I were speaking, she'd placed four items at my place: a rock, a feather, a flower, and a shallow bowl of water above the feather.

"Now, what is it that you feel?"

"Feel?" I asked, mulling it over. "Cold draft from the door behind me, your eyes on the side of my head, Rowan farting around with my brother and Peabody out in the graveyard."

"The items on the table, child."

"Ah, from the stripes and brown dots, the feather looks to be a hawk's tail feather. The rock is granite, probably from a nearby loch, and the flower...feverfew, *Tanacetum parthenium*, genus *Asteraceae*."

"You are closed to it," she finally said.

"Wouldn't you be? I want none of that man."

"He is you, in you, of you; take what he's given you, child. Or forever be haunted by him as you run from what you cannot escape."

Ethel and I sat for a long while, me counting the seconds, Ethel, staring at me, making the side of my head feel the heat of her gaze. I wasn't sure if it was disappointment or a challenge to try harder.

"Fine," I said and picked up the rock; it was cold. I put it down and picked up the feather; there was something about a feather that always invited a touch down its smooth spine. I did; the silk of the pennaceous barbs was slippery against the pads of my fingers, and I couldn't help but imagine that bird employing each feather it possessed to take flight, to soar through the heavens and touch the sky, looking down on us like ants in a field.

"Stop."

I was on my third stroke of the slippery feather. I looked over at Ethel. She had dipped the fingers of one hand into the water, and the other was held open, palm facing the floor.

"That's enough for now. Do you know how you did it? Are you in control?"

"How I did what?"

"You traveled there, became the bird, and were connected to it, flying through the sky. You did not notice?"

"I mean, sure, I was imagining that," I retorted, not liking how clearly she was able to view my thoughts.

"Look to the table once more."

The flower had changed. "Oh," I said, "it's dried now." I looked at the shriveled thing and could only think, *How long have I been sitting here?*

"Just the moment," Ethel answered my thought aloud, "but you've journeyed far, and to do so, drew on energy around you. It is a light thing that you've done, compared to recent events, but this was you in control. It's what I expected." She dried her fingers off as she added, "What I expected you to be able to do this time *next year*."

"Oh," I whispered, then looked at my hands. "What does that mean?"

"It means that your emotions are making you volatile. We will focus today on working through those emotions. I'll have you focus on naming them so that you may drain yourself of residual energy like you did making the field grow." She gave me a knowing smile, a confession that she'd been watching my progress from afar. "Then we will work on balance and intent."

"Do you really think she won't mind?"

How Peabody clutched his meter to his chest as he breathlessly asked that made Rowan think of a schoolboy asking about his crush. In a way, he was, the academic studying magic desperate to meet the ancient magician inside the church.

Rowan sighed and looked away from Peabody. There was a pleasant view from the graveyard, not as pleasing as the one off the top turret of Castle Laoch, but he had to give this view its due as the only pleasant thing about the place. His skin felt like it was going to crawl off his bones as he stood there on the consecrated ground where Minorys had been laid to rest for the better half of the past thousand years.

He sighed again and turned back to Peabody, whose wire-rimmed glasses were catching the mist from the onshore breeze. He answered the man's question: "I dunno, shall we ask?"

Cole's brother caught a hint of the conversation and, like the chaos creator he was, came up next to Peabody, cocked a hip as he put his thumb through his belt loop. "She might shrivel your dick if you don't ask right proper like."

How could the beautiful rogue woman inside be related to this creature? Rowan would constantly wonder. Where she'd been gifted with intellect and a powerful sense of fortitude, TJ was like kelp in the loch: He let the water roll off him as the tide rose and fell back. And like kelp, it wouldn't be wise to disregard him; they both could be strong as rope and easily clog the propellers of progress.

Rowan cut in, putting the intellectual at ease. "She will not; she fought beside us on the field and supped at our table." It was more like Ethel drank them all under the table the evening after the battle. "Yes, she is passionate about her descendants. This means she is likely to be open to learning about these energies that you study."

TJ shrugged. "Or that." He took a beat, then looked at Rowan. "What do you think is going on in there?"

"Ethel is teaching Cole the way of the earth, the way it was, is, and can be."

"She said Ormr was still in her; he blew up who Cole used to be to make her into the thing she is now. He gave her his magic."

"She's no' 'a thing,' as you say. But, aye, she's magic-touched now."

"If Ethel is teaching her all that, she's gonna be in there forever."

Rowan thought about his wife with copper fire for hair, the only outward evidence of her lineage and its zeal for life. "Aye, she's a whole lot more comfortable with facts and science than the unnamed forces that surround her."

"Sure. We call it pigheaded."

Rowan's retort died on his tongue when his cell rang. He pulled it from his pocket and excused himself. He'd barely gotten out of earshot before he said to the caller, Charmaine, "Ye have it?"

Rowan could hear road noise behind Charmaine's words. She probably had him on speaker in the car. "Unfortunately, no. And it seems that Murdoch has moved it, as the recovery agents searched the Otey manor house and found nothing. Well, not nothing. They did find sensitive bank files that were not secured. I presume he left the place in a hurry after the bank notified him that they were going to conduct the search. His superiors are leveling disciplinary charges against him for those files and, at my behest, removing him as an officer from your loan. Something that might be more ceremonial, but it cut Murdoch. Apparently, his superiors heard from him immediately. He's outraged."

Rowan underestimated the lengths to which Murdoch would go to get his revenge by playing hide-and-seek with his family's artifact, and it made his blood boil. "Not yet, he's not."

"Now, Rowan. Please, do not do anything so rash as to go there and beat him to a pulp. That will put us in a bind with the picture I am painting of the clan being victims of theft. If you put him in hospital, we'll look as if we're not as innocent as we are."

"Twenty-four hours, Ms. Chevalier. That's all I can promise before I find him and *interrogate* him to get back what's mine." He severed the connection and walked farther away from TJ and Peabody to the cliff edge. The wind tossed his collar and blew his short hair back. There were stronger forces in the world than him; that wind was his reminder that this thing he wrestled with was a small thing, that he'd get through it, and god willing, no one would be murdered. Only the quiet he normally felt after several deep breaths at the ocean's edge did not arrive. His blood still boiled. His mind's eye was obsessed with the image of Murdoch's fine-pressed shirt caught in his fist as he lifted the human pustule off the ground, cutting off the man's airway.

He didn't feel or hear Cole until her boots were swishing through the tall grass behind him.

He tried to shutter his thoughts, but it was too late. Her hand was on his back, and she came around his shoulder, a question in her gaze. He closed his eyes as he pulled her into his embrace. He breathed in deeply, taking in her scent—spring, pollen, and warm sun—and felt the knots in his stomach loosen. The thought of pummeling the banker slid back into the shadows of his mind.

"Walk home with me," she whispered up to him. "Let Peabody and Tee stay on. Walk with me through the forest. I know it takes Clive a while to walk it, but it can't be that far, even if the trail meanders. It takes hardly any time to drive here."

"Nae. I need tae get back and make some calls. Murdoch will be the sorriest sod tha' ever walked this earth when I'm done with him."

"Sure. Or we can walk home, and cool off." He felt her go up on her toes, and her lips gently kissed his cheek. He knew he should do it, walk it off, but it was all too much, especially now that he knew the man was working out a vendetta, well outside his capacity as a banker. It had been too recent that he'd needed to defend his clan, and now again. *Mark tha'*, he thought, as this was different. This time the man threatening them was mortal.

"What is it with men trying tae take the things I love from me? What I'd give to be a lone sod in a cubical in the city with every evening filled with pizza, beer, and movies."

He opened his eyes then as she responded with a wry smile. "Been there—not as amazing as it sounds. It ends in antidepressants and wishing for a life like this one. Well, maybe not exactly like this one, but one with a little more action."

"Fine, just a week of pizza and movies."

"Done. Walk through the forest with me. Ethel said I need to try emptying my energies; the forest is a good place to try."

Rowan was about to respond when she continued.

"Well, she said to get rid of my excess magic, but I think my scientific brain is still wrestling with calling it magic."

"Same beast, different name, aye?" If he hadn't been raised with the curse as his daily bread, then the thought of doing magic in a kitchen off the coast of northern Skye would have him thinking the lot of them was bonkers. If Ethel said she needed to expend her excess magic, it was wise to heed the request.

She was quiet for a moment, and then her green eyes returned to curiosity. "So, tell me, on a scale of one to pissed, where are you about the Rembrandt?"

"I'm not drunk."

"No, pissed as in, never mind, how about one to homicide?"

"Multiple homicide."

Cole grinned, her dark humor the match to his. "We have the entire walk back for me to get that down to 'cursing his good name.'"

Rowan scoffed and looked back out at the ocean, but Cole's gentle fingers hugged his chin, bringing his gaze back to her steady one. "You doubt me?"

"This time, love. Aye, I may well be beyond saving from my temper this time. This time it's a mortal human who's trying to destroy me." He felt his fist open and close. It had the feel of Kelly and his father all over again. The two who tried to take Cole from him just last year after the gala thinking they were the rightful heirs to the MacLaoch seat. And with Cole's hand in marriage, they could end the curse and bathe in the perceived MacLaoch riches. Instead, they got a Lady MacLoach–class lightning bolt to the head and he got a bullet to the shoulder.

"Destroy? I don't doubt it feels like that, but because he's mortal, he has to obey laws. Eventually. We'll get him."

Rowan gave her a look.

"Don't look at me like that. Between the two of us, I'm the one with the temper problems." She gave him a soft smile. "Come." She tugged on his hand, and he let her drag him toward the far side of the property where the MacLaoch forest began.

She waved to her brother and Peabody and pointed toward the woods.

TJ called to her, jogging a few paces closer, "Throw me the keys!"

Cole fished the keys out of her pocket, and Rowan snatched at them. Cole yanked them away and, with a laugh and the arm of a cricket captain, whipped the keys to her brother.

TJ caught them easily. "Don't fall off a cliff!" he said and went back to Peabody who was now talking with Ethel at the back door of the church. When Ethel turned and saw Cole, she relaxed her hands, palms down. Rowan caught Cole nodding.

"Cole..." he said to her. "This is different. There's no amount of corporate punishment that is enough for what he's done. And what if he's destroyed it?" The thought made his guts twist; he needed to bash the man's face in until he told him where it was.

"Rowan," she said and walked backward toward the forest. A smile he couldn't place was on her lips.

"No," he said through gritted teeth. "I'm getting back to the castle now, and it looks like without ye."

"Nah, come," and her gaze squinted as if she were trying something. Her palm opened toward him, and just as he was going to turn from her, crashing waves blew through his body. He staggered back, his arms going out to center himself. As he heard waves crash around him, the memory of Cole in his arms, in the water, washed through him. He was making love to her in the loch, calming the fire in her veins with another kind of fire. Her legs had wrapped around his middle and with a grip on her thigh and the other in her hair, he drowned himself at the altar of her love. It was intoxicating to his senses, the icy chill of the water and the warmth of her body against his, and he remembered the way her hand dove down between them and undid his fly. He remembered the way he plunged into her, making her head fall back with a groaning gasp. Then thrusting into her until— Then suddenly it was gone.

Cole's hands in the distance were relaxing down. Her eyes were on him, and he was woozy with the ride. It took him a moment to return to the present, but what was left was a settling in his bones and the onshore misty gusts. It was as if his mind was clearly focused and derailed from his dark tirade. The earth was beneath his feet, the love of the ocean was washing up his backside, and beauty and love swirled in his guts.

It was as if the anger he had been nursing formed a woven tapestry, and the threads had rearranged to show a different picture.

"Did it work?" she called to him.

"Fuck" was all he could manage. "Ye did tha'?"

"Yeah." Then she sobered. "Are you all right? You didn't get zapped or anything?"

She made her way back to him.

"No, aye, I'm fine. But just a moment ago, I was fucking ye in the loch."

Her eyes went wide with satisfaction as she flattened her palm over his jumper front. "Well, then, I'd say it worked."

Rowan blinked to clear the last of the dream from his mind, but the desire to be calm with her, to place ocean-wet kisses on her lips, lingered. "Aye, but now I want tae fuck you in the loch."

Her grin returned. She nodded to the trail. "Let's go?"

"Let's, but I have to warn ye. I'll not make it back to the castle with these feelings in my belly. You'll have to run, if getting home is your aim."

His words did as he'd intended and sparked mischievous joy in her gaze. "Oh, really?"

"Run like the wind," he whispered over her lips, "because if I catch ye, there's a cove halfway down I've a mind to explore. And it will be without yer clothes on."

Chapter Twenty-One

❧

"So...where's this cove?"

I had run the first part of the trail, a little bit to tease Rowan but a lot out of pure joy. There was nothing like running downhill with the wind in your hair. Then tight switchbacks edged close to the cliff edge, and I took a break.

The breeze kicked up, tossing my hair about before it teased Rowan's collar, then zipped into the stocky forest behind us. The trees, spruce and fir, were all angled back from the nearly constant wind. The understory grew scrubby and squat out of the litter of gnarled bark and pine needles underfoot. The sea spray and insistent foul weather created a tough environment where only the hardy survived. And even then, only to dwarf size compared to their inland counterparts.

Rowan was still panting. He braced his hands on his knees. "Oh aye, yer fast."

"Downhill, I'm like lightning; uphill, I'm a tortoise. How far until we're on MacLaoch land?"

"Right when ye stepped off the lawn of the church ye were on MacLaoch land."

"Is the castle another hour or so?"

"Half if ye run. But it drops down onto the rocky beach here and there, so it might be longer at tortoise speed." He grinned and kissed me. "But here is where I wanted to stop anyway. Come."

He pushed aside the deep green, leathery leaves along the downward slope.

"The cove is just below—can ye see it?" He called back. I followed Rowan to a goat trail. Some enterprising shrubs and herbaceous plants grew in the craggy rock face.

"It's a little farther," Rowan said as he slipped on some loose rock.

"Rowan!"

He grinned back at me. "Now that you know magic, I'll expect never to have to go to hospital again."

"Ha!" Holding onto a scraggly branch as long as I could, I picked my way down the path, "You've got high hopes for my skill set, sir. Let's not put it to the test today."

"Ye'll get there."

"From what I learned today from Ethel, I think I might be able to bring the cairn knoll back to life."

"Tha's a big deal..."

"Ethel's got a theory. She said that the field, my energies, the drama of Ormr—"

"Ye mean trauma."

"Whatever. Thanks to all that, I am sucking the life out of that area, and out of others I'm connected to."

Rowan looked at his hands. "Me too?"

"Maybe? Probably." I thought of the way he fell back down into the bed the other night, "We're definitely sharing energy.

"That spot of land since it's where we held the ceremony, and I've spent considerable time there, is taking the most absorption. But mostly, she said it was the m-ma, hell"—I cursed, I still couldn't say *magic*—"metaphysical energy–laced slurry we drank. It transferred the powers from Ormr to me permanently. She thinks it was a prank Ormr played."

"Prank?"

"She said it was a plan of his. But prank feels more accurate."

"Aye, right."

"He was all: I'm off to Valhalla, but let me leave a fat chunk of my essence with my granddaughter so I can live on in glory."

"I detest the man, but I can say for certain that his bloodthirst was tamed only in the moment ye were punching his lights out. In a verra, and I mean *verra*, strange way, I think he's proud of ye."

"Gross."

"He recognized that you were stronger than him in both mind and heart. Then, in a narcissistic display of love, he left ye what he felt was missing from your life: his power."

"Ugh. Sucks."

"Aye. I can imagine."

And then Rowan jumped.

I finally stopped staring at our feet and looked fully out. We'd made it to the concealed rocky beach. Protected from the waves, it was peaceful at low tide. The water lapped up onto the rocks in a lulling, sleepy rhythm. It felt secluded, secretive, and rocky.

"Rowan?"

"Aye?" He raised his arms, ready to catch me.

"This looks real rocky, babe."

Instead of jumping into his arms, I used his hand to brace myself and jumped down to the beach as well.

Keeping hold of his hand, I took in the high moody clouds of that afternoon. They added sultry darkness to the private cove. Rowan hugged me in against him. He gave me a kiss that was both an *I love you* and a question: *Are we really doing this? I can't decide.*

I breathed him in, letting my lips linger on his, and reiterated, "It's all rocks down here."

He kissed me again. "Come over here."

Much like the loch at Castle Laoch, this too had an imposing cliff face that, at first glance, was solid rock. Then, as my eyes adjusted and absorbed the edges and juts of the gray basalt, the nooks and crannies were revealed—and also, where Rowan had disappeared.

I followed his lead along the rocky face and found what he knew was there: a cave.

Hands momentarily lingering at the edge of the opening, I slipped to the side into a narrow passageway then slipped back as the path serpentined in. Then the mouth of the cave opened wide.

"Whoa..." I murmured as I took it in. It was the proper idea of a cave. Over the millennia, the water had surged into it and cleaned out a ten-foot high and wide cave. A big basalt bubble. It tapered toward the back like a teardrop, though didn't seem fully closed back there, as I felt a cool stream of air feeding into the cave. In balance, the dark basalt rocks at the entrance heated under the sun, transferring their warmth throughout the cave. It was good enough to live in. And live in someone, at some point, had. A stream of light beamed into the cave, illuminating a fire pit. The fire pit hadn't seen fire in a very long time. There was also a flat rock that looked wide and long enough to hold a twin mattress.

"Does high tide clean this place out?"

"A good storm surge will clean the floor, but at high tide, only the beach is gone. This cave remains dry. And with that corkscrew entrance, it's protected from the spray."

I touched the walls and felt the smooth rock face bump under my fingers. I was in awe; someone had spent time in here, and somehow it felt familiar.

"Who lived in here?"

"Lived?" Rowan asked, confused. "No one. Why?"

I made it to the flat rock I envisioned as a bed and sat; there was a definite feel to the place, it was as if hands were reaching for mine, trying to tell me something.

"Nothing..."

Rowan leaned against the opposite wall, tossing and catching a rock he'd picked up. "I used tae pretend when I was a wee lad that I was meeting a fair maiden here, and we'd neck until the sun went down."

I laughed and lay back on the flat rock mattress bed. "Where? Here?"

His eyes held mischief. "Aye, right there."

"And what did this maiden look like, sir?"

He grinned at the memory. "It'll give ye goose flesh."

Thoroughly intrigued, I asked, "Snakes for hair? Raptor eyes?"

He shook his head. "Nae. Different kind of spooky."

"Hmm..." Watching him, his eyes going soft as they rested on me: "A seal goddess, what is the Gaelic term for them?"

"Selkie, and nae, it would be like bedding my own kind. She was a manifestation of what a young boy thought true fair maidens looked like."

"Mmm," I murmured, "so, like, a *Penthouse* centerfold?"

Rowan laughed out, playing along. "Oh aye, maybe that's where I saw her."

"Tell me, what did your fantasy woman look like?"

"Luxurious copper curls that cascaded down her back and green eyes that set my guts on fire."

"Not last year, Rowan—when you were a kid."

"I told you it would make you shiver. I dreamed of ye when I was just a wee lad and being back here reminded me of how vivid those dreams were."

That settled down into me. Rowan as a teenager was mooning for a woman who looked like me. "Ohhh."

The hands that seemed to be trying to touch me since I'd arrived at the cave finally did.

"Oh!"

Rowan heard the tone change. "Oh, what?"

I sat up, looking around. "Rowan?"

"Aye."

"What exactly happened in this cave, Chief?"

He came off the wall and to stand in front of me. He let the stone fall with a clink to the cave floor and held his hands out to me. I put my hands in his.

"It's best if I show ye."

"Excellent. As you know, I am a visual learner."

He slid over me as I lay back. His fingers walked up over my sweater, brushed my cheek, and dove into my hair before gently tugging my hair tie out of my curls. Then, with a soft touch, he fluffed my hair out until he was satisfied. "Aye, like that. Spread wild as if ye'd been tossed down in a fit of passion."

Watching my lips, he added, "Yes, then"—he kissed me—"a wide, sultry smile, just like tha'." Down onto his elbow, he brushed another kiss over my lips. "There is a small but consequential part of me tha' feels as if I'm fulfilling a long-held fantasy and will likely want tae to do this over and over and over again."

I laughed out, and Rowan kissed my exposed neck and murmured, "Aye, that too, lots of lust-filled laughter, and when in a few moments I whip out my cock, lots of sounds of admiration and comments on it being the largest one you've ever seen."

Our laughter was the bond of our next kiss, sealing the joy within our comingled breath.

"In this fantasy, do I call you chief, sir, or my liege; like, 'oh, my liege, your cock is so *huge*'?"

The deep sound of Rowan's laugh rumbled in his chest before it escaped. "Just like that." His lips brushed my ear before he continued, "Nae, I only remember her knowing what to do. She'd tell me tae take my clothes off and, at some point, to hold verra still. I'd lay here with my cock out and wait and imagine her taking it deep inside, but it took forever because I had to make the hole. She was a virgin, after all."

"Make the...hole? Oh, sweet boy Rowan." I put my hand on his cheek and fell in love with him all over again. "You thought you had to make the hole?"

He was matter-of-fact. "Oh aye. All I'd caught was snippets of conversations that led me to the assumption tha' it was my job tae make the hole—that's why it was so tight, and that was why there was blood on a virgin's wedding night."

My lips felt the smirk at his youthful naivete. "When did you discover that's not exactly how it works?"

He laughed then at his own ignorance as he worked my sweater up and off. "Actually, it was in basics."

"Sorry? Basic training? RAF? Not, like, say, high school health class?"

"I thought they were full of shit in secondary. It's hard tae learn things when ye think you know it all."

"Mm-hm. I see, and I remember you were a bit of a Lothario in those days. You probably thought, 'Thank god all these women have already slept with guys who did the hard work of making a hole.'"

"Oh aye, glad the work was already done. I didn't like the idea of causing pain in casual hookups. I was trying to get to this moment"—he paused to kiss me and smiled—"without having tae do the work to get here." He kissed the tops of my breasts, plumped out the top of my bra. "To be clear, that 'here' I was aiming for was where my fair maiden found me, saved me, and for all the reasons in the world that she shouldn't, she did pick *me* to love. Then picked me again tae wed and to bed for the rest of her life." He let his body relax down onto mine, and I wrapped my legs around him.

"That's right." My thumb traced the contour of his cheekbone as his pewter-blue gaze went hazy with contentment. "I was zapped into action to cross the Atlantic and found you, an arrogant Scottish chief I thought I might murder before I'd kiss, much less get naked with."

His grin was back. "Aye, but then I trapped ye in my hunting cottage tae keep you safe and realized that you were the woman I'd dreamed of. It was the curse talking to me. I knew then in my heart of hearts that you were sent to break it because I'd never felt love like tha' before. I'd only met you, a wild American who set my belly on fire, and suddenly I couldn't think of a future without you. It was like you'd always been at my side. I'd never felt that way before. I was intoxicated."

My hands wove up into his hair and gripped. I agreed, "Intoxicated." And pressed my lips to his. I inhaled the ocean spray smell and exertion of his run down the hill off his skin. The memory of us in the loch came back to me. His arms were tight around me then and now the warmth of his weight was on my front.

Rowan's hand smoothed over my stomach before he found my jean's buttons and yanked; each one popped out of its hold, yawning open my fly. His fingertips scoured over my hip and pressed my waistband down as I made quick work of his undershirt. I breathed in along the skin of his shoulder as I scratched my nails up his back. We'd made love plenty over the past year, but there was something unique in that moment. The sound of the ocean lapping on shore beyond the cave wove around me until I was consumed with its rocking lullaby feel.

I undid Rowan's fly as I kicked off my shoes and he his, and I pushed his jeans off with mine.

My knees spread as Rowan moved to notch into me, his cock in his fist, when I remembered my line.

"Oh right. Mm! My what a large cock you have, sir. Or is it my chief?"

Rowan paused, and for a moment he didn't have the mental capacity to remember what he'd fantasized about. He was purely in the moment, and it took him a few heartbeats before he recalled what I was talking about.

A grin broke across his face. "It had been chief, but when ye say sir, it feels exotic, very American. I'll be sir, tae-day."

"It's a magnificent erection. Sir, I've never seen one so *large*."

Rowan laughed and settled down on me, his forehead resting against my temple. "This is not going as I imagined."

"Maybe if you lay on your back, you can poke up to make that special third hole— Mmm..." Rowan pressed into me, and my train of thought was lost as he filled me, stretching sumptuously into our connection.

I pulled his hips in until his pelvis bumped mine, and he settled there. He relaxed out before pressing back in again. There it was again, the ocean waves, the heady mix of exertion and desire. A small flame seemed to break across my skin just as I felt I was the only one feeling it, Rowan groaned in pleasure.

"I'm back in the loch making love tae you."

His slow and deliberate hip presses created a slip and slither until they gradually crescendoed into earnest thrusts, making me moan and bite his shoulder. I'd forgotten how good it felt to be possessed by him. And this time possess him.

My skin took on a golden sheen that coated us and heightened our touch and immersed us within the memory of Rowan, his hands on my hips, my arms wrapped around his neck and straddling him in the icy waters he rammed his thick erection up inside me like a man possessed.

Dampness from our own sweat or the loch water of our memory slickened our skin. His lips found mine, and our tongues tasted as we shared one breath and one body. Electricity of our lovemaking built. I arched my pelvis up, taking Rowan deeper. He followed suit and pushed himself farther in, stretching and tapping into that elusive erogenous zone deep inside.

My body shuddered. The stones we lay upon seemed to quake along with us, as if they were possessed with our erotic energies as well.

"Cole..." Rowan murmured in longing. "You have me, all of me, for the rest of time, mind, body and soul."

His words were a spell and a promise. The ground shook as a groan escaped over my vocal cords. My head fell back as the power of our lovemaking shot through my body in a powerful orgasm.

At my groan and pinch of my insides, Rowan lost it and wild with his own release thrust erratically before he cried out with me.

I could feel Rowan's chest rising and falling with each of his breaths, and his heartbeat thumped in the vein at his neck. Rowan gave a small push in, making me giggle. Our skin glowed softly in the dimly lit cave.

"Are we glowing?"

I lifted my arm off his back and took in the soft golden light.

"I think we are. I might have finished that loch memory."

Rowan kissed the tip of my nose.

"I noticed. I think I like it, this new skill ye have."

We smiled like fools as we locked gazes and swam in our connection.

I wet my lips that had gone dry with our kissing. "That was fun."

He took a deep breath with his nose to my neck. "Aye it was. Tha gaol agam ort."

"I love you too."

He made a pained face. "Though, next time, I need padding under my knees. The rock is no' fun. Not like the loch at all."

"You hurt your knees?" I looked down past our joined bodies, his thick erection slowly fading out of me. He lifted a leg. That knee indeed looked roughed up.

"I am nothing if not dedicated to the fantasy."

. . .

IN OUR LITERAL POSTCOITAL GLOW, I TOOK IN THE CAVE ONCE MORE. It was in a nice location. A deep little inlet for a boat, and the cave was a little like an ancient stone cottage set into the hillside. And a grand old place to avoid authorities if you were distilling whisky in the bad old eighties.

"When did you discover this cave?"

"The cove we've always known of. It's a fine location for harvesting langoustines and mussels. Clabbydoos and the like. There are bogs and marshes not far from here that were good before climate-controlled architecture. Like butter—"

"Whisky?" I asked. Rowan grinned. He was on his back next to me, his hands resting under his head. The black of his armpit hair matched the hair at his navel that dove down.

"Aye, whisky. But it gets transported over the bog and to the road on the other side. No' stored in the bog."

"So your family knew of this cave forever. Because there's one thing that I've been curious about with the Lady MacLaoch curse," I said, using her formal name, just in case.

"What's that?"

"How did she and Ormr develop a relationship?"

Rowan made an acquiescing noise out of the back of his throat. "Mm-m."

"I mean, she wouldn't decide to throw away everything that had been laid out for her in life for a Viking dude. I mean, he was an enemy. How'd he win her heart? Because we both know—"

"That she'd come to be his better half. She quieted the wildness of his soul."

We'd seen it on the cairn knoll. The way her presence gave him pause in his quest for retribution, and eventually with her ghostly hands in his, he gave in to her love.

"Right. So, how'd it happen?"

Rowan pulled me in close, resting a leg over mine as the bridge of his nose rested on my temple. "Ye are the only one with the connection to the man who can answer that."

"This cave... There's something about it. What was it like when you came here when you were a kid? What was the condition of this cave?

"You think they met here?"

"I mean...besides it feeling consequential? It's private and close to the castle. I wish she'd kept some record of her life." I added, "Peabody says she was likely illiterate. Most people outside the clergy were. And 'paper' would have been expensive—papyrus or leather—so her writing a diary, or letters to Ormr, for that matter, would have been rare and probably completely unlikely."

"What about that sheaf from Clive? Tha' one you thought was runic, and you read it before Ormr fully showed up."

"The one Clive and Deloris were having a bit of an argy-bargy—as you'd say—about."

"Tha' one."

"It was from the book Ethel had and that I helped her digitize. I wonder if that book has the day he met Ora—"

"Shh..."

"Right."

Rowan shivered. "I just got a wee tingle up my spine."

"Sorry, when he met Lady MacLaoch. I wonder if it's in there, him meeting Lady Mac," I said.

"Or..." Rowan said.

"Or what?"

"Or...?" His brows rose up in pointed meaning.

"If you're suggesting that I chat with Ormr..."

"I am."

"Can't."

"Ye haven't tried."

"Not gonna." I sat up and rummaged through our clothes for my pants.

"Don't you want to know the part of their story that was beautiful and legend-making? We know the end, the brutality, and curse, but what about the soft and lusty beginnings?"

"He probably brutalized her, and in a fit of Stockholm syndrome, she acquiesced to feelings she had under his capture, and in a fit of fantasy, they married for a brief second on his dragon ship."

Rowan scoffed so hard I could practically hear him say bullpucky.

"Ye know that's not true."

"Could be." I got my bra on when he grabbed the back of my pants and made me sit again. Sitting on the edge of the flat stone, he pulled me in against his naked chest, wrapping me in a hug.

"Look, maybe ye start a journal of your own? Ask him questions there. Maybe he'll answer."

"What, like, 'Hey, Grandpappy, how'd you and your lusty lady meet?'"

"Nae. 'Why'd you possess me, ye bastard?'"

"I could try something like that."

"And if he does answer, ask him about the coffers coffin."

"I'm not sure I want to know where he got those coins…"

THAT EVENING, I SAT IN THE FRONT ROOM OVERLOOKING THE DUSKY evening of the tidal flats beyond the cliffs, notebook immediately in front of me. Rowan, much calmer now after our "walk," had taken seriously what I thought was a joke. He'd met with Clive after we'd gotten back and Clive had given him a blank notebook with an indeterminate origination date to pass along to me. Or, in Clive's words: "Don't tell Deloris I've given it to you to write in." Since the moment I had demonstrated skill at reading runes that day in his office, Clive had gotten keen about helping with my gift. The pilfered old journal from the library was just one example of that.

The evening chill sent me breaking kindling for the fire in the small wood stove behind me. Then, with a cup of tea (with a tipple of Glentree Gold) and a wool blanket tucked tight around my shoulders, I resettled at the antique writing desk. I uncapped my fountain pen—also a Clive gift—and opened the notebook. It was leather-bound. Each page was translucent like filo dough and had slight imperfections of visible pressed plant fiber. I put my hand to the upper right-hand side of the page and took a deep breath, praying that my pen wouldn't offend the creators of the notebook. And that I wasn't cursing myself once again.

I scrawled the date. Then, in an instinctual scientific urge, I wrote the location, weather, and time of day. I had no idea what I was doing or if any of the questions I was about to ask would work, but I did know that, much like scientific research, if I didn't try, I'd not earn a different level of understanding than I had now. With a steadying breath, I set my intention—kissing the ring on my finger that was my link to the ancients—and with the crackle and snap of the fire behind me, I penned the first entry.

Chapter Twenty-Two

CLAN MACLAOCH LANDS, YEAR OF OUR LORD 1210

It was an unforgiving way to end his wretched day. The winds from the sudden gale pushed the boats off course, and with the casualties of his last raid, he had to man his ship alone back to the isle. It would be a gift from the gods if he didn't succumb to their rage. As he limped back home along the coast of Scot Land, the waves frothed and churned, smashing against the hull of his wooden ship. It would be a matter of time before it was shattered onto the rocks. He detested the place called Scot Land—and the man, more detested, named Laoch. He was an unforgiving pike in the eye who likely had the blood of a thousand Danes in his veins. He'd been a fool to sack that fishing village, to have believed the rumor that Laoch protection didn't cover that wealthy port.

Never again. He would kill Laoch if it was the last thing he did in this star-crossed existence.

A gust blew salt water into his face and made the sea roar with anger.

The sails caught, and the canvas filled, tipping the dragon-headed longboat dangerously sideways. Cursing the gods for having forsaken him, Ormr downed the main sail and, with two hands on the steering oar, gave up on completing the journey home today. Instead, he would end this day now.

Ahead, a narrow inlet could be seen over the tops of the waves and through the driving rain. Shifting tack, he turned toward the inlet. He prayed it was deep and that he could control the ship through the narrow opening. He would either live to see the morning or be crushed against the rocks.

Feet braced, he gripped the wooden handle of the rudder and held on tight. The next wave in the frothing set of three, one under and two directly behind, caught the Viking ship and sent it scuttling down its front and toward the cliffs. He leaned back, keeping the bow from catching the wavefront. Just as he seemed doomed to plunge straight into the depths, his momentum faded. The wave left him behind in the ocean foam, and the second in the set was directly behind. He felt the ship lift, and bracing his feet once more to the boards, he rode the wave thirteen feet in the air. The precarious position of being solo in a vessel that required a team to drive as well as being under the command of the ocean gods were acutely felt by Ormr. Then there was the thrill, the wild abandon that his future was out of his hands, and for a moment, just that moment in the driving rain and frothing sea, he'd succumb to his fate.

The ocean drove him toward the rock face, and like threading a needle, he was blasted through the narrow inlet. Too late did he see it was a short ride to the rocky shore. The bottom of the hull struck, and he was thrown forward. He felt weightless arcing through the air, salt water in his nose and mouth, and he thought to himself that there was more, much more, that he wanted to do. But his life beyond this one, he hoped, would be one of riches.

AFTER WEEKS TRAPPED INSIDE BY THE WEATHER, LADY ORABILIA had had enough of domestic work. Just as the mere sight of the stones of the inner keep was about to make her go mad, the sun dawned bright and blissful. It was as if the near month of foul weather had been only in her imagination.

Back into the kitchen, she slipped her foraging apron on and her sturdiest leather boots. The cook was in desperate need of fresh stock to feed the many hungry mouths. She pulled up her skirts and knotted them to keep them dry from the dampness of the meadows as she moved along the muddy trails to her favorite spot an hour's walk into the hills. With a bladder of water on her hip and a leather satchel over her shoulder, no one would know her to be the firstborn daughter of the fierce Skye chief: Laoch. Her black hair was pulled back and plaited; she was ready for the day's work. Other wealthy clans across the high- and lowlands boasted servants for every one of their needs; she prided herself on her dedication to her people, that her back would know hard work and her hands would know how to heal the wounds of both the body and the heart.

In a half day's work, her leather bag and medicine bottles were full: herbs, roots, leafy greens of burdock, wild garlic, and nettles filled the satchel to bulging. The weight of the pack and the day's muggy weather caused by the rare bright sun made her undergarments stick to her skin. It also brought on Orabilia's thirst. Looking over the meadow, butter yellow and frothy white with flowers, she emptied the contents of the skin into her mouth.

"Och," she grumbled. How she wanted to stand beneath a waterfall.

Atop the farthest hill, she looked down upon the ancestral land, watching small wisps of smoke rise from the hearths of the village far below. Orabilia knew the path back would be unnecessarily arduous without water, so she set course for the coastal path that would wind her down and back over a burn or two.

Sweat dripped into her bodice and pooled under her breasts. It was hot work carrying her load home, so thankfully, there was just time enough to stop at her secret cove—her private spot to gather the small red crustaceans, clabaidh-dubha, and other ocean delights. After a long hard winter and a moody wet spring that refused to succumb to summer, spending the rest of the daylight at the cove made her insides jubilant and her muscles relax. Peace would soon be upon her.

At the hidden path that headed toward the cliff face and the narrow trail down, Orabilia picked her way through the shrubbery. When she broke through the greenery, her cove was not hers. A Viking ship lay on its side like a bloated beached whale, the casualty of a war with the ocean gods.

She felt panic surge through her limbs. Vikings? She should run. *Now.*

But behind the panic was reason. She felt her heartbeat pulse under her burning skin. If it were just dead men, she'd not want to waste her chance for at least a good dousing of icy water down her bodice.

Leaving her heavy bags at the top of the cliff, she moved carefully down the steep path. Orabilia looked keenly at the wreckage as she descended. Even half-dead Vikings were dangerous. The trail ended at a short stone cliff not much higher than a farmer's stone wall.

She leaped down onto the rocky beach and froze, listening. The water lapped against the rocks and echoed in the empty wooden ribs of the Viking ship. Her spine tingled, and Orabilia knew she had to be quick. She rushed across the short beach to the spring, swollen from the rains, that gushed from between the rocks and soaked her bodice and filled her mouth and waterskin. Still sensing no one, Orabilia took a chance to observe the wreckage. Her father's men would want details.

She inspected the beach, then the water. There were no bodies. They'd been drowned at sea, she assumed, and the ship tossed up onto shore. The ship was shattered at the nose but easily salvageable. Painted in Laoch red, it would make a fine addition to their arsenal.

Just then, the bird calls ceased as another sound rose. A deep groan came from behind the boulders against the cliff face.

Orabilia felt the tingle of danger move up her spine. With a light foot, she made it back over the rocky beach to the short wall and up to her things. She pulled the short blade from her waist.

The voice rose again, echoing through the cove below; the agony of the human was palatable. But it was surely a Viking, and leaving him to the ravens was his due justice. She picked up her things and put them back on. Vikings rarely traveled alone, and where there was one injured, there'd be a ship of them coming to collect what remained. Cooler now, she had to get back to the keep and warn the clan. Her father and a few of his men were still in the south at the Uig fishing village, assuring the Uig people that Vikings wouldn't be so bold as to travel that far south into Skye territory.

On the trail, her boots slipped in the mud as she moved swiftly back toward home. The forest was dark, blotting out the late-afternoon sun. Another chill ran up her spine, and this time, she thought she heard a voice in her ear: *Help*. She skidded on the mud and turned sharply, holding out her short blade. The path behind her was empty.

Fear moved her; she began to run until the forest broke out into a sunny meadow. She ran and ran until she could see the keep ahead. With her heart beating a steady tattoo, she slowed then paused in the daylight to catch her breath. Walking to the cliff's edge, she peered down to the calm lapping of the ocean waters against the rocky face below. There were no ships crashed, nor were there any on the horizon clear to the north or far south. The green humps of the isles off her father's lands looked happily situated as if nothing of consequence had ever happened there.

Chapter Twenty-Three

Upon her return, Orabilia found the keep bustling with the end of the day's sunshine chores. Wood was being split to cure; freshly laundered bed coverings and undergarments were being folded into baskets after drying all day the rare bright sun. Woven floor coverings and tapestries were being taken back in after being thoroughly beaten and left to breathe in the fresh air.

Through the delivery of her goods to the kitchens, the evening meal, and lying on her pallet that evening, she thought of the voice that seemed to have called to her. And cursed herself for not finding her own voice in the bustle of the evening's doings. She didn't make the effort to take aside her father's man in charge, despite him sitting not two persons away at the evening meal. And most disturbing was the list she was making in her mind of things she would need when she returned on the morrow. Bandages, yarrow, tinctures, rope, and her sharpest blade. The pain in the voice she heard had wormed into her mind and sat like a toothache.

The next morning, she was up early, her racket collecting bread and ale bringing the cook to the kitchen door. "What has ye up before the cock crows?"

"Patch of dew-touched thistle in the upper forest lands; then I'll hunt in the cove and bring you langoustines."

His only reply was a laugh at a joke he didn't understand as she left without the traps for the small crustaceans.

Orabilia was back at the cove as the sun was cresting the far hills, throwing long shadows over the land. It was quiet, almost peaceful. The tide was out, as she had hoped. The dragon ship had been pulled lower down on the beach by the evening's high tide and was listing dangerously in the deep water of the inlet. It likely would not be salvaged in time before it fell into the water and drowned. 'Twas a pity.

She set her things down and quietly went to the serpentine entrance of the cave she thought of as her own. In the low light, she saw that it was empty. Once, she found a fox sleeping on the chiseled bed she'd made.

With her skirts drawn up in a knot, she slipped her blade out and left the cave.

Over the rocks and toward the far cliff face, Orabilia carefully stepped; her soft leather boots made no sound. The chill of the inlet's stone facade from the overnight dip in temperatures cooled her superheated skin. She was likely on a fool's errand and knew if he wasn't fully dead, he might need to be killed if he was one of the wilder ones.

With her sharp sgian-dubh gripped tightly in her fist, Orabilia hopped onto the next large gray rock. It was there that she found him. His honey hair, still plaited, was copper-streaked with dried blood, and he lay slumped, his chin on his chest and palms lifeless, facing the sky. It was as if he'd made his way to sitting and that was all he could do.

Crawling like a beetle over the rocks, Orabilia made her way to his feet. His eyes were closed, and his mouth was slack. He was not the right color. But she'd seen enough in life to know that sometimes color lied about the vitality of the spirit within. She kicked his foot, and he groaned. His head rolled to his other shoulder, and Orabilia heard the sound again. His voice was in her mind while his groan was in her ears.

Help.

She whispered in wonder and awe, "How is it that you do that?"

He did not respond. His boots were torn and hung off his feet. His tunic was ripped, exposing a shoulder, and the furs she knew Vikings wore were gone. The gold on his wrists and dragon torque around his neck said he was no common berserker; this was a Viking of means and wealth. He was of value. Orabilia then understood why the fates had called upon her to rescue this death dealer.

The ground beneath him there between the boulders was fine black sand. With great effort, she pulled his ankles and laid him flat. With fresh water and a clean cloth, she bathed his face. Then she searched his body, looking for the wound that was killing him. She found it on the back of his head. He groaned when her fingers probed it. Orabilia was familiar with war wounds and knew that had a sword made the slash, he'd be dead from fever. Instead, this was saturated with the healing waters of the sea; he'd gotten it in the wreck, and that, she knew, was the only thing that had saved him. There were powers the sea held that even she could not explain. She knew an old woman with joints that pained her could swim in the loch each day for three cycles of the moon and walk freely again.

Gathering more seawater, Orabilia rolled the Viking to his side and washed the wound deeply. She plaited his hair away from the gash that had nearly knocked him into the afterlife, padded it with masticated herbs of willow bark, plantain, and yarrow, then loosely dressed the wound with clean remnant cloth to keep the healing poultice in place.

From her bag, she retrieved the nourishment she'd planned for him. Putting the skin to his lips, she poured drops of broth into his slack mouth, and like all folk, his throat automatically swallowed. She fed him until he choked, a sign his body could take no more. Leaving him there, she went to the water's edge. Mussels were easily got with her short blade and a quick twist. And below the water's edge, the clabaidh-dubha were in abundance. They would do well for a midday meal. The Viking ship groaned at the edge of the inlet. The next high tide would see it taken as a sacrifice to the gods. There was nothing she could do save to watch it drown.

As the sun set, Orabilia fed the Viking again.

"On the morrow, I shall return, and when you are awake, I will bring you bread soaked in rich milk. You will need it to regain your strength. Enough to get you to the cave where I can build a fire, or a chill will set into your bones and take you from the living just as surely as the wound at your head might."

When he choked, she stopped feeding him and then gathered her things.

"On the morrow," she said to his limp form there on his side. She made a note to bring a woolen rug to place over him. If he survived the night.

For several days, Orabilia returned to the cove. On the fifth, the Viking's eyelid cracked, and she glimpsed the piercing green gaze of the man she had brought back to life. She had expected blue. To see the green felt like a sign. It felt like the abundance of the forest and kelp in the sea.

"You're awake."

He made to speak, but his mouth was dry.

"Come now." Orabilia kneeled and fed him cool spring water.

His eyes closed as soon as the water coated his tongue, and he greedily drank it down.

"Hold off." Orabilia pulled the flask from his lips. "You will be sick if you drink too much at once."

With a grunt, he grabbed her wrist. His grip was surprisingly firm. *Even half-dead Vikings...* With her free hand, she slipped the sharp, short blade of her sgian-dubh from its scabbard at her hip and brought it to his throat.

"'Tis a pity if I kill you now, after all the work I've put into getting you whole. But slice your neck and have you bleed out, I will."

He looked at her blade and then her face. "Water," he croaked in her native tongue.

"You'll have more. I'll put you under the spring myself once you are better and let you drink until you drown. But suck it down like a lamb at the teat, and you'll retch it all back up. And ye have broth and milk in your belly. I'd like to see that settled before ye retch."

He gave a faint smile, and his hand slipped off her arm as he lost consciousness again.

Orabilia didn't know how to interpret the slow smile that had spread on his face. Had he been happy with her chastising him? Was it sarcasm?

She sighed at the man. He might be a bit touched from the head wound.

"Now ye've gone and done it. Grabbing me has used all your strength. Just rest." She gave the large man's shoulder a pat and then left him.

After some time foraging for late-spring mushrooms in the upper forest, Orabilia returned to the cove, set her things down, and pulled the broth from her pack. It was then that she realized the Viking was sitting on a rock, hands on his knees.

Slowly, she reached back for her pack and pulled out a thick loop of rope. She shouldered the rope and dropped her pack. Pulling her sgian-dubh, she approached. With hands and feet tied, he'd be a nonlethal threat she could still feed but also escape from.

He looked up and squinted across the cove.

Orabilia made her way toward him, the waterskin held up high. "Are ye hungry?"

When he didn't respond, she added, "Lunge at me, Viking, and I'll spear ye through."

When she was within arm's reach, she heard his rough, unused voice ask her, "Are you a Dane?"

Orabilia tsked. "Had yer head bashed, and finally after seven moon-rises, ye get the strength to stand, walk, then sit again, and yer first question to me is if I'm a Dane?" He looked as if making eye contact was hard; his eyes squinted against the daylight. "If I were a Dane, ye'd be dead."

He found something humorous in her words, and with that light-ening his features, he closed his eyes. "True."

Orabilia didn't say she was something altogether worse: Laoch's firstborn who would likely release him to men who would kill him slowly while they extracted every secret he held. One thing at a time was best.

"Come. If ye can stand, you should come with me; just beyond is a cave—"

There was a great creaking groan before the ship behind her slipped into the inlet with a splash. It floated on its side for a moment before the hull gulped seawater, slipping with a gurgle below the surface.

She wondered if the words the Viking uttered at the sight were as foul as they sounded.

She couldn't help looking back at him and asking without mercy, "Oh, was that yers?"

He could only bare his teeth at her, like a wolf threatening to bite.

"Aye, easy..." Then she held the bladder out to him. "Sip this, verra slowly, and I'll get ye a bed made and a fire to warm your bones."

His hand was slow, and when he missed the skin, she grabbed his massive hand and shoved the bag into it.

"Drink. Slowly."

Orabilia made her way to the cave—one last look back before she entered; he was raising a shaking hand to his mouth. "Aye, good boy," she whispered.

In the cave, Orabilia set down a woolen rug, then another, and her fur coat, which she'd worn to the amazement of the keep guard, who'd commented, "Aye, 'tis looking to be another sunny day, yer ladyship!" before giving her coat a pointed look.

Next, she set to work on the fire. After several tries, the dry kindling caught a spark, and the pine needles went up with the small sticks next. In a moment, the fire was good enough to stack small logs. Satisfied, Orabilia dusted her hands and headed back out. She stopped short outside the cave. The Viking was now staggering toward her. Orabilia made to reach for her short sword when he caught himself on a boulder and doubled over, retching.

The empty bladder hung from his hand.

"Och. I told ye not tae suck it down like a wee lamb. Now ye've gone and lost it—"

He teetered, and she rushed to his side. "Och, no ye don't. Inside," she commanded.

She wove him through the entrance, then to the bed near the fire. His weight became heavier and heavier with each step until, at the bed, she let him collapse. He sat first, then lost consciousness, keeling backward into the blankets.

"Oof!" Orabilia grabbed the back of his neck to keep his head from striking the bed and was pulled atop him with the force of his flopping body weight. She saved his head, but as she lay atop the man, she caught her breath and looked down into his unconscious face and said, "Why am I going through all this trouble for ye? When I should take yer fine jewels and leave ye to your fate?"

She let his head slowly relax down, cushioned in its bandages, then rested her chin on her fist and observed the man up close. His beard was unkempt, of course, but it was done in three small plaits so it looked like he had kept it tidy before he fought the rock face and lost. Like the Viking nobility he surely was when he was not dying in enemy territory.

Slipping off him, she gathered her things, leaving the bread and bladder of milk with him. He was a miracle. She'd never seen a man his size recover from a head wound like he had nor so swiftly. If his traveling voice, haunting green eyes, and luck were any indication, he was blessed by the gods.

She left that day and knew that tomorrow, she would have to tie him up. He was getting stronger each day; each day she returned, she was that much closer to danger.

Chapter Twenty-Four

Ethel's kitchen was warm as I sat at her ancient wood table for my next lesson in controlling the powers that Ormr left me, which included putting the cairn knoll back to rights. That morning, herbs were hanging upside down from hooks in the beam above me.

"What does it mean that Orabilia would chance her security to save him? For all intents and purposes, Vikings were not welcome here, right?"

"You sound like a MacLaoch."

"I did fall in love and marry one; it makes sense that I sound like them. Vikings then were considered pirates, intent only on raiding whatever their kings and jarls, or war chiefs, demanded, right?"

Ethel poured hot water over the black tea leaves and herbs in the porcelain pot next to the stove.

"Was my ancient grandfather a jarl?"

"He was…" Ethel was thoughtful about her response before saying, "He did not wear the official title of jarl, or earl. His brother was a jarl in the northern isles. However, his status as a war chief and loyalty from the men who sailed with him, as well as the people who lived under his brother's rule, made him more powerful than his brother.

Despite Laoch owning much of the land out that window"—she pointed out the small rectangular window over the sink to the sea and the Lewis and Harris isle of the Outer Hebrides—"Ormr pushed the boundaries and laid claim to much of it."

I took the notebook out and flipped to the last entry. The entries, questions and answers, were written in my handwriting, but I didn't remember writing the answers. had penned my questions to the ancestors, and then it was as if I'd fallen asleep. I had awoken, the wood stove had died down, and I was sitting looking down at the scrawl on the pages. My pen was gripped in my hand, and my ring was warm on my finger.

"Orabilia was risking everything she knew for that ocean-going terror that haunted the isles at that time."

"She did."

"I hope I get to see why."

"Was any of her life her choosing?"

I thought about Ethel's question as I helped her get the teacups down. I slipped a brown-and-tan cozy wool sweater over the teapot before rescuing the cookie tin from the top cupboard beside the stove.

We settled in companionable silence as Ethel doled out the cookies, buttery oatmeal cookies with warming cinnamon, rough raw sugar crystals embedded into the tops. The cookies were like a warm hug—not too sweet or too plain, but just right, with a hint of nourishment from the chewy oatmeal.

Coming back to Ethel's question, I said, "I can't imagine a young woman in the thirteenth century getting to choose much of anything that happened in her life."

"So then, what happens when she discovers a man with golden clasps on his wrists, a dragon-shaped golden torque around his neck, close to death? She is in full control over whether he lives or dies. Does she take the opportunity to change his fate? Or is she satisfied with her life and choose to ignore him?"

"Choice is a powerful tool in our human arsenal, I suppose."

"Quite."

"I still have so many questions for them..."

"The notebook you have will facilitate dialogue between you and

Orabilia, especially now that you are wielding your grandfather's powers. Albeit reluctantly... Should you find yourself with greater gaps between responses, I recommend you revisit the cave." Ethel's face had gone from her usual serious consternation to one of suppressed laughter.

"Oh," I said, realizing belatedly that the cave in the cove was linked through our shared DNA. "Yes, we were able to find it on our hike back to Castle Laoch. It's quite profound to know that they were there as well. I assume she nurses him back to health in there? Peabody likely would get amazing readings there."

Ethel snorted. "I doubt the readings will be tragic enough for him and his meters."

I took a sip of tea as she continued.

"Although I shouldn't suppose to know what he'd find. Mayhap losing your virginity on the mighty cock of a Viking is a tragedy."

I choked. Tea sprayed over the table. I clamped a hand over my mouth as my teacup hit its saucer with a clang. "Ethel!"

Ethel threw her head back and cackled wildly.

Chapter Twenty-Five

CLAN MACLAOCH LANDS, YEAR OF OUR LORD 1210

The cove the next morning was quiet. The clear water showed the Viking longship perfectly upright, well below the surface. The birds high up in the forest called back and forth as small black crabs scuttled over the rocks in the mouth of the inlet. Orabilia made her way to the entrance of the cave; she dropped her things and pulled her short sword.

Inside the cave the Viking sat. Milk-soaked bread was in one hand and, in the other, the skin of milk she'd left for him. The fire had more wood on it from the pile she'd left, and he with effort turned his head toward her.

"I cannot see you well, but I know your step and fresh spring smell."

"I see yer up and around..."

"I am. I also am— Is that a sword?"

"I thought you couldn't see."

"The light behind you tells me there's something glinting in your hand. I'm no fool. You are Scots. I do not want to fight you now. I am injured. It will not be an honorable fight. I wish to see you clearly as you shove that blade betwixt my ribs."

Orabilia wasn't sure why, but what he'd said was humorous.

"That, and," he continued, "I am finally feeling the pangs of hunger and would like to finish my meal."

Orabilia slipped her blade away. "Aye, no sense in killing ye before ye've supped. Go on, then. I've things to take care of. I'll be back, Viking."

"Ormr."

"What was that?"

"My name."

"Oh…I see. Ahmhair."

"Ormr."

"Yes, Omerrr."

He gave up and asked, "And you are?"

"The woman who saved ye." Leaving the cave entrance, she tossed over her shoulder, "I'll be back before sundown."

Squatting in the field, her favorite wooden digger in her hand, pulling up the wild garlic to plant in the fields closer to home, Orabilia thought of the Viking. He had been calm, and his eyes keen, but they also had held a fire in them that spoke of pain. She had tinctures for that. What he really needed was a swim in the inlet. But if he could barely see, that would be foolish, she argued with herself.

She uprooted the last of the garlic for the home kitchen and hurried along the path back to the cove, her heart light and full of exhilaration. She would not look closely at why she felt that way, nor at the reason she had yet to inform anyone, much less her father who had returned from Uig, what she had found. She knew now that the Viking had been a part of the battle her father spoke of. And for that, he must be questioned before he was hanged.

The thought of him being executed after all the work she'd done to keep him alive made her stomach twist. The gods would show her the path soon enough. She just needed to be patient.

Back in the cove, she dropped her things and entered the cave. "I have returned—"

Only he was not there. Her mind whirled. He was stalking her. Or she had been followed by her own people, and he discovered, and that meant he was already as good as dead. She rushed out of the cave and grabbed her things when an exhale sounded from the inlet.

The Viking was there, surfacing. He was...swimming. Orabilia watched as he swam gracefully back toward shore. He didn't indicate he'd seen her. For reasons she also could not explain, she stepped to the side of an outcropping of rock to spy on him as he got out of the water.

He was the enemy and should not be admired, but she supposed she could appreciate fine things even if they were venomous. His shoulders were wide; he was built for wielding a weapon, an ax or a sword. His abdomen rippled with muscle, though she could tell he needed more food. She should not have looked between his thighs to his manhood, but like a child in the farmyard, she could not help but be curious. The inlet was cold, and his privates were tucked up in and tight. It would be a pity if he were brawny in all ways but one. The gods could be cruel. He squatted down, picked up his breeks from behind a rock, and slipped them on as he stood.

He was still for a moment before standing and turning toward the cave. He called, "Back so soon?"

She stayed still, knowing there was no way he could see her from there.

"I can sense you. I cannot see you. Come. I need your assistance."

Against the wall of the cave entrance, she scoffed. "Nae!" she hollered out.

"Come. The water is too deep, and my head pounds in pain."

She gathered her things and came around the cave entrance.

"Oh," she said at his form, which stood immediately before her. Crystal droplets hung off his lashes and beard. He smiled at her. He was still wearing only his torn pants. His upper body, up close, was sculpted into the physical manifestation of a god.

"Come," he said again, this time softly and looking deep into her soul with sparking forest-green eyes.

"Oh?" was all she managed. It felt as if she'd lived within that moment hundreds of times before. His word, *come*, slithered over her skin before it wormed its way into her ear and embedded itself deep into her consciousness. It was clear then. He was a secret she was keeping. He was something she had to share with no one, and in a clan that depended on self-sacrifice and going without when others were in need, he'd become something of a hidden treasure. With this human who was her sworn enemy, she could be herself: acerbic and demanding. She did not have to be "the chief's daughter." She could command his attention with the power of who she was, not the facade of a woman born to a powerful clan leader.

A wince crossed his face then, and he wavered.

Orabilia commanded him, "Sit." And with a hand to his upper arm, she gently sat him on the flat rock behind him. Then, she pulled out her tinctures. "Stick out your tongue."

He obeyed, taking his medicine. Then, elbows on his knees, he let Orabilia examine his head wound.

With light fingers and gentle eye, she determined it had healed; now the skin was pink and fresh. She took her time undoing the plaits around the scar and gently combed them out with her fingers before pulling all his wet hair back. She gave the base of his neck a rub, as if he were her pony, and a gentle pat.

She heard a guttural sigh escape his mouth before: "Thank the gods for you, friend," he whispered.

The word *friend* rolled around in her belly before attacking her heart, making it squeeze with pleasure.

She tsked. "Do not butter me with fine words before gutting me, Viking."

He straightened up and gave her a genuine smile. "You remind me of the woman who birthed me. Tell me, do you also hold witchcraft in these fingers?" He reached for her hand, and it was too soon to allow his touch. She yanked her hands away.

"Do not touch me so familiarly, Viking."

His smile vanished, and a keen fire erupted in his gaze. "I meant it in kindness." Orabilia kept his gaze until he nodded in understanding. "I am what I am. Aren't I?"

"The monster of my nightmares."

"And yet you brought me back from my promised death—why?"

Orabilia shook her head. "I have asked myself that same question every day since I found yer body. I cannot explain what I myself do not know."

"And I have silenced everyone who has ever spoken to me as you have, and yet...I am blind to it with you. Abuse me, friend. Gladly, you may be my downfall, and to Valhalla, I'll go, with your blade sending me there."

Orabilia laughed out. "Kill ye? Nae, not after I've brought you back to the living, but if ye try anything, Viking, I will choose me over you, aye?"

"Yes."

She held her hands out to him, palms up, and said, "Now, what do you want with these?"

He grasped her wrist, turning her hand so that her fingers pointed to the sky. He touched the tip of his pointer finger to her index finger. After a moment passed, he groaned. "I'm still too weak. I cannot."

"What is it that you are attempting?"

"It's better that I show you."

"Fine," she said and resisted the urge to tuck one of his golden locks behind his ear. But then he did it as if she'd asked him to.

Orabilia looked out to the inlet and then back to him, shaking off the feeling of deep connection with the Viking in her hands. "Now, tell me, Viking, what is it that you were doing in the water?"

"There is something very precious to me that sunk with the ship. I can see it."

Without thinking, she moved to the water's edge. The Viking was at her shoulder—her heart quickened as she felt his breath on the curve of her neck—and they both looked into the crystal clear depths to the ship that rested peacefully below.

"'Tis stuck in the boards, right there. But I cannot manage it yet." In his pause, they both realized something, but only he voiced it. "You are well versed in the ways of the water; surely you can make it down and back in a single breath."

"Yes, I could..." She couldn't tell him that the act of slipping her clothes off while he watched was something that created feelings in her that she could not identify. "I'll not have a Viking standing here while I do it."

"Naked as the day you were born? Are you shy, Scotswoman? What is it that you are afraid of? Is it that your patient will see the skin of the doctor's arse?"

She tsked at his obstinate nature and corrected his thinking. "Not *afraid*, Viking."

"Ah," he said. Then: "Afraid that I'll fall to my knees in abject wonder?"

Instead of laughing him off, she pulled her sword. The tip of it was sharp, and she had a point to make. "You mistake me, enemy. You have raped and plundered your way through our lands. What I see as mine, you lot see as a market where the goods are free for the taking."

He was solemn and raised his hands in surrender. "It is fair."

Orabilia narrowed her eyes at him and waited. For a sarcastic follow-up. Or the laugh that some men too long at war were too quick to, propelling the person of their ridicule into shame and subjugation. Neither came.

"It is fine, Scotswoman. I will not pressure you more. I have spent some time thinking of you. As foe, I understand. I want friendship from you, but I trust foe from you."

He turned from her and moved back toward the cave, seemingly content to leave the thing he wanted in the sea until he was well enough to retrieve it himself. Orabilia was taken aback by the ease with which he let go of his quest. It made her do something that she would look back on with curiosity. "Oye! Why it is so important to ye?" she called to him.

He stopped where he was, halfway over the rocky beach, and turned back. "I traveled long and hard to acquire it. A sword. It is superior in every way: light yet strong, balanced yet brutal. It is my power. Without it, I am not Ormr. It is my right hand, and it gives me strength."

"Mm," she said, giving herself a moment to think on it before saying, "If that is the way of it, then I feel I have a solution."

Chapter Twenty-Six

Ormr thought he must have struck his head harder than he'd assumed. He was sitting on a makeshift rock bed in a cave being tied up by the Scotswoman. Being expertly tied up. As he twisted, testing them, he felt the knots tighten. She was not a young maiden with no worldly experience; she was a seasoned woman dabbling in a maiden's fantasy. Her eyes told him that the ocean swam through her veins. It bled into her eyes, making them change like the ocean tides. A mortal goddess, nae Völva herself, as his people called such a powerful witch, had come to him in his time of great need. Once his strength returned, he would show her who she was.

"These are tight, Scotswoman."

She gave him a wicked grin that held a spark of mischief. "Doubting yourself now, Viking?"

"That...I am."

Holding his wrists in her hands, she gave him a sly smirk before a rich, throaty laugh bubbled out of her. The melodious sound filled the cave. Ormr felt as if he'd struck his head again, only this time he was in Valhalla, and the riches that were awaiting there were this woman and her laugh. He would find a way to make her do it again.

She tightened the last rope that bound his hands to his ankles and stood. She patted his hands and said, "Now, then, I will be back." Halfway to the door, she turned back to him. "Roll after me, and I'll push you into the water and watch ye drown."

He scoffed, feeling petulant at being tied.

She read his face and replied with a soft smile. "Oh, yer all right." She walked back to him, and bending low, her hair in its tight plait swinging forward, she put a gentle breath of a kiss to his cheek.

Without a thought, he followed his desire.

She made to leave and found that her dress was caught in his fingers. Wrists bound, he held on tight and watched her face as emotions crossed her features as surely as they did his. She had kissed him, and with the music of her laugh still filling his ears, he wanted another one.

Instead of slapping his hands aside, her gaze kept steady on his. "Oh, you liked that, did ye?"

He didn't want to beg, but... "More."

Dress still caught, she slid in next to him, her blue ocean eyes demanding: "More of what?"

He had punished women who teased him, testing his restraint and desire. They thought that because he chose to bed them, they held sway over him, but at that moment, it didn't feel as if she were keeping herself from him but rather making him state aloud what he wanted, and if he could do that then, she would give him what he'd asked for.

"Kiss me."

"Why?"

"You feel it too." He objected to having to explain himself. Doing so felt too revealing.

"Maybe I need to measure your thoughts against my own. I need to hear it from your lips, my formidable enemy-friend."

"I desire you."

She studied his eyes and mouth as if searching for some part of him that would tell her a different story. Satisfied that his words were not a lie, she gently kissed him. "Yes," she murmured against his lips, her eyes a crystalline blue he'd only seen in small purses of the most precious jewels in the vast cities of Persia. "It is the same," she confirmed. He released her captured dress as she pushed his tied arms up and slipped under them, going astride his lap.

Ormr's chest tightened at her response; he was indeed in Valhalla. First, her laugh sent bells chiming up his spine, but now she was confessing to feeling as he did? He had died. Or he was in a bitter death haze, and she was a wild seal who had discovered his body, and it all was a fever dream. He'd thought she was his Völva, but really, she was really what the Scots called a selkie. It was the only explanation for the feelings that were so new and violent that he felt as if he were drowning while holding her tight in his arms against his chest. Her touch, her weight on his lap, was electrifying. He wasn't at the bow of his ship or in war but in a quiet cave with a woman loving on him. The feeling was the same, only with her, there was also warmth in his groin.

Her warm, soft lips and rounded hips filled something deep inside of him that he hadn't known he was missing. He wanted to eat her, crush her, and breathe her into his lungs until she was of one body with him. His affection was startlingly necessary. And with the bone ache of his desire for this Scotswoman, a peaceful silence rushed in. He had felt no other equivalent except free-falling in deep water. Then, as now, his mind let go.

"What is this that you are doing to me?"

She breathed him. Her nose traced his jaw beneath his beard. Her lips found his. "I was going to ask you the same. What kind of magic have you placed upon me? What is this thing you hold that calls to me, Ormr?"

Hearing his name properly roll off her tongue sent a shiver down his spine; he knew then that this Scotswoman was destined to be his. He cradled her closer and rubbed the apex of her spread thighs over his firm arousal.

Orabilia groaned in pleasure before gripping the hair at his temples to make him stop. "None of that."

Her eyes blazed blue, and within them, he saw the ferocity with which she could love someone and also hate them.

"What is it that makes you command me to stop, Scotswoman? I crave you; you crave me; there is nothing but time before us this day."

She shook her head as if he wouldn't understand and rested her forehead on his shoulder.

"We— *I* have gone too far. What is this that we are doing? My father has promised me to another. I should not have started this. It is impossible."

Ormr felt her soft breasts in the fine linen cloth of her dress pressed against his chest. He longed to undo it all. To slide his hand under her hem and check to see if her body was ready for him, slick and slippery like an ocean stone. But he also held fear. She was talented with her sword, yes, but it was more than promised death that stilled him; if she rejected him because he'd gone too fast, he'd curse himself, and for that, he slowed. Patience, his grandmother had always warned him; it was patience that got the fish, the gold, the power. This time, patience would see to it that he'd get this woman, betrothed or not.

"Break the betrothal. I will give you a life of luxury."

Her smile was soft with joy, but her gaze was tinged with pity. "If only it were that easy."

"It is."

"I am Lady Orabilia, daughter of Chief Laoch of the MacLaoch clan."

Ormr's guts twisted. Of all the women... Of all the powerful, beautiful creatures he'd ever held, why... Why did the one he desired so much have to be that man's daughter? He was no longer in Valhalla. It was real. He was far from death, and she now held the barbed story of life's truths to his heart: torment.

She continued, "I can see in your face that you know who my father is."

"I know of him."

"Then you know this can never happen." She kissed his lips, and it felt like goodbye.

He gripped her tight. "Do you know who *I* am?"

"Ormr."

"Ormr Minorisson, brother of Harald Minorisson, court-appointed *jester* to King Hakkon of Norway. My brother is the mouth, and I am his fist."

"Oh." He felt her pull away at the name of his king. "You are... I must go."

He watched dread cross her features as she swallowed and tried to slip from his arms. He held tight.

"Understand, Orabilia—"

She murmured, "What have I done?"

"I can take you from this place."

"I don't want to leave!" She leveled her fiery gaze onto his. "We have been fools."

"We have."

"The people you have killed in his name..." She breathed firm breath. "I must go *now*."

"Why? You always knew who I was. I am a Viking, woman. And yet, you have come this far. There is no hiding what I am." He gestured to his blond hair, towering body, necklace and cuffs. "And now, I know who you are. What is different about this reality now that we have names?"

"Sunlight has shown starkly on my betrayal, and I cannot have it. I have betrayed my country, my people, by being with you, having the thoughts I've had..."

He nodded. "So have I. You are a fine ransom. Maybe the best I've ever come across. I should tie you up, pull my ship from the depths, and take you home."

She gritted her teeth at his idea.

"But all I can fathom is doing none of it. I want to see you at the prow. I want to see the sail snap in the wind and your onyx hair ride along with it. I want this..." He removed his arms from around her to grasp her hand and held it still while he put his finger to hers.

"What are ye... Oh." Orabilia shivered.

Golden light arced out of his finger and touched hers. *Can you feel the hum within?*

"Yer lips dinnae move."

Because you are a woman who can speak to me on the wind. We are beyond what others see us as. Instead, we are connected because we are the few who are gifted.

"I hear ye. But I... How?"

"You are what my grandmother calls Völva. I see you and will heed your words. But I understand now that you have not been taught the way. Stay, Orabilia, and let our bodies talk while our minds rest."

"I'd rather my mind talk before my body does. Who is your brother to the king? You say jester, and I can hear the sarcasm in your words."

"My brother controls the politicking on our lands, but I command the men. And it is I who command fealty. I have planted the fertile seeds to continue his lineage, and while he reports to the throne, it is *my* command that the people follow."

"If it is politicking that your brother is good at, then it is fortunate that you have him because the only way you can have me is if you play a very fine politicking game."

Ormr was silent for some time, then added as if a minor side note: "My brother understands the power I wield; I have been able to wield it because I need nothing from him. He grows irritable of my command of the people. If I need this from him, he will gladly assist."

Orabilia heard the caveat in his words. "At what cost?"

He grinned with dark delight at her understanding. "A fiery boat journey into Valhalla."

Her thumb brushed over his lips. "Then we will have to be more cunning."

"Cunning, yes, but I have secrets that he wants to have buried. He would be dead if he did not have the king's backing. But he has a mouth that weaves golden thread."

"You would kill your own brother?"

"We are the result of merely the coupling of our mother and father; we have no bond. He has attempted to kill me every year since I did him a service that kept him in power."

"Killed you because you did him a favor?"

"He could not father a child. A flaw that would end his privilege in the court. His wife sought me out, and I provided my services and promised my silence. But she is still indebted to me—a way to keep a piece of power over him."

"You have a child?"

He shrugged. "He looks much like his mother." Ormr warmed at what looked like jealousy in Orabilia's gaze. He put his arms back around her and pulled her in tight. "I have a strong desire to see you round with my child. To watch you birth my first true son into this world."

"It sounds like you have too many already."

He grinned, liking her barbed reply. "None would mean as much to me as the one you would birth. He would be gifted and loved tenderly by you and have your heart of a bear."

"It could be a girl, you know. Are you so war-hungry that you don't see the use of a girl?"

"If she is like you, she will be a queen."

Having her there on his lap and talking of his child in her belly, he followed the urge and rocked her along the thick length of his throbbing manhood. The thought of spilling his seed inside of her and taking his life in a new direction was thrilling. The likes of which he'd not felt before. He'd pursue it, even if it meant certain death.

Her eyes fluttered shut. He could see the pleasure his stimulation was causing, and for the first time in his life, he had the pungent desire to give another human, a woman, more. She was a goddess possessing him.

"Untie me," he whispered over her lips.

Intoxicated, as if she'd been at the ale all day, she nodded and languidly kissed him. Then, she proved she was his match when she bit his lower lip. "Nae," she responded to his request to be untied. She kissed him again.

She slipped out from under his arms and skated backward toward the cave's entrance. Her nipples beneath her bodice were taut with arousal, and her eyes shone with excitement.

"I have a sword to retrieve." Then she disappeared.

Ormr groaned; she was one unforeseen moment after another, and he needed days naked with her before, he fathomed, to get enough of her. Maybe even a lifetime.

He groaned again—outside, she was about to take off all her clothes, and inside, he was tied like an animal headed to the spit.

"You're a wench!" he called after her. He heard her laughter in response.

Ormr inspected his bindings: hands tied and feet tied. Also, the tent of his erection. He had no choice; he had to roll or hop his way out the entrance to watch her and do it quickly. He did not want to miss the moment she unveiled the landscape of her entire body before diving into the water.

He was up and at the entrance in time. Her forest-colored dress was off, and she dropped her ivory-colored undergarments. She took a steady breath, bent, and jumped into the water. With the splash still ringing in his ears, he closed his eyes and remembered every detail: the curve of her hip, the cleft of her buttocks, the hourglass shape of her body. He imagined the curves of her rear would be generous enough for his large hands to grasp, and grasp he would. He desired to see her bend again, only this time his hands would smooth over her soft skin and grip her hips. He'd luxuriate in connecting their bodies and watching the carnal possession he'd have when pressing his manhood into her. He wanted the slip and slither of her aroused sex on him and for her cheek to turn as she looked over her shoulder at him before her mouth gasped in pleasure.

A dark cloud interrupted his heady, love-lust daydream of Orabilia. The slip and pat of wood over flat water sounded before the red-and-white-striped sails of his army's longship sailed into the tiny, deep-water harbor.

His men had come for him. First, he felt joy at their discovery of the obscured inlet; then, he felt panic for Orabilia. His real life—the one he'd been consciously ignoring—and his lucid dream life collided. He cursed under his breath and had the strong desire to roll to the water's edge and kick Orabilia's clothes into the water to keep her safe. But he doubted that help, and then she'd suffer the humiliation of being naked during her capture. Instead, he swallowed down his panic and made his way, squirming, toward the far end of the cove. He was the vision of a captive man waiting for his rescuers. He called to them that they had to hold the ship farther out, lest it be lost in this treacherous rocky cove like his, and send just one man to get him.

In their hurry to cut him loose, retrieve him, and retreat from the enemy's shoreline during the dangerous light of day, her clothes went unseen. Aboard the ship, he was genuinely happy to be rescued, making his fabricated capture story believable.

His men, glad to have outwitted the enemy, sailed with the wind and the northern current away from Scot Land.

Out of the inlet and into open water, Ormr took his place at the back of the longship and righted himself into his present moment. Watching over the ship as they sailed into the calm waters of the late afternoon and set course for home, he let the thoughts of his past days wash over him. He'd left two loves in Scot Land that day, his Ulfberht and a woman he'd never forget.

His grandmother's words came unbidden to him then: *Seek the unobtainable, and you will be blinded by love. She will outlive you and, in your absence, will suffer a fate worse than death. And your spirit, unable to succumb to the call to Valhalla, will roam these lands for eternity.*

He should heed his grandmother's advice. Only he was nothing without the Ulfberht, and that woman... It was several moments before he chanced a glance back. Movement caught his eye. Something pale was crawling up the dark basalt. It got to the top and stood. He squinted, and there, in the distance, was a tall, hourglass figure stabbing a sword into the sky. *Orabilia.*

A smile broke across his face, and his grandmother's warning faded away. He'd be back.

Wait for me, he called to her, hoping their connection was strong even though it was so new.

To his surprise, her voice filled his mind: *I will.*

Chapter Twenty-Seven

"So, you see," I said to Rowan, "it started as an accident. He wasn't supposed to be there. Instead of murdering him, she gave in to her humanity and caregiving instincts and gave him a fighting chance. She made it seem like it was in the hands of the gods, but really, it was her skill set that brought him back to life. He would have croaked right there in that inlet had she not found him."

Rowan had been working all morning like a madman at the kitchen table—as he had done every morning since the whisky business got restarted and even madder so this morning with the Rembrandt missing—filling out distribution tables in his spreadsheet for Glentree Gold. His shirt was his old RAF training shirt, well-worn gray and fitting tighter now over his musculature than it did back then.

I took a big slurp of the coffee I'd poured right after settling Rowan with his. His was heavily laced with milk and sugar for sustenance. Mine was giving me rocket fuel to boost my already jubilant morning. I felt like the battle memory and the trauma of it had been lifted off my shoulders after working with Ethel, writing in the journal, and having my dreams transform into useful stories. It was progress, and while I still had work to do—Ormr was still within me and the land was still inert—progress meant hope, and hope was intoxicating.

"The MacLaoch plaque up in the castle infers she was stolen away. Honestly, the way she took to Ormr—oh, look, I said his name without flinching!—tells me she wasn't happy under the leadership of her father. Her father was the chief, but as we all know, women were popular trading items in those days. Her father seemed to be gaining power and wanted to keep it, so he arranged to have her wed a man with ties to the crown and land. Ethel says Ormr and Orabilia do the humpity, which...they must not have done it a ton because she never got pregnant from him."

"Mmm," Rowan said, thinking of something, looking up from his laptop's spreadsheets. "She would have known what herbs tae take to avoid pregnancy. Any chance he told ye where he got a coffin full of coins?"

"Oh, right! I did ask. But he didn't answer." I thought on it. "I wonder if I need to be clearer in my question or intent. I'm still new to all this."

"Or it might be one of life's mysteries." Rowan refocused on his data and tossed my way, "Although, DNA."

"DNA?"

"DNA test it. Maybe Peabody has an extra kit."

"Ha! Peabody's kits are for the living. The bones in the coffin would need an entirely different setup. What are you thinking?"

Rowan looked at me pointedly. "Yer kind does nothing by half measures, so I'll bet my left nut the bones in there are a matched set to some of your DNA."

"Like..." I didn't like where this was going. "Peabody last year said they never had kids so... He killed a nephew or something as a gift to Laoch, so the Vikings lost power in the outer isles, and Laoch could be all-powerful or something?"

Rowan shook his head. "Nae, more like 'here are things tha' are valuable to me,' like my child who didn't make it..."

I choked on my own breath. "But you made a good point about Lady MacLaoch taking precautions to not get pregnant..." Then added, "We'll check it against your DNA test too, then..."

His eyes opened a bit wider in surprise. "If it's a close enough match?"

"Could Peabody be wrong?"

We held a whole conversation in our gaze. If Ethel was to be believed, a love match between Orabilia and my ancestral granddaddy was fated to never work. But they'd tried, maybe? If we tested the bones in the coffin and they matched us both...

"Shit," Rowan mumbled under his breath.

"But why would he do that?"

"Obvious, isn't it?"

"I've got four hundred theories swirling around right now—please tell me which one you're referring to."

"What better way to tell a man—the man who refuses to let his daughter marry ye—tha' he's already had all the benefits of marriage, a child too, and if it's money you want, I'll give you that too. The wedding would have been an important ceremony, but the meat of uniting the two families was already done."

"What, like, in a way he was saying, 'Give me your daughter; we're doing this anyway, and you're either with us or against us'? That'd mean she spent at a minimum—because their dresses hid a lot back then— the last trimester away from home..."

"Aye."

"We know where your ancestor, Chief Laoch, fell with those two questions."

"Definitely against." Rowan tapped a few keys then thought of something and added. "I can't imagine Lady MacLaoch approving the coffin with coins."

"Right? Maybe she thought he was going to present her father with money. But Ormr couldn't resist the dig at Laoch. The one that said, 'I've already had your daughter—here's the proof. What say you now?'"

"Or, more likely, the coins were separate and Laoch buried them together after beheading Ormr."

"But before that, it's 'load up the ships, boys; there's a murder I'm gonna have.'"

Rowan grinned at me. "Ye sound like you're making a wee history documentary...after spending the afternoon getting pished."

"What are you saying? People don't serve up murder like a menu item?"

Rowan came over to me and put my mug aside on the kitchen counter before setting me up there next to it. My university tee just covered my bum. "Nae. Most just say they're out for revenge, then oopsie-daisy, aye?"

"Back then?"

Rowan nodded, conceding. "Aye, back then, they likely had different societal qualms about murder."

I agreed and then brought up the real issue. "So, she did bone him before it all went horribly wrong."

"Until then, it went right for them," he said, cradling my cheek in his hand and gently kissing my lips. "Wed and sharing a bed every night. We just need to fulfill the fantasy your ancestral grandfather had. I will grow my hair out, stand at the prow of the dragon ship you build, and let the wind rush through it while heavy with your child."

I wrapped my arms around his middle. "Speaking of heavy with child..."

He leaned back quickly. "Are you...?"

"No, no, nothing like that. I was just thinking we might want to talk about it, you and me and a wee one," I said, using his term. I was suddenly shy talking about this very real and life-altering question. "Do I take my IUD out or keep it in?"

"Make a baby...you and I?"

"Maybe not right away, but later? What do you think?"

His mouth opened and shut like a gaping fish.

"Too soon?"

"What? No. I want that. It's as if another one of my blue-sky dreams has found me and it's taken my breath away. I want to be ready, to be a good father."

I gave him a soft kiss. "Of course, no rush."

"Until then, we can practice."

I wrapped my arms around his neck and my legs around his middle, and inhaled his sweet scent into my lungs, "Uh-huh. I love practicing."

"That way when we're ready, we will know what to do."

I smothered my smile against his, and our shared breath held our laughter.

"Let's start right now."

He bent, and with a toss, I was over his shoulder. My laughter bounced off the slate floors of the cottage as he walked with me into our bedroom and tossed me onto the bed. I was still laughing, wiping tears from my eyes as he shucked his pants then shirt.

He stepped between my legs. "Oh aye, there's the hole. Step, one, aye?"

I gathered up my university tee and tossed it, "Yes, step one, locate the hole. Luckily," I said teasing him, "I'm not a virgin—"

"Thank god I dunnae have to make the hole," he said, playing along. "And there he is." Rowan took his firm erection into his hand, the red sweating tip of it protruding from his fist.

"What's next?" I asked, and slipping two fingers down below, I spread my soft lips, giving him a good look and a hint at what I thought should come next.

Rowan's gaze followed my fingers, and his inhale told me he thought she was beautiful, the kind of beauty that squeezes the chest with smoldering desire. He picked up my ankles and drove me deep into the pillows of our wide bed before following me in. His mouth was on my inner thigh, breathing me in, then exhaled the heat of his breath over the apex of my thighs and my tight nest of copper curls. His fingers replaced mine and with a tentative touch, his tongue tasted the pearl hub of my erotic center. Him teasing my clit with the tip of his tongue made me groan and grip the comforter. My knees fell wide, and Rowan slipped three fingers inside, deliciously stretching me to accommodate him. Open like a clam shell to him. Rowan worked my pearl nub with his mouth and tongue, sucking and licking as his fingers thrusted into me. He worked me hard, his hand slipping in the slick warmth of my excitement. My hands found his head and gripped his hair as if I could ride the orgasm that was coming.

As it built through my body, I crooned in pleasure. Rowan stopped and with a last lick had the wherewithal to say, "I thought we were practicing babymaking."

I didn't understand what he was saying, my body thrumming with a near orgasm, and wanted his face, hands, cock, all on and in me at once.

"Get in me, right now."

He crawled up. "Your wish"—he settled over me and notched into my opening—"is my command." Then groaned with his own suppressed need before thrusting in.

His hard thrusts brought my orgasm bursting to life, and it shook me as Rowan lost himself in our tangle of limbs. My arms gripped him to me as his hand grabbed my hip. Braced on an elbow he pounded into me with his engorged, overexcited blood-red cock. It stretched up to my cervix, and his pelvis smacked against my opening like an erotic, rhythmic clap until he was crying out. My name echoed through the room as his abdominals constricted, making him crunch with a groan. He emptied himself within me as his body shone with the outward sign of his sensual efforts.

His head rested against my temple, and we sealed our lovemaking with a kiss.

"Tha gaol agam ort."

"I love you too."

WE SPENT THE NEXT HOUR ENJOYING THE SOFT AFTERGLOW OF OUR connection. I lay on top of him, my head rested on Rowan's chest as my left hand lay in his palm. I tapped our rings, making a slight clinking sound. Warmth lightninged up my arm, startling Rowan's gaze. "That's new."

"Magic," I whispered then kissed him. "Oh, speaking of, at our last meeting, Ethel said that she thinks I'm ready to put the cairn knoll back to rights. It'll take quite a few people to accomplish it in one go. I suggested doing it by myself, and she said it would take a year; I don't have the energy source."

"Mmm," he said and kissed my naked shoulder. "How many people? Tonight, while we have a moment?"

"Yes, and maybe all the battle clanspeople? That many?"

"Aye, that will help with the energy too. They were there for the original doing."

"Exactly." I was impressed with his intuition. "This comes naturally for you, doesn't it?"

"What does?"

"Magic."

"When ye grow up as I have, it's second nature."

"True." I ran my hand through his wild hair, deliciously tousled by our romp. "Eli definitely needs to be there. Hopefully, I can unplug my brother from Charmaine for a bit to come; I think the balance of Minory and MacLaoch will add to the potency of what I want to accomplish."

"Oh aye, Tee will be there; ye know he comes running when ye call."

"I think I need some time to get used to this new part of him that is in love with a woman who tried to exorcise me like I'm some demon. I mean, real recently, as in, less than a month ago. It's fresh."

"I'll keep Charmaine off the list, then?"

"If she's bold enough to touch this metaphysical body again, she can go full in and hold my hand," I said, holding up my free hand.

I heard the smile in Rowan's voice. "She'll likely have sudden business to attend to."

Chapter Twenty-Eight

❧

A few hours later, the light faded into purple gloam as the orange sun set in the west. Even though it was a last-minute invitation, folks turned up, and we stood just inside the forest, where the singed edges of the field touched the undergrowth.

Our head gardener, Reggie, stepped over to me. "Miss, the chief said a wee bit about why ye wanted us all out here again today. I want tae tell ye that even if all this is for naught, if the field doesn't reawaken, I've begun rehabilitating a meadow on the other side of the castle, planting the ones you've said are native to the land here." He turned and pointed to the opposite side of the castle's main entry.

The conversations were buzzing around us, and I was greeting those still arriving, so it took me a beat to register what Reggie had said. I finally turned. "What now?" It was barely visible from where we were standing, but I knew of the place he mentioned—a tender new meadow adjacent to the entry and before the other forest started.

"It's still a wee meadow yet, but it has the potential to have that increased diversity ye've mentioned."

His taking my words to heart about the importance of native species and then taking action made my heart swell with affection.

Tears stung my eyes with joy. It didn't hurt that it'd been a rough few weeks, and this was an act of pure thoughtfulness and beauty.

"Reggie. That's amazing. And even if we bring back this field, this knoll, your efforts over there will matter. A duplication of the plants would ensure—no, it already *has* ensured—that the native species survive."

I threw my arms around the gruff older man.

"Thank you," I mumbled as I hugged him; his fresh cedar and clean, crushed-green-foliage smells enveloped me.

"Och, come now, lass. Yer welcome." He gave my back a pat then gently extricated himself before dabbing his eyes. "Ye know you've been a godsend since you've arrived, aye? The laird is well again, the land has taken on new meaning, and the castle will stay standing and in MacLaoch hands because you've come. You've touched all of us. Brought with ye a new wind and new life that these old stones and tragic history needed. It is bonny right tha' you're ours come home tae roost, and a wee ray of sunshine." He sighed like a proud father and wiped a tear off my cheek with a calloused thumb. "And with the magic in your blessed hands, you'll whisper to the soil and bring it back tae life. I know it." He tapped his fist over his heart. "Right here."

Rowan's warm hand was on my back and skated up to my shoulder, where he squeezed. "He's right. I've told ye what you mean to me. Now you know what you mean to *us*."

Hoo-boy, I thought and choked on the happy, humble, and shy feelings that welled up in me. I found that life had a way of forcing our foot to the accelerator and asking us to never let up, but in this moment, time was standing still. What had been accomplished over the last year was monumental. It was to be savored, relived, retold, believed, and given thanks for. How far we had come. And the people —the lives we touched along the way, the impact of little conversations built brick upon brick to form the spiritual castle that housed us as a community. Five thousand miles from home, and yet, here I was, *home*.

I looked out into the sea of faces here now: Clive, in his tweed. Deloris, her glasses on her chain as if she'd just left the library desk. Marion and Flora, still in their own tweed, in skirt form, but with their wellies on instead of their sensible heels. Eli towered in the back, his wife, Elise, next to him. The MacDonagh brothers smiled softly at the moment, their eyes resting kindly on me. Bernie and Angus had done something similar to this last year. It was they, however, who did the magicking within the storm of putting Lady MacLaoch's curse to rest. Tonight I was hoping for just magic and no ethereal storm.

We were all there except...

"Hold up!" Tee was jogging up the hill with Holly and her father and the Whisky Boys behind them. Out at the Circle Garden, Mickey stood next to Charmaine, keeping their distance as if what we were about to do was catching.

In the forest to my right, up into the oak and pine, I could feel Ethel's presence. And someone stood next to her. I smiled when I realized it was Peabody's silhouette.

Holly was panting as she and Tee caught up to us on the charcoal-colored hill. "Did I miss it? Are you going Viking?"

There was a collective inhale, and Tee said, "Too soon, I gather?"

"Aye, right." She looked around. "And what do you expect? You got tae fight by her side while some of us missed it all."

Rowan soothed the crowd. "No Vikings tonight."

I heard Double-A mutter of his daughter, "Such a high-spirited lass, dunno where she gets it from." Then a collective snicker from the Whisky Boys. They knew exactly whom she'd inherited her pizzaz from.

To me, Holly smiled. "You ready for this?"

I blew out a breath I hadn't realized I'd been holding. "I've maybe just come to the realization: I think I am."

There on the cairn knoll, we linked hands—Tee held my right as Rowan held my left. Clanspeople grasped hands and listened as I explained that we would walk down over the field and then walk back. A rope of people sweeping over the land. My hope was that my bottled surplus Ormr energy would unite us, and in our footsteps, we would return what had been taken from the field. And settle the thing, the place and time, that had gotten broken.

I took a deep breath, and with my husband and my brother beside me, different families, different continents, all home, I took the first step.

Then another. I thought of the soil and the life it held, as Ethel had taught me. When it didn't seem to be working, I paused. I took a deep breath, closed my eyes, and quieted my mind.

In the quiet, in the deep recesses of my brain, a tiny sparkling raindrop of calm light wavered, a beacon for me. I took another deep breath, holding curiosity in my hands, and mentally reached for that calmness. When I touched it, a melodic wind blew through me.

Falling into the breeze, I said to Rowan, *Guide me.*

Aye, I have you, mo ghràdh.

I took a step, and Tee followed, anchoring my other side. The quiet, melodious breeze continued to pull me into a place I saw in my mind's eye: It was warm and sunny. The haze of that summer moment sent motes of fluffy dandelion seeds into the air over the lush green meadow. Tiny dots of insects danced and fluttered in the cornflower-blue skies. I could feel that calm breeze move through my chest and swirl around my heart, and like grief's tears, it bled off my overburdened soul and into my hands.

In the distance, I heard the intake of astonished breath. The breeze moved off and out into the distance. I understood somewhere in my consciousness that the clanspeople and I—through our linked hands—were putting my experience and *their* experience of that cairn knoll back into the soil.

I floated in the melody for some time, my feet moving as if of their own accord as my mind danced on the summer breeze. Eventually, the night air cooled my skin, and foliage softened the crunch of charcoal under my boots until my boots swished through meadow plants, clover, grass, and yarrow.

Finally, I opened my eyes. The music had faded into the distance, and now I was left with the peaceful aftermath. Standing at the top of the meadow looking down over the cairns and out to the darkened sea beyond, I stopped.

There was the chirp of crickets and other night bugs then the chatter of the forest birds before they bedded down for a long night's sleep. I could feel Rowan's gaze on the side of my face, and turning to him, I saw there was a blue glow that hummed off him and, as I looked around, all the MacLaoch blood who'd fought on the cairn knoll shimmered in blue while my own skin was golden, and threads of it wove around my arms and over Tee. Eli in the distance, touched by Ethel's power in battle, glowed along with us. Ormr's gift was shared and returned to the soil.

Well done, child came Ethel's voice. *What has been done has been undone.*

As night bloomed, white trailing vines glowed in the half-moon light. The field was returned. As we unlinked, voices murmured, and we all took in the foliage and new smells. We'd performed a miracle.

Rowan turned to me and putting a warm hand to my cheek said, "Bonny well, lass. Mo chridhe, look at what you've accomplished." His eyes stayed on mine, and their depths held admiration and awe. "Bonny well," he reiterated before sealing it with a kiss.

My heart felt light. I hugged him and squeezed with the fervor of joy and delight at accomplishing something so incredible, so unbelievable, that I could practically hear Peabody take his spectacles off and whisper, *Incredible*.

In Rowan's arms, I rested my cheek on his chest and admired the field, the laughter from our clanspeople at the miracle they'd helped perform, the magic that swam through our veins and restored the soil. A season's worth of growth happened as though in a timelapse video, in an instant.

Tears streamed down Reggie's cheeks as he came over. "Ye've done it, lass."

"We did. I couldn't have done this without you. Without any of you." I slipped from Rowan's embrace to give Reggie a hug. Like a magnet to iron, my brother came in behind and added his hug to us. Then Holly and Rowan were at my side, and soon there were arms and gentle squeezes as we all celebrated, giddy like season ticket holders to an underdog team that made it to the Super Bowl and won.

Rowan cleared his throat and said, "Let us mark this day. To the quiet goodbye of the MacLaoch curse and the resurrection of our native miracle."

"Aye, I'd toast tae that." The crowd murmured their agreement.

The MacDonaghs chimed in. "It's good we brought some mead we've been abrewin', then, ain't it?"

Rowan smiled. "It's as if ye knew this would happen."

Angus answered, "Who, us?"

"While we crack the MacDonagh mead that will surely blind us all—"

Bernie called back, "Aye, but you'll be happy before it does!"

"—I'll add to the moment with the first of Glentree Gold. Double-A, you've brought some, aye?"

"Aye, and it's a good one."

"Hear, hear!" came from the crowd.

With many hands to help, cups and the food meant for tea the next day were brought out and tartans were spread on the new meadow ready and sturdy to receive us and our evening festivities.

Ethel with Peabody ambled down and shared in the frivolity. Ethel settled in by my side as Eli and Tee stayed close too.

Her gentle hand rested on my shoulder as her warm milk chocolate gaze settled onto mine.

"Granddaughter," she said, and then her gaze touched Eli and Tee. "My grandchildren." She indulged in a long, comforting look before her gaze returned to me. "You have his powers, his ability to wield magic—you are a woman born into it. Unlike him, you have the kindness and wonder a woman of science has for the world around her. Your life here will be full and meaningful, satisfying and complete."

For the first time, I gathered Ethel up into a hug. Her shawl was buttery soft, and her body's cuddliness reminded me of my late grandmother. As her arms returned the embrace, I felt it again: I was *home*.

A song broke out at the edge of the group. A fiddle and skin drum had been found, and they struck a lively tempo. I released Ethel. "Thank you."

Ethel patted my arm. "It is what we do. Mothers follow their instincts. You are my child reborn. I cannot do anything but love you and help when you are in need."

Tee tucked in on the other side and slung his arm over my shoulder. "Feels like home, right?"

So he could feel it too. "Yeah" was all I could manage as I smiled so hard my cheeks hurt.

"Like we've been out cruising the world not knowing this was right here waiting."

Holly, carrying a multitude of sloshing glasses, said, "Here," and started passing them out. "Some's Da's whisky, some's mead, ye get what ye get."

I inhaled the perfume off my cup and knew I held Glentree Gold. I smiled at Rowan.

"Uncle's whisky that the Whisky Boys saved."

Holly stepped aside, and behind her were visible the faces of the clanspeople again. The song died out in anticipation of me saying a few words in a toast.

I stood with Ethel and Tee. "Thank you, all, for coming out tonight." I smiled at each face, letting my gaze touch them with the gratitude I felt. "What we accomplished here, I think I'll only start to understand twenty years from now, if ever. Some things, I suppose"—I looked at Rowan—"are just *magic*."

He gave me a knowing smile at my use of the word *magic*. I finally could say it out loud. I finally believed it.

"Destiny took my hand and brought me here. It knew this was where my future lay. I've returned to the place that once held so much meaning and purpose for my ancestor. I'm glad I've come, I'm glad you're here, and I'm especially glad to now call you kin, of blood and spirit." I didn't know what possessed me, but I held my hand up and rubbed my fingers together as if dusting glitter from the tips, and out from them, fueled by spirit and love, flowed glowing sparks. The fluttering golden light floated up and settled over the clan like bioluminescent fireflies.

"Whoa" came from Tee, looking at the lights.

I raised my cup, and the rest followed.

"Slàinte mhath!" came from the back, and it rippled through the crowd.

"Silante," I whispered before tossing back the Glentree Gold. The whisky heat stung then puffed into warm vanilla tones with smoke and sea spray.

"Mm," I said.

Tee agreed. "That's some damn good whisky."

Rowan, next to me, hissed, "Oye, fuck me." He looked at his cup. "I've got Mac Mead." He coughed. "That *is* going to make me go blind." Then hollered to the MacDonagh brothers, "Oye! Mac!" He lifted his cup. "Good fucking shite!"

Bernie lifted the earthen jug high with a glowing smile. "Aye, it's good for two things: degreasing engines and making everyone around ye pretty."

Angus guffawed, looking hard at his brother. "Not everyone."

Rowan grinned. "I'll take another."

Chapter Twenty-Nine

The next morning, Rowan and I lingered in bed. The cool morning fog dampened the sun in a gauzy haze. I rolled over, feeling heavy in the head and cotton in my mouth.

Rowan put his hand to his forehead. "Mac Mead," he groaned.

I tucked my pillow under my cheek and smiled at his rough side profile. We'd all gotten good and sauced then stumbled home or into the castle. The cottage sitting room had Holly on one couch and Tee on the other, and the castle held the rest. I was sure after a shower and a coffee, when I went up the knoll, I would find more bodies snuggled into the new grass. The frivolities had been music-filled, drink-sloshing euphoria that was starting to be common with Rowan and me.

"How many cups of mead?"

"Too many." He squinted at me. "Is my head still attached?"

"It is."

"Feels like it's been knocked off my shoulders."

"Nope, it's still there. Where do you think the MacDonagh brothers learned to make it?"

"Hell."

I snickered. How did something that started as honey end up as Scottish moonshine?

"I'll make us all a greasy breakfast; then we'll go see what we did last night.

"Och, sounds good. May I have two ibuprofen with my breakfast? Nae, make it four."

I kissed his cheek and slipped out of bed, feeling light in my heart and soul. "You betcha."

Our small dining table was crowded with four of us around it. Plates were piled with eggs and bacon and biscuits thick with butter and jam. Cups of coffee and tea jostled for space. We were all slowly coming alive. Rowan's ibuprofen had kicked in, and he was looking almost perky.

"Is it like this every time y'all get together?" Tee asked, downing his second cup of coffee.

Holly and I answered in unison.

"Yes."

Rowan's phone interrupted the conversation. The caller ID said: Casswell Agent; he answered it on speaker.

Charmaine sounded like she was driving. "It's come to my attention that today the constable will be doing a walk-through of the Otey house. There are several eyewitnesses outside your clan who have verified that it is indeed at the home despite the bank's agents having gone through it and not seen it above the mantle as it was originally reported. I have to file verification of artwork ownership papers with the constable's office—they're woefully behind the modern age of email and need my signature inked in person. I'll be filing those this morning in Laoch County. Meanwhile I'll need you to be available to meet the constable in person. I will try to be with you, but I'm unsure how long the filing will take—it's often I get there and not only have I been given the wrong forms but two more are needed. Please be ready when I call again."

The table was a bustle of activity. Chairs were pushed back, dishes were rushed to the sink, the last of the coffee was drunk, and tea was put down the hatch.

Charmaine continued after a pause, sounding almost vulnerable. "Is... Is Tiberius with you, by any chance?"

Tee, a biscuit shoved in his mouth, was at his phone that was charging by the window.

Charmaine said, "Oh, he's calling in. Goodbye."

She was gone, and I heard Tee as he headed out the door, slipping on his jacket: "Hey baby, you coming to get me? Yeah, I crashed on Pipsqueak's couch after the party. I know, I missed you too."

Holly was tugging on her boots. "Meet you up at the castle in ten!" Then the door slammed shut.

"Wow, that was…" I trailed off, seeing I was alone. I turned back around as Rowan came rushing out from the back room of the cottage, pulling on a thick wool sweater.

"Love you, bye" and gave me a drive-by kiss before he too left the cottage. The door closed with a decisive click.

To the empty house, I answered, "Bye, guys!"

We were at the back of Rowan's ancient boxy all-terrain Mercedes that looked like it had been a service vehicle in WWII. The rear hatch was open as he loaded the items Charmaine texted he'd need to transport the Rembrandt home. I'd taken the short walk to inspect the wild field we'd brought back to life and beamed with pride at each blade of grass, clover, and herby shrub that grew. Now, at Rowan's vehicle, the buzz of retrieving the Rembrandt was palatable.

Charmaine called again, and Rowan paused to hold the phone while on speaker and was looking impatient at her nasal instructions.

"As I mentioned in my text, it is vital that the painting is carefully handled. Hopefully I'll be there and you won't have to do any of this, but it does mean you'll need gloves and properly prep it for transport with a witnessed transfer to your vehicle. Again, the detailed instructions are in our text thread. Violate any of these steps, Chief MacLaoch, and it will void the insurance policy on that piece of art. Understood?"

He replied with an impatient "Aye, is tha' it?"

"I cannot impress upon you the importance of this; without the insurance backing of the item, it could become worthless."

I made a face at her use of the word.

Rowan matched me. We were solidly just barely tolerating the woman.

"Aye, got it, fuck up the *priceless family heirloom*, and we're fucked."

"That's not exactly what I—"

I could hear TJ in the background of her call coach her: "Say yes. They understand the importance and your instructions." Charmaine into the phone said, "Yes."

"Goodbye." Rowan jabbed his thumb into the screen severing the call before pocketing his phone.

I put a gentle hand on his shoulder to get his attention, and to give him some of my calm. "Remember," I said to him as he loaded a metal munitions box into the back that he swore on his father's life was "just some tools." "You'll politely ask to go inside. He'll say no. And Rowan, that's fine. The constable will go in next. They'll confirm it's there, and then you can go in and remove it, handling it in the way Charmaine says it should be handled. But honestly, I doubt the constable will let you enter his home. Let him retrieve it. That is also fine." Rowan had his pilot gaze on, one where he was so focused on his task that nuance was lost to him.

"Aye," he said absently as he rearranged moving blankets.

I had a feeling he'd not heard a word I said.

I switched grips to his wrist and gently turned him to face me and got even more pointed. "No breaking and entering."

He put his hand over mine and said quietly, "I want tae promise ye that." His gaze held rage and determination. The kind that was useful, even necessary, two hundred years ago, to keep the land that his clan had settled a thousand years prior. This had the feeling of an old-timey feud that required guts and cunning, but it was the twenty-first century, and while the stakes were certainly high—the loss of the castle and jobs for many—this was not a physical battle. Or shouldn't be.

"Fine," I said, letting my resignation sound in my voice. "Where do I send Clive and Charmaine if you're arrested?"

He grinned then. It was a smile that was laced with what I could only assume was "I'm gonna fuck shit up and have a grand ol' time while I'm at it."

"I'll drop a pin."

"Don't forget to *before* you're handcuffed."

Holly arrived then with a surprise passenger. Only it was a surprise just to me. Rowan seemed to know he was coming. Mickey got out of Holly's car. He grabbed a duffel bag out of the trunk and came around to the rear of Rowan's vehicle.

"For the record, I don't approve o' this."

"That makes two of us," I responded.

To Rowan, he added, "But if it makes us even, I'm in."

"Says who?" I asked.

His gaze went Holly, who had made her way to us, then back to Rowan. "She says it does."

Holly was pocketing her car keys when Rowan asked her, "Ye said that?"

"Let me come?" she said in response, but it sounded more like a rebuttal to a conversation they'd had prior and she already knew Rowan's answer.

"Nae."

"Aye, then." She threw her thumb at Mickey.

Rowan was silent while assessing Mickey, trying to figure out if he could toss him out of the car on the way to the Otey place.

"When this is over, I'll decide whether or not we're even."

When Mickey looked to object, Holly whispered, "Take it."

Mickey ground his rear molars as if he were grinding his free will into submission. "Fine."

Rowan pointed his chin toward the front. "In, then."

I reminded Rowan, "Everyone is on alert. Charmaine will have the paperwork for all the legal fancy footwork she wants. She'll get it. He can't have hid it just anywhere. It's four feet tall, for crying out loud. Just remember to get back into your rig and come back here. No funny business."

Holly held her cell in her fingers and gave it a short wag. "I got my eyes and ears out there. We'll find it, Chief. And if he wants to go missing again, we'll find *him*."

I didn't like the sound of the last part.

He held his hand up to her, and she clasped it before they gave each other a one-armed hug.

"You're a good lass."

She tucked her phone away and said, "Aye, I'd do better for you in tha' front seat."

"And your dad and mum would hang me from the old oak tree in town square if I did. Not tae mention that the castle is unguarded without ye."

He gave her a wink as I said, "Hey. I'm still here, along with Clive, Peabody, Marion, and Flora. I have data due to the Fund to submit, but I'm still here."

Rowan gave me a funny smile and dragged his thumb along my jaw before giving my lips a kiss. "I know."

I didn't know how to interpret that, but Holly slung her arm over my shoulders. "I'll protect your bride, my liege."

He gave her a knowing smile and stepped back, closing the rear hatch. "I know ye, Holly—careful what ye wish for."

Holly gave him a wicked grin; they were having another conversation that sounded like one they'd had before. Like siblings who were able to pick up and put down conversations even if they were hours, days, or years apart.

"I know *exactly* what I'm wishing for." Then she turned her face into mine; she was close enough I could see the ebony freckles on her brown cheeks. "Come on, let's get hammered."

"It's barely half past noon. And I did that yesterday."

"Yer point is?"

AFTER INSPECTING THE FIELD AND PUTTING THE FINISHING TOUCHES on the report to the Fund, Holly and I retired to the cottage. I crouched by the wood stove, adding kindling before striking a match to get the whole pile started. Holly was getting something from the boot of her car. The fire gave a pop and then caught the rest of the dried wood with crackling snaps. I was closing the door to the wood stove when Holly fumbled with the cottage door and fell in, a box in her arms. It had golden lettering across the side: Glentree Gold Whisky Co.

We gave each other a grin. The bottles tinkled as Holly jostled the box, keeping upright as she kicked the door shut.

"The ones last night didn't have labels on them."

"Aye, that was the tasting whisky Rowan had with my da and the gents. This is the official first bottling. The rest are in boxes and are set for distribution. Exciting, aye?"

"The unlabeled stuff was good." I picked up the bottle and admired the emerald label with embossed gold lettering.

"This is the aged set. Last night was the young five-year. Here I have twelve and twenty-five."

"Twenty-five, how is that possible?"

Holly waggled her eyebrows at me. "It's the whisky from the raid. Care for a taste test of the best, and once considered bootleg, whisky in Glentree and maybe even all of Scotland?"

I grinned. "That sounds like an outlandish claim, and one, frankly, I won't believe unless I witness it myself. And by witness, I mean, taste."

"Aye, best we do our own research."

I raided the kitchen cupboard and pulled down two proper glasses. Rowan was casual enough to drink whisky from ceramic cup, quaich, or even a mug, but when he wanted to sit by the fire and look out the large living room window as a squall moved onshore, he enjoyed his amber fire in a crystal whisky tasting glass. Some of them were antiques, some of them were pinched from the castle gift shop and were etched with the clan crest and MacLaoch motto: Bellator ad mortem. A warrior unto death.

Holly ceremoniously opened the bottle. The corked cap came out with a satisfying pop. She held the bottle and murmured something in Gaelic. As she poured, I asked what she'd said.

"Oh, just a little something my mum taught me. A prayer ye say over an auspicious moment. This is the whisky that my da helped care for since the laird was a wee one, and with the help from his boys, they're ready to go to market. Everything they've worked so hard on made the chief weep. Feels powerful and consequential, aye?"

"Yeah, it really does."

"So, I asked that this moment be protected, observed, and cherished for the life it's giving and the health it's preserving—and that the angels take only their fair share."

"Slàinte."

"Slàinte mhath."

The whisky was mellower than the one last night, but with a honey-bold fire on the back of the palate, warming my blood as I swallowed it down.

"Mm." I smacked my lips in satisfaction. "I'm pretty sure in any other situation, none of us would make enough money to afford a bottle of this.

"It's something, aye?" Holly looked lovingly at the amber legs the whisky left on the crystal.

We settled in on the couch like two old married folks enjoying an afternoon dram, looking over the bottles lined up by year on the coffee table out the window to the ocean beyond.

"It's been a wild few weeks, aye?"

"It has."

"With the Rembrandt coming home, we can finally put it all to bed."

We finished off our little sample, and Holly picked up the bottle and gave it a tiny wag. Another?

I gave a cough as the last sip warmed my stomach. "Let's do it."

Chapter Thirty

They'd been in the gravel drive of the old Otey manor for over an hour. Rowan was listening to Charmaine, to Cole, to everyone: He was being a good boy and waiting for the constable to arrive. Him waltzing in there wouldn't accomplish much, at least not yet. The men the bank had sent days ago had been in, supposedly, and not found it, but reports continued to come in saying that it was there. Something in his gut said Dick was actively hiding and revealing it, over and over, but for what purpose, he didn't know. The old Otey manor was full of nooks and crannies. It'd take a man like him who had lived his life in another centuries-old building to spot where the walls connected a wee bit too far apart and understand that gap between them was worth looking into.

Mickey Gillian was pacing outside the SUV looking like someone who'd smoked his last cigarette at noon and had needed his next one since noon.

The air through the open car window was clean and cool, but the wind, the onshore breeze that was so prevalent at Castle Laoch, was absent at this place. It made Rowan feel like a storm was brewing.

The old Otey manor house had been built with the monies from Robert the Bruce's coffers in the thirteen hundreds. Now the grounds were distantly wooded, but probably back then, the forest had been allowed to creep much closer. Rowan could look over the expansive lawns that led down to a small river inlet that led to a larger loch at the cloudy horizon. The property eventually came to be the Blackhart estate. In the seventeenth century, the Oteys made their fortune in textiles and purchased the nine-thousand-acre estate away from the ailing Blackhart family. In present day, when Old Man Otey, as Rowan affectionately called him, couldn't pay the taxes the British government levied on the estate, he sold it. Now, it was with Murdoch. And now it felt like a piece in the pocket of an anal collector. The stone facade was mint, as if it had recently been bleached and scrubbed clean; the grounds, while beautiful, were stark. Rowan remembered visiting several years before Old Man Otey sold it. He'd needed the retired physician's advice about Uncle Jacky, who'd had cancer.

Back then, roses twisted up the entry and a sculpture sat to the right of the front double doors. The sculpture had seen better days back then, for sure, but it was a prized part of the house. It had been a present from an Italian aristocrat who'd visited before the First World War. He'd returned every summer until his death, each time leaving behind bottles of his favorite wine—something Old Man Otey shared with every guest and did it with pride.

Now, the place was sanitized: The roses were gone, and not even a weed grew in the crevice between the foundation and the gravel parking area. The statue was gone too. And Rowan would bet his left nut the cellar was empty. The place's history was scrubbed clean.

Activity caught Rowan's eye in the rearview mirror. He recognized the forest-green van. It was Double-A and the Whisky Boys. If they were here, that meant their task hadn't gone to plan.

Double-A stepped out, a cigarette hanging from his lips; Rowan met him halfway between the vehicles. The air felt humid and heavy.

"What is it?" Rowan asked.

Double-A nodded toward the house, his eyes on Mickey. "Found 'em." He was talking about the banker.

"Where?"

"He was speeding south. Caught 'em in Fort William."

Rowan squinted his eyes as if trying to figure out that mental puzzle. "South...?"

"My brother-in-law's nephew pulled him over just south of Fort William."

"And?"

"It's not in his boot. Had to let him go."

Rowan turned away then, his blood boiling. "Bloodyfuckingshitpig!"

Double-A agreed with his reaction. "Maybe we should take a look; see if it's still here?" and nodded toward the manor.

Mickey slowly made his way over, having overheard them. "Feels like a trap."

Double-A snapped the cigarette out from between his lips as if he'd been rudely interrupted. "Ye think? Maybe my daughter did ye a favor when she knocked ye about. Got ye thinking clearly, for once."

Mickey's blood drained from his face, and Rowan could only assume it was from the realization that the man was Holly's da and the person who taught Holly how to do the knocking about.

Double-A went to him, popping his cigarette back into the corner of his mouth. "All right, son. No hard feelings. Right, boys?"

The two Whisky Boys creeping about the perimeter gave verbal grunts of agreement.

"Aye," Simon called from the van. "No hard feelings. So, we send him in first?"

There was a low twitter of humor. Double-A had one hand on Mickey's shoulder as the other squeezed Mickey's bicep. "What'd ye think, pretty boy? Wanna go first?"

Mickey was about to reply when Rowan cut in.

"We wait for the constable; there are other things at play we need to heed."

Double-A tsked and let Mickey off with a friendly double-pat to the back. "Off the hook." Mickey's body shook with the force of the pat. Then to Rowan: "All right, Chief. We'll wait." And he promptly went to the house's front windows and put his hands up, shading his eyes to get a good look in.

Rowan felt the thread of control slipping. Double-A and the

Whisky Boys had been with his uncle through his law-dodging days, and as Rowan watched them case the exterior of the building, it was obvious that old habits died hard.

"Double-A. *Uncle*," he called to Holly's dad, with respect. "Nae funny business, aye?" He heard Cole in his words.

Instead of confirming, Double-A asked, "When did ye call for a constable tae come?"

"They were to meet us a half hour ago."

Mickey found his voice again. "At least." Then to Rowan: "Look, I'm not saying I'm an angel—we both know I'd sell me dad for twenty quid—but this isn't good. We need to go."

Rowan didn't want to agree, but he did. It wasn't worth giving Murdoch the satisfaction of besting him in this ludicrous game of retribution. Watching the Whisky Boys, they looked like they would not heed his example of not breaking into the locked manor. They needed to go. If they got nicked for B and E, the whisky business would be over before it started.

Mickey pressed, keeping his voice low, "You know when I say these old chaps know how to canvas, break a window, slip a lock, and leave no trace. But times have changed since they learned to hot-wire a coupe. This place is old; I get it—they think they're in their element. But if your banker, that Murdoch, is as cunning as he might actually be, this is a fucking trap. There's likely monitors on all entrances, and if he's a confident sod to keep it displayed over the fireplace like Holly said it was, it'll be covered in trip wires and sensors that will set off silent alarms."

Rowan slid his dark gaze over to Mickey. "Bank agents came in and found nothing."

"Sure."

"And if it's there with trip wires, that's what you're here for."

Mickey didn't like that blunt response but kept at him. "I know that. But do *they*?"

The thought of the gray hairs being loaded into the back of a police car made him shiver. "They have orders to wait for police—"

Glass shattered.

Rowan's attention snapped to the front of the manor, and beside a broken window, Charlie shrugged as if saying, "I'm not sure how that happened."

Double-A called to him, "Oye! What are ye doing? We've orders."

"Shit," Rowan said under his breath as he called to them, "Get back to your van and go. *Now*."

At the tall, metal-cased window, Charlie put his hand to his ear, his hearing aid tucked behind the shell of his ear. "What's that?"

Mickey raised his brows. "If you didn't hear him, I'm the fucking pope," he yelled back.

Double-A shouted again. "In tha' fucking van!" and pointed, the cigarette between his fingers.

Only Charlie was bent over now, listening at the rectangle that was now missing its glass. "Oh no," he said dryly, "I hear someone calling for help."

"Oh, you do, do ye?"

"Maybe that constable arrived early, the Murdoch tied him up, and we're the only ones who can save him. We have a duty to save an officer of the law."

Mickey murmured, "Clock's started."

Rowan ignored the pressure Mickey was putting on him and pointed at Charlie. "Don't unlock tha' window. Don't ye go through tha' fucking window."

"But I heard—"

Double-A cut in, stomping toward Charlie. "No one believes that crap."

"What? We have a duty to help that person."

Double-A bent over, listening at the window. "And... nothing—"

Just then, the curtains moved, and the window clicked and swung open, pushed from inside. Standing there was Shepherd Rupert in his dark blue windbreaker and lithe form looking confused. "Why'd ye break the window? The back door was wide open."

There was a collective pause, each of the eight men standing still, digesting what it meant that the rear door was wide open.'

Rowan knew then it indeed was a trap. "Get out of the house. *Now*."

"Aye. But the Rembrandt is sitting over the fireplace. Want me tae grab it first?"

Rowan blinked. "It's where?"

"Over the fireplace." He pointed behind him

Rowan felt like he had been hit sideways with a rage missile. "How..." Rowan couldn't think. His elder clansman was in the building. Trespassing. The clan heirloom that had been stolen from the halls of Castle Laoch was mounted like a trophy just beyond the open window.

"Fuck it."

Those words electrified Double-A. He rammed the cigarette back into the corner of his mouth. "Rupert, get out. Charlie, stand watch at the front. Josh, get tae the back."

Rowan added, "Double-A, tell the rest to keep a lookout on the drive; clock is ticking." To Mickey: "How much time do we have?"

"Not enough."

Rowan bit back, "That's not an answer."

"Five minutes at most. I timed it on the way in. That driveway takes a full two minutes—"

Rowan cut him off: "Double-A, wheels up in four." To Mickey: "Ye have ten seconds to get your things and get to the front door."

The old Otey manor was a solid stone-built manor house. Rowan took a beat in the foyer. The grand entry and sitting room immediately beyond were no longer filled with opulently carved wood furniture, heavy velvet curtains, and glass curios packed with knickknacks. The lush houseplants that had softened the corners and crawled along window frames, making the house alive, a true part of its natural surroundings, were gone.

Now, the aesthetic was starkly modern, making the place look twice its size. It held a chill. All the walls were bare and painted dark as midnight; even the ceiling was flat black, making the occupant feel like they would fall up into the void. Glass tables and metal chairs with gray leather seats took up the seating area beyond the foyer.

The ornate mahogany stairs that had swept guests up to the open second-floor hall had been replaced with a metal-and-wire industrial staircase. Rowan could see beyond the open cement treads of the stairs to an elaborate glass and stone dining hall with a table made of...was that concrete?

From the rear of the house, Rupert rushed in with a ladder. The fireplace anchored the main wall in the sitting room. The fireplace had been built to impress, and as far as Rowan could see, it was the only thing about the house that was as Rowan knew it. Its opening stood five feet high with a raw-edge wood mantel that looked to be made from one solid tree trunk. It was the only warmth in the place, save for the Rembrandt that hung above it.

"Take it down," Rowan said, but he didn't have to. Rupert was already on the ladder, Double-A at his hip, while Mickey came in with his bag of goods.

Mickey hollered at the balding Rupert up on the ladder. "Just wait one bleeding moment." To the rest of the men: "Just wait." When Rupert looked at him, Mickey pointed to the ground. "Get down."

Rupert looked to Rowan, and he shrugged in agreement. Rupert did as Mickey asked, and Mickey practically passed him on the rungs, they exchanged places so fast. Rowan noticed Mickey had put on surgical gloves since he had returned from the car. Charmaine would be pleased. He ran a finger around the edge of the ornate frame of the Rembrandt then the pocket it sat in on the wall.

Mickey looked back to the men in the room. "You're not going to believe this..."

Chapter Thirty-One

Rowan looked at the man in the portrait. What would he, his great-great-great-etc.-uncle, think? Being the subject of this strange tug-of-war. The man was in full formal wear, his red tartan expertly wrapped around his hips and tossed over the shoulder of his kilt jacket. He stood with his foot on a low grassy knoll looking out to the loch behind the viewer, with the forest and castle behind him.

Mickey's brow pinched in confusion. "You're not going to believe this..."

"It's wired, isn't it?" Rowan asked, feeling the time slipping away; they needed to go.

"No. It's recessed."

"Aye, so?"

Mickey ran his fingers around the pocket that held the painting. "There're grooves in this. I think there's a sliding door here."

"Like a secret compartment?" Rowan shook his head, understanding. "A laird's lug," he said. "If you're a man about court in Robert the Bruce's time and you needed insider information, ye could get it there. It's a faux vent shaft."

Mickey knocked. "Yes, sounds hollow behind."

"Och, knock off the history lesson—we need to be out!" The last word was a punch-to-the-gut *oot* in Simon's thick Scots.

"Get the things ready in the boot, Simon. Josh, ye go with."

As they left, Mickey lifted the four-foot-tall portrait off the wall, and the heavy weight of the gilded frame tilted back.

"Careful!" The room erupted with calls for caution from the Whisky Boys.

Mickey glowered at the remaining old men who seemed to have little faith in him, and sent the painting down. Rowan stepped in to receive it, and despite Charmaine's request for him to wear gloves, he was glad to feel the warmth of the wood against his naked palms and have the sight of his ancestor back in his hands directly.

"I'll make sure they're ready for ye." Double-A ran out. Mickey was off the ladder, lifting his bag as Rowan repositioned his grip on the painting. Mickey murmured, "I suppose we don't need these things—" Rupert grabbed the ladder, tucking it under his arm.

The room began to ring.

The three men paused.

"What is that...?" Rowan looked around for the source of the phone call, which seemed to be coming in at full surround sound.

The ringing device was answered, and Dick Murdoch's voice filled the room, "Well, well, well, what do we have here?" There was shuffling and panting as if Murdoch had rushed to arrive on speaker.

"Get the f—"

"You appear to be breaking into my home, MacLaoch, and you're not alone. Who else do we have here? Let's see. Ah, yes, Mickey Gillian, son of well-known felon Lou Gillian. And who else..."

Rowan went for the door. Double-A and four of the Whisky Boys were running back, ready to take the Rembrandt from Rowan. Rowan, feeling like the painting was a child who needed rescuing, tossed it, "Catch!" The painting sailed through the air at the startled men. All of them lunged for it as Rowan grabbed the thick wood door, slammed it shut, and threw the bolt.

There was a scuffle, swearing, then, "Oye!" from the other side.

Rowan returned to the sitting room where Mickey and Rupert

were paralyzed, wondering where the disembodied voice was coming from.

"What is it, MacLaoch? Did you just run for your life?" Rowan couldn't see the man, but it sounded like he couldn't see them either, at least not all the time. "Are you trying to run away? It is incredible how naive you MacLaochs are. This day, I have to say, is going swimmingly. You do realize that video evidence is irrefutable," he called out. "Your uncle might have gotten away with his drug activities, but it'll be his nephew who pays the price."

Rowan was about to respond when the crunch on the gravel outside the open window caught his attention. Edging to the far wall, he worked his way to the open window where the Whisky Boys were coming around. Their chatter was peevish and wanting answers that no one had.

"What'd ye say?" Rowan answered the voice in the room.

"Ah, there you are, MacLaoch; I thought you'd run for your life."

Staying by the window, he motioned for Rupert to put the ladder down and for Mickey to join him.

Double-A arrived at the window. "Have ye lost yer bleeding mind?! I nearly dropped it! We're packing it up now. Come on, git out—" He heard the disembodied voice. The cigarette stub fell out of the corner of his mouth to the gravel. "He's in there? What the bloody hell is happening?"

"Nae. He's talking through some device," Rowan whispered back.

At the window, Rowan could hear the wail of a distant siren.

"Get going with the Rembrandt. I'll buy you some time." Charmaine would likely arrange for his dismissal as chief for treating the clan artifact like they were, but they didn't have a choice. "You two, out," he said to Rupert and Mickey.

Mickey and Double-A helped Rupert get his leg over the windowsill; then Double-A pulled him out as Mickey followed with a hop over the sill.

Double-A held his hand out to Rowan. "Out you come, son."

"No, go. Murdoch went too far. I have a mind to find out where he is and share my thoughts with him. I cannae bring ye or the men into this; I've got this."

"Fine, I'll send the boys off. I'll tuck intae the boat out back and wait for ye there."

He held his hand up, and Double-A grasped it. Rowan pulled him into an embrace and, with his temple next to his, said, "I appreciate you, Uncle. Ye'll not wait for me. Take the rear operations road and *go*."

"No—"

He leaned back. "Leaving is an order, from yer chief."

Double-A's lip curled back, hating the directive. "Son—"

Hearing the sirens in the distance, Rowan punctuated his order with "Now." Then closed the window on his old friend.

The disembodied voice of the banker hollered, thinking he'd completely lost his audience.

Double-A walked backward a few steps, waiting for Rowan to change his mind. When he didn't, he pivoted and ran toward the van. Before his bottom could hit the passenger seat, Charlie, behind the wheel, hit the gas. Gravel spewed out from under the front wheels as they tore out of the drive toward the maintenance access road.

Rowan stepped farther into the room, and the tirade stopped.

"Aw, MacLaoch, are you there all alone now?"

Rowan stopped where he was in the center of the room. So, Murdoch could see him, but only middle of the expansive foyer was in his frame of vision.

"Do you think you can save them from jail time? Some of them seemed old—it would be a pity if your actions caused them to spend the rest of their lives in prison. But let's be real: They should have been in prison in '89."

Rowan reminded himself that the Rembrandt was back in MacLoach hands. And that was what mattered.

"Where are ye, Murdoch?"

Laughter filled the room.

"If I remember correctly, *Dick*, my uncle gave yers a black eye the day he came to Castle Laoch to take what wasn't his tae take. Come on out, and we can have a second go-round. What do ye say?"

"You look so mad, MacLaoch."

Looking around, Rowan said, "I'm well beyond mad, ye fuck. Well into cursing ye and everything you hold dear."

"Cursing me? Ooh, what a threat."

Rowan whispered as he searched the shadows, "That's what a man who's not heard of a woman named Lady Orabilia MacLaoch would say." A shiver went down his spine as if he'd accidentally run his finger over an electric wire that was trained on a dragon's tail. Then, louder: "Come, Murdoch, let's do this face-to-face, aye?"

"Why? This is so much more fun."

"I take it ye like to torture caged animals, do ye? How'd you get to work for the bank for as long as you have without a psych eval?"

"Haha, MacLaoch. You're the only animal in a cage I want to watch."

Rowan kept him talking, hoping to catch a clue about where he was. "Why'd ye take it, Dick? Why'd ye steal MacLaoch property? Why break the law and ruin your career?"

There was a long pause, and when Murdoch spoke again, he was seething. "My career isn't over! Your overreaching solicitor thinks she has me, but she's the one who did the stealing; she's headed to prison right alongside you. You think you have bettered me, but you haven't. I have you and your clansmen on record for trespass. You'll go to prison, and while you're in there, I'll take Laoch. The Oteys didn't stand a chance; inheritance tax is mighty formidable." He sounded as if he were the tax collector himself and it was 1805.

"Do you like the remodel?" he goaded. "And once I have Laoch, I'll be able to unite all the ancestral Murdoch lands—"

Rowan hissed, "Murdochs never owned—"

"Ye ignorant bastard!" The speakers crackled as his volume exceeded their capacity. "You have too much land—so much you don't know how every inch was gotten. You're a disgrace. Your eastern forest was Clan Murdoch land. We were hung in the cattle raid, and you got our lands for the cost of the missing cattle. Our men took a few cattle the wealthy MacLaochs would never have missed."

Rowan felt the blackness in him shift into deep worry; Murdoch was unhinged. What broken narcissistic mind held a grudge so penetrating that he'd let it darken his heart and play tricks on his mind so that he'd see to it Rowan went to prison for what his ancestors did three hundred years ago?

Movement at the window caught his eye; Mickey silently pushed it back open and was coming back through.

Rowan heard the banker laugh. "Are you worried, MacLaoch? You look as if you've realized the sirens are for you..."

Mickey slunk against the far wall to the grand opening of the massive fireplace and began pulling things out of the bag he'd brought in with him. He paused and, orienting himself, looked up into the flue. He stretched up slowly, then paused. He sank back down, put a finger to his lips, and pointed up into the chimney. Rowan watched as the younger man connected his phone to what looked like a cigar box with stubby antennae on it before opening a small laptop and connecting them.

"Murdoch," Rowan said, keeping the conversation going. "I'll never forget this. Yer one man—I've a clan standing behind me. Where are the rest of the Murdochs?"

"I'm holding you accountable *on their behalf.*"

"You haven't told them, have ye? Because they'd tell ye to stop, that what you're doing isn't what's done anymore. Get yourself some psychiatric help, plant a nice veggie garden, take up birdwatching, anything to help calm your mind, man."

The Murdoch took a long, deep inhale. He spoke his next words in a tone that sounded as if he were an overstretched balloon being sat on.

"I think I shall. I've grown rather fond of renovating these old homes. They need so much tender care and oversight. But you know what, I've been to Castle Laoch, and I think there's nothing worth renovating there. I'm thinking when I purchase it out of bankruptcy, I'll...*tear it down* and build atop the rubble."

Rowan felt that verbal blow smack him in the chest. He was ready to rip apart the chimney to find the source.

He shouted, "Where are you at, Murdoch?"

Again the man's laugh showered down into the room. Finally, Rowan spotted the black speakers set flush in the dark-painted ceiling between the painted wood beams. Mickey's fingers flew over the keys. He made a rotating motion with his arm, which Rowan interpreted as *Keep him talking.*

"And how exactly do ye plan to take Castle Laoch when you're no longer agent for Scottish Trust Bank?"

"Oh, don't worry about that. I've made enough off these old estates to have a tidy amount set aside to purchase Castle Laoch. Maybe I won't wait for bankruptcy to buy it." He giggled like a man who just watched his last marble roll out of his mind and down the hall. "I'll reveal something to you: I pushed forward the foreclosure status on your account. The bank tried to take me off your loan, but this is destiny—it cannot be stopped. MacLaoch estates, the castle and all its assets are forfeit. Bank owned. It's up for grabs. It's mine now. And I look forward to setting charges to its base..."

Rowan felt as if he had been dunked underwater. Had that been the real reason for the diversion? Those halls were sacred. The feet that trod those hallways were of his kin, and the stones that made up its foundation were placed there by Glentree's ancestors as a beacon for all those who called that spot of Skye home.

His fist opened and clenched in restrained anger.

"What ye've done is not legal, Murdoch. None of it is. And there are people who live in tha' building. Are you so lost tha' you'd add murder to your list of things tae do?"

"If they're there, they're trespassers and will be dealt with as such."

Rowan needed an outlet. He grabbed the back edge of the metal-and-calf-hide couch and, with a grunt, lifted. With a roar, he threw it, and it crashed against a glass bookcase. Books, all with the same blank gray covers, and glass knickknacks went flying.

Mickey gave him a glance as the banker asked, "Did you think I was hidden behind the pillows?"

"I'll destroy this place before ye get me in cuffs, Murdoch. And when they release me like they did my uncle twenty years ago, I'll find ye and rip ye—"

Rowan flipped the matching chair, sending its cushions flying.

"—limb." He tossed an onyx table and matching lamp with a crash. "From limb."

The man tittered. "Ooh, my decorator will be so *mad*."

In the fireplace, Mickey rotated his laptop to show Rowan his monitor. It was an image of Rowan panting in the middle of the space.

The couch was upside down, and the cushions were tossed. The camera was set into the mantel somehow. The rough bark edge of the massive wood shelf hid the tiny lens. Rowan was impressed with how Mickey had hacked into the camera's signal. With a keystroke from Mickey, he was impressed again. The screen shifted and showed the heavy-faced banker leaning forward on his desk, not knowing the camera on the top of his own monitor had gone active, and Rowan was now seeing him in a small office piled with papers, artifacts, and empty soda cans.

Rowan felt his lip lift. "Maybe I'll get to punch yer lights out after all." He walked toward the mantel and looked along it, his fingertips following, doing their own search. And then: There it was. A pinhole lens. It was disguised as a shadow.

"Got ye."

Rowan could see the man's hand tap keys on his keyboard in Mickey's monitor below him.

"Sure, MacLaoch, you found the camera, but you don't have me; I have *you*."

Rowan turned and grabbed the first thing he saw, a solid glass orb that had so far survived. He picked it up and pivoted. The orb flew across the room and struck the mantel with a crack. Bark and glass shattered.

Mickey cursed, throwing up an arm to block his face as pieces rained down. Outside, two police vehicles skidded into the gravel drive, one on each side of the old Mercedes, sirens screaming.

Rowan began picking at the broken mantel. Mickey was snapping his equipment closed and stuffing it into his bag. He stood in a crouch, looking out at the gravel drive, then to Rowan. "How well can you pretend you're a pretentious asshole?"

Rowan, holding the excavated tiny camera in his hand, watched as the officers rushed to the front door. "How pretentious?"

"Like you own all the land from here to Inverness. Including this house, if you catch what I mean."

"OK," Rowan said, feeling the rage still in his veins, giving him the arrogance to have a chance to get out of the trap Murdoch had set. "But what about the video?"

Mickey grinned. "His laptop is actively rebooting. When it does, everything will be written over with FurryFan pics."

Rowan snorted. "How well can ye pretend tae be an IT sod?"

Mickey's grin brightened, and his accent moved from lilting Irish to Southern California. "Why else would you call me, dude?"

Rowan watched Mickey's body language morph too: His shoulders slouched, and his gaze turned bored.

"Yer frightening."

The officers rushed in. "Hands!"

Mickey dropped his bag and put his palms up over his head.

Rowan ignored their command and, with the camera in his fist, put his hands on his hips and dug deep for his best Clive impersonation. "What in God's name is all of this!? Stop right there, or my solicitor will have your heads! Look at my home! Everything is just trash! Look at what they've done!" He indicated the tossed furniture. "The only thing left of substance are these floors! Those are *original* Georgian-era marble floors installed over two hundred years ago, and now you fools will no doubt destroy them with your boot scuffs!"

Mickey whispered under his breath, "And *I'm* frightening?"

Chapter Thirty-Two

The one-room police station was equipped to handle only the lightest of offenses and basic medical care. With the interrogation room doubling as a holding tank, the rural station was mostly a counter for pushing papers. The little bit of public seating involved a few folding chairs around an industrial table laden with pastries and employee morale questionnaires.

It was adjacent to the northernmost tip of MacLaoch land, and while half the staff had no clue who Rowan was by sight alone, those who did stayed mum as he filed a police report on Richard Murdoch for voyeurism. It would hold just long enough for Charmaine to arrive and change the charges to something more hard-hitting or whatever it was that she did in such situations.

Mickey drawled around a huge bite of oatmeal scone, "Can I go now? You guys have all you need, right, man?"

The intake officer tsked at Mickey while her administrative assistant hung on the counter, making eyes with him. Just then the front door to the station opened, and Charmaine breezed in, her black satchel on her arm, her hair pulled back, and her eyes bright. She'd changed clothes and now looked like a very expensive solicitor from some futuristic metropolis. TJ followed, taking in every detail.

Charmaine said to Rowan, "Where is it?"

Rowan dropped his act and said calmly, "Making its way back home now."

"Has it been documented?"

"We have bigger issues at the present moment," he said, nodding at the desk clerk who was at first curious about the newcomers and then began exhibiting impatience as Rowan's accent morphed.

Charmaine was sharp. "No, we don't." To the clerk: "What are you holding him for?"

"Holding him? He's here to file a complaint for voyeurism."

Charmaine looked from the woman to Rowan to Mickey and then back, assessing the situation, and deciding she needed no further information, she said, "Shred that form." Then to Rowan and Mickey: "Get in the car."

"Hey, wait a second—"

"Listen up, I have every judge on speed dial and very little time, so if you think you have reason to pursue any of these men for anything other than a pleasant greeting, I suggest you bury that idea. Because if you don't, I'll—"

"Out." The officer pointed to the door behind them. "Get out. A waste of time this has been. Just be on with you."

"Yes, ma'am," TJ piped up.

The officer scoffed as Mickey gave a 'sup chin nod. As Rowan left, he heard the lovelorn administrative officer ask Mickey, "Are you really from San Diego?"

"Totally."

Rowan heard the wink in Mickey's voice.

She said, "Cool," in a single exhale as the door to the station closed behind them.

TJ drove them out onto the rural road and worked them out of the village and back toward Otey and Rowan's vehicle.

Charmaine turned in her seat. "Explain. Everything."

Rowan did as Mickey looked out the window, feigning boredom.

"How'd you know the camera was in the chimney, Mickey?"

"Where else would he get a good signal in a solid stone building with a slate roof?" He sighed, "That, and I saw the antenna when I got back into the car."

TJ piped up. "Dude. San Diego called; they want their accent back."

Mickey let a small grin slip over his lips. "I travel a lot. Accents come and go."

Rowan remembered then that Mickey had no idea who TJ was, yet it was apparent TJ knew exactly who Mickey was. He watched the exchange with pleasure.

"Jackson," Tee said from the driver's seat.

"It's Mickey."

"No, I was trying to remember what my sis calls folk like you. I just did: Jacksons. Well, she did when we were kids. You see, she's always had a thing about the natural world giving us the tools to understand humanity. There's a reptile called the Jackson chameleon. They change their colors depending on their environment."

"Mmph" came from Mickey, and Rowan almost smiled.

"No worries, *dude*," TJ quipped. "I'm not some chameleon-eating raven. But you should stay away from my sis—she punches guys like you in the dick."

"She sounds fun," Mickey said, back to his natural acerbic tone.

Rowan smirked. "Mickey," he said, waiting for the man to meet his gaze, "that's TJ." Mickey shrugged. "My brother-in-law."

They held gazes for the length of time it took for Mickey to connect the dots.

"Huh," Mickey said, but he seemed to shift uncomfortably.

Rowan met TJ's gaze in the rearview mirror.

"Yeah," TJ said, taking his eyes off the mirror and putting them back on the road, "I'll be sure to let my sis know you were a big help so when that Viking I've heard so much about comes back, she won't rip your nut sack clean off." He sighed like it was hard having a sister who was so violent. "Like grapes off a vine." He made the hand gesture of a man pulling fruit from its stem.

Rowan smiled for the first time in a few hours. He was beginning to feel brotherly love for TJ—he was a solid man to have in his corner.

"Come now," Charmaine said, wanting them to get back on track, "what else did he say?"

The county pastures whizzed by. Rowan finished his story with the worst of it: "He said that he's acquired Castle Laoch. Somehow, he's pushed it, I'm assuming fraudulently, into foreclosure status. He plans tae level it. Ye might think it a farce, but I'll tell ye, it felt real."

Now that Charmaine was with TJ, Rowan and she were finally back to being civil, and it was nice to remove someone from his battle list.

"That's a crime."

"Aye, and would lead me to commit one in retaliation."

"Even if it were empty and in some psychotropic fantasy he indeed held ownership of the castle, leveling it is an *actual* crime: Castle Laoch is a historical landmark and cannot be altered without Historic Council approval. That's why we do alterations to the building and lands through the Fund. If he did do that, he'd go to prison and likely lose the property in the process. Not to mention that amending a loan he no longer has access to into default so that he may buy it out of foreclosure? That is another surefire way to spend time in our prison system."

They went silent as they reached the Otey property's long driveway, each thinking about whether a man who booby-trapped his own home to capture Rowan on camera would demolish a historic building out of spite. And if he was the kind of man who would wait for the law to tell him it was his first or he would rush the timeline to get what he wanted.

For Rowan, he wondered if he could find the blasted man in time. He'd gone from worried about losing Castle Laoch in bankruptcy to worried a madman would attempt to level it.

He sighed, letting his head fall back against the headrest, and in his quiet, he felt that his fingers had gone numb. He looked down at them and tapped them together. The tap felt icy. Moving them one way and then the other, he saw his fingertips were turning blue. The blue felt electric, and a soft light glowed out of them. His heart skipped in anxiety as he recognized the glow before the spirit of Cole, possessed with Ormr, breathed through him.

They arrived at the Otey manor, and TJ pulled next to Rowan's vintage SUV. As he parked, he said to Charmaine, "Hold on, my pocket is blowing up."

In the back seat, Rowan blew out a breath as if preparing to dive underwater. The blue was moving up his arms, and he felt as if he was being squeezed.

"Ho-fuck," Mickey said at Rowan and scratched frantically at the door handle. He caught it, kicked the door open, and leaped out of the back seat.

"What's up with him?" TJ pulled his phone out and turned around. His brown eyes went wide. "Holy shhh…"

Rowan swallowed down panic and, forcing himself to talk, said, "Check your phone."

TJ, mouth agape, did. His eyes stayed on Rowan until he had the app open, then read quickly.

Charmaine turned to look into the back seat to see what the fuss was and covered her scream with her hand.

TJ, reading off the texts, said, "Holly says we need to get back. Cole's gone Viking."

Rowan gripped the door handle and tried to pull it but couldn't. Charmaine ejected herself out of the car as TJ sprinted around to Rowan's door and yanked it open. He caught Rowan's upper arms as he slid out.

As soon as TJ touched him, energy flooded into TJ's body. His head snapped back. "Ugh," he groaned and went to his knees.

Rowan felt the instant relief of TJ taking the power from Cole. "I didn't think this could happen off MacLaoch property."

TJ was now catching his breath as Rowan hung half out of the rear of the coupe. "What the fucking hell was that?"

"Well, shit." Rowan swallowed. "You *are* her brother." Rowan gave him a wan smile, thankful for the relief that his brother-in-law was enough Minory and enough magic-tied to him that he could hold Ormr's power and siphon off his opposite, Orabilia. TJ's tan seemed more golden—as if the sun had come out and shone only on him.

Mickey was wary as he came around the coupe's rear.

Rowan explained, "Cole needs me."

TJ was recovering on his knees. "Shit, that was a rush. Is that what Pipsqueak had going through her when she was ancestral Grandpa?"

"Aye." Rowan noted TJ was taking all this very well.

"No wonder she's got the slug of an MMA fighter."

"Later, we'll talk about how calm ye are about all this. But, aye, when she pulls, I give... This is stronger than she's been since working with Ethel. And it means she could be lost to him. Like before." Rowan shivered, remembering the battle on the cairn knoll, her power uncontrolled and ruthless.

TJ took that information too and calmly asked, "Need me to drive?"

"Um" came from Mickey. "Holly's da just texted. They got to the castle, and there were men there, trucks piled with furniture and boxes of clan antiques. Her da left to get reinforcements. Some of the men are armed."

"What?" Charmaine exclaimed. "Oh no, no, no." This didn't seem like news to her. "He-he wouldn't have. He couldn't. That's, but it's *vandalism.*"

Three sets of eyes landed on her.

She explained, "Richard Murdoch said he had a surprise planned. Today, *now*, is the surprise. It has to be. I thought it was over. The ransacking he dreamed of doing, was referring to, was a crude description of taking the Rembrandt."

Mickey clarified, "It's not. Is he a war-reenactment nut?"

"I've no clue, but Chief MacLaoch, I'm afraid now. Those explosion threats might not be a bluff. The constable should be notified, and *they* should bring reinforcements, not Holly's father. I don't believe the man he's solicited for this work is above hurting people."

Mickey said, "He'll shoot his own son if he deems it worthy."

All eyes were on Mickey.

Knowing that Lou Gillian, who took the Rembrandt off Charmaine, likened himself to a gangster and fixer, Rowan asked, "And I take it you have the bullet hole to prove it?"

Mickey gave a wan smile, and Rowan thought he saw the true Mickey Gillian surface for a moment before he smothered it back down. "O'aye."

TJ stood and was dusting off his knees when Rowan got out. "Get in the front," Rowan said to TJ.

Mickey tossed Rowan a cell phone. Rowan caught it. "Thanks, but I don't need yer phone." Rowan did a double take. "Wait. This is mine."

"I needed it for the trace."

"Fine. Do you need the keys to my rig, or do you have those too?"

Mickey pulled the keys from his pocket. "All set."

Rowan slid into the driver's seat as TJ kissed Charmaine when she refused to go with them.

TJ climbed in as Rowan let off the clutch, and gravel pinged the undercarriage as they launched out of the driveway.

TJ fastened his seat belt as the scenery blew by; Rowan shifted, giving them more speed.

"Good" came from TJ. "I like to play it cool with others, but I'm glad we're on the same page about hustling to the castle."

"Is tha' why you were so calm back there?"

"Ye-up. Pretty sure I shit my pants when you shocked me. I'll take care of it later. I have a feeling it won't be the last time I shit my pants this day."

"If Cole is Ormr, I guarantee it won't be."

As they blew out the drive and blasted down the country road, TJ added, "And I'm mighty glad you're a trained fighter pilot. I'm definitely not screaming in my mind as you take this next turn"—his hand went to the roof to brace himself as Rowan engine-braked through the wide turn, then shifted up, flying them out the backside—"at eighty."

Chapter Thirty-Three

Peabody had spent most of the day with the lovely woman from Misty Cliffs, Ethel, and now was using the evening to measure the castle's rooms. The light from his headlamp bobbed along the walls of the old servants' quarters, which had never been electrified, as he moved around boxes and gently set dusty antiques into other boxes. The meter was gently ticking, a low, happy sound of lives that had once taken up residence there. Occasionally Peabody's thoughts drifted. Cole was still a phenomenon, and now her brother deepened the complexity of the curse's powers and the timing of when it had become active in Rowan's generation. He wished that he'd been at the castle a few days before and witnessed the rebirth of Orabilia and the appearance of her one true love, Ormr. All had said that seeing Cole as Ormr had been frightening. The MacLaoch solicitor had described it with disgust and fear, calling Cole a snake molting. Peabody had advised her to seek out counseling with a good therapist. So, there in his happy place, thinking and measuring, Peobody was startled when he heard noises from lower in the castle.

Making his way down to the second floor, he distinctly heard whispers, then a crash. Without the buzz and hum of daily life—Marion and Flora had been the last to leave, after letting him know that there were extra sandwiches from the tea service in the main dining hall for him—sound traveled farther in that ancient stone castle.

At the crack of plexiglass, the meter outputs in his handheld device shifted, clicking with a kind of urgency that he'd not seen before. Curious, he continued to investigate, plunging on down to the artifacts hall, hoping to get a moment with Cole.

It was not Cole. Three men were ransacking the room.

The sturdy plastic storage boxes had been yanked from under the display tables and were now open on the tables around the room's perimeter. Their protective stuffing had been removed, and instead of holding just a few delicate, precious artifacts each, they were now packed up to their brims. Two of the men were older—Peabody's age— and the third was younger and had a pistol tucked into the back of his jeans waistband.

The younger man, whose blond hair was pulled back into a pony- tail, was reaching into the broken case of the Ulfberht. Peabody felt his body react to the sight of the man's hand preparing to grab the handle of the ancient Viking sword that belonged to Ormr. He'd only heard tales of it, but he still pictured Cole holding it above her head. Lightning had rained down over the field she had been studying just days before she "became" her ancient grandfather, the field that was also the final resting place of her ancient grandfather's men. Rowan had shared with Peabody that the only thing the Viking loved more than his one true love, Orabilia, was the Ulfberht sword. Little wonder: The sword, as Peabody knew, had been forged in fire in Persia, or present-day Iran. He would have had to travel the long and treach- erous Volga Corridor of the Silk Road, a route that connected the Baltic and Caspian Seas. And retraced his steps back home. Then to have it be a superior blade in combat? Well, Peabody could understand that Ormr believed the sword made him into the dominating force he'd become in his lifetime. And now, someone other than his grand- daughter was about to grasp it.

Peabody held his breath as the younger man, hand within the case, wrapped his fingers around the hilt. In Peabody's arms, his equipment shifted and began a low ticking, a second hand counting, Peabody hoped, something other than what was left of their lives. The pulse was in the frequency he'd recorded previously. They were Cole's metaphysical energy readings. Peabody was suddenly more curious than afraid. Was that young man Cole's relation?

He looked up to find all three men staring at him and his ticking device.

"Oh, hello."

The young man pulled the sword out and gripped it with two hands, making the meter's notation hiccup as if energy were coughing into the pulse.

The shorter of the older men, with a deeply etched face and who looked like he drank hard, smoked cigarettes from sunup to sundown, and punched before he asked questions, said, "The fuck you?"

Peabody answered calmly as the ticking increased. "Who am I? I'm Dr. Edwin Peabody; I'm here researching the MacLaoch curse."

The other older one, tall, lean, and who also seemed to smoke more than eat, told him to "Get the fuck—"

Peabody interrupted, "Young man with the sword, are you by chance a Minory?"

Taking note of his elder comrades' demeanors, the young man mimicked their ready-fight attitudes: "What the fuck is a Minory?"

"Hmm." Peabody looked down at the meter; it was clicking faster. He was trying to figure out what it meant if the young man was not a Minory. Could it be signaling something or someone getting closer, like a sonar?

"Is that a bomb? You about to fuck us up?"

The question interrupted his thoughts, and it became apparent to Peabody that to keep them talking would also keep them from entering a physical altercation with him. An altercation he was now not sure he could leave his place at the door without entering—he doubted these were men fit for much of a gab. His main reservation was that the men might think his foreign-looking equipment was a threat and smash his things, which he'd gladly engage in fisticuffs to prevent.

"Young man, this is a metaphysical energy meter." At their blank faces, he added a Tiberius-ism: "A metal detector. -*Ish*."

All three looked at one another. The lanky man asked him, "That finds gold?"

The detector had started to click so swiftly that it was almost a buzzer.

Peabody was about to explain when a muffled boom shook the castle's stone foundation. He flinched before he recognized the sound of the heavy rear castle door being opened.

A shiver rolled down his spine; the meters whined.

"The fuck was that?" the young one asked as the older two snapped to and grabbed boxes.

"I believe, young man," Peabody explained, realizing it *was* a sonar signal they were hearing, "that sword's owner has arrived."

Swallowing down apprehension at what would come down the stairs, Peabody stood frozen in the doorway. Tales of the Viking battle on the carin knoll swam in his head. The only way the young man was not going to die was if he were Orabilia herself.

There was shouting. Peabody recognized the voice of the head research assistant, Holly Alexander, then what sounded like a body hitting a wall.

Then, more shouting.

He caught: "Holy fuck" from a man. Then another: "Run! Lou! She's possessed—"

A body came tumbling down the stairs. The man bounced solidly on the bottom two on his back before going head over heels into the wall. He groaned and went silent.

Peabody, a stone's throw from the unconscious man, held out his meter's receiver node. He could feel his chest pumping in time with the footsteps pounding down the stairs.

He heard Holly again: "Hey, Mickey's da! Where are ye, ya bastard!" Then, like a witch from a fairy tale, she cackled and sang, "Come out, come out, wherever you are."

The older, hardened man in the archives room shoved past Peabody. His shoulder struck Peabody in the chest, sending him backward into the stone corner with a crash and knocking his wire-rimmed glasses askew.

"Oof." Peabody slid to the ground. Meter gripped to his chest, he looked down the hall frantically, adjusting his glasses so as not to miss the moment.

The rough man saw his acquaintance slumped unconscious at the foot of the stairs and went red with rage. He shouted, "Is that you, Alexander, ya cunt?"

Holly laughed. The sound echoed off the stone as the thing on the stairs stepped down and into view. There, towering in the lower hallway, with the man sprawled out at her feet, was Nicole. Peabody sucked his breath through his teeth as adrenaline mixed with fear surged through his body.

Nicole was lit with golden light. Each one of her curly copper hairs looked to hold power, snapping and crackling like a halo around her head. Around her neck was a dragon torque; on her wrists were golden cuffs, whether physical or metaphysical, he couldn't tell. They sparked along with the neon green of her eyes. It was unlike anything he'd ever seen before. This was...unbelievable. Except he was witnessing it with his own eyes.

"What did you say?" Nicole asked. The timbre of her voice shook the stones, and Peabody scrambled upright and pointed his machine at the confrontation.

His movements grabbed her attention, and she watched him with goblin-green eyes. Halfway to standing, he crouched, waiting for her reaction. He prayed to Madam Curie that he wouldn't perish that night in the holy pursuit of science.

"Peabody," her voice echoed, "you've been tossed about. Has this man harmed you?"

He opened his mouth to reply, but her eyes went to the man before her. Now seeing her compared to another, Peabody was reminded how human she really was. In her Wellington boots, she was only the man's height. She was bare-legged and in an oversized plaid shirt. Yet she was also not human.

Holly popped into view. "Peabody?" She was scared for him. "Shit, you gotta go."

"What about you?!"

Holly pointed at the pants-less demon. "She's about to fuck shit up; someone's touched the Ulfberht—"

The hardened man stepped in with a heavy fist at Cole's face.

Holly shrieked.

Cole dodged it and in the same movement, stepped in under his swinging arm and punched the man in his abdomen. The man blew off his feet. He hit the ground, went ass over teakettle, and came to a stop next to Peabody.

"Fuuuck" came from Holly at the stairs.

With dedicated footsteps, as if moving toward a lover, Cole moved to the archives room with the intent of retrieving Ulfberht written in her gaze.

Peabody read her energy as she passed by. At the doorway, she paused and turned her gaze onto Peabody. She gave him a look of interest. "Good readings?"

He swallowed down a scream as her neon eyes locked with his, and he felt cold air blow through his body like an ethereal wind through his atoms. He was weightless in her gaze as the past, present, and future were being measured and assessed.

He choked out his response. "The best."

The men in the room shouted, shaking off their paralysis.

"You fucking cunt," the tall one snarled.

"Lou!" the youngest shouted at the rough man on the ground.

Peabody watched Cole smile at the tall, older man who'd called her a name that Peabody thought would do the man no favors. Cole was an American, and she'd take that word's meaning like one.

"Cunt," Cole said. "A slang word for a beautiful organ made for fucking and birthing new life. Unlike *dick*. A fragile reproductive organ that swings dangerously from the body and renders its owner paralyzed when hit. What are you? A dick or a cunt?"

The taller man slipped something onto his knuckles; the brass of it shone dully in the fluorescent lights.

"Interesting choice." She then brought her wrists up and struck them together with a clang. Peabody was sure the clang shook mortar from between the stones beside him.

On the far side of the room, the younger man held the Ulfberht sword with two hands, ready to stab Cole if she moved.

"You"—Cole pointed at the younger man—"will pay most dearly

for touching her." Then back to the taller man: "Once I'm done with my demonstration."

She stepped farther into the room, and the taller man put his fists up by his face like a boxer and moved in an arc. Cole turned with him like a queen facing her heretic accuser, hands out, palms flat as if welcoming his first shot to her sternum.

As she did, Holly made her way down the hall and next to Peabody.

Peabody could only watch the possessed fight and his meter read-outs. Cole was taking and giving energy in a pulse that was new to him as the ancestral energy coursed through her. He could almost feel the sizzle, and he had a strong hypothesis that something would happen once the Ulfberht touched her hand. And he wanted to be there to capture it.

At his and Holly's feet, the man Nicole had knocked off his feet stirred. With a violence Peabody was unaccustomed to seeing from his peers in the science field, Holly stomped her foot down on the man's jaw. It happened so quickly that Peabody thought maybe that wasn't the first time she'd been in violent fisticuffs. The man slumped back down.

Holly grabbed Peabody's arm as the fight erupted. The man who was still upright yowled and leaped. His first jabs missed, but his third landed. Cole stumbled, and the practiced fighter moved in. He punched her abdomen. It knocked the wind out of her, and she hit the back wall with a thump and crashed into a display table.

"Oye!" Holly stormed into the room.

The man, arm back, aimed for Cole's face. Holly kicked the man's knee sideways as the younger man shouted at her. The taller man's leg buckled, making his fist miss as he hollered in pain.

Suddenly, the fracas was all on Holly. The taller man turned and swung. Holly ducked and struck out. Her slugger's punch landed on the man's chin, and the young man charged with the Ulfberht.

Cole, unnoticed by the two men, braced her hands against the wall and lifted her boot. Peabody heard her low growl before the lights crackled, the air simmered, and she struck the taller man in the back.

He was knocked clean off his feet. Like a projectile thrown across the room, he hit the youngest and took him to the floor. The Ulfberht was knocked loose and clattered to the stones. The men hit the ground in a tangle of legs and arms as Holly moved in and kicked the sword to Cole. The younger man pushed and shoved his way out of the tangle.

Cole watched the Ulfberht spin slowly on its handle, showing its precise balance. She bent with reverence and humility to it as Peabody moved closer, his energy receiver out.

She lowered her hand to it, paused as if asking for permission, then grabbed the hilt. A shockwave snapped out and shot through Peabody. His machine let out a single scream before going silent. Peabody shook his meter, then gave it a smack before flicking the switch on and off. It was broken.

Standing, Cole tossed the sword up, letting it spin on its vertical axis before catching it again in a small, practiced movement.

"I wondered what that would feel like again."

Holly was beaming, and then her face crashed as all three saw the young man pull his pistol.

Holly, the closest to him, kicked, but the young man was fast. He lifted the pistol and then brought it back down, cracking against Holly's cheekbone.

The calculation in Cole's calm gaze said that while she wasn't screaming in fury, she *was* taking note of his actions and would repay him in kind.

Chapter Thirty-Four

Threw young man pointed the pistol at Cole.

His face had gone blotchy red with rage and fear. "I don't know what the fuck you are, but you fucking die."

He pulled the trigger, and the explosion startled Peabody. He gripped the meter to his chest as if he'd been the one shot at.

Cole was already moving. The speed of her spinning blade felt like it created a kind of vacuum. Or that obtaining her speed required an energy pull so strong it created negative pressure in the room. He heard a metallic clank and the ricochet buzz of a bullet before a *thunk* as it hit a plastic case next to him.

Cole's blade slowed down to a single twist. She gave the blade a decisive flick as if she were removing blood from its tip before moving in on the younger man.

"What the fuck?" the blond-haired young man asked no one in particular before doubling down on his attack.

Peabody shouted at him to stop. But it was too late. He pulled the trigger again and again.

The room siphoned. The pull made his knees weak, and the stones next to him creaked as if they were being ripped out of their mortar. Peabody felt his fillings ache as Cole's blade whistled.

Peabody flinched when her blade struck the bullets, then ducked as they ricocheted past him.

The next moment, Cole was in front of the man. Her blade came down with a decisive swipe. The pistol flew from his weakened grip, and Cole put the tip of the Ulfberht to the base of his throat and walked him back against a display table.

"No one hits my friends."

IN THE ARTIFACTS ROOM, I STARED DOWN THE TWENTY-YEAR-OLD turd who looked like he'd sell his dignity to Lord Voldemort for a buck. I felt the need to make a point—specifically, with the tip of the Ulfberht. I desired a nice long trip down his frontside, yawning his clothing open before gently tucking the blade in next to his genitals.

I shoved that desire down; though my temper was inherited, I wasn't Ormr.

Then he spit in my face.

Ponytail was slumping to the floor before I knew I'd punched him. A goodnight switch was located in the jaw, something Ormr knew and gave to me to use. I wiped my face clean with my shirt collar as Holly stirred, her cheek red.

Pulling my attention off the younger burglar, lest I follow through on the new urge to put my sword tip through the man's cranium and twist, cracking his skull open like a walnut, I helped Holly stand.

"Oye, fuck," she said, "I think he broke something." She worked her mouth open and closed.

"Your jaw?"

"Och, no, he broke a chunk of my pride off and took a shit on it."

I grinned at her, and she gave me a matching one.

"Yer a bit of fun like this. I'm glad my praying to meet Ormr paid off. But we better call the constable. Then figure out a way to get you back to...dunno, regular Cole?"

"Agreed." To Peabody, I said, "We came across three men upstairs. They'll be stirring by now; at least two have pistols. There's a lower sea gate passage you can use. I want you to leave now. Whatever's going on here, I don't think it's over."

I felt a shiver down my spine as a warm hand pressed into mine. I heard Ethel's voice: *Balance.*

The castle's stones seemed to shudder as if they were resettling themselves. I hadn't realized I'd upset the balance of the place, but it was now evident I had. I tried to remember to keep the energy in balance, but the desire to fight and protect was strong. I wasn't sure I was centered enough to do both.

I will try, I replied.

"I'll get him out," Holly said. She hissed in pain, putting her fingertips to her cheek. "But I need to go out the front to make sure my da stays clear," she said through gently clenched teeth. "They're coming back with the Rembrandt. I didn't tell ye earlier because, well"—Holly looked around, letting her eyes do the talking, encompassing the unconscious men and the Ulfberht sword—"the chief got stuck."

"What now?"

"Dick had a trap set and sprung it with him inside the Otey house."

What little bit of Ormr that had faded—drained from my body and into the stones—surged back.

I took a deep breath to find balance and reminded my soul that I was a botanist in the twenty-first century.

"Is he still there?" I asked.

Holly looked at me expectantly. "No idea. I thought you could *reach out*, ye know?"

I knew that was risky, as Ormr's residual powers coursed through my veins. The last thing I wanted to do was incapacitate him in the power surge.

"Can't" was all I supplied. Feeling the urgency of time, I redirected Holly's attention to Peabody. "Take him. And when you come back, be careful."

Holly held my gaze for several beats before she extended her hand up for me to clasp. I'd seen her do this a dozen times with Rowan and felt its significance. In the blend between Ormr and myself, I responded. Instead of grabbing her outstretched hand, I cradled the back of her head with my palm and gently touched my forehead to hers. Our breaths blended, and in our shared life force, Ormr recognized her as a chieftain, the right hand of her chief, and now we were bonded by battle.

Holly let me hold her, and after a moment's pause, she copied me and gripped the back of my head. The sound of our connection crackled like electricity in my ear.

"Yer frightening as hell like this, but if this now means we're warrior blood sisters, I'm in. And if you tell Rowan any of this, I'll deny it. As we MacLaochs say, bellator ad mortem." She continued in Gaelic; Ormr interpreted: "You have my sword and with it my fealty. I will stand beside you until the cold hand of death takes my last breath."

I smiled at her. "The wind is at our backs. Victory will smile upon us. Go."

She stepped toward the basement stairs. "I'll meet ye around front once Peabody is safe."

"Go."

Down the darkened hall she pulled Peabody, who looked both reluctant to go and full of awe at what we'd done.

I set to work. Grateful for Ormr's strength, I pulled the incapacitated men out of the castle and to the gravel at the base of the front steps. I headed back in for the sixth man, the first I'd struck.

He was gone.

I stood there in the hall, looking into the dark corners around me.

A light flickered from Clive's library. I ran toward it.

The paper-laden shelves behind his desk were ablaze.

The room, with all of Clive's papers and books, was a veritable tinderbox. The whole thing would catch in just moments. The closest fire extinguisher was in a kitchen on the next floor. Fear gripped my guts. Beyond the loss of Clive's nest of historic items, fire in stone buildings destroyed mortar and took impenetrable rock and turned it against itself, causing collapse. The fear was like gasoline feeding the feeling that tore through me next. A heady anger stole through my veins.

There was a great iron screech, and I turned to look: The man I'd belted off his feet pelted out of the castle. His head was stronger than I'd assumed.

My anger, like the fire next to me, found its outlet. The men who'd been there that night were there to destroy artifacts and stop anyone who stood in their way, then burn it all to the ground. I knew then how a berserker found their psychopathic rage.

Without fully understanding what I was doing, I clapped my hands around the Ulfberht and raised it upward. Through the hallway windows, I saw the sky billow and roar, filling with unstable cloud cover. Energy laced my anger, and I felt the Ulfberht engage. I tilted the sword down. Lightning streaked. The man had gotten to the top of the stairs that led toward the sea gate. Thunder clapped before roaring out over the loch; the lightning struck him off his feet.

Ethel's voice hissed into my mind, *Balance!*

I looked back into Clive's office.

Paper smoldered and sat inert in an ash heap behind his desk. The fire was out.

Ormr's ancestral knowledge had me flick my sword as if flicking excess blood off its tip, but it was energy I was returning to the ground. His knowledge and the spirit of him, as I let him in further, had me reassure Ethel, "Cloud fire for paper fire. We're even."

Standing in that rear hall as Ormr's ancestral knowledge came trickling in, I knew that as a biologist and research botanist, I was out of my depth when it came to a castle sacking. What was obvious was that the banker had zero intentions of letting the castle return to MacLaoch hands. Foreclosure was likely a legal maneuver he'd employed to accomplish his goal, and without it, he'd gone to plan B: Burn it down, damn the consequences. He was a man possessed.

He attempted to trap Rowan in that manor house and send him to jail while he paid dangerous humans to burn Laoch to the ground. And because my ancient grandfather walked with me, his experiences were mine now, and in those ancestral memories, I understood that on every floor, the four corners of the castle were ablaze. He'd been a grand nightmare in his time with the living. He had raided with impunity and knew how to take a structure to the ground in the time it took to strip it of its valuables. At least, that was what Ormr would have done, so I guessed that was what Dick would do.

Moving into a jog, I went up a floor, and the smell of smoke confirmed my thoughts. In the castle's western corner, the tearoom drapes were ablaze. A meal of leftover tea sandwiches was laid out and untouched on the dining table. But it was farther up that drew me; the smoke was getting thick, making me cough. I made it to the base of the main staircase, then up it, taking the stairs two at a time. My body coughed at the dry air in my lungs, but the golden hue that made my skin glow kept my air filtered and me moving. At the top of the stairs, the door to TJ's quarters, Rowan's old studio up in the turret, was open. Smoke was so thick in the room above that it pressed down and billowed out the stairwell.

The castle was ablaze below me, above me, and on the eastern and western flanks. The Persian rug down the hall caught embers that floated to the ground, and the walls still held the clan's priceless art. Some were MacLaoch portraits; their eyes seemed to fix on me as if commanding me: Do something!

The air shifted, throwing the smoke into eddies as the fire caught a new oxygen source. The fire snapped and thundered in a continual roar. Down below, the front door opened.

Moving to the top of the stairs, I could see the commotion beyond the gravel walkup. The three men who had been in the artifacts room moved back in. I had a feeling that those three were the captain, sergeant, and lieutenant of their band of turds. No one in their right mind would reenter a burning building with a specter of death inside unless the riches they were promised were immense. Another pistol had been found, and two entered with pistols raised; the other still had his brass knuckles on. A filled pickup was in the roundabout, and my stomach lurched. They'd plundered more than I'd realized. And even that wasn't enough for them.

But what made my guts bottom out was the sight of Rowan in the middle of it.

Chapter Thirty-Five

The borrowed car skidded on the gravel around the last turn approaching the circle drive. Once the view straightened, Rowan and TJ saw him: There in the wide gravel circle, Dick Murdoch stood at the rear of the open bed of a pickup truck full of MacLaoch goods.

"Oh, shit," TJ said, watching as Murdoch began circling it, shaking what looked to be a can of petrol.

Rowan hit the brakes with his fingers on the door handle, though as they skidded to a stop, TJ had his door open and was out of the car first. He sprinted toward the petrol-carrying banker. Seeing that his time was up, Dick frantically pulled something from his pocket as he dropped the can of petrol. Fluid splashed out the nozzle, hitting the stones and the banker's shoes.

He flicked the lighter open. "Stop right there!" Murdoch shouted.

TJ skidded to a stop, his hands up, wordlessly telling him he'd obey. "Now, hold on one moment—"

Rowan slammed his door and was about to shout at the man that he'd best start running when a flicker of light caught his eye from the castle turrets. In the upper windows, light flickered and waved.

"What the..." Rowan recognized then that it was fire. The upper stories were ablaze.

TJ added, "What in the hell is..."

The banker reluctantly looked to where they did and then back, a feral grin on his face.

Rowan cut to the chase. "You burning my home, Murdoch?!"

"And you thought you could escape me!" He held the lighter closer to the tailgate. "I have contingencies upon contingencies! My ancestors lost the battle with their arrogance; they thought they were better than you MacLaochs, but didn't prove it. I will prove it, and not by a casual battle, but with forethought, intelligence, and attention to detail."

Rowan bent and picked up a stone. "Ye've gone and done it, haven't ye? You've hit rock bottom, and nothing will ever be enough, will it?"

"Is that stone supposed to be my lesson? That's my visual aid? I think not, MacLaoch! I am hardly at rock bottom. I think you and your clan have underestimated me, and it's to be to your detriment! The Murdochs will flourish in your absence! Your lands are ours now; we'll step out from under your shadow and rule all of Skye as we were destined—"

Rowan whipped the rock.

It struck the banker in the eye. "Oof!"

The lighter dropped from his hand as his palm went to his eye.

TJ leaped forward and grabbed the hot lighter in midair. "Shit! Ouch!" He hot-potatoed the extinguished lighter into his other hand and grasped it by its base. "Gosh damn it, that's hotter than a tin roof in midsummer."

Rowan approached and pulled from the truck bed a fuel-laced rope that had once held open the formal dining room silk curtains. "I need to get inside," he said, handing TJ the cord. "I can feel Cole is still in there. Tie him up."

Rowan was almost to the castle when through the newly mended stained glass above the open doors he saw an unmistakable figure. He stopped and stared at his wife.

Rowan wanted to talk to her and open their connection, but she was ablaze. Only then did he also notice the unconscious men littered about the gravel.

Behind him, TJ breathed, "Holy fuck, is that Pipsqueak?"

"Aye." Then: "The banker?"

"He's tied up at the moment."

Rowan looked back and then gave him a dark grin. "Didn't know they taught that kind of knot in basic."

"They didn't. That's all country boy."

Murdoch was squirming, wrists tied to his ankles—behind his back.

"I got a little crafty with that silk. I thought it'd be nice and smooth against his skin, so I didn't want to waste it using it on just his wrists."

"He's appreciating it, I'm sure." Rowan saw TJ had found some tape to cover Murdoch's mouth. "Though, not as much as I am."

"Hey, look." TJ directed him to three very conscious men moving about the foyer. "I believe those men—"

"Don't know they're about to die?"

"Seeing my little sis look like she's channeling 240 volts out her every pore, I'm worried for them. I wouldn't care, except I'm thinking she'll be real upset later when she finds out she killed those three idiots."

"Best flush them out." Rowan cupped his hands and shouted, "Oye, ya fucks! Get tae—"

TJ interrupted, "Not sure you know, but they have pistols—"

The gravel at their feet exploded.

"Oh, shit!"

"Duck!"

Rowan and TJ each dove toward the shelter of the low stone wall that funneled guests to the front from the parking circle. Rowan crouched in one bump-out beside its informational placards while TJ did so in another.

Gravel stopped spewing as the air began to pull. The soft breeze of it wiped Rowan's cheek—it was as if the castle were inhaling.

They both chanced looking around and saw Cole's hands extend, her sword held firmly in her right and pointed at the three men.

. . .

Rowan's gaze met mine as he and TJ moved, crouched, up the gravel path like the military men they were. They'd both known close-quarters combat, and their alert postures and hand signals told me that it was knowledge that had never left them.

Coated in the golden glow of Ormr, I held the Ulfberht high and out to my ancestral grandmother, whose cold chill told me she was standing, grounded, in the tidal pools. "Prepare us," I said.

Her voice breathed through me. *Yes. Just once more, child. Ormr will be your guide.*

Relieved that she could provide balance, I prepared to do something I so far could only do in a limited capacity.

The fire snapped and crackled, licking up the wood-paneled walls and coating the ceiling in black. I gave a test of my sword hand, pulling on the fire. Incredulously, it moved toward me as if a wind behind it blew it in my direction. Emotionally leaning into it, I pulled harder. It moved but was not removed. I was burning the castle down faster.

I cursed under my breath.

Breathe, child. Let Ormr guide you.

I coughed. The smoke was really beginning to billow, and I was suddenly conscious of how much I had inhaled. I should be passed out. Was holding the Ulfberht really creating a semi-sealed bubble of clear air around me?

The glow on me began to fade as fear took hold of my mind. I'd done the fire thing downstairs in Clive's office, but this was an entire floor, no, the entire castle. How did I move that much fire?

My heart thudded at the enormity of the task. Out on the cairn knoll during what I'd come to think of as the Healing, I'd held hands with the entire clan to move that much energy. I was solo now. And it was so much energy—too much. The frames of portraits were getting consumed; the MacLaochs were burning where they stood. A burning ember landed on my thumb and sizzled through my skin. For the first time that night, I felt pain. I hollered and dropped the Ulfberht.

Flames reached for me as smoke filled my next inhale. Coughing racked my chest, and I bent then went to my knees there at the top of the stairs. On all fours, I watched as my skin lost its glow. The

Ulfberht lay inert an arm's reach away from me. I was a fool. I needed to get out.

Mo ghràdh—came Rowan's voice clear and cool—*Ethel cannot reach you.*

I coughed and tried... *Can't breathe.*

I could hear his cursing, but I was sinking. His voice came again: *Tee says if you don't get your ass up and come outside right this instant, your mother is going to serve pecan pie at your funeral.*

I smiled, but with the effort of a tired soul ready to lay down and sleep for eternity.

Where's your pig, mo ghràdh?

It took me a second to remember my pig, and as soon as I thought of her, I couldn't quite remember what a pig was.

Breathe close to the ground; I'm coming.

Something moved into me. My ring heated just as cold, outside air entered my lungs as if Rowan were blowing into our connection.

I heard Ethel. *Grab the Ulfberht! Orabilia's grandson is coming for you, child; I've given you his breath through your connection so that* my *grand-daughter can save* him.

Save Rowan, I thought.

Save Rowan came clearer into my head until the protective sow Rowan had asked me about came tearing back. I needed to get the fuck up and get the fuck out.

My eyes watered as I searched the carpet around me.

The back of my hand hit the hilt, and then with seemingly the last of my clean air, I grabbed it. The connection was like lightning to my mind and body. My lungs filled with pure, breathable air as if an oxygen mask had been put over my face. I gave one last lung-clearing cough and sucked in the freshness of that golden glow.

"Oh," I said softly. This was magic.

Shouts and grunts from a fistfight in the lobby. I came up to my knees and looked down as the man with brass knuckles clocked Rowan.

Over the roar of the fire, my own voice, my cry of rage, echoed off the cathedral ceiling. The golden clasps were around my wrists again, and this time, when I pulled on the fire, I did not drag it. I carried it.

The fire wound around my body like snakes to Medusa. It came off the walls, down the stairs from the turret and up from the lower floors. Arms full of it, I shoved them out and sent the fire through the skirmishing men and cut off new men trying to rush inside.

It had been a good effort, but I'd intended to circle the castle. Instead, it left the front doors and collapsed like a fiery pile of molten lava. Frustrated, I gripped the Ulfberht tighter; holding it out, I let the connection, the talisman to the violent, talented man who wielded it in a former life, guide me. The castle shuddered, and the stones groaned.

The unbridled connection to Ormr's powers created a cacophony of rioting energy. I sent my arms out wide again. Heat of the flames snapped and crackled around me. Reaching for all four corners of the castle, I pulled the snapping, biting fire once more and let it build until it was heavy like a lake and I a dam. With that pressure, I pushed my arms out, the Ulfberht pointing.

With intention, I bent the laws of physics and laid the rest of the fire line. It sailed out the front like a heavy rope falling out a window and drew a circle protecting the castle.

Shouts of alarm crescendoed as I guided the crackling rope into place.

The last of it slithered and snapped, closing the circle as I descended the stairs. The men at the base of the stairs forgot about Rowan and Tee, who'd been knocked into a door frame, and instead stared at the fire funneling out of the castle.

The fire within kept the circle burning, and once set in motion, it continued. It undulated past me as I worked my way down the stairs. Tee and Rowan, whose blood dripped from his nose, turned on the men.

I spread my arms and raised my voice to a booming level. "Did you find what you came here for? Was it me you wanted, or was I the snake in the grass?" I clapped my hands, and the fire that still clung to me sparked and sizzled out.

Three sets of eyes landed on me. The shorter, grizzled man raised his pistol.

"No." I pointed the sword at him. The undulating line of fire grew a root and struck him in the chest. He was knocked off his feet. The other two on the other side of the river of fire were left to Rowan and Tee.

Rowan's body softly glowed. He was magic-touched, with Orabilia's moonlight glow coating his skin; her ethereal breath had blown into my lungs with the aid of Ethel. TJ, Minory like me, wore a golden dragon torque on his neck, a metaphysical manifestation that matched the one around mine. I tightened my grip on the Ulfberht, and everything our magic touched flared.

I smiled.

Tee was on the man with brass knuckles. He put a fist to his kidney like an army-trained bare-knuckle boxer—a practice he found as valuable in combat as he did back home when he was escaping from promised women's beds.

Rowan had the trained fighter in him too, and when the ponytailed kid turned to run, Rowan stepped in and punched him off his feet. The man TJ had struck was open-mouthed, holding his back in a silent scream.

I nodded at Rowan and my brother. "Let's move them out."

Rowan, I noticed, refused to make eye contact with me, and opposite him, my brother could do nothing but stare open-mouthed.

"What?" I asked. "Do I have something in my teeth?"

TJ shook his head. "Not unless your teeth are towering over you in a face that looks like Granddaddy's."

I looked up, and sure enough, the Viking was back. He felt a part of me like a visible memory—keen to do as I asked and lend his lived knowledge to me—then fade when the need for him was gone.

I grinned at him and felt the air crackle with sparks. "TJ, meet Ormr."

Tee gave the glowing transparent silhouette following me a salute.

"Come. Grab a man."

We grabbed the collars of the downed men and moved through the front door. There, I could feel the heat of the circle of fire; it was still siphoning its power from the flames within. But as I dragged the young man through it and down the walk, a chill ran up my spine.

A gunshot rang out, and something clipped my shoulder. I was only one part metaphysical being. I felt a sting as my shoulder snapped back. I lost the grip on the man I was dragging and stumbled. I was flat on my backside on the gravel, staring up into the night sky, before I knew what had happened.

Rowan was quickly on all fours over me. Then there was TJ. The wave of his soft golden light made his tan seem darker, and his eyes glowed delicately within their sockets like a night animal used to the dark.

"It's OK. I'm OK," I said and sat up.

I rolled my shoulder. TJ saw the wound as Rowan braced me with my good arm. He then put his hand to my cheek. We were below the opposite wall of the walkway, and it gave us temporary shelter.

TJ murmured, "Just nicked you. But it's a decent gouge."

Rowan and I shared a long gaze in which he connected us. The cooling buzz of his power washed over and through me, and he asked for something I didn't understand.

"Protection? Of course. I'll protect you; stay behind me."

"Not tonight." His lips crushed down onto mine, and his passion made it evident that he'd spent the day watching his clan, his loved ones, his family artifacts come under fire. What he was about to do was retaliate. He was going to find the man who had pulled the trigger and put him in the ground.

Then he was gone.

"Rowan!" I fell forward in his absence and shouted as he cleared the wall and disappeared like a Scot moving into battle.

"Pip—"

"Goddamn it." I felt anguish move through me, mixing with the power I was consuming. The fire arc dimmed with it, and TJ looked from the fire, then back to me.

"Pipsqueak. He needs to do this."

"I can protect him. He—"

"I don't know how all this magic stuff works, but how about you use whatever it is that feels like it's pulling my fillings out and weakening my knees and put it into Rowan."

I felt like wailing. "He'll drown," I managed to say.

"He won't."

I looked askance at my older brother. I really wanted to believe him, but I couldn't take his word on this one thing.

"This afternoon he—we—discovered that he can funnel your overflow of energy into others. I'm thinking it has to do with people you connected or Ethel connected that night on the cairn knoll. If I was a guessing man"—TJ held his hands out, indicating his golden glow—"this is coming from him." He rubbed his fingers together. "Has that brother feel to it." I noticed the blood on his hand where it had been on my shoulder. "If this light is residual from him, and it feels like you're taking it, like a loop of energy, then something tells me that whatever you two have going on, he can likely build up that energy to become as powerful as his great-granny," he said, talking of Orabilia. "He's not gonna drown, Pip."

I blew out a breath at the hope he gave me. "Damn, Tee."

"What?"

I hugged him tight. "I'm so glad this one time you did your homework."

He grinned. "Yeah, this time felt like I should pay attention to what I was being taught." Then he chanced a glance over the wall. He ducked as a bullet hit the opposite side, spraying rock fragments into the air.

"Now seems like the right time to give it a go."

Looking at the empty space where Rowan had been, I spoke into our connection: *I give you all that I am and all that you need until you tell me to stop.* Then, I released into it.

Chapter Thirty-Six

Cole getting shot had activated an old part of Rowan. The part that made a promise at Vick's wake to do all he could to never lose another person he loved. And that night, with the moon's glow coming out of his pores, he had the power to do a lot. He'd reminded Cole about her sow, and he knew his was at his side. He'd gone to war with reanimated wraiths on the cairn knoll. Tonight, this enemy was mortal and would stay down when he put them down.

He moved in silence over the narrow stream and up the opposite embankment. The air was moist, and his footfalls were hushed on the mossy ground. Squatting in the brush on the rise of the other embankment, he heard voices. They were debating if they'd hit *it*, if *the thing* was dead yet. He knew they were talking about Cole.

A twig snapped to his right, and he held his breath. Squinting into the dark, he saw his clanswoman make her way to him. Holly, eyes on him, moved silently up and in next to him. She had dried blood at the base of her nose and was in high spirits like a woman finally getting her battle wish.

She held up five fingers and said under her breath, "Listen, there are five down 'round back, and there're skiffs on the beach. Peabody is out of the castle and safe with Ethel in the tidal flats. Da is coming.

Said he had to pick up reinforcements and will be here with the constable. But"—she emphasized—"the constable might be late."

Rowan knew what that meant. The constable would finish his cuppa. Polish his badge. Make sure his boots had a high shine and check in on his neighbor before making his way to the castle. Everyone who'd grown up in Glentree understood: Man had their laws, and they'd be seen to, right after the laws of fairies were dealt.

"Two here," Rowan whispered back. "One shot Cole."

Holly's eyes went wide. "Oh, fuck, is she OK?"

Rowan's eyes closed, and he inhaled as Cole's power pushed into him. This time, he didn't try to hold it but pushed it out to those he was connected to.

"Aye, she's fine. She's not in danger of dying. But her shoulder was grazed by a bullet that was meant for her head. She's still carrying Ormr within her, but that doesn't mean she's bulletproof."

Holly was solemn for a moment, and then her eyes set on his. "After tonight, I've realized something keenly. I dunnae want to meet Ormr without Cole in the driver's seat. He's a nightmare come real."

They were quiet for a moment as they agreed on how true that statement was. Cole with Ormr was disturbing, and Ormr without her would surely be death unleashed. Rowan understood now what historians tried to convey about berserkers—modern times had a narrow vocabulary for the brutality of those Vikings. And he was glad he could stop having to explain to Holly why she shouldn't wish for Ormr's return.

"Aye," he finally said.

From where they were crouched, they could see the flat grounds and meadow that Reggie had planted. It was a point of pride, at Castle Laoch, that they could take Scotland back to its native roots, one plant at a time, setting a precedent for the rest of the ancestral estates. All in that field the men were tramping through.

"There has to be at least ten more," Rowan added.

"Aye. Those skiffs on the beach aren't ours. I think they knew that it would raise suspicion if they tried to leave through Glentree. By boat, they'd never know."

"Or it was part of Murdoch's plan."

Holly took a beat and then got it. "Ye mean that he's trying to reenact that 1989 raid?"

"That's exactly what I'm saying."

Holly digested that. "He's a nutter then?"

"A nutter hoping to receive the love he'll never have from a father he never saw and a clan who doesn't know who he is."

"Dangerous. A love-hurt man wanting to burn the world."

"All to win the hearts of men who don't know he exists."

"If you're trying to make me feel bad for him..."

"No, but if you don't understand the man yer up against, you're on perpetual defense. And this time, I want to be on the offense."

"Aye, right, well, they've guns, Offense," she said, giving him a new nickname. "And you're lit like the moon; once we're out of the bush, they'll shoot ye." She looked around him to the men on the other side of the bushes, then back. "Best ye be my distraction and let me put them down."

Looking past him, she gripped his arm as though she'd thought of something to add but let it go with a soft yelp: "Your skin is like ice." Recovered, she said: "Over there, in the forest. What's that, then?"

Rowan saw it too, a golden glow moving through the trees toward them. He squinted, but the picture didn't clarify.

"Is that Cole? How'd she get there?"

Rowan inhaled, recognizing the connection. "Eli," he breathed.

"No. Fucking. Way." Holly made the sign of the cross before kissing her fingers.

Rowan grinned. "Now or never, Warrior."

She grinned at her new nickname. "For what?"

"Retribution and a clan battle the likes of which we have never seen."

"Oye. I need details; I've never been in battle!" she hissed.

"Aye: Knock the teeth out of these two. Lead the charge to flush these marauding eejits down to the boats." He looked pointedly at her phone. "And text yer da. We'll need water support."

Before she could respond, Rowan erupted out of the brush with a screeching call that startled the two men there. It triggered his clanspeople, who were, as he'd suspected, right behind Eli. They swarmed out, their rudimentary weapons held high as their own skin-crawling screech returned their chief's call.

Eli wielded his claymore replica. It glowed with golden light, as it had on the battle of the cairn knoll.

Rowan heard Holly curse from behind him, but she had his back. Rowan leaned in, bringing his fist through with the power of his entire body, to connect with the first man's cheek. With a crack, he crumpled to the ground. The second lifted his pistol. Holly's hand was on the shaft, and she shoved his shooting hand down. The man panicked and pulled the trigger, shooting himself in the leg. He howled as Holly struck his nose with her forehead like a pro footballer, knocking him out.

Cursing from the banker's invaders rose to a crescendo. Rowan heard the shout to "hit the boats."

Holly released the magazine from the downed man's gun, opened the slide, and popped out the chambered round. It hit the ground as Holly separated the handle from the shaft and threw the two pieces in opposite directions.

Rowan and Holly shared a glance. "I see yer da taught ye a few things before your mother came and got ye."

Holly grinned. "Just a few things."

Rowan watched the banker's men scatter. "Let them flee," Rowan said.

"The boats are loaded with artifacts from the dungeons and the fairy tower."

That took Rowan a moment to process. The pickup had been full and now boats on the loch too?

He cursed resoundingly before looking for the pieces of the pistol. "Maybe we should've kept tha'."

Eli worked his way toward them. He punched a man clean off his feet with his sword fist. Pleased with the power that surged through his magic-touched body, he stepped up to Holly and Rowan.

"Thanks, brother, for the power." Eli held a golden hand out, and Rowan clasped it.

After a brief embrace, Rowan said, "Ye can thank your cousin for that."

They both looked to where Cole was descending on Dick Murdoch. The banker had tried to take the MacLaochs to their knees, using their finances as leverage, and when that didn't work, he took a page out of their shared history. He was still tied up behind the pickup, which Rowan now recognized as a mere decoy.

Love, he reached out to her.

Cole's head snapped in his direction. He could see her glowing green eyes even at their distance. Ormr stood a full head height above her but was fading, a sign she was using less of his ancestral energy.

There are boats in the loch.

She nodded. *I will come to you there. Be just a moment.*

He pressed into her mind. *You are not Ormr.*

She understood his meaning. *I won't kill him.*

Tha mo ghion ort.

And I you. She kissed her ring. The one on his own finger warmed with her breath.

Rowan returned the kiss before saying to Holly and Eli, "Come."

Through the brush, along the stream's edge, he led them down to the loch's rocky black beach.

Holly said, "I want to glow too. Any chance I can get in on that? I am MacLaoch by blood. Can I be on Blue Team?"

Rowan came to the short drop-off where the stream emptied onto the beach in a small waterfall. On the rocky beach, it meandered like a freshwater snake before fanning out and emptying into the loch. He crouched, moved foliage out of the way, and inspected the beach. Eli bent behind them, keeping watch on the hillside.

"Best we have at least one on this team that's invisible, aye?" Eli whispered.

"True. But I'll counter that feels a bit exclusionary."

Rowan grinned. "As I've said before, Ms. Holly, be careful what you wish for."

She was also peering out, counting the men and the two skiffs. "I've come to realize I've gotten everything I've wished for, so I'm making new wishes. It's an auspicious night, feels right."

Rowan gave her a dark grin. "Say yer prayers, conduct a blood ceremony, and have a witch make ye drink tha' blood, and I bet ye can have Orabilia's powers too."

"Right." Squinting into the distance, she revised: "On second thought, I'll take my dark skin on this dark night and play to my strengths."

"Didn't like the blood-drinking part, eh?"

"Fucking repulsive."

Turning his attention back out to the beach, Rowan murmured, "That's a lot of open beach for us tae cover before we get to them."

"They've not fired their guns," Holly added.

"So they've maybe got loaded pistols."

Rowan sighed, not liking that it was a mystery how many bullets were still out there.

Holly suggested, "We can skirt around the edges, then? Swim through the loch and come from behind?"

"We'll be exhausted before we get to them," Rowan explained.

"We need coverage."

All three were quiet for a moment before Holly scooped up some water and let it drizzle back down into the low stream. "Any chance ye know a witch who can make fog?"

Rowan quieted his mind and sent the message to Cole.

"What now?" Holly asked.

"We wait."

He looked back out to the black-rock beach from which he'd launched himself countless times to swim away the stress that plagued him. Now, it all seemed like a distant memory as strange men wanting to tear down his castle and clan at the behest of a wealthy deranged banker swarmed it. He could see from their perch the shadowy boats rising on the foam of the incoming tide. They'd timed it perfectly.

"I'm trying to think what my da would do," Holly muttered.

"He was Jacky's right-hand for a reason," Eli said. He turned to Rowan with a grin. "He was always nice to Rowan and me, wasn't he, Row? Even when he had to come get us when we took the boat out that one time."

Rowan grinned up to Eli. "Oh, right."

Holly asked, "Was it that ride on the Orkney current ye two took at eight?"

Eli's low rumble of a laugh seemed to vibrate the air. "Oh aye."

Rowan explained, "Holly's ma brought her home before too much of Double-A's city life rubbed off on her."

"Yeah, well, I might have had some of it rub off on me when my mum and da first separated. Da didn't take to losing Jacky so well, and Mum left him right after. Weekends in the big city were real enlightening."

Rowan nodded and put a hand on Holly's shoulder. "I'm glad he came home for ye, though."

"Aye. He had his head up his arse for just a wee while."

Eli asked, "Did your mum know of the city shenanigans?"

"Is my da still breathing?"

"Ahh. Right."

Holly's breath caught. "Oye, fuck."

"Wha—"

She shook Rowan's hand off her shoulder. "Is that...coming *out* of ye?"

Where he sat crouched next to the water, fog rolled off him. The tingle of Cole's power was moving through him.

Holly encouraged him. "Here, hold yer hand out over the water." Grasping his hand, she put his palm over the water. "My mum says, set your intention into your mind, then connect it to your heart. Your heart is connected to your hand through your blood, so you must think hard about getting the fog tae build. It's using the water."

"Right." He wasn't sure if it would work, but he knew it certainly wouldn't if he didn't try. A receptive vessel would work better than one just sitting like a lump.

Like a cat that had discovered a receptive petter, the fog wound around him and began to billow in earnest off the short waterfall and pour out over the beach.

Holly gave a tight, incredulous laugh. "I know I sounded sure of myself, but...I always thought she was full of it. Now I'll have tae go apologize.

"Eli, go to Cole and TJ and help them sweep the men down onto the beach. We'll take care of the boats."

"Aye."

"Let's go—I can do this fog business while we walk." And Rowan leaped.

Chapter Thirty-Seven

A shudder went through me from Rowan. He needed coverage down on the beach. He asked for Ethel's help, but Ormr had known the trick for fog, and using the power I was pushing into him, I also sent the words Ormr taught me.

I'd join Rowan on the beach, but the banker was at my feet.

"What do you want to do, Pipsqueak?"

"Murder."

"Besides that?"

"Tie a rope around his neck and find a sturdy tree. Let us see how long it takes before his hatred becomes a plea for mercy."

"Ormr, take a beat. Lemme talk with my sis."

I grinned at him over my shoulder. "What would you do if he really took full control?"

"Impossible. Probably tell you jokes until you pissed yourself. You can fall down an elevator shaft but crawl right out with a well-told joke. Ormr could try to take over, but you'd come right back."

I nodded. "Catnip. I love me a good laugh."

"He's gone now, and are you losing your glow?"

I looked at my arms. The pain in my shoulder felt stronger. "I think I am. Maybe I'm calming down? Do you want to arm wrestle?"

"No, thank you, ma'am."

Over his shoulder, a golden, glowing Eli was moving toward us, then disappeared as he entered the shallow ravine.

He jumped over the wall, startling TJ.

"Ho-shit!" Clutching his shirt front, Tee leaned against me. "Damn near gave me a heart attack, man!"

Eli was grinning as he always did when we were together. The present we'd gotten a year ago of a newly found family relation was perpetually playing in our minds' eyes.

Eli finally met my eyes and then glanced away. "Is there a being also attached to you? His outline is faint."

Tee was keen to the fear caught in Eli's gaze. "Ye-up."

Eli leaned next to TJ's ear and spoke.

TJ reassured him, "Yes, sir. She's in the driver's seat."

"Come, Eli," I said, holding my hand out to him. "We've fought together before. Let us resume our camaraderie."

TJ amended as Eli clasped my hand, "Mostly."

I grinned. "The fun part is that you can't be sure who is driving at any given time."

TJ gave me a dry look. "Don't fuck with us, Pipsqueak."

Movement at the rear of the pickup had TJ look around me and call out, "Whatcha doin', Mac? I tied you up nice and purdy and now you've gone and wrecked it. Looks like someone helped you. Let's correct that."

Eli asked, "Why is he tied?"

"He is a liar and a thief. He is a dishonorable man with intentions that can only be done behind honorable men's backs. Until his punishment can be decided, he must be detained."

TJ gave me a look as if it was an overly long-winded answer.

"Let's redo those ties, sir." As TJ bent for him, I put my hand out, stopping him. Flames dripped off my pinkie. "Wait."

TJ halted, throwing his hands up. "Hold up. There's gasoline spilled everywhere, Pip."

"I see." Back to the banker, I said in Ormr's baritone, "Is this what you wanted, Dick Murdoch? To burn us all to the ground?"

He was wriggling in earnest now, making TJ state the obvious.

"He's two seconds from slipping out of his ties."

"And the time it takes for him to loose them, stand, and run for his life is the time he has to answer my question before my blade asks the next one."

Eli butted in. "Please, Cole, tell Ormr, no killing."

"Worry not, Cousin. I'll only take what he's not using. And his mind has been damaged for some time."

"That is wholly unreassuring."

I focused then on Dick, who was sweating and pushing off his ropes.

"I asked you, Banker Murdoch, was this what you desired? To burn us to the ground?"

He grunted and wriggled to all fours, then struggled to get to his feet.

TJ hissed in displeasure. I moved in, kicking the man in his rear, sending him sprawling into the gravel. As he rolled over, I walked a circle around him, the Ulfberht tip pointed at his abdomen.

"Do you wish to die here today?"

He grunted, pushing himself away from the blade and the fiery electricity that was actively dripping off me. "What— What are you?!"

"I asked you a question." The blade nicked him, severing a button off his shirt as a wide paw grasped the front of my arm. Eli's grip was firm on my bicep and stayed my hand.

"Cole. Cousin," he whispered. "You are not a killer."

I knew the hand I had to play, and with my brother close, I could do it in code. I didn't want Eli to relax. To TJ, I said, "Death is the only *confessional* man knows." Then, I gave my brother a TJ-class wink.

Eli gripped harder. "Death is no confessional!"

TJ pulled out his cell phone and moved to frame the banker in the lens.

"TJ!" Eli hollered, shocked. I yanked my arm out of his grip, and with two hands on the hilt of my redeemer, I swung down.

The banker screamed, "Yes! That was my intent!"

My blade stilled.

He was panting, his eyes darting to Eli, TJ, and reluctantly to me. "You deserve nothing, you MacLaochs. Death will be too kind a mistress for your chief. The hell made for the Murdochs ends today. By me! I did this!" He gave a small hiccup as laughter and fear blended in his diaphragm.

Eli's hand was back on my arm, this time on my forearm, and gently pressed it down.

Surprised, I took my eyes off the banker to study Eli's profile. He was beyond livid. He, I realized, hadn't heard Dick spouting his nutter hatred before.

Murdoch knocked my blade to the side; it sizzled when he touched it, and with a yelp, he scrambled to his feet before taking off down the drive. He screamed something incoherent as he blasted away from us.

"He's out of his nut," Eli said, astonished.

Coming up the driveway at a good clip was Rowan's SUV.

"Uh-oh," I whispered.

Too late, the driver saw the running banker in their headlights and slammed on the brakes. The tires caught, and the vehicle slid on the gravel, bumping Dick Murdoch. He flopped against the hood as the driver in the car screamed. We heard Dick groan before he fell back onto the ground.

Mickey stepped out and looked at the man on the ground and then at us. I watched him take in the ethereal glow and the fire behind us. He gave a shrug that seemed to encompass the entirety of the situation and called to us, "Got him."

Charmaine was next to him, taking in the sight of the man's prone body then the fire encircling the castle.

"What in god's name..." Then her eyes found me.

TJ was sprinting for her as her eyes rolled up into the back of her head. He caught her just before her face hit the gravel.

Mickey stepped over the banker, adjusting his cuffs. "What'd I miss, chaps?"

"Gilliansson," I commanded to Mickey and heard Ormr in my words, "how deep does your contempt for the elder Gilliansson go?"

Mickey cleared his throat as if hearing his name in Norse tradition, with the *-son* at the end of it, made him want to run and he was swallowing down that desire. "To the bone."

"Then tonight is the night you'll get retribution. The clan has flushed him and his men down to the loch."

Mickey's handsome symmetrical features contorted with suppressed venom as his lip lifted. "Death or prison?"

"You've earned my respect. I'll give that decision to you."

Eli was clearheaded. "Prison. No death, please. This is not a thirteenth-century fight."

I held my arms out to Eli so he could see my glow and his own. "It is not?"

He grimaced. "Magical, yes. Thirteenth century? No."

TJ joined us. "Charmaine"—he tossed his thumb behind him—"will wait for the constable. What'd I miss?"

"Tee, it's time." I grinned. "Gopher hole."

He blinked, then smiled, understanding the context shift. "They've gone to ground?"

"Down to the loch."

The gold in his gaze sparked with mischief. "Then it's Foxhole."

"They're escaping on boats," I argued.

"Then Pirates."

"Goddamn it, Gopher Hole. They're scrambling into the brush."

"Foxhole Pirates!"

I could feel my hair crackle. "Gopher. Hole. Flush them out."

"Gopher Hole, with Foxhole Pirates."

I could feel the ground shake with my frustration. *"Fucking Gopher Hole."*

Eli put a hand on TJ's shoulder to stop his rebuttal. "Tha's enough." His eyes were on me and scared.

TJ patted Eli's hand. "Don't worry, big guy," he said as Mickey backed away. "The key to Gopher Hole is to blast the varmints out of their holes. I'm assuming that she can't do that if she's calm." He grinned at Eli. "Isn't that right, Pipsqueak?"

Gritting my teeth at his asinine antics, I went to the low walkway wall where Rowan had disappeared earlier. I put the Ulfberht against my back, where it tucked into its metaphysical scabbard. Clapping my hands together, I shot lightning through the sky.

I heard TJ behind me. "Fuck yeah."

TJ was a real dick, but he was effective.

I had to get down to Rowan; I could feel his struggle in the fog, his worry that Holly would get another damaging hit to her face, and his concern for the Whisky Boys, that they might fall on the rocky shore and break a hip. His siphoning off my energy was new for him, and even as I fed him the dying fires from behind me, I could feel the toll it was taking on him.

The boys followed me down through the brush to the low ridge that formed a natural storm wall. The fog was so thick, I couldn't see my own hand.

Ethel's voice whispered over my skin as if carried by the fog: *When the fire is out, this castle will crumble. The energy in its stones is the only power left to feed you. When that fire dies, stop, or it will cost MacLaochs everything. The castle will fall.*

Anxiety rolled through me; now we were in trouble.

And yet... "Gopher Hole," I whispered and concentrated. It wouldn't take much more energy...I hoped.

"Remember, Pipsqueak."

"Please dunnae antagonize your sister," Eli whispered.

"What? Pipsqueak?"

"Aye."

"That's her nickname, and the name I'm using to keep myself from shitting my pants—again—today."

I turned from the fog below us on the beach to grin at him. I could see him but could barely make out Eli. TJ gave me a matching grin in return.

"Is it the eyes?" I asked.

"They're beautiful—"

"Thanks!"

"—for a space alien."

The fog cover crackled. "Asshole."

He just waved to the fog and antagonized me further. "Batshit crazy-looking goblin alien."

I sucked in air as I watched his stupid face retrain his focus and squint into the distance.

"Not working."

Turning back toward the beach, I opened my arms. I felt the soil beneath my feet all the way to the cairn knoll and north to the end of MacLaoch land. I connected to the root system of every flower, shrub, and tree then, using that energy pushed it out like a wall of light.

I heard TJ whisper to Eli behind me, "Bloody fucking hell, I feel that in my bones."

Chapter Thirty-Eight

Rowan had quit making fog a while ago, but it was thick enough now that he could practically scoop it with his hands, and there was nothing he could do but feel around for the next rocky step and listen for footsteps that weren't Holly's. And hope he bumped into the Rembrandt-thieving Lou Gillian, Mickey's da, so he could set the man's teeth straight. With his fist.

A figure moved out of the fog. Rowan cocked his arm, and then relaxed—it was Double-A. This was a great example of why he preferred no guns; they'd have done something irreversible before realizing their mistake.

Lightning crashed overhead, and Rowan felt Cole was coming.

"Tha' yer bride?" Double-A asked. Then he swore, as he lost his cigarette. He finished popping one boat motor's cover and pulling its starter wire.

Holly answered, "Maybe she can clear some of this fog. Ye were a little too good at creating it, my liege."

Double-A gave him a grin. "Yer uncle would be proud of ye. And on this night? He'd tell ye: *You know what tae do.*" Double-A lit a cigarette.

"Da," Holly said to him as he put his lighter to the tip of the cigarette. It sounded like an old argument that no longer had words, just a tone.

He answered, "I know, love. This is my last. I promise."

Holly tsked. "Love ye, Da, but I see why Mum left yer arse."

"Fuck, I'll quit today, then."

Holly corrected him, "Not your smoking. You lie like a pastor quotes the Bible."

"I'll quit smoking *and* take up the Bible, then."

"Och, fuck nae."

"Ye don't think a pious life is for me?"

"No, I'm pretty sure the Lord would ask ye to stop smoking, and you'd tell him, 'Right after ye provide world peace.' Then you'd find yourself in hell."

Double-A's laugh was cut short as golden light blew out from the MacLaoch stream. There were shouts as Cole moved toward them onto the rocky beach. The fog billowed and blew eddies.

"Good, I can get to the other boats now."

There was a hammer click, and Lou Gillian stepped out of the moving mist. "No, ye ain't." With the eye of his gun trained on the group, he added, "Do as I ask. Or the pretty bird gets it."

Rowan felt his guts bottom out, but Holly had no reservations about the gun being pointed at them.

"Aw," she said nudging Rowan, "he called you pretty. Isn't that sweet?"

Lou scrunched his face at Holly. "Yer a daft one."

Rowan realized, when Double-A was suddenly there with his arm over Holly's shoulders, what was happening.

"Oh, come now, she's not daft. She's just had me for a da, so don't hold it against her."

Holly gave a sloppy guffaw.

Lou pointed the pistol at Holly. "What the fuck is wrong—"

Double-A was at Lou's side, twisting the pistol down and out. In the next moment, Double-A hammered the bridge of Lou's nose with the butt of it.

Lou cried out. "Oye, ye fucking wank, you broke my nose."

Holly moved in. "And now for yer nuts," then punted his crotch like a game-winning football strike.

Air hissed between his teeth before his knees knocked in, and he went down. Double-A put the muzzle to his cranium, and that was when Rowan stopped him.

"No. Constable is on his way."

"Och—"

Lou was as much an old fighter as Double-A and, with a shout, launched himself into Double-A, knocking him back and the gun loose.

Holly grabbed it midair, and in the lightened fog, Rowan saw ten men hurtling themselves down the beach toward the waiting boats.

"Oye, fuck," cried Rowan. "Holl! Put a hole in the motor cases!"

Lou was on Double-A. Double-A fell and hit his face. Rowan raised his boot and slammed Lou sideways.

Double-A blinked, his nose bleeding. Rowan held his hand down for the elder Whisky Boy. "Ye all right, Uncle?"

"Oye. I think I've gone a bit daft, yer liege. There's two of ye now."

He looked around for his lost cigarette and found it on his chest. After popping it into the corner of his mouth, he grasped Rowan's hand and let himself be pulled up to standing.

Shots rang out as Holly put holes in boat after boat.

"The hulls if you can't sight the motor!"

"What? It's got our stuff in there!"

"Better the sea has them than these fucks."

Fog now hung only over the middle loch, where the low drone of a motor was adding to the shouts and chaos around him.

The Whisky Boys were grabbing at Lou's men, punching and scrambling to keep them from the boats. The young blond was running like his life depended on it. He was making his way to the far boat on the beach.

On the upper edge of the beach was Cole. She was flanked by TJ and Eli, with the glow of her ancestor behind her, and she was harnessing power that seemed to come right out of the ground.

The stones began vibrating and then rising off the earth.

"Oh, shite."

The clouds overhead rumbled and spit lightning.

"Get down!"

Yes, mo ghràdh, he said into their connection as groans rose. On the beach it seemed each of the banker's men had been struck. They writhed on the rocky shore as if they'd experienced a shock. Rowan smiled. But then he saw Ponytail. Rowan took off after him. His footing was solid, as if Cole's effect was for everyone but him.

Rowan was close to the kid when a bullet whizzed by. Rowan ducked but kept running. The bullet crashed through the side of the hull of the boat the man had jumped into. The boat's motor revved, and with an incoming wave, it tore back off the beach. Rowan ran into the water then leaped.

Cold water collided with his shins and blew up the front of his body. Rowan caught the edge of the boat, but his grip was ripped off when the next wave brought the nose up and threatened to crush him back onto the beach.

Rowan tumbled in the surf, and when he caught his breath, he made it to standing. Water streamed off him as he watched the boat turn and gain speed out of the calm loch.

"Goddamn it!" he shouted, as water sprayed off his upper lip and dripped into his eyes. "Fuck!"

Holly was next to him and took aim. "That little son of a bitch owes me some brain cells..."

Rowan put his hand on her arm. "I want to say yes. But later we will regret it. It's with the gods now."

Holly and Rowan waited a moment until the lapping waves next to them were the only sounds they could hear. The boat was a gray speck out in the distance as they slowly returned to the chaos. Double-A had Lou pinned, and Rowan watched as Mickey approached, squatted down, spoke to the man, and then stood. Double-A released Lou, and before Rowan could protest, Mickey brought his boot down. Holly hissed next to him, watching the violence.

A shadow moved out on the horizon, and Rowan squinted at it. "What is tha'?" he asked and got his answer as the HM Coast Guard vessel threw on its lights and, with a spotlight on the fleeing skiff, commanded it to: "Halt. HM Coast Guard requests your compliance. Refusal to obey will result in the use of force."

Holly giggled. "This *is* an auspicious night."

Back to the beach, Rowan saw that the rest of the banker's men were either unconscious or being tied up by Whisky Boys as the constable moved down onto the beach, handing out temporary loop restraints.

Cole was approaching him, a soft smile on her face. Her passenger was gone, and her golden glow was fading.

"Got 'em all." She looked up to the towering castle perched on the hill like it had been for centuries. "And she's still standing."

ROWAN, WET AND COLD, PULLED ME INTO HIS ARMS AND HUGGED ME tight.

"Aye, we got them all."

After a long squeeze, Holly said from behind him, "Aw, the boat stopped. I was hoping he'd try to outrace it like it's 1989."

"Och, I'm glad it's—"

I felt the ground shake beneath our feet.

Rowan looked at me. "Was that ye?"

I shook my head. "That felt farther away..." I looked at the castle, and it seemed to be flexing on the horizon as if someone were playing whack-a-mole with its foundation boulders. One would slip out, and they'd smack it back in, then another would pop out.

"Uh-oh."

Rowan whispered, "The castle."

He saw it too.

It was no longer ablaze, but something was seriously wrong.

Holly pipped up, "I could be mistaken, but that sounded like a detonation."

"He didn't..." Rowan uttered.

My insides felt as if they were tumbling down an elevator shaft. "I need to get to Ethel. She said if I didn't stop using my power, I'd use the power in the castle's stones."

"No, Dick Murdoch," said Rowan and started moving toward the castle.

"No," I said, still focused on what I believed to be true, "she's in the tidal flats!" and I waved for him to follow me over the rocky shore. As we were reaching Ethel, so too was Peabody, running back through the sea gate toward her, throwing wide his arms.

"Oh, fuck" came from Holly.

The castle gave a massive shudder.

Rowan made a sound that I could only assume was the sound one might make when their guts are yanked out of their bodies via the mouth. He choked and staggered back as the first turret broke. Chunks of it tumbled down, crashing onto the back stone patio and off the bowling green.

I choked too on my scream when Castle Laoch groaned and then in a terrible roar fell to its knees like a massive cliff imploding upon itself. Boulders and rock fell off the cliffside and what was once a beautiful castle crumbled into a rockslide down toward us.

I screamed.

Holly shouted.

Rowan grabbed us both, and we ran to the tidal flats and then into the loch. We dove off the rocks, following Rowan, who knew the depths of every part of the loch at every tide level. Cold water splashed up around us as the earth shook. We panicked, swam, grabbed each other, and swam harder as boulders hit the water, rolling into the sea behind us.

Then suddenly, it was quiet.

The chill of the water hit our bones, and we came up for air as we tread water off the tidal flats. A jagged horizon of rubble gut-punched us. Holly choked as Rowan struggled for breath. It was as if the castle were his lungs, and now, he couldn't breathe.

Castle Laoch was gone.

IN THE DISTANCE FROM WHERE WE WERE, I COULD SEE THE BEACH with our clanspeople, the constable, and the men who'd ransacked our lives, and the Coast Guard vessel behind us in the open loch waters. They were alive. But Peabody had been close to the castle, and Ethel nearer still, and their lives called me to swim, swim as fast as ever.

Up onto the tidal flats, I slipped on algae-covered rocks and searched in the broken pieces of Laoch's walls for Ethel and found her kneeling.

I crashed to my knees, splashing in the saltwater next to her.

"Ethel." I grabbed her shoulders. She wasn't awake but rather in what I could only assume was a trance and she existed elsewhere. A soft firefly light swirled off her, and as I was going to shake her, Peabody was there.

Thank god he was alive.

"She's not here. There's another plane of existence that she's currently inhabiting with her energies. The castle required too much of her."

Emotion squeezed my windpipe. "It was me; I thought I could use the fire energies, but—" I grabbed her slender, soft shoulders. "Ethel, my ancient grandmother, come back. I'm sorry."

I felt her words move into me. *No, child. I am sorry. I underestimated the actors who move to keep the curse alive. I assumed all was well now that the Chevalier woman was linked by love's hand to your brother and Minory descendant, Tiberius. However, it found a willing participant who set charges to the base of the castle. I couldn't counteract that level of energetic expulsion.*

"He"—I choked; it hadn't been me—"Dick Murdoch blew up the castle."

I heard Rowan behind me groan, and he slowly went to his knees; his head hit his hands, and from within them, I heard him say, "At every turn this night when I've thought he couldn't be serious in his vengeance, he has been. The fire should have been enough, but—"

"Ethel says he's set to make sure the curse in all its forms stays true. It had been Charmaine, but love made her give it up. So, the curse found another."

Rowan's anguished gaze met mine. "What?"

I shook my head as if I couldn't believe it either. Then I had an idea.

He nodded, following my thoughts. He looked at me with hope.

"Gather everyone. It's worth a try."

Holly heard us and ran over the rocks to the shore on the other side.

With Ethel's hand in mine, I spoke to her. *With all of us, can you help us return the castle to standing?*

The energy necessary is too great. The kind of power needed would have to be more than I know of.

All of the clan linked?

Maybe...but it will cost a life.

"That's too much," I responded aloud.

"What is?"

I felt Rowan at my side and spoke to him with my eyes closed and still linked to Ethel. "It will take a life to restore the stones."

Rowan agreed, "Too much."

I had another thought. "What about lives past?"

Who?

Holding Ethel's hands, I said, "Let me show you."

It took me some time to connect fully with Ethel. The cold of the water was too much, then the rubble behind me. Peabody was explaining to Rowan what I was doing, but then finally, I found Ethel and connected to her. My sense of self wound out from me, and like the tender shoot of a vine, its glowing energies wound around Ethel's. I took us up the dark, rocky shoreline to the cove that Rowan showed me. And it was there that we found a pool of glistening energy that felt pure and powerful.

This, child, helps. I haven't seen it in this plane—do you know what this is? The power of it?

No, but I feel it.

This is Ormr's love; he has hidden it here in this cave. This is not a life, but it is powerful.

I touched it, and like fuel to an engine, it moved along our energy lines back down to the castle, where I found my body standing. Rowan's hand was in mine, Ethel's in my other, and TJ's in her other hand. One by one, the clanspeople held on, and with the pressure building in my heart, I pushed it out to the stones that were the foundation of MacLaochs for centuries. The same stones that I'd walked upon, the same that I'd touched, and I wondered how many hands had done the same. The stones that witnessed Rowan's rage and then also he and I make love within their shelter.

In the distance, I heard castle stone grind upon stone, and someone gasped, "They're going back."

I touched on Rowan's memories, the ones at his uncle's knee, the whisky in the breezy, dark lower levels, and the raids they'd dodged before the eighties. I thought of the first settlement, the keep that Orabilia described, and the land that supported it.

Every phase from that moment to the next filled my mind…until I eventually saw myself making my morning tea in the kitchen less than forty-eight hours ago.

I heard Tee curse in disbelief.

"It's finished."

Not yet. A life to bind it.

Ethel's hand felt loose in mine, and within the ethereal winds of the plane we resided in, I looked at her. She had become translucent; the fireflies glowing about her were moving in rapid succession as if busy putting her to work. Then, in a swarm, holding her essence, they flew toward the castle. The sparks of her life struck the rear of the castle and spread out, coating the towering structure in glitter. Each rock beneath the concrete facade smoothed and locked into place with a spark. The spark molded into mortar, moving like blood through veins. In that whipping wind of her ethereal plane, I saw Ethel's smile before it faded.

I was suddenly back standing in the tidal flats; it had begun to rain as if the heavens were weeping for the thing it had just witnessed.

Cheers went up around us, but Rowan, Tee, and I looked at our hands. Ethel's clothes fluttered to the ground where her body had been; the last soft sparks of light grew dimmer until they vanished altogether.

"No…" I said and went to my knees, gathering up her clothes. "Nope, Ethel, that's too much." My golden light was gone, as was Tee's, and Rowan's blue moonlight. The castle stood proud in the dark night;

glowing from within its stones was the light from each of us, making it seem like something from the land of fairies.

"She's gone," said Peabody. His equipment lay among the wet rocks, dropped in shock.

"No," I said again, feeling the rain dampen my cheeks as the realization and sacrifice of what she'd done settled down on me.

Chapter Thirty-Nine

Back up at the front of the castle I stood, flanked by the Whisky Boys, Rowan, and Tee. The clan milled about behind us, waiting. Grief and sadness mixed with the sweet joy of having the MacLaoch heart restored.

Dick Murdoch, Lou Gillian, and cohorts sat shoulder to shoulder in the back of the police van, sullen looks upon their faces, some with bloody noses, with their hands cuffed together in the front. The constable had called for backup when a "pushy lass" told him he should. I assumed that was Charmaine. Blue-and-white lights strobed in the dark, bouncing off the castle stones that had me looking at it repeatedly to make sure it wasn't suddenly going to crumble again.

Dick shouted that he'd done it, he'd done what no other Murdoch had done, and for that, he'd get a medal.

The officer helping to load them into the rear of the police wagon piped up, "Oye, keep yer head, man! I'm a Murdoch, and none of what you've confessed to is legal or loyal to the clan honors." He slammed the door shut. With an exasperated look that seemed to be the trademark expression for any who spent time in Dick Murdoch's presence, he said, maybe to us, maybe just to the night air, "I know I need to be unbiased about the accused, but he's a one."

Rowan responded with a short nod and agreed, "He's a one."

THE SMALL LIVING ROOM OF OUR COTTAGE FILLED WITH CLAN members, while many more milled around outside. I sat curled up on Rowan's lap while Tee sat on the couch opposite us.

"We were just getting to know her..." I said of Ethel.

We'd finished the police reports, and the sun still did its job even as it set, lightening the calm and clear horizon. A structural engineer from the Fund would be coming in the morning to review the castle.

I shook my head, still feeling Ethel's hand in mine vanish.

Holly meandered over between the Whisky Boys to deliver me a dram of whisky in a mug. "I'm good," I said to her proffered cup.

"Ye don't look good."

"My guts say I missed something. That somewhere in this whole thing was a piece I missed that could have prevented all of this."

Rowan's hand ran slow, soothing circles on my back.

"Oh, ye mean that you should have known that a nutter banker was a greedy sod susceptible to the MacLaoch curse and played the part that would always need to be played, by somebody?"

"When you put it like that," I said and took the proffered cup. I looked at the liquid within and whispered, "Slàinte," before throwing back the contents. I choked and sucked air through clenched teeth; it held the hellfire of ethanol with some teasing sweetness on the backside. "What the heck is this? Firewater?"

"Heehee, firewater. That's appropriate. Grandda makes it with Bernie."

"Ooh," I said, feeling Rowan's laugh beneath me.

"Mac Mead," he said.

I coughed. "Pure moonshine." The fire was still sweeping up my throat and out my nose. "Hell, pure rocket fuel." I coughed again as the fumes burned my throat and nose.

In the silence that followed, I muttered, "I want to know how he did it and why. I mean, we already know he was a little on the edge and maybe a bit curse-touched—"

"A bit?" TJ interjected. "Try full-blown. No one loses their marbles like that without social conditioning."

I beamed at my brother who was bantering about the minutia of curse logic with me. "Not too long ago, you stepped into my life up here and told me I was full of baloney; now listen to you."

TJ nodded. "Yup, went full cult. I'm in."

Rowan said, "Good. Blood sacrifice in the morn—see you there?"

TJ looked at his watch. "Gonna be busy. I'll catch the next one."

They grinned at each other, and I couldn't help but feel the lightness in my heart at their connection. Their original meet-cute was dark as hell, but now their bond was tight, as if they'd had it as long as Rowan and Eli. Eli now knew he was the original Minory for Rowan and wore it like a badge of honor.

"Charmaine is managing the charges being leveled at the banker and his gang?" I asked Tee.

Rowan had rested his head on the back of the couch; his eyes were getting heavy post-adrenaline rush and within the calm comfort of home. Still, he spoke up. "Yup, and I've already gotten a warm message from the Murdoch clan chief, who is doing his own investigating. He sent his apologies that a man was doing harm in the name of the clan."

"That was kind of him."

"Aye, what we do, this seat that we keep, he and I, is rare in modern times; we're here to keep traditions alive and celebrate our history by being good stewards. Making trouble is precarious to the position."

"You should send a message to the MacLaochs, then. I don't think we got the memo. Since I got here, we've had nothing but trouble."

TJ had gotten a text message and read it before laughing. "Speaking of trouble. Mother just texted."

"Oh no."

"Oh yes."

"Flight number?"

"You know it."

"Ugh."

"You know," TJ said, "trouble follows you wherever *you* go. I don't think it's the MacLaochs' fault." He raised his phone with the text message from Mother, making his point.

I squinted at him. "Who are you?"

He waved, playing along: "Hi, I'm TJ. I'm your older brother. I invited myself here, like I always do."

"Right..."

He looked over his shoulder at the door. "Should I see myself out?"

"Man, you are one smart dude."

Holly stood and stretched. "Sounds like nothing more can be done right now." To the room: "Come on, fam, let's let the lord and lady of the house have their home back."

We said our goodnights, gave hugs, and promised a full Scottish brekkie in the castle in the morning. After the structural inspection.

Rowan held me in our empty living room, my arms around his middle and my ear resting on his chest. I listened to his heartbeat and found my own, matching his beat for beat.

"I'm sorry about Ethel," he said before giving me a soft kiss on the top of my head.

"Me too. That kind of sacrifice... I wasn't prepared for it. I understand on some level that she's always been a supernatural being and now is part of the stones of the castle, but there's also another part of me that is grief-stricken to have lost a friend, a woman I was growing to love as a grandmother here. I wish there was some other way to accomplish what we did..."

"I know, mo ghràdh. We all wish that she hadn't gone."

I gave a long, loud, heart-wrenching sigh.

"I know too tha' we also need to respect her decision. She was much older and wiser than all of us combined."

I nodded; there was comfort in that. "You're right. I hate it—the loss feels sad—but you're right."

I looked up at him, and he took the opportunity to kiss my lips. "I like hearing tha': 'You're right.'"

I was about to respond when I thought of something pertinent to Ethel. "How'd she live so damn long?"

"Human sacrifice?"

"Is that the same body or a new body a spirit inhabits?"

"What, like Dick Murdoch? Possessed by the spirit of the curse?"

"Maybe...that sounds too ghostly. That doesn't exist, right?"

Rowan's eyes illuminated before his smile broke hearing my sarcasm. "Those reanimated skeletons on the cairn knoll were ghosts."

"Were they?"

He added ignoring my sarcasm, "Mo ghràdh, tonight you held the power of your ancestor Ormr and wielded magic like I have never seen before. Ghosts are just one paradigm shift away."

THE NEXT MORNING, I BROUGHT THERMOSES OF HOT COFFEE UP TO the castle and passed out mugs of it. Marion and Flora, with the help from Clive, passed out hot breakfast sandwiches. Rowan and I walked the castle with the Fund's castle architect, structural engineer, and fire recovery expert. There was almost no damage, not even from smoke. It was as if Ethel simply pressed rewind on the event. With the OK from the structural engineer to resume regular activities, the looted artifacts were being loaded into the main ballroom. Canvas was laid down over the hardwoods, and one by one, chairs, paintings, silver hairbrushes, dishes, and sgain-dubhs were being delicately placed for review and restoration from their time being jumbled about, dropped into boats, or doused with gasoline.

Surprisingly, the charges in the foundation's corners were still intact, another thing that seemed to suggest Ethel had sacrificed her life to rewind time. The police got usable fingerprints from the explosives, a smoking gun of evidence to put away the entirety of Dick Murdoch's accomplices.

We were heading up the stairs to the main dining room from the lower ballroom when Rowan grasped my hand.

"What is it, hon?" I asked as he came up to the stair I was on and gently laid his hands on my cheeks; his gaze was amorous.

"I was thinking...how many times have ye saved me? Yesterday, the year before... Thank ye. I'm grateful to you every day, and I have to tell ye, if I haven't said it before, thank you for all you've done, for me, the clan." He looked at the soaring ceiling of the castle's entry that we were walking up into. "The castle. I went to my knees, felt my breath collapse at the explosion. It killed me, the rubble of it was my broken body, and ye...you drove us forward, pulled power from tha' cave—how you even thought of it in that moment, I'm in awe—grasped hands, and led us, me, here. You and Ethel put it right. She has my gratitude, but you..."

Sparks of light flickered in the air around us.

"Luaidh mo chèile, I've fallen in love with you all over again. You hold my heart and my soul in your hands, and I hope in the rest of our lives together I can return the favor, that I can show you with the whole of my body and my actions how much I love, adore, and..." He swallowed down the emotions that his words were pulling from him. He took a deep breath and, with a shimmering gaze, continued, "I"— he kissed my lips softly and lingered there, letting our breaths mingle before picking up my ring hand and speaking into the gold filigree— "give you all of me, again, body, soul and in every plane of existence. Tha mo ghion ort."

I wrapped my arms around his neck and pulled myself up onto my tiptoes, glowing now with the honesty of his words. "I love you with all my heart too. Now and forever."

"Aye, forever."

Epilogue

With flowers in hand, we stepped from the car out into the bright, watery sun at Misty Cliffs. TJ was headed back to base soon, and we—Eli, Rowan, and the Baker kids, with Peabody—wanted to pay our respects to Ethel's memory before he did.

Rowan had one warm hand on my back as he opened the white-painted gate of the churchyard. He paused a moment, collecting himself, and followed us.

"Each time I open tha' gate, I swear I can hear the souls in this yard scream."

Peabody asked, "Is this true? What do they sound like?"

Anyone else might have left that comment alone, but of course, ever the researcher, Peabody did not. And of course, ever the gracious host and friend, Rowan could not leave Peabody's question unanswered. As Rowan peeled away from me to step beside his old friend, TJ took his place. He held store-bought flowers wrapped prettily in brown paper and tied with twine. My bouquet was from the field and forest and held together with my fingers.

"Those are beautiful, Tee." I bumped his shoulder with mine.

He looked at my bouquet. "She was more into weeds, though, good call."

At the door to the church, we paused.

"Feels weird to be here without her," I said.

"Feels weird to feel like I lost someone important when I knew her for such a short time."

I watched his soft brown eyes lose a bit of their spark as his face processed the last weeks. I added, "I liked the way she knew things and understood the way of the world. She understood the connectedness of things, just in a different, but parallel, way to mine."

"Yup, hers was the study of magic; yours is science."

Peabody caught up with us, and Rowan was again at my back, his palm resting softly on my waist.

"Interestingly enough, you both understand the world in the same way; it's just that science is magic explained. And the unexplained magic is the bit science has yet to discover," Peabody suggested.

We heard tires crunch behind us and turned to see Eli waving as he exited his car.

He caught up to us, with a smile for each of us. Then, as if touched by a supernatural force, his eyes widened, and he said, "Whoa. Is this place haunted?" He shivered.

TJ gave his shoulder a pat. "Yeah, man. Wicked haunted."

"The readings of this graveyard alone will fill my book. It's a gold-mine of data," Peabody enthused. "I'm sorry she is gone; she was a wealth of information and a special human being."

"Aye," Rowan added. I knew he was still processing. There was too much MacLaoch in his blood for Ethel to embrace him wholeheart-edly. It was as if they both agreed to be kind to each other but also to respect the past. Yet in the end, she gave her life for the MacLaochs.

Eli pointed at the flowers. "That was a good idea. Maybe I should have an offering as well?"

TJ said, "You want a few out of this bunch?"

"No, I think I have something." He reached into his pocket, pulled out his wallet, and fished something out.

We were curious. Eli held up what looked like the wrapper of a small packet of shortbread cookies.

Tee was the first to ask, "Is that trash?"

Eli grinned broadly at his cousin. "Aye, right? Why keep a bit of trash? Unless an old woman gave you a packet of biscuits and you met your best friend that day. And that old lady when she gave it to ye said, 'Today, child, you'll have a brother.' And I thought it was my mum and da having another bairn." Eli grinned at Rowan behind me, who, in my peripheral, I could see had a matching smile; he remembered the day just as clearly.

"Ye shared that packet of shortbread biscuits with me."

"I did."

"Impressive," Peabody said.

I was awestruck. "She's been trying to break the curse for a very long time..."

Eli, the first of the Minorys to come to Rowan, grasped him up into a hug and gripped tight. Rowan returned the fierceness. And when they came apart, he quickly wiped his damp eyes.

"Brother," he said to Eli, then to Tee, "Brother. I was twice blessed by this woman. And that's just counting her bringing you two to me."

"Yes, you were." I smiled at him and then reached down to his hand. "Come."

I opened the door to the church and stepped into the entry of the cavernous space, pulling him in behind me. We made a small procession to the back kitchen. We didn't know if the church would replace her or who even knew she had passed. I made a note to figure that all out.

We placed our items on the kitchen table, and each of us said a few words.

I was surprised when Rowan pulled a coin from his pocket with the Roman Colosseum on it and set it down with the flowers and cookie wrapper.

"Is that—"

"Aye. It was her grandson's donation to our clan, and he was beheaded for his troubles. He might have been an enemy, but I'd like to think," he said, finding my hand and interweaving his fingers with mine, "that we're passed all tha', and moving on, and healing now means giving her back something her grandson touched."

Tee wrecked the moment by saying: "What about that dead baby?"

I gave him a sharp look. "It was a long time ago. The Fund has the coffin and bones now and is examining the remains. I'm sure he didn't put coins on top of...it."

"Then how'd they wind up there together?"

"Fucking hell, Tee...Let it go."

"Tiberius," Peabody interrupted, "what we have to understand about that time is that death wasn't something that rarely happened; it touched a person's life nearly daily, and what might be abhorrent today, back then was commonplace, for everyone who lived so close to death. They processed grief openly and without hesitation for as long as they needed. Those coins, whether they came with the coffin or were added later by Laoch, is a mystery we might never get answers to. But maybe in time we will get a better insight into what really happened. Especially with the Fund examining it now."

Tee shook his head. "I'm just saying, I've got friends who'd say that thing has some serious juju on it."

Rowan agreed. "That's exactly why I gave it."

The group moved to disperse, and I asked if they'd mind if I lingered a bit. "Take your time," Rowan assured me with a kiss.

I couldn't help but make one last cup of tea in that kitchen. I set the kettle to boil on the stove, opened her cupboards, remembered the moment she'd performed a chemical mix that settled things down when Ormr was gaining strength from his long spiritual sleep. That had been a while ago, and yet, as I pulled down her special Darjeeling mix, I couldn't help but think that had she stayed alive, I could learn an infinite amount from her.

I jumped when something hit the tabletop behind me.

I turned to find the book that Ethel and I were digitizing open on the table. It must have fallen...from a shelf? I didn't know how that could be, though. I carried the pot to the table and set two teacups and went to put the book away when I saw what page it was open to. One filled with runic symbols, which Ethel could read.

"I wish I could read that," I mumbled, because it felt like a sign from Ethel. I sat with it a bit longer and recalled that not too long ago, I'd read a page in Clive's office that also held such symbols, a page that Ethel had taped—much to my horror—back into the book. Without the Ulfberht and not currently in an emotionally heightened state, I didn't think I could repeat that. But I sat anyway, and with Ethel's voice in my mind's eye, I quieted myself, and after a few moments of deep breathing, I set my intention to reading it.

Opening my eyes, I saw the runes, and as my eyes took in the angles and shapes, a memory came to me. It was as close to a translation as I'd get. Ormr didn't write it; Ethel wrote it, but not Ethel, a woman who was transferring her power to Ethel. The symbols at the end were clear: Völva of the Misty Cliffs Church.

I sat with that knowledge for several heartbeats before I scrambled up. "Ohh!" Grabbing the book off the table, I made for the door, but stopped. Even if I could learn how she transferred her power from one generation to the next, there was no one to take or give.

I returned to the table with a sad sigh and poured the tea. I whispered the incantation that Ethel always said over the tea, knowing it was the last time I'd do it there in that kitchen, which was so special to Ethel. That held all her things, her life force in physical form.

I put the pot down and went to the doorway. Tee was coming back in with Eli in tow.

TJ's gaze went over my shoulder. "Holy damn. What's going on there?"

"What's that?" I heard Eli suck in his breath as he saw what TJ did.

Turning, I understood why they were gap-mouthed. Over the table, weaving between the objects left on the table, was a soft sparkle of violet light. It was as if small dots had been stabbed in the fabric of this plane of existence, and UV light was coming through them.

"Oh my...lordy," I said channeling my inner Southerner in the emotional surprise. "Is that getting all misty with purple?"

"Ye-up..." came from TJ.

"Guys?" I said.

I felt Rowan come up behind me.

The church itself seemed to respond, along with all four men, "Yeah?"

"I'm gonna need the Ulfberht."

Glossary of Terms

bellator ad mortem: Warrior unto death.

clabaidh-dubha: A northern horsemussel; also called clabbydoo.

claidheamh mòr: Known in English as a claymore; a two-handed basket-hilted sword.

dinnae fash yersel': Don't trouble yourself.

ghràdh: Love.

luaidh mo chèile: Love of my life.

laird's lug: also known as lord's ear. A listening peephole typically found in Scottish castles.

mo ghràdh: My love.

mo chridhe: My heart.

sassenach: Derogatory word for outsider; English person.

sgian-dubh: Small, single-edged knife.

slàinte: health or cheers.

slàinte mhath: good health.

tha gaol agam ort: I love you.

tha gaol agamsa ort fhèin: I love you too.

tha mi gad ionndrainn: I miss you.

tha mo ghion ort: I love you with all my heart.

tanist: The chieftain who is the clan chief's successor; second-in-command.

tòiseach: The eldest/most respected of a clan's chieftains.

Acknowledgments

First and foremost, thank you, dear reader. Your continued support is the reason I can keep pursuing a dream so wild I can hardly believe it myself. Who knew a Maui girl could grow up to do what I do? I get to call myself a writer and an author, and I have you to thank for it. Mahalo.

Thanks also go to my early readers, Annie and Diane. Your feedback is essential to keeping these sequels as good, if not better than the first. Thank you to my father-in-law, retired US Air Force Master Sergeant Mike Mannthey, for the military insights. Any gross exaggeration for fiction purposes is totally my fault. Thank you to the absolute gem, Bess Austin, RN-FNP, for double-checking my medical terminology. Any errors or oversights are on me. Thank you to my editor, Kristin Thiel; you are the pro behind my prose.

Thank you to my Scottish ancestors who fled the Clearances and workhouses of Glasgow in the 1700 and 1800s to find a new life in America. Your stories and sacrifices grew legs and sprouted wings in this land of opportunity.

And a big thank you to my family and friends—the past year was one for the record books, and I couldn't have done it without you.

One last note, with thanks about health. As you can imagine, my creativity falters when I'm in poor health. Creativity is my lifeblood and my career. In June 2024, I was diagnosed with a tiny but cancerous tumor in my right breast. I'm in my early forties; my mammo should have been crystal clear. While that road I had to travel last summer was morbid, life-altering, and a real test of my strength, confidence, and will, something beautiful happened that I couldn't see while I was knee-deep in surgery, tests, radiation, and recovery. I was surrounded by women. My surgeons, the support staff in the operating room, nurses, techs, my oncologist and radiation specialist...all were women. Each was a guide, each operating at the top of her game in her respective field. Each one carried me in some way through that darkness. I'm cancer-free and will stay that way because of the dedication of these women who decided decades ago to go into a field dominated by men to make a difference. To all the women who carried me through the darkness, I feel the difference you made and are making—and you are my heroes. Thank you. Now, reader, please get your mammogram today. It could save your life.

Author Bio

Becky Banks is an international bestselling and award-winning indie author from an old Hawai'i family, who lives in Portland, Oregon, with her husband and two kids. Becky is a breast cancer survivor and likes to craft dark romances that stem from her past and require love to see her characters through. When she's not writing love stories, she's planning family adventures and making her kids laugh with fart jokes.

Visit Becky Banks online at beckybanksbooks.com and follow her on social media for updates on new releases and more.

facebook.com/beckybanksbooks

instagram.com/authorbeckybanks

amazon.com/author/beckybanks

goodreads.com/beckybanks

bookbub.com/profile/becky-banks

Also by Becky Banks

CLAN MACLAOCH CURSE SERIES

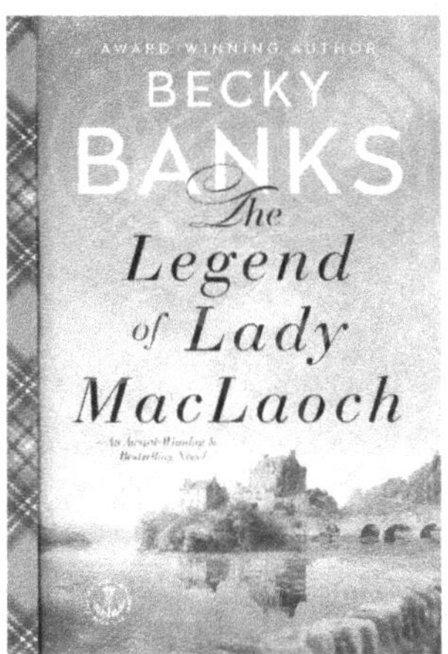

The Legend of Lady MacLaoch. *Book 1 of the Clan MacLaoch Curse Series.*

Centuries ago a vengeful curse buried itself deep into the history of the MacLaoch clan and became a legendary tale told by all those not cursed by its words.

In present-day Scotland, the laird and chief of the MacLaoch clan is an ex-Royal Air Force fighter pilot who has been past the gates of hell and returned a changed man. Rowan MacLaoch does battle with wartime memories and a family curse that threaten to consume him—unaware that his life and that of the history of the clan will be changed forever by the arrival of an American woman.

Cole Baker, a feisty recent graduate of a master's program, stumbles upon the ancient curse while researching her bloodlines. Moved by the history of the MacLaoch clan and the mystery of its chief, she digs into the legend that had been anything but quiet for centuries.

On their quest for answers, Cole and Rowan travel to places they have never before been and become witnesses to things they have never before fathomed.

The legend—one started with blood—will end with more shed as its creator
finally exacts her justice.

Book 2 of the Clan MacLaoch curse series, The Legend of the Viking.

In this second book of the Clan MacLaoch Curse series, we see our favorite
characters, Rowan and Cole, return in their most passionate selves yet.
Coming off the loss of the Gathering and the thought-to-be-extinguished
MacLaoch curse, Rowan finally has a chance at his happily ever after. That is,
until everything that he loves is put at risk, sparking events, that once set in
motion, will not be stopped—except by love.

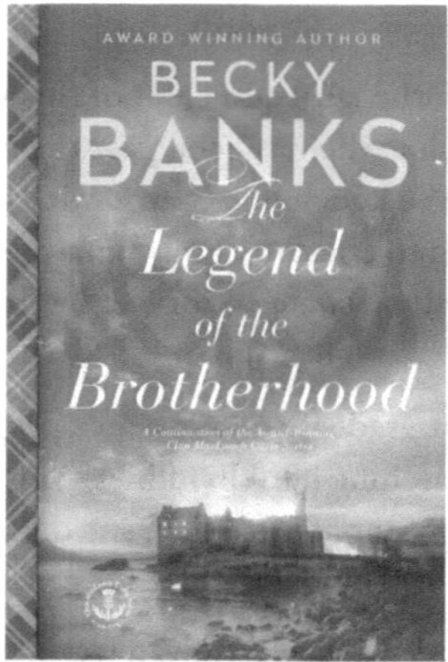

Book 3 of the Clan MacLaoch curse series, The Legend of the
Brotherhood.

In this third book of the clan MacLaoch curse series, Cole's two worlds collide when her brother, TJ, stops by Castle Laoch for a surprise visit. His presence upsets more than the status quo at Castle Laoch, as he and Rowan have a score to settle. Cole and Rowan - fresh off the battle on the cairn knoll - are bonded even more profoundly as they move to save the castle from financial ruin and a curse-touched banker set on a generation's old revenge. Can Rowan's determination, the Baker kids' ingenuity, and residual Viking power within Cole save the castle and clan from ruin?

ROMANTIC SUSPENSE TITLES

Flux. *Can one notorious hacker protect the women she's saved before her dark past finds her?*

Vega Flux, a notorious hacker whose single mission in life is to protect the weak from online trolls, crashes up against an impenetrable powerhouse of a man who wants nothing more than to slip the dark shroud off her persona and protect her from her torments.

In this smoldering high-stakes game of defense and one-upmanship, Vega takes a bet she knows she shouldn't and starts the largest hack she's ever attempted, against the only worthy opponent she's ever known, tech billionaire and ex-NFL tight end, Hoyt Kahoʻokalakupua. Master of his domain, Hoyt, welcomes the chance to flex his power in a true challenge. With the stakes dangerously high, and his heart on the line, he enters a game with a woman he wants it all from. There's only one fatal flaw: Hoyt and Vega are following different instructions to the same game. He's a law-abiding billionaire, and the world Vega lives in breaks every rule.

Dark passions ignite in this fast-paced thrill ride from award-winning indie
author and Maui girl, Becky Healani Banks. As the torments of Vega's past
breach her defenses, she reaches for the one man who is uniquely capable of
providing the shelter she seeks. And in that process, she touches a power she's
never known, real-life love.

Forged. *First loves, dark pasts, and fast cars collide in this high-octane
thrill ride.*

Managing editor of a Manhattan fashion rag, Eva Rodgers, couldn't believe she
would ever step back into her old life, but the day her father called with his
diagnosis, she had little choice. Returning home, and to the past she left
behind, Eva signs up as editor-in-chief of the struggling Portland magazine,
Rose City Review. There in the drizzling Portland metro Eva still holds firm to
the New York city values that defined her time there: compromise on nothing.
When her European auto, one luxury she missed in the walking and hired car
world of Manhattan, needs fixing, she doesn't compromise. Even when the
best European auto mechanic her assistant finds turns out to be an ex with a
vendetta, Eva doesn't flinch.

Nathaniel Vellanova can't believe what the fuck just showed up at his garage.
He'd gotten his life together, buried his dark past, and definitely put Eva
Rogers in his rearview mirror. Right?

But fuck him if she wasn't standing right there in the pouring rain needing his
help. He'd do it—help her out—just this once then forget all about her. Again.

In this dark and suspenseful story of broken first loves, readers will ride the smoldering heat of high-octane fast cars, glitzy club fashion, and tainted love and ask themselves, are first loves the only love?

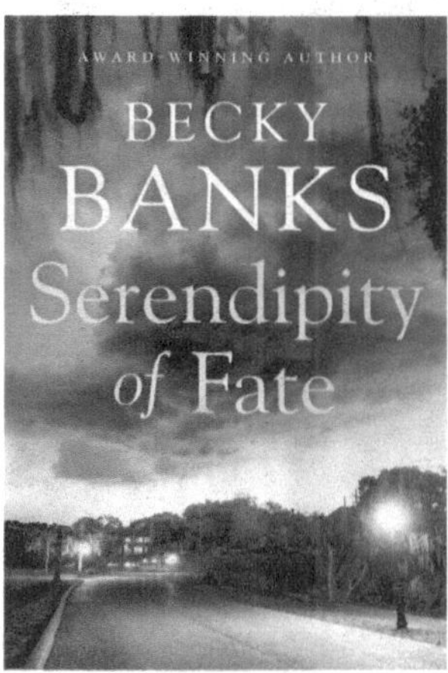

Serendipity of Fate. *Enemies to lovers romance. One war, one blood promise, and the love to save it all.*

It has been two years since Cason McPherson watched his best friend, Ryan Sparling, die in his arms. Now, with a blood promise tied to his heart, shrapnel in his hip, and a war behind him, he's focused on building a useful civilian life in his hometown of New Orleans. Living with Ryan's mother, a widow and retired nurse, he gives back the protection and care his best friend wanted. Only Ryan's sister, a woman whose well-worn picture got him through the darkest parts of the war, does not see it that way.

Savannah Sparling has spent the last five years building her career and life to the exacting expectations needed to achieve partner at Knight Interiors. And nothing could derail them except for the one person from her past who returned home a changed man. Cason McPherson and her brother Ryan had been her entire world once, but now she no longer recognizes him with his caustic attitude and effort to turn every conversation into a verbal sparring match. When a potential client, one large enough to secure her place as partner, requests her as lead designer, Savannah sets a plan for her final career move and Cason's eviction.

In a series of unstoppable events, Savannah's carefully laid plans backfire, and an unfathomable truth is revealed. In the aftermath, Cason and Savannah find that the only people strong enough to save them from themselves are each other. But will either one of them accept the help—and the love—that is offered?